NUDGE CANYON

Where the Real world

meets the Reel world

Edward, St. David's

Contents

For Dad
A lover of westerns from start to finish!

"Saddle up, pardner!"

Introduction

A little research on the subject will tell you that modern day America began to be settled, in earnest, from the early 1600's when the Mayflower, carrying its brave cargo of 101 surviving (out of 102 pilgrims), docked at Provincetown Harbour. This gradual forming of the America we know today was completed in 1912 when the last western territories became states. This entire time period is known as "The American Frontier".

You may or may not have heard this name before.

By comparison, "The Wild West" as the world has come to know it – mostly through the eyes of Hollywood – lasted only a short time. The general consensus is that it ran from circa 1850 to circa 1910. Hard to believe, isn't it?, that the period of history which made household names out of John Wayne and Clint Eastwood, lasted 60 years at the most!

So you have very likely heard of "The Wild West" before, haven't you?

It is the world where, if the "University of Hollywood" curriculum can be trusted, "Adventure" and its unfortunate twin, "Danger", lay around every bend in the road.

And one cause of that danger was outlaws.

Since those days, the classic "Wanted" poster has become something of an artistic icon that has inadvertently, at least to a degree, romanticised robbery. Back then, no town lacked at least one such poster at a time when the law fought with all its might to gain the upper hand.

Bearing the generalising and almost slang name "The Wild West", this was a bizarre civil war battle without a fine name such as "Gettysburg" or "Vicksburg" to dignify proceedings to future students of history, for how can you dignify rank evil?

A breed of voluntarily dangerous creatures in their own right, outlaws lived from moment to moment and every moment was of bad intent. They rode stolen horses, wore stolen and ill fitting clothes and were armed to their rotten teeth with stolen weaponry. Every day they lived had to be stolen also; stolen out of the hands of the hangman. Not *completely* without feelings, the average outlaw regularly showed fondness . . fondness for train robbery.

Unfortunately for those smelly vagabonds, the law of the day *also* had a fondness . . for chasing outlaws and their company, with the sole intent of destroying them all.

***

The "Liberty Bell" was the world's first ever one armed bandit; invented, unsurprisingly, in 1894 when outlaws were on the go. Once seen everywhere, the passing years and the dawning of other entertainments saw these three reeled rascals rounded up by the posse of "Time", to be incarcerated forever in history books. The odd "parolee" can be found under house arrest in museums and private collections today.

But be careful, for a few are still out there, having never been caught.

Unwilling to submit to authority or change their ways, they stalk the unwary.

And they are not called "Bandits" for nothing . .

Prologue

It was April 26th 1901.

The New Mexico desert spat up a dust storm under the thundering hooves of a twenty strong posse. This posse was utterly focused on their hunt and slowed for nothing. Following the southward flow of the Rio Grande, over hills and dunes, across rivers and along mesa sided canyon tracks they flew. The whole noisy unit sped as one, keeping formation, even over terrain unpredictable. They were in pursuit of a criminal element that spoiled the founding of a new nation and simply confirmed that, wherever people went, there would always be trouble.

Suddenly, the front rider lifted his hand to halt the justice machine. His horse stopped first then the other riders fanned out as they slowed, coming to a halt in a rough semi-circle around him. He dismounted and walked – spurs clinking – up to a camp fire someone had left. He kicked the embers. They smouldered and sparked a little when disturbed, betraying their youth. A posse member spoke:

"Is that what we're lookin' for, Sheriff? Is it them?"

The sheriff stared at the embers. His face was as craggy as the surrounding mountains. He had a walrus moustache with matching eyebrows and days of dusty stubble from days in the saddle. Born in to, and fully betrothed to, the rough life, he looked up and seemed to stare past the posse and in to the mind of his prey, seeing the end from the beginning. He had the expression of a person being forced to read a book already read. A tired expression, yes, but still in control of events. His men saw this and awaited his reply.

The sheriff looked straight in to the eyes of the man who asked the question. The posse member saw in the sheriff's eyes exactly why life had qualified him to be the law keeper he was. Who needs a gun when you can stare like *that*? The sheriff nodded then glanced back to the struggling embers that, to him, were something of a metaphor for any outlaw's future.

"What we're lookin' for sat here less than four hours ago and tonight we're gonna bring them all to justice."

He mounted up. Reins whipped horse necks. Dust flew.

Thundering hooves thundered on.

***

Cedric simply *loved it!*

His 5th birthday had been pretty good. He didn't get a games console but he got the next best thing, for the time – 1901 – and that was a soccer ball. *BOUNCE BOUNCE BOUNCE!!!*

The number of games a child can play with a soccer ball are endless! There's "Kick it and see how far it will go!" then "Throw it against any surface and see how well it bounces!", "See if it floats on water!" and "Make your parents regret ever giving it to you!". And of course, if you have the desirable, that makes *you* desirable! For a time, anyway, young Cedric would have lots of friends, well "friends" if you catch the drift.

Mum and Dad were themselves children of immigrants from afar. They owned a hardware store in the oddly named town of "Clean Getaway". This was a very nice place to live – again, for the time – with near no crime. Nothing is perfect, of course, and sometimes during the night a crowd of ruffians rode through, but thankfully never stopped, Clean Getaway probably being en-route to their hideout. What was needed was a bypass for such people on the run. The odd tumble weed would roll on in to town, looking for some purpose to its existence.

Today, the family had been in a neighbouring town. What is work without its rewards after all? They were at the railway station. Dad was getting tickets and Mum looked simply lovely in her new hat! Being a Saturday, the beautiful wooden station, adorned with hanging baskets, forced veneers of respectability and social pleasantries, bustled with holiday cheeriness. Even back then, Saturday appeared to have an atmosphere of its own.

"Have I got this thing on back to front?" muttered Mum to herself as she stepped close to a window on the last carriage, checking her reflection and turning the hat this way and that. The window made a good reflector as the carriage seemed to be filled with utter darkness like it was filled to the ceiling with black tar. Cedric, instinctively using the license to transgress that his age bestowed upon him, bounced the ball off the window right next to his mother. She jumped with a start.

"*CEDRIC!, give me that thing!*" scolded Dad in that "Restrained because we're in public – through his teeth" voice, sounding like a snarling dog with the volume down at 2. He grabbed the ball and glared at his boy. Mum would have told Cedric off also but then noticed that when she had jumped with fright a happy accident had occurred as the hat had slid a touch and now sat at a very pleasing angle.

A whistle blew.

"Next stop – Clean Getaway – All aboard!"

All aboarded, but none boarded that last carriage, the one filled with darkness. The platform went from packed to deserted in 60 seconds as the train chugged and spat and hissed, then moved off.

***

"BOO!" shouted Gemma as she whirled around in her seat.

Two of her friends, Kyle and Lisa, had been creeping up on her but Gemma had seen them reflected in a chrome surface she sat next to. Gemma was convinced she was the prettiest girl in the world and her reflection never argued the point . . so.

It was busy at the mall as it always was on a Saturday. The three friends sat and compared notes of the past week's soap opera that was their lives. A debriefing meeting with colleagues, if you will.

"Sorry we're late Gem, we thought we'd give you time to reflect. Where's Lenny? I thought you and he were a "thing" now!" said Lisa.

"WHAT! Don't even *joke* about that possibility!" replied Gemma.

Lenny was a character in town that people – including Lenny's own reflection – tried to avoid. He had asked

Gemma for a date the previous week. She had given him "July 4th, 1776" and left him standing with a puzzled look.

"And where's Buck Rogers today?" Kyle inquired then realised the pointlessness of the question. Kyle was referring to the fourth member of their social group.

"Oh he's on the corner of Jarvis and Kinnoul." replied Lisa. She looked at her watch. "And if I'm not mistaken, he's currently on level 84."

"I believe you Lis." said Gemma, "I worry about him sometimes. He should be here with me . . er . . us. Spending too much time in those places may not be good for him in the long run."

***

Another nub end hit the ground.

The person who threw it was of large build, well overweight and looked really quite scary. He had been out the back of the local amusement arcade, which he owned. He had sometimes stood smoking and worried for his hearing, such was the heaving noise that his establishment could produce; but, if you wanted maximum return with minimal effort, there had to be a catch *somewhere* along the line; no free lunch, remember? The back alley was the closest he could come to the countryside and he appreciated it for what it meant to him, perhaps hinting at a side to his personality seldom seen.

Well, some back alleys are born litter filled, some back alleys achieve litter filled status and some back alleys have litter thrust upon them. The discarded nub end bounced and rolled off the small heap of fallen comrades. At least they were generally thrown in the same place. He moved the nubs in to a rough pile with his foot. If you're going to be untidy then at least be tidy about it.

His attention then returned to something, for he was standing in front of a one armed bandit. It had *definitely* not been there yesterday, *definitely!* It had flown well under the radar of perception, admittedly easier to do at night, and had just appeared when no one was looking.

"You've come late to the party, buddy! What happened? You get lost in the backstreets?" He thought someone left it there so it could join its "family" of coin guzzling, trendier relatives.

"You look like you've been given up for adoption!"

He was of course referring to the fact that one armed bandits may have been hot stuff back in the day but the people who saw their emergence and played them were now either in retirement homes or cemeteries. Vegas still had bandits of course, but none were as quaint and well crafted as *this* one. It was a real specimen. The youth of the present, however, were not interested in "real specimens", just 8 bit blast gratification. A teenager knocked on the arcade back door as if it was the door of the CEO's office. A creak open then a young voice spoke, unseen, through the gap.

"Can we get some change here please?"

"Sure buddy, comin'!" replied the bemused owner as he stepped back inside.

So it was a bit of a stalemate. The one armed bandit had apparently hit a dead end full of nub ends as it stood alone in a back alley that had just become one nub end dirtier. It, however, had not come to meet the madding crowd nor to make loads and loads of new friends . .

. . just one would do.

1

Ambush at "Side Alley"

It was April 26th 1981.

The amusement arcade was just heaving with youth, spending, for the most part, money earned by the next generation up. There were several arcades in town but this one was the best, with, usually, none of the rougher elements seen here. Roughly ten or so game cabinets lined three of the walls. There were three pool tables in the middle. The change booth sat in line with the middle pool table and in the booth sat Al.

Rotund Al would pass for an extra in any gangster movie, standing on lookout as someone got shot to bits, but, he was friendly, and that's all any person wants from another. Noisy it certainly was too! The babble of weekend youth is at the pitch of freedom from school, mixed with beeps, blasts, tyre screeches and 8 bit music. Saturday oh Saturday, where would we be without you!

At one game stood 18 year old Tom. Tom loved the arcade and video games. The dopamine release he got from simply walking in to the arcade and seeing the machines was exquisite to Tom. He fell prey to the rush the games could give . . every time! A recent school leaver, he wanted to make these games for a living and had enrolled in a college course in the autumn with that goal in mind. Tom was 6 ft tall and, having extreme youth on his side, was slim and naturally fit. But the best thing about Tom was that he was friendly and WYSIWYG, and that is all any person wants from another.

But, as youth has its rewards, so too, does it have its curses. You see, one hour earlier, in Tom's home . .

"Tom honey, it's such a nice day, could you nip to town and buy . . ?"

His mum, Sheila, handed Tom a list with 4 or 5 things. Just the usual grocery list. She also handed Tom a $5 note which included a taxi home, should it start raining.

However, Tom "kinda" forgot and Sheila "never even knew" that, between Tom's house and the grocery store, lay the arcade. It *was* a beautiful day so Tom happily walked the two miles in to town, occasionally taking the $5 note from his pocket and looking at it. He looked at the picture of the man on the note and wondered what *he* did in his free time back then, when almost nothing had been invented. Tom also wondered how many of these notes he would own in his life and who had owned this note before him and who would own it after. He was surprised at just how many questions arose from simply staring at a $5 note!

Well, *Al* became the next owner of the $5.

Tom was just cast adrift on Saturday morning ecstasy, his moral compass lying where he had dropped it, somewhere on the verge of the two mile walk in to town. Standing in front of his latest favourite game, Tom was the last piece of the jigsaw, found and placed. Some of his school pals were there and some from the other school in town.

Somebody else who was there was Lenny.

Lenny was 28 and had never had, or desired, a job. Usually seen leaning against any wall in town, today he was at the arcade. At six foot four inches tall, Lenny the brute looked – and smelled – as he acted. Not completely without cunning, he watched as Tom inserted a coin then stepped in front of the game machine, pushing Tom aside easily.

"Well gee thanks Thomas buddy, don't mind if I do!"

Lenny's sarcasm was a skill he'd not need later on down the line in prison. Tom had this treatment from Lenny once before and just moved to another game.

Like a magicians slight of hand, the sights and sounds of the game distracted Tom from noticing the coins disappearing from his pocket, for glorified pick pockets these games were. Soon, Tom was absorbed and Lenny was forgotten. Right along with memories of Lenny also disappeared memories of why Tom was in town in the first place .. and that $5.

***

And so, inevitably, about 45 minutes later, the moment arrived.

Tom put his hand in to his pocket for another coin but felt nothing. He panicked and turned his pocket inside out; still, nothing. His mouth and eyes opened wide in stark realisation as he suddenly envied, with all his might, people who have no interest in video games.

"Oh *NO!*"

He thrust his hand deeper down in to the same pocket, hoping to hit a rich vein of coins. It was a futile gesture. This time, Tom's exclamation was a little louder as he looked in to the fairly near future.

"NO WAY, MY MUM!"

But there it was: Al had the $5, the machines had the coins and Tom had one big problem. The machine Tom had been playing saw Tom was of no more use to it so simply turned its back on him. Lenny certainly wasn't going to push Tom aside and take his place *now,* because, when *things* desert you, *people* generally will too. Until this predicament Tom found himself in was resolved, he would temporarily see beneath the arcade's veneer. He covered his face with both hands because there was nothing fun about what he now saw.

***

"Let me get this straight, kid, you want ME to give YOU money?" said an incredulous Al. Monetary flow in *any* arcade is strictly a one way street and now Tom was asking Al to go in to reverse gear.

Tom pled his case with feeling: "I spent my mum's shopping money and if I don't get this sorted I'll be grounded 'till I'm like 60!" His supplication to Al was clearly heard above the racket of the setting. Some gamers glanced at Tom during a break in play.

"Well bein' grounded might be a good thing for you 'cause you might have a bit more common sense!" replied rotund Al. Tom's case for the defence was repeatedly interrupted by having to step aside for a second to let someone else trade notes for coins.

"C'mon Al man, *please!*"

The very fact that Tom felt he could approach Al for help said a lot about Al. He may work in an arcade but that did not mean he was an *ambassador* for the arcade. If closing time came but you were on a roll for a high score,

Al would wait till you were done before flicking the switch. He would also emerge from his booth if it was quiet and take on someone at a game of pool. A gangster in appearance only, friendly and approachable to those who knew him even slightly. Now he beheld foolish Tom and smiled, perhaps remembering his own reckless youth.

"Ok kid, the money's yours with one condition."

"What?" replied Tom.

Al grabbed a broom sitting in the corner of the booth and gave it to a relieved Tom.

"Sweep the floor and I'll pay you $5."

Tom grabbed the broom. It's funny, isn't it, how, in the right context, the utterly mundane can become so utterly pleasurable! Sweeping, for the moment, was more fun than any game Tom had ever played. With "Mother's Wrath" averted, life was worth living once more!

***

The arcade side alley was typical.

Litter, like inner city tumbleweeds, drifted, ironically, past trash cans. Traffic could be heard a few streets away. The buildings rose sharply, causing a ravine effect. The perfect place for an ambush.

Tom emerged from the arcade back door. It had taken him about 30 minutes to sweep the arcade floor. It would have taken him 15 if people were a bit more considerate with litter. He never realised just how messy himself and his "colleagues" of the arcade could be and felt embarrassed about it. Today was turning in to a "See it the way it really is" kind of day.

He carried the broom and a makeshift bin bag which appeared to be a ragged old blanket Al had produced from somewhere. Dust and a drink carton spilled from the improvised bag, leaving an easy to follow trail. Tom emptied the blanket in to a trash can then just threw the old blanket in as well, like Al had suggested. Tom was blinded to his labours by the high of "Mother's Wrath Reprieve".

While bending down to pick up the drink carton, he noticed what was obviously a gaming machine of some sort, casually covered by a dirty sheet. Laying the broom aside, Tom lifted the sheet tentatively. The machine was an old fashioned "One Armed Bandit".

Sitting there, half under a blanket, neither plugged in nor making any sound or movement, the machine held Tom's gaze in a way those other machines could not. Tom was intrigued with the air of history and mystery about it. This initial spell was broken, for the time being, as Al emerged from the back door.

""Here's your $5 kid!" said rotund Al as he handed Tom a fist full of dollars and some change. He noticed Tom's interest in the machine.

"You ever seen one of those before?" asked Al.

Tom, now spellbound free, pointed to the lever.

"Is that the joystick?" he asked.

"Yeah, right!" chuckled Al. "This is a one armed bandit. See that handle on the side that you thought was a joystick? Well, that's his arm. He's one armed, see? You pull that to make those reels spin and hopefully win some money. Put in a coin and give it a pull!"

Tom inserted a coin, already eating back in to the retrieved $5, pulled the bandit's arm but it was stuck solid, supernaturally solid. He tried again; nothing. Around their circumferences, the three reels displayed beautifully painted pictures of lemons and crowns and other things; all very alluring, making it all the more painful that they wouldn't spin.

"It's broken!" he said, a touch disappointed.

"And that's what it's sitting here." replied Al. "That and the fact that no one plays them anymore. Not dangerous enough or loud enough I guess. It wouldn't work if you put in 100 quarters!"

"So it's a bit of an antique?" asked Tom.

Al replied "Maybe in another 100 years! She too old to be new and too new to be old."

"How long has it been sitting here?" Tom asked.

Al stretched and yawned. "Well now that's the funny thing. I've been running this place for three years and am out here every day. Day in, day out, I come back here for a cig, and nuthin'. Then about a month ago, I come out and nearly trip over the thing. Beats me really but it just appeared! Maybe somebody thought they were doin' me a favour. The trash man never takes it away. You wan' it?"

Tom is astonished at Al's offer. Al sees this in his expression and is inwardly pleased.

"You serious?" asked Tom, a touch delighted.

"You did a pretty good job with that broom, buddy. Sweep up for a month and she's yours!"

Tom's tone deflated just a bit. "A month? And hey, I lost that quarter!"

Al turned and entered the back door again. Gangster look and words came in to conjunction:

"It ain't called a bandit for nuthin'!"

2

Attract Mode

A month had now passed and Tom was working on repairing the one armed bandit, having faithfully swept the floor for Al. Over the next few weeks, Tom unscrewed this and oiled that. He visited the library for help but there was scant information available. The garage at home was quite big and Tom could easily fit his new acquisition on one side, conveniently next to his dad's workbench. Tom's dad, Andrew, passed as he came and went to/from the office. Sheila had the washing machine housed in the garage also and would offer Tom words of encouragement. The gaming machines had kept Tom in the arcade and now a gaming machine was keeping him out of it.

Tom's initial interest in the machine had matured significantly and he had now come to realise the value of his quirky acquisition; not the re-sale value but the value it possessed in terms of beauty and history. Neither Tom's parents, nor even Tom himself, noticed this new found streak of maturity in the young man as none of them expected it yet. The honour he felt in just owning such a machine made Tom very careful, never forcing or turning anything too much. It became a case of simply inserting coin after coin, and, slowly but surely, seeing where the fault lay.

Now and then, Tom stopped repairs and just stood, admiring the one armed bandit. There was that feeling again that he had when he first laid eyes on the machine. Yes, a person could look and see the bandit, could reach and touch the bandit *and* be impressed, but what Tom experienced was on another level altogether. Like staring at Egyptian hieroglyphs, Tom knew there was meaning in there but, annoyingly, could not cross the finishing line of understanding.

Eventually, the day came when everything appeared to be fixed and renewed. During repairs, a smile had come to Tom's face when he retrieved the coin he lost inside the bandit, out the back of the arcade. He now stood, holding that very coin, as he summoned his parents to witness the first spin of a new era. Both parents were elated.

"Well, Son, I gotta hand it to you, your mum and I thought you would lose interest but you saw this thing through!" enthused Andrew.

"He saw it through alright, he's a winner like his mum!" came Sheila's echo.

They all stood and admired the machine which had a western theme and was called "NUDGE CANYON". While the reels span, pictures of a bandit and a posse were lit from behind by various light bulbs. If the reels lined up and gave a win, the bandit made it to the town of "CLEAN GETAWAY". If the reels did *not* give a win, the posse caught up with and apprehended the bandit, bringing him to the town of "JUSTICE". If a "Nudge" – the option to move one, two or all three reels a notch and make a winning line – was offered, the bandit got to ride through Nudge Canyon, which was a shortcut to the town of Clean Getaway.

Build up over, Dad took the coin from Tom's hand, then handed it back to him.

"Here, Son, the first spin's on me!"

"Eat your heart out, Archie Karas!" laughed Sheila, rubbing her SOS pendant she wore, being a diabetic.

Tom inserted the coin and pulled the bandit's now smoothly working and beautifully chromed arm. A gunshot sound effect sounded, taking them all by surprise. Sheila jumped with a shriek. The gunshot had plenty of "Wild West Ricochet" that just brought the whole garage alive. Spin spin spin went the reels. One by one they stopped to give three lemons in a perfect line. The pictorial bandit made it to the town of Clean Getaway, represented by the flashing town sign, accompanied by raucous cheers from all present.

"And we have a winner!" said Andrew, punching the air.

"Looks like our boys a high roller!" gushed giggling Sheila. There was a short, silent pause which then got the hang of it and became a longer, pregnant pause.

"What did you win, sweetheart?" asked Sheila, her smile and tone trying to avert pending disappointment. Tom gave the machine a fairly firm shake; nothing.

"And we have a loser!" came the predictable punchline from Dad, his trademark ham fisted way of soothing a situation.

"Oh now Dad, don't!" said Sheila. The telephone rang.

"That'll be Pete." Andrew went to answer the phone, patting his son on the back.

"Oh gosh, *the oven!*" Tom's mum ran off, leaving Tom staring at the now un-fixed machine. The rapid exiting of, coincidentally, *both* parents seemed mighty suspicious. *Was that really Pete and was it really the oven?* thought Tom briefly. He tried to insert another coin, the one he lost at the start, but it wouldn't go in. The machine wouldn't let go of this coin, now it won't take it. The arm refused to budge an inch and Tom didn't want to force it. Being an avid gamer, feelings of defeat at the hands of a gaming machine weren't all that new to Tom, but c'mon, all that patient work! A mouthwatering smell from the kitchen limped to the rescue of crestfallen Tom. Sheila had made it to the oven in time and the evening meal was ready. Tom sighed and plodded towards the kitchen to comfort eat.

"An entire month of sweeping!"

***

The next day and dawn was well underway, about to hand over to early morning. The weather promised to be simply beautiful! It was a nice area Tom lived in; just far enough from town to feel safe and not too far in to the sticks to feel safe. Nice weather in a nice place! Tom yawned and stretched under the duvet, which tried to talk him in to staying and would have won its case but for an objection, for from outside came the sound of a prolonged honk on a horn followed by a screech and a crash. Tom jumped up to look out his bedroom window, as did half the slumbering street. A show of synchronised curtain twitching.

"*Wow!*" Tom cried, and no wonder.

A lorry carrying lemons had swerved and screeched to an abrupt stop directly outside Tom's house, spilling its unusual load right in to the driveway. Literally a thousand lemons rolled and splattered among smashed wooden fruit boxes, nearly to the front door. A good few neighbours emerged and gawked. Tom's parents, always wanting to "keep up with the neighbours", emerged and gawked also.

A sight like this casts a stun of a spell that defies all speech. The lorry driver jumped down from his cab, swithering as to either face the music or resign on the spot. He angrily pointed to where the dog had run off; the dog he had swerved to miss.

"*Was that your dog I nearly hit?*" he said angrily to Tom's dad. His tone was of someone who had decided not to resign on the spot.

"*No, are these your lemons I nearly fell over?*" was Andrew's sarcastic reply with, also, angry pointing.

"Stinkin' mutt. I should'a kept on goin'."

It was never mentioned at the time, understandably, but one thing all present agreed on, the smell was overpowering and simply wonderful!

***

An hour later and Tom handed the last crate of intact lemons to the lorry driver. The clean up job wasn't too arduous due partly to that wonderful smell and partly due to the fact that a good few intact lemons had magically disappeared. Would it be coincidence or something else that lemon ice cream would be on the dessert menu in several houses on the street in the coming days?

The truck driver, who, to be honest, spent too much of his life in the cab, as rotund Al did in the change booth, gasped and sweated as Tom handed him that last crate. He was glad he'd faced the music as, massive inconvenience and total embarrassment and potential loss of job and earnings and house aside, nobody had been hurt or property damaged, thus making the music he'd bravely faced fairly melodic after all. He had chatted to Tom as they laboured and now that rapport was about to pay off for the helpful lad.

As Tom handed the driver the last wooden box, they both looked around at where the mess had been. Now there were just a few box fragments which Tom would sweep up afterwards. Splattered lemon remains lay around and a dog – not *the* dog – was already licking them tentatively.

"Here, Kid, you were the only one who really helped!" said the driver as he handed the last crate of perfect lemons back to Tom. Tom was delighted. Labour should *always* be rewarded!

"Alright! Thanks!" He took the lemons in to the garage and dumped them next to the fruit machine.

A thought now came to Tom.

This thought didn't just arrive but seemed to have been waiting in the garage for him. It didn't come to Tom, Tom came to *it*. He stood bolt upright and looked at the line of three lemons the one armed bandit displayed. He whirled round, mouth agape, wide eyed and speechless as he watched the lorry drive off. The thought had tapped Tom on the shoulder, then stepped from view.

"Nah! No way!" he said, shaking his head slowly. Just then, Andrew came in to the garage and picked up the crate of lemons. He's cooled down now. All's well that ends well.

"Your mother wants these inside." He, too, noticed the the bandit lemons.

"Well how's *that* for a coincidence?!" He took the lemons inside.

Tom put another coin in the machine and gently tried to pull the lever. The arm moved as intended. The bandit suddenly worked perfectly again! The gunshot sounded. From the kitchen, Sheila shrieked. Reels span and came to a stop at three perfectly aligned crowns. The pictorial bandit once again made it to Clean Getaway; he's pushing his luck, surely. Tom was elated the machine worked again and wanted to make sure it continued, so went to insert another coin. This time, Tom was side swiped by the "too good to be true" side of life as the bandit's arm, again, stuck in place. Not only did the arm stick but the coin slot closed, halting any interaction except unscrewing the back and . . Tom felt dejected to say the least. He walked away.

***

Next day and Tom was in town helping his mum at the supermarket, being designated "Trolly Pusher" for the hour. They walked back out to the car and both began to load shopping in to the vehicle when . .

"Oh wait wait! Tom, honey, nip back in and get some kitchen roll for the barbecue. Just any kind." said flustered Sheila.

The twice yearly barbecue Tom's parents held was this coming Saturday. Tom never usually enjoyed these events as they were mostly attended by people his parents' age. If Tom had a penny for every time he'd been told "My, you are getting so *big* now Tom!" he could stay at the arcade forever or maybe even buy the place. But, Tom being Tom, he'd trotted back to the store happily. Too bad the job of "Trolley Pusher" never paid overtime.

Upon re-entering the store, Tom heard a fanfare, loud and jubilant. He looked around and saw a whole crowd of people closing in on him, blocking his way to the store depths. Flashing lights, streamers and confetti swamped Tom amidst cheers from staff and customers alike. Just *wow!* The beaming manageress gave Tom a smacker of a kiss on his cheek while handing him a bottle of champagne. It was her first day at the supermarket and what a way to start!

"*Congratulations Sir, you are our one millionth customer!*" she gushed, "*You are King for a day!*" A camera flashed, capturing the moment for the local newspaper.

"How does it feel, Sir? Have you any words?" asked a reporter. Tom replied by asking what isle the kitchen roll was on, which caused much laughter.

***

Later on, in the evening, Tom stood staring at the row of crowns on the fruit machine. He was deep in thought. Did what happen this afternoon *really happen*? It did, of course but the real question was *why* did it happen? He was the one millionth customer but *why* had that honour fallen on Tom's lap? Tom spoke out loud, slowly and deliberately, to the fruit machine or to *someone:*

"King for a day . . King for a day. You gave lemons and I *got lemons!* You gave crowns and I became a *king!*" A crack had been found in Tom's thoughts and now a wedge of possibility was being driven down in to his realisation.

Yes, the question really was . . *why?*

3

Becky

The family barbecue had been going for about half an hour. Good weather and good spirits abounded! Yummy smells of beef, pork, bread rolls and sauces filled the air. Guests arrived, some carrying six packs, others home made barbecue sauce and homemade just about anything. Being a barbecue and not a formal dinner invite, it was partially a laid out buffet spread. These always have the advantage that, if you didn't like the look of someone's "Home made" whatever it was, you could just bypass it and no offence taken as nobody knew who'd eaten whatever and nobody knew who hadn't! Three or four children, half Tom's age, ran through the maze of grown ups. Tom's dad manned the barbecue with Tom as co-pilot.

"This is the Captain speaking. Hey buddy, we're running short on burgers!" said Andrew.

"No problem Captain Daddio, I'll nip to the freezer!" replied Tom, jogging off to the garage, where the freezer was. The shade of the garage brought pleasant relief from the summer sun and the stifling barbecue, but when the freezer lid was lifted "*Oh my!*" The large white rectangular box was maybe where winter hibernated during the summer months. Such an escape from a garage full of heat!

Tom was about to reach for a pack of frozen burgers when he saw the one armed bandit nearby. Unable to resist, he abandoned burger duties and slotted a coin. Just then, the beautiful antique grandfather clock in the hallway struck 1pm. Tom momentarily paused to listen then pulled the lever. The gunshot duly sounded but went unheard at the noisy gathering. The reels danced, stopping at a perfect row of three love hearts; shiny, ruby red and oh so *romantic!* Tom was delighted by the hearts and that the machine actually worked.

"No *way!*"

He had, strangely, never noticed the heart symbols before while mending and playing the bandit, yet there the hearts were, and a perfect row of them, no less! The spell cast by the machine which Al had accidentally intruded upon that day was momentarily re-cast. Just *who* was in charge here and just who owned *who?* A voice stopped the answer from forming.

"Hey Tom, did you hear that noise?" asked "Captain Daddio".

"What noise?" replied Tom.

"The sound of rumbling stomachs!"

Tom closed the freezer and jogged back to his dad's side, already regretting bringing so many burgers out as now he had no excuse to return to the garage and claim sanctuary from the heat. The front lawn was simply packed with people, chatter, tasty smells and drifting smoke.

"Good man!" said Dad, "For a while there we were cruising at 30,000 feet with no burgers! Hey lookee, it's our new neighbours. Howdy pardners!"

Tom's mum was welcoming a new family to the neighbourhood. She ushered them up to her well smoked husband; quite an achievement considering he was at 30,000 feet. She did the introductions.

"Honey, I want you to meet John and Susan Hart from across the way! They've moved all the way from Ohio!"

"Hi John, Hi Susan!" came Andrew's voice from somewhere within the smoke, sort of like a Genie. "Well I hope walking all the way from Ohio gave you an appetite!" Everyone ignored a joke that was so old it was originally spoken in Latin. Sheila continued:

"And *this* southern beauty is their daughter *Becky!*"

She put a comforting arm around Becky and gently brought her forward. Becky spoke understandably shyly:

"Hello!" was what they heard . . barely; blushing was what they saw.

Tom was instantly smitten. Becky was the most beautiful thing he had seen, so far, in his short life and surely the reason he was born, *surely*. On a subliminal level and, to be honest, a more blatant level, the amusement arcade was bumped in to second place by potential romance. Tom's mum enthused:

"Why Becky, you're just a year younger than Tom! Now Tom, you be a gentleman and help Becky out here! *Y'all hungry?*"

***

An hour or two later, Tom and Becky were sitting astride the low garden wall, facing each other. Tom was eating his burger with both hands while Becky picked at her food with a plastic knife and fork. During the meal, both made fleeting but sincere eye contact, both dipped their toes in to the unexpected.

Could it be that, this early in their lives, the two of them were being granted centre stage at the greatest show on Earth? Was the curtain rising for *them*? Did the footlights shine on *them*? Was the applause of the waiting, watching and appreciative world sounding for *them*? Tom had only just finished school and Becky was within sight, just two years behind. Neither had even begun to live but now each had stumbled in to the other at the foothills of experience; and you can forget your 15 minutes, this was *surely* forever!

Rookie Tom was dumbstruck and shy. His face hurt from smiling so much, but he managed to strike a seam of backbone from somewhere and said:

"So hey, listen, why don't I show you around tomorrow Becky? I think it's going to be nice out!"

"Sure, I'd really like that!" replied Becky.

Oh, both were *so glad!*

***

Well, the next day *was* indeed beautiful as the weatherman had told Sheila who then had told Tom who then had told Becky. Understandably, Tom was in high spirits, due to the fact that he had discovered why he existed. Now Tom had found the reason for being alive, he had no thoughts of the arcade or of the need to eat or anything else for that matter. As he left the house, heading over to Becky's, he passed his dad who was washing his car.

"Quicker you pass your driving test the quicker you can take Becky out for a spin in *this!*" came the obligatory quip.

"No, it's ok Dad. When I take a girl out I prefer to make a *good* impression!" came the obligatory reply. The double act had been going for years now. Sometimes Tom's dad was the straight guy and sometimes it was the other way around. Dad playfully pointed the hose at Tom for a second as Tom ran out of range of water and quips.

Five sunny minutes later and Tom arrived at Becky's. The house was beautifully kept outside and Tom didn't know whether to attribute this to Becky's family or the previous occupants who had said goodbye to the area with their own barbecue just a week earlier. He rang the doorbell and feasted on anticipation. *What* arcade? A very welcoming Becky's mum answered.

"*Hiii Tom!* How's things? Beautiful day, huh? Becky's upstairs. Go right up and follow the loud music!"

Tom finally got a word in: "Uh hi Mrs Hart! Ok, thanks!"

As Tom started up the stairs he saw Becky's dad out the back washing his car as his own dad had been. It didn't look fun. Incredibly, Becky's dad was dressed nearly the same as Tom's dad. Didn't either dad know what life was *really* about?

Sure enough, the slightly too loud music, and that was from *outside* the room, drew Tom, siren like, to Becky's room door. A trace of perfume filled his nostrils, garnishing, right to the hilt, the feast of anticipation. He knocked and set phasers to "Bliss". Becky answered from within. She sounded harassed.

"*Yeah, hang on a sec.*" preceded the sounds of cardboard boxes being moved and stacked in a corner. Becky then opened the door. Tom didn't know what to react to the most; the too loud music, which she never lowered out of politeness, or the fact that Becky was still wearing her pyjamas with her hair a total mess. Tom tried but found it near impossible to muster a smile when expectations and reality didn't quite match up. Becky spoke loudly over the blaring music:

"Oh it's *you*. Sorry, what's your name again?"

She may as well have said "Do you have any last words before sentence is carried out?" Tom struggled and replied, loudly:

"*Tom, it's Tom.*"

"Right! I think I met you yesterday."

"That's right, yesterday." said Tom, now staring at the floor. "I said I'd show you around."

"Did you? Well maybe some other time huh? Thanks for calling!"

She closed the door on Tom, who now wished he was 30 years older and out the back, washing a car.

4

Nudge Canyon

"Hey, lover boy, back so soon?" was a fine parental tonic for the way Tom was feeling as he plodded back up the drive. Dad was now polishing the car. As Tom passed, he saw himself reflected in the car door and momentarily wondered if his reflection fared any better with *his* potential girlfriend.

Now, dad was "Dad" and all that, but he saw his son was crestfallen and knew exactly why, as, unbeknownst to crestfallen Tom, his dad had plodded those very same steps many years before. It hurt to see this, so he tried to help.

"They've only just moved here, buddy. Give it a few more days then try again!" Tom only half-heard this over the sound of his entire world falling apart. He had just been so *sure* he had found the reason for being alive.

In to the garage then, plodded Tom, to escape the heat and recent events. He stood in front of the one armed bandit which still proudly displayed the three love hearts. They seemed to actually beat, or was that a trick of the light? *Oh my*, how Tom was hurting! Wouldn't *anyone* hurt if the pretty girl next door tore out his heart, spat on it and threw it in to a clump of nettles?

Tom took a coin from his pocket. It was the very coin he'd lost to the machine the day he discovered it. Tom had intended to keep the coin for some sentimental reason but now all he wanted to do was spin the reels to move the mocking hearts from view then go and lie down till he turned 100.

So, he slotted the coin, pulled the arm, gunshot sounded, bandit fled, reels span. One by one, clunk by clunk, the reels stopped, giving two love hearts in a perfect line with the third heart sitting just one space too high. Tom sighed heavily at the sight. The tantalisingly incomplete line of love hearts was an all too apt metaphor for "So near and yet so far".

"Tell me about it!" mumbled Tom at the end of his first taste of adult life. He would have put another coin in but didn't have any so just walked away.

Suddenly, the gunshot fired again. Tom whipped round to see the machine acting as it had never done previously. Every light on the display started to flash in a beautiful, hypnotic sequence. The bandit's arm shook very firmly as if prompting Tom's next move. The word "NUDGE" flashed altogether too brightly, making Tom squint. This almost frantic behaviour from the machine caught Tom unawares, making him forget the last half an hour with ease. Could it be that, in giving Tom a chance to bring the three hearts in to line, the one armed bandit was offering to help Tom with his love life? No one was around to hear the gratitude in Tom's voice as he pulled the lever.

"Thanks buddy, don't mind if I do!"

Suddenly, Tom felt like a fish out of water, trying to breathe but not accustomed to an alien way of doing so. He stood there, gasping and gulping. Every time he blinked he saw a new world, one of confusion and unreadiness and full moon mystery. He saw things as vividly as the normal world. When he closed his eyes for the third time and opened them, this new world remained. Either the new world was visiting Tom or he was visiting *it*. Fear, the like of which Tom, in his admittedly short life, had never known, sprang from nearby, where it had been waiting, and plundered his heart.

For Tom was no longer in the garage at home but way out in the desert at night; way *way* out in the desert at night. This change of location, and the rudeness of that change, struck loud fear in to him, almost to knee buckling point.

It had been bright sunshine when Tom had entered the garage but here it was true midnight with a soaring full moon. Nocturnal animals could be heard as Tom's eyes adjusted. A fully saddled horse stood nearby, snuzzling the ground nonchalantly, looking for greenery. Tom, at this point, understandably bewildered and stun-shocked, still did not understand that the *real* reason he became owner of the one armed bandit was now being revealed to him.

Now the meeting of Tom and the one armed bandit was finally consummated.

Now Tom stood in Nudge Canyon . .

.. the *real* Nudge Canyon.

The terrain was desert but rough desert; home of the cactus, night creature and those forced by circumstance to pass this way. Tom saw he was indeed in a canyon as either side rose fairly sharply to hem in all inhabitants. He thought he could hear a river somewhere off but couldn't pinpoint it. A fair breeze was blowing.

What was there to do now but move and explore and account for this new location Tom found himself in? He took a step forward and was momentarily glad his legs still worked. He heard a crunch underfoot accompanied by sparks, both of which caused Tom to jump back with a yelp. He had stood on a nearly extinct campfire, scattering embers and sparks and nearly re-igniting the thing. Suddenly:

"Tom, Tom, over here!" cried a woman's voice. Her cry faded in and out on the wind like a hampered radio signal. Tom was astonished to hear his name called but also relieved somewhat. He looked and saw Becky in the distance, waving her arms. He also saw a group of about eight or so men on horseback, just past Becky, riding away with all speed. Who

those men were or what on earth Becky was doing there Tom didn't know or care, he just set off at a jog towards her. With his first few steps he passed a sign that read:

CLEAN GETAWAY – 1 MILE

Becky seemed to be standing next to a small wooden building. A hut maybe? Popping noises with a slight crack in them caused Tom to look behind, where he saw flashes out of sync with the popping. Suddenly, Tom heard a quirky sound like a short, jabbing, laser pulse. It sounded like any sound he'd heard at the arcade.

The ground around Tom's feet burst open from bullet strikes as the wind suddenly became forceful, causing tumbleweeds to hurtle past. The quirky laser sound was bullet near misses from the posse, the now frighteningly real posse. Tom was now all out sprinting towards Becky. He had been chased by things in his dreams before but this was in another league, the league of reality.

"Hurry Tom, they're coming!"

Tom was close enough now to see the fear on Becky's face. He was also close enough to see that she was not standing next to a hut but to an overturned stagecoach. There were other people there apart from Becky but none were without injury. Two bodies, either dead or as well to be, lay on the ground amidst a sickly syrup of blood mingled with sand and another, a woman, was half in/half out of the carriage, moving spasmodically, moaning terribly. Torn asunder luggage was strewn everywhere. Two of the four horses pulling the stagecoach were dead. The other horses, caught up in it all, pulled to flee the scene and the fallen but were stuck, pulling the immovable stagecoach of death that would journey no more.

Becky cried again but Tom could not hear her over thundering hooves with an horrific reputation. Had he been middle aged with your typical middle aged physique and stamina, it would have been curtains for Tom as he had run nearly a mile. But, the wheel of "Extreme youth attributes/drawbacks" stopped spinning at "Youthful Fitness". Ten more yards to Becky, who was now close enough for Tom to see she stood next to a sign which read

CLEAN GETAWAY

This sign was just outside a little town that, bizarrely, oozed with friendliness and safety. With just a few yards left to run, a lasso, thrown by a maestro of the art, caught Tom, pinning his arms to his side. Becky just screamed.

"*It's over, Ketchum!*" shouted the sheriff.

The lasso was on Tom but the momentum of the sheriff's horse took time to slow and gave Tom just enough straining steps, over dead bodies and all, to reach Becky and pass the sign. When that happened . . *FLASH!!!*

With a thump and an awful grunt, Tom returned to the real world, dropping an awkward height or so on to the garage floor. He lay there in terror, thrashing and gasping.

"*NO NO NO NO!*"

The lasso the sheriff caught him with was still around him. Tom looked down at it in terror then threw it from himself like you would throw off a rattlesnake. For what seemed like an age, Tom just lay there, totally shaken to the core and utterly unnerved with shock. Who knows what Tom's dad would have thought had he walked in to the garage at that moment. Mercifully, no one *did* enter the garage, giving Tom time and privacy to deal with the experience at his own pace.

He rolled over on to his front then rose to all fours with his head hanging down, clawing the garage floor again and again to convince himself it was real. Leaning on the fruit machine, Tom raised himself to his feet. His eyes went straight to the CLEAN GETAWAY sign, which was now flashing. Breathing deeply, he looked and saw that the three love hearts were now perfectly in line. The pictorial bandit had made it through Nudge Canyon, escaping to Clean Getaway with his spoils.

Five minutes later and Tom was in the the bathroom, shirtless and throwing water on his face. He repeatedly looked at his reflections in both the mirror and water. If what had just happened had been real, he never wanted it again; if it had been purely *imaginary*, he never wanted it again. Tom's physical return to his world was instantaneous, his *emotional* return would not be so quick. He had thoughts of burning the lasso, if he could bring himself to look at it, let alone touch it. Whichever way Tom cared to see it, the last half hour of his life had been a "*Wow*" and a fairly brutal one at that. In the midst of these insistent and jarring thoughts, Tom thought he heard the doorbell. He was right. Sheila shouted up to him:

"*Tom, it's Becky!*"

Tom heard the cheerfulness in his mother's voice and wondered just what she had been doing when he had been way way out in the desert in the middle of the night, nearly dying. He felt an incredible urge to run downstairs and tell his mother everything, just to unburden himself from the weight of the experience, for it sat heavily on his shoulders like a giant scorpion; ugly and viciously undesirable and just waiting to get the angle right for another sting. Tom could almost feel its segmented, bony legs digging in to him. He put his shirt back on and plodded downstairs.

I'll burn the rope and smash the one armed bandit to bits immediately I've finished chatting to Becky, he thought.

Tom opened the slightly ajar front door and Becky's beauty and the sunny day both rushed for Tom's affections.

Becky really did look stunning! Tom had seen Becky a few minutes ago in Nudge Canyon when his usual world had been unexpectedly spliced with that of the fruit machine and just stared at her, wondering if she was here or there. He looked around at his surroundings as if he'd just been born.

"*Hi again Tom!*" smiled Becky.

Tom just blankly stared at her. Becky noticed this but was on some sort of an emotional high, be it by her nature or some other force.

"*Hi Tom!*" She gave a tiny wave. "Is my tour guide ready for a tour! I'm sorry I seemed so off putting but we've just moved here and everything. I think you're really nice!" Tom blinked hard twice and smiled meekly, the best he could do, considering.

"Boy, I'm glad to hear that!" he said.

Becky's sincerity, smile and scent gave her full absolution in Tom's eyes. Becky had beaten the sunny day in the race for Tom's affections but there would be other sunny days. A delighted Becky realised this and her smile beamed.

"*Well, let's go!*" she said.

With the the three ruby red and "oh so romantic!" love hearts now perfectly aligned and Becky's "feminine to the hilt" affections now within easy reach, the one armed bandit had kept its part of the bargain.

5

The Catch

Tom and Becky spent the rest of the day walking the walk of the utterly carefree. Tom's outlook on life went from zero to 60 in 5 seconds then 60 to light speed over the next few hours. They walked closely, every now and then coming in to slight contact, which thrilled both. Tom's jokes were just the funniest in the world and all his opinions were the right opinions! Becky's jokes were the funniest in the world and all her opinions were also the right opinions! Call it Utopia or Shangri la but who would quibble with a set up like *this?*

The local park was extremely beautiful and had a boating pond. On a day like this, there was fun at every turn and at all points of the compass! Tom had bought ice creams and Becky offered hers up to Tom, who took a bite. Tom would have reciprocated this gesture but he was a guy, so completely forgot to.

While out on the pond's safe water, Tom looked at Becky more than he listened, and not because she was pretty but because he wanted to ask her why she had been in Nudge

Canyon. He did not want to invite ridicule from Becky or blow this beautiful day with her so he just smiled and rowed. Becky stood up, making the boat wobble, and sat down next to Tom, taking one of the oars from him.

"I wonder if this will make us go twice as fast?" she asked.

Tom couldn't work out if she was joking or not, but he wasn't going to explain her absurd grasp of physics right at *that* moment as she was sitting right up against him! Of course, as centuries of those very physics predicted, they went round in circles; big, wobbling, splashy, laughy circles and it was obvious neither wanted it any other way! Tom put his arm round Becky and his hand over hers and that regained enough seamanship to make it to shore. Tom climbed out first and offered Becky his hand to help her disembark, which she accepted. It was difficult for both not to vocalise their delight and both blushed a little when neither let go of the other and both walked off holding hands.

Oh, the joy of new experiences!

To gaze upon something you have only ever heard others tell of; the Northern Lights or a meteor shower! To hear something you have only ever heard others enthuse about; a valley full of a hundred calling cuckoos or your first ever visit to the opera! To touch your newborn's skin and realise that the millions before you who gushed about it endlessly weren't lying! To hold your darling love in your arms, where – just the very day before – all you held were your dreams and longings! When the new introduces itself, shake its hand and your world will stand still!

In the twilight, Tom and Becky, arm in arm and heart in heart, arrived at Becky's front door. Tom was thinking of what to say that didn't sound too cliché. Becky saved him the trouble by putting both her hands round his neck fairly tightly. *Wow*, those beautiful eyes of hers!

"Now *that's* what I call a *tour!*" she said in a tone surprisingly sultry and tantalisingly peppered with italics. Tom put his arms around her waist and also spoke "Italic".

"Now *that's* what I call a *tourist!*"

They kissed their first kiss and the new introduced itself. Tom shook its hand and the world indeed stood still. What arcade? What Nudge Canyon? What lasso? What *anything?* Becky released slightly.

"Can I call you tomorrow?" she asked.

"I'll be a waitin'!"

Becky gave Tom a quick peck on the cheek then went indoors, blowing Tom a kiss before closing the front door. The one armed bandit had indulged Tom right from the start. First an avalanche of lemons then a town full of kingly admiration for the young man and well . . well *now!*

The machine was letting Tom know it never did things by halves. He turned and looked up with eyes closed.

"*YES!*"

He pumped the air like he was trying to wrench the moon from the sky.

***

The clock at Tom's bedside read 11:30 am. Becky had wanted to call Tom straight after breakfast but Tom said he would be accompanying his mother first thing. Hearing this only made Becky like him all the more, judging her tone of voice.

Tom was now lying on his bed, kicking his leg out as he chatted to Becky. He had just returned from town, where he and his mum had been at the "King for a day" store. Tom's King for a day experience had been fun. He had received, among other things, several substantial "money off" vouchers, some of which his mum used today. Most customers knew Tom by name now and one or two of the floor staff teased him by calling him "Majesty" whenever he shopped. Like his dad at the barbecue, Tom was cruising at 30,000 feet, the exact altitude of Cloud 9. If you'd eavesdropped on him, you'd have easily known who was on the other end of the line. This was, again, the season of *italicised talk!*

"Yeah, I think *you're* pretty cool too!"

"You looked *stunning* yesterday!"

"*OK, OK,* it was *my* first kiss too!"

And so on and so on. That beautiful clock in the hallway would strike its gently exquisite chime dutifully, the gorgeous sound trying to break it gently that, as much as it would like to, time has no favourites and cannot wait for us.

Time, what *is it* with you? Just whose side are you *on?* Yesterday, the best day in Tom's life, had already drawn to a close when some secretary, somewhere, filed it under "M" for "Memories". Whenever we attempt to make "Today" last forever, time always has the last say, hence the existence of diaries and photo albums. The very fact that we have the word "Tomorrow" should drop a huge hint that "Today" will not last. A person could wonder if time was ever embarrassed to break up a party when it was all going so well.

"Hey, fancy going bowling midweek?" asked Tom. An easy question to ask and a doozy to answer.

"Wow, you *bet!*" sprang forth Becky's italicised answer. Wednesday, usually a bland milestone to mark the halfway point of the week was now bestowed with the power to thrill beyond comprehension. *Eat your heart out, Saturday!*

"Great! I'm not much of a bowler though! said Tom.

"Don't worry, *no one is!*" replied Becky, laughing almost musically.

Just at that moment, the grandfather clock in the hall chimed 1pm. Tom looked at the bedside clock. Where has the time *gone!* Becky fell silent as the 1pm chime faded away. Silence of a weird kind now joined the party. Like receiving a hard, unexpected, slap, the change in the atmosphere was frighteningly sudden and palpable.

"Becky?"

Nothing.

"*BECKY*?"

Nothing but the most awful silence. The most awful awful silence dripping with contempt and indifference. Tom could hear Becky breathing on the other end of the line. A thunderclap of cruelty broke the eerie stalemate as Becky spoke;

"Look, why don't you go and bother someone else, OK?" and then "*CLICK*", call over.

Now there was another kind of silence, a mocking aftershock of a deadness as Tom sat on his bed. His breathing deepened and deepened until, with a cry of anguish, he threw the phone against the wall. Tom had been riding the crest of a wave and, in the revelry of his heart, had failed to notice that, sometimes, those kind of waves lap not up on to a beautiful, secluded beach, but shatter against mockingly sharp rocks so ugly that they could hail from another planet. His majestic and viking like galleon of joy had sailed clear off the edge of the world to tumble endlessly through sad space.

Tom's inexperience banged its nose when it ran full tilt in to this very steep learning curve. His parents would have gently warned him about this potential pitfall but it was so early on in matters! Nobody expects their new television to break down after two days but, in this eerie case and with no manufacturers guarantee, it had done just that.

"What is *wrong* with her? What is *WRONG WITH HER?*" fumed Tom. "One day hot, the next day cold!"

Suddenly, Tom's emotions unexpectedly subsided. The wave he rode stopped sadistically and repeatedly crashing upon ugly alien rocks. Thoughts formed clearly. Emotional pain was flicked off at a switch, leaving Tom speechless; relieved but speechless. He didn't know at that moment but a flicker of emotional maturity, just a pilot light's worth, a down payment on emotional strength passing years would bestow, happened by at the most opportune time.

In this calm, Tom could see forever and knew every in and out there was. He thought back to the day after the lemon spill and the conversation with his mother:

"*PHEW!* Tom honey, can you get rid of these lemons, I was just about to make a lemon . . lemon . . *something* when they went bad, right in front of me!" said Sheila as she wafted her hand in front of her look of disgust. "They were so fresh up until a moment ago!"

Back to the present and clarity of thought counselled Tom. He now pondered the "King for a day" experience. He saw the scene. He heard the applause. He remembered the script now, completely:

"King for a day! You are King for a day! You rule the town till *tomorrows sundown!*" gushed the manageress as she handed Tom a bottle of champagne amidst streamers and applause.

"Everything I win lasts only 24 hours." said a tad more mature Tom. He covered his face with his hands and slouched the slouch of the broken within.

"Including Becky!"

A pattern rose to the surface, because there's *always* a pattern, isn't there? The catch, seizing the heartbroken moment, declared itself unashamedly, because there's *always* a catch, isn't there? All rewards and all fun and all "love of a pretty girl" lasted only 24 hours.

Tom sat, with clarity moving on and emotional pain returning. If the one armed bandit ever had a smile, that smile had now slipped a little.

6

Second Visit

One week later and things were different. Those influences that had rocked Tom's boat had lost their venom and weren't so scary to think about anymore simply because Tom had not made contact with them. He hadn't seen Becky for a whole seven days, that's a long time in the "Puppy Love Calendar"! The one armed bandit was unplugged and with a thin layer of dust on it, its stomach rumbling for coins.

Tom came down the stairs looking fresh and happy. He was whistling to himself. Mum heard this as she was chopping vegetables and smiled. She also smiled a tremendous smile inwardly. Sheila was totally happy go lucky and just took life as it came. "If life gives you lemons, make lemonade and if it gives you rotten lemons, make *rotten* lemonade!" was her basic outlook. She never looked round but kept chopping as she spoke:

"Hi Honey! Whatcha got planned for today? Gonna see Becky?"

"Nah" replied Tom, "Haven't seen her for a week now." He stared out the window, saw a beautiful day and didn't need Becky to make it any more beautiful.

"What a beautiful day not to have a girlfriend!" said Tom as if it were a one sentence declaration of emancipation speech. "I thought I might meet up with the guys at the mall and take it from there."

"Is it also a beautiful day to mow the lawn?" asked Sheila, cautiously. A wry smile came over Tom as he turned to face her.

"Sure!" he said, already halfway out to get the lawnmower.

***

As Tom was getting the mower out, he heard someone four or five houses away doing their lawn too. It *was* a beautiful part of the world Tom and his kindred gardener lived in, and would continue to be so if all would just play their part. Tom pulled the cord and, dormant season over, the ravenous mower growled in to life. One row was cut, then another and on to the third. Oh those dark and light green lines looked *so good!*

Suddenly, Tom did a double take as he saw Becky cycling past with some of her girlfriends. The sound of the mower was now drowned out by the sound of Tom's thumping heart. As his eyes followed the group until they were out of sight, his breathing became deeper and he became flushed. Covering his face with his hands, Tom suffered once more.

"Oh no, oh no, oh NOOO!"

Tom was utterly ambushed by emotion and in that ambush, common sense was slain. In a few blinks of an eye, he abandoned the lawnmower, stepped over the battle fallen common sense, headed to the garage and plugged in the one armed bandit, slotting a coin before the machine could even get in to "Attract Mode".

Pulling the lever and hoping for the best – having previously experienced the *worst* – Tom watched as the reels span. They stopped at one love heart in line but the remaining two just one space too high. *Two* nudges would be required this time to align all three hearts. Colourful and sequential lights shone in an alluring pattern and the machine's arm shook as it told Tom the two nudges he needed were exactly what was on offer.

He reached out to the lever and hesitated, turning to look where Becky had just cycled past. The invisible countdown, that began after Tom returned from Nudge Canyon the first time, now reached zero. With eyes tightly closed and knowing full well what he was letting himself in for, he pulled the bandit's arm.

In a heartbeat, Tom stood again – and alone – in the awful loop that was Nudge Canyon.

Everything was as before: the full moon, the waiting horse, the gentle breeze that pushed reluctant tumbleweeds to somewhere. There was that river sound again.

Using what little, if dramatic, experience he had in this place, Tom immediately looked to where he had seen Becky, but saw only the sign she had stood next to. No friendly face *now*. There was no upturned stagecoach with dead occupants either and this brought comfort, albeit stone cold. He also saw the exact replay of the eight or so rough looking riders, past the sign, fleeing. A train's whistle sounded, quite powerfully but obviously far off.

"*BECKY!*" shouted Tom in vain hope. The only reply he heard was the popping sounds and muzzle flashes he had experienced before. He knew what that meant.

"Oh *NO!*"

He may have escaped by the skin of his teeth last time, but some bizarre history book now read that he *had indeed escaped!* The after effect of actually escaping the posse *once* gave Tom an injection of bravado disguised as courage.

Whatever it was that coursed through Tom's veins would be needed right now as he glanced at the nearby sign which read:

Bravado took a low blow and hit the canvas at the sign's declaration an extra mile stood between Tom and all he held dear. He ran to the horse in panic, hoping he, or it, would know what to do. The horse resisted and kicked out a few times in response to Tom's bridle grabbing fumblings but then acquiesced, allowing him to mount up ineptly, as if it was all a black comedy. The breeze matured instantly in to a howl that gave a somber warning of impending doom as the posse approached. The wheels of justice were turning in Nudge Canyon. Spiked wheels these were with axels unapologetically greased with outlaws' blood. Tom knew from before that it was all, every bit of it, every ravenous "justice in full momentum" bit of it, coming for *him*.

Finally on the horse, which still pirouetted and reared slightly in confusion, Tom screamed "*C'MON!*" The horse suddenly became itself again. It seemed to know what to do and took off at a blast that nearly toppled Tom off backwards. He grabbed handfuls of bridle and mane as he hugged its neck tightly, forming a sleek silhouette with his speeding ally.

All parties hurtled through Nudge Canyon with only their shadows keeping pace. Bullets and shouted threats from the posse were tearing past. One shot splattered a cactus Tom was passing inches from. Nocturnal creatures scattered at the violent intrusion. Moonlight was not designed to shine down on *this*. Off to the side, Tom heard the train whistle. Not too far to the next sign now.

This rickety old sign that had stood alone in the belting desert heat for years was now a monumental hinge on which Tom's future swung. No gateway back to Mum, Dad, and Becky, just the portal to more nightmare.

The horse, oblivious to anything except going as fast as it could in a straight line, stayed strong for its rider, tearing past the CLEAN GETAWAY – 1 MILE sign. Somewhere way off, out of reach in an intangible other world, a love heart symbol on a fruit machine dropped in to place, making an incomplete row of two.

***

Tom's mum, who was walking past the one armed bandit carrying some laundry, heard the metallic clunk of the reel moving a notch and looked around for a second before loading up the dryer.

***

Off to the left and getting closer, the train sounded its horn again but in a more prolonged manner. On and on went the straining whistle. The train seemed to be screaming for its life and screaming for help. The path of the train was gradually splicing with Tom's flight through Nudge Canyon.

The group of rough looking riders Tom had seen before were level with the last carriage. They were, thankfully, on the other side of the speeding train. Some had mounted the outside of the carriage and were walking the walk of death along the speeding carriage tops towards the engine. They looked like monkeys clambering over a car as it drives through a safari park. One of the outlaws was just shooting his pistols in to the air over and over, either to frighten the passengers into submission or just out of sheer mindlessness .. BANG BANG BANG BANG.

The passengers in the last carriage, outnumbered in maliciousness but certainly not in courage, bravely engaged in a gunfight with the desperados, the nocturnal desert lighting up with flurries of muzzle flashes from both parties. One outlaw was struck by a shot and tumbled off, his body falling awkwardly and disjointedly, discarded by Nudge Canyon as mere collateral damage. Screams came from the carriage as outlaw bullets hit home, more from luck than skill.

Tom's gorgeous horse drew level with this last carriage. Realising he was in the loop with no one but himself to blame, Tom just held on for dear life as his horse ran for such. Just how many bullets did everybody *have?*, because the shots just kept flying. Tom just wanted to stop it all and explain to posse and passengers that he was nothing to do with all this and that all he was guilty of was squandering the money his mother had given him for groceries that day.

Suddenly Tom saw Becky in the last carriage before the engine. She was all alone and obviously in distress like the last time, reaching out to Tom and pleading with him to hurry. A bullet grazed Tom's shoulder and nicked the horses ear. Tom shouted in pain for himself *and* the horse, but nothing slowed and the engine was finally drawn level with, the noise becoming utterly tremendous and brutal with a sound so loud it could induce vomiting.

Tom reached for the handrail just as a volley of bullets sank its teeth in to his horse. The beautiful, swift creature, Tom's friend, turned in to a tumbling mass of blood, muscle and devotion as it rolled endlessly, coming to a halt as a rare feast for the vultures of Nudge Canyon.

Now grabbing both handrails, a bullet grazed along Tom's shoulder blades. He screamed in pain, thinking a hot poker had been placed across his back.

Falling on to the floor of the engine cab, Tom immediately felt a sustained and ice cold prod to his forehead. It was the barrel of a pistol held by the driver.

"Stand up real slow now!" said the driver, loudly, over the racket of the scene. His voice was full of caution mingled with concealed surprise. He was as nervous as Tom was but at least he held the gun. A good thing trains can steer themselves at times like these because Tom – and whether he would still be alive 10 seconds from now – was all either man could think of at that moment.

He grabbed Tom by his hair very tightly, causing Tom to grimace. This anguished look gave the driver even more psychological leverage as the bizarre encounter continued. In the background, dangerous bang bang noises of this eventful evening went on unapologetically.

Eventually eye to eye with the driver, Tom saw a fairly aged and fairly plump face covered with sweat which was covered with soot. A frown from the depths of righteous indignation sat upon the driver's work worn face. What a situation! From both parties viewpoint, life was bad enough, but *this!*

Letting go of Tom's hair and taking half a step back with the gun still pressed against Tom's forehead and with the screaming steaming train about to break the sound barrier twice over, the driver sarcastically asked:

"Can I see your ticket please?"

The moment was just too much for now pleading Tom:

"*No please, no please . . I . ."* But "please" was simply not going to cut it here. The driver's expression and voice became totally angry.

"*You've got 3 seconds to tell me yer name.*"

Tom half screamed "*IT'S TOM . . IT'S TOM.*"

At the hearing of this, a macabre smile swept over the drivers face, like he had just seen his ex wife fall in to a cactus patch. He seemed to pause, relishing this moment, which would one day become an anecdote for drinking buddies and gawping grandchildren.

"Goodbye Blackjack and *hello reward!*" said the driver, unable to believe his luck. He cocked the hammer and pulled the trigger without hesitation just as the train passed the CLEAN GETAWAY sign. When that happened . . *FLASH.*

✳✳✳

With a thump and an awful grunt, Tom landed on the garage floor. The shoulder and back wounds were clearly visible along with a red circular indentation in his forehead where the barrel of a pistol had been pressed. He lay, gasping desperately, reaching out with stiffened arms to defend himself from the train driver who wasn't there anymore.

"No please, wait. No PLEASE!" The lawn mower sat purring in the half cut garden.

All three parts of Tom's young, barely touched psyche, had just been twisted out of joint with a three reeled cackle. Distraught Tom needed time, and very likely, medical attention, before he could return to any semblance of normality. He heard his mum speak. She must have heard Tom's plea to the train driver.

"Tom, did you say something, honey?"

He heard her enter the kitchen. Three more steps and she'd be in the garage. Mum seeing Tom like he was would do nothing less than open up a Pandora's Box of questions from his parents that Tom could never answer, well, answer and be *believed*. Tom rolled under his dad's pick up truck, rolling over his wounds and yelping slightly. Thankfully the lawn mower mostly blotted out his cries of pain. He could only hope his mother wouldn't see blood on the garage floor.

"TOM?" she cried, a little louder. Luckily for Tom, the one armed bandit was placed on the far side of the garage and she would not walk that way to go in to the garden. He watched her feet walk past and gave her a few seconds. He heard the lawnmower being turned off then rolled and yelped out from under the vehicle.

"Just taking a break, mum. Goin' upstairs for a minute." he shouted. He waited till she replied "Ok darlin', just thought you needed me." to make sure she would not continue looking for him and see the bloody floor, then ran, and yelped, upstairs to his room.

In the midst of all this nerve jangling predicament concealment, it went completely unnoticed that the three love hearts were now perfectly in line.

***

Tom was in the shower washing very, *very* tentatively. He yelped and jumped from his wounds. It was a terrific relief when he realised they were deep grazes but nothing more serious.

"I nearly died. I could have died. I nearly died."

This was serious.

Last time it was a lasso, this time it was actual wounds; real, bleeding injuries. Like so often in life when a product is seen in a glitzy television commercial and purchased hastily – ignoring the small print – the one armed bandit, at first oh so benevolent, now demanded potentially lethal penalties for its helpful nudges.

This was serious.

Blood is the ultimate confirmation that any given situation is perfectly serious. Tom stood in the shower with bloody water swirling at his feet. There was blood on the garage floor. There were blood soaked clothes Tom would have to burn.

This was serious.

Tom had succumbed to the peer pressure of circumstance and indulged in his first "Hit" the day after the barbecue, and now, another hit. In the joy of receiving rewards, the pain and disappointment of the comedown that always followed – emotional or physical – had been snatched from Tom's attention by cunning misdirection and promises of greater treasures ahead.

Young and carefree Tom, who loved fun first and foremost, was being forced to scale the north face of a very steep learning curve with no ropes or crampons and no climbing companions. Was he a pioneer of Nudge Canyon or had others passed that way? When Tom had first found the machine that day at Al's, he had, to his credit, sensed an indecipherable "something" about it. He had now graduated from the University of Betrayal, enabling him to read the hieroglyphs which stated quite categorically that the one armed bandit and Tom were enemies.

And had been . . all along.

***

Tom had wanted to rest for a while but, sensibly, had quickly returned to the garage to hose blood from the floor. The family first aid kit in the kitchen had been a real pal and patched Tom up fairly well. He was wearing a black t-shirt to hide any bleed throughs. He stood, staring blankly at the three love hearts when a hand tapped him on the shoulder. He whirled around very quickly, for a variety of understandable reasons.

"*YEAGHHHHH!!!*"

It was Becky, and *then some!* Some girls are just born with it, it would seem!

"Sorry, Cowboy, did I startle you?"

In a tenth of a second, Tom nearly cried then nearly laughed then nearly cried then nearly laughed. Eventually, with his heart unable to choose, he just smiled and sighed.

"It's ok, I'm getting kinda used to startling experiences!"

"So more boating today Tom?" asked Becky.

"Well ok if you . ." he realised the hose was still on and he and Becky were in a growing puddle. " . . *oh wow, sorry!*" Becky put her arms round Tom's neck like a necklace of soothing balm, the ingredients of which only women know. She stared in to his eyes, lovingly.

"Can I get a *kiss*, Captain?"

Since the dawn of time, no man has ever *spoken* the answer to such a question as *actions* speak louder than words!

Later that evening and the couple were in the local hang out in town: a large, neon lit place of pool tables and juke box satisfaction. A couple of gaming cabinets stood in a corner. Tom had played these games a few times. It slipped by him that the positioning of the games, standing in the corner, alone, was something of a metaphor for the shift in Tom's priorities. Alcohol was available, and consumed, but it garnished the fun as opposed to summoning its sidekick "trouble" like it did at the harsher drinking venues in town.

The large and extremely atmospheric room was a microcosm and government unto itself, with all citizens harmonising with ease. Tom's friends: Lisa, Gemma and Kyle, were there and, well, what more does an 18 year old guy called "Anybody" want?

For, as awful as his second visit to Nudge Canyon was, it had the effect of unlocking Becky's love for another day. Tom just truly, well and truly, well and well and truly and truly, could not believe who was sitting on his knee!

What more does an 18 year old guy called "Anybody" want? .. *THIS!* A two piece jigsaw he and Becky were as they sat at a booth under neon up lighting. Lisa sat on Kyle's knee, leaving Gemma the rank of fifth wheel.

"Oh now Gemma" said Becky "that is so unfair you sitting there alone!"

Gemma replied: "Yeah, kinda sucks, huh, but Lenny said he was busy tonight." Lisa part spluttered out her drink as they all laughed.

"Yeah, I know!" said Kyle "I've heard they put his name inside misfortune cookies." A few more splutters then two hours of much the same, followed.

***

"Oh boy, is that the time?" Lisa exclaimed "Better get going. Got work tomorrow." When she said that, Tom's heart sank. Time and its sidekick "Tomorrow" were the things he didn't want to think about. He had glanced over Gemma's shoulder at the trendy clock repeatedly throughout the evening because Becky's love, so intense and custom built for Tom, had a shelf life and was little more in true, lasting value than any prize you would win at a fun fair. The taste of Becky's affections did indeed do what it said on the tin : "Will blow the mind of the user!" but, as Tom sadly knew, that wonderful and exotic taste lasted about as long as the flavour in a piece of bubble gum.

Lisa, Gemma and Kyle left. Tom and Becky had a slow dance, Becky leaning her head in to Tom's chest. As they slowly turned, Tom kept seeing the clock which seemed to deliberately jump out at him.

About and hour later and the couple walk up to Becky's front door. Becky's affections remained undiminished. She hugged Tom's waist. Amazingly, Becky's hugs and embraces, throughout the entire lively evening, had missed all Tom's wounds, but the sadistically slow draining of sand from the hourglass of Becky's love had not missed Tom's heart. Every smile and response to any of Becky's jokes had been forced and it had been a real drain on the poor boy.

Before he even knew it, Becky kissed Tom.

"Well thank you very much my handsome outlaw!"

At the mention of the word "Outlaw" Tom could almost feel desert beneath his feet and boiling gunfire. He staggered ever so slightly.

"Why do you say that?" he asked and was genuinely afraid of the answer.

"'Cause you've stolen my heart!"

Hardly a crime.

Becky went inside, turned and looked at Tom.

"See you tomorrow then, handsome!" she said with a finger wiggle wave, closing the door. Tom nodded and, for some unknown reason, smiled his first genuine smile of the evening.

"Sure, see you tomorrow Becky!" passed Tom's lips, bourne on a knowing sigh.

Ten minutes later and Tom stood in front of the one armed bandit. It seemed to stare back at him. Having had several murderous dress rehearsals with the machine, Tom knew his lines and spoke them bang on cue:

"I know what you're going to do, buddy!"

He slotted a coin and played. The reels stopped at three love hearts, all sitting just one space too high. Three nudges would be required to bring them in to line this time. The lights flashed and the arm shook, offering exactly that. Tom sighed and a look of maturity that neither he nor his parents nor the world at large would expect to see for another twenty years, appeared on his face.

"Sorry Becky, but either your love dies or I do!"

He unplugged the machine, shoved it in to a corner, face first, then covered it with a tarpaulin.

7

The Final Hunt

It was Saturday morning, one month later.

The shopping mall, unfailingly, was the place to be. A welcome change of scenery for honest workers, the building was a three storey vacation. Even your boss could be seen in a new light as they were sometimes seen with family members out for some joy. You could even be tempted to think your boss was human after all. Anyhow, the mall was very busy and generated the most happy atmosphere.

On the first floor was a vibrant jingling of a coffee shop called "Pit Stop". A totally open plan affair with a racing car theme. Several outlets of this new chain had opened up recently and were riding high on the honeymoon period of the "something new in town" novelty effect, which maybe accounted for the extra bustle in the place. An autographed, sellotape-mended poster of a whitened teeth racing driver was on the wall. It had been torn in half the week before by the driver's ex-girlfriend, who happened to see it. Open plan allowed that beckoning aroma to hook customers, causing them to veer off course just ever so slightly for caffeine fuel or a milk shake, if that revved your engine. So much in life is about the luring, isn't it?

At one table sat Tom with his buddies, the same buddies from the neon night out. They were speaking young speak and laughing young laugh, operating according to the manufacturer's instructions exactly. It was a testimony to the fun aspect of Saturday at the mall that Tom was there and *not* at the arcade. All that Tom was had been shuffled and shuffled over and over by recent events and all of it against his will. In Tom's private thoughts and feelings, the cards were now in a new order but at least the pack was still intact and, for the most part, Tom had regained his old self, enough anyway to make people who knew him think nothing had happened at all. The physical injuries he received were all but healed and he was now able to sleep better at night. Just a little while more of this and Tom would be home free with his whole life in front of him.

"Maybe I'm single because guys don't like my cooking?" said Gemma as she admired her reflection in a nearby chrome surface, even though it was distorted, "Don't know why 'cause I make textbook lasagne!"

"Yeah you do!" chirped Kyle, adding "It tastes like an old textbook!"

"So Tom, where's Becky and where have you been?" asked Lisa.

"Somewhere else and somewhere else." said Tom, answering both questions. The reason Tom hadn't been around so much was that, barring helping his mum at the supermarket, he'd been spending lots of time alone, either in his room or just wondering out in the sticks. This had been necessary to allow the traffic jam effect of loving and hateful incidents to ease off. The tarpaulin covered one armed bandit was exactly as Tom left it: covered and facing the wall – out of sight and mind.

Suddenly, the mood changed for the worse as it became apparent someone in town had cracked a misfortune cookie, causing neighbourhood brute Lenny to come in to view. The group were agog to see him arm in arm with, of all people, *Becky*. Tom drew a sharp and very powerful intake of breath. Lenny saw the group and made a B-line for them, half dragging Becky with him. He stood six foot four victorious in front of the now subdued youths, causing the air to be filled with the bizarre odour of cheap perfume and a fortnight's worth of sweat. Lenny may have hidden talents *somewhere* but no employer would employ such a person, even as a doorman at the dingiest dive in town. Where Lenny lived, no one ever knew. *How* he lived was never speculated upon in polite company. He grinned at Tom, cruelly.

"Hey, Thomas, thanks for this girl, that's good of you buddy!"

He gave Becky a fairly rough kiss which she seemed to enjoy, nearly going limp with unconsciousness in Lenny's selfish embrace. Passing shoppers, a good few of whom had vile Lenny anecdotes of their own, shook their heads, quickened their step and passed hurriedly.

"Don't mind if I do!" he quipped, slightly breathless, as he ended the kiss of near death to Becky, who laughed as she was grabbed away. She had been used by the one armed bandit and was now used by Lenny. Even if you *could* actually have a rational conversation with stinking Lenny, you'd never convince him that the only reason he had Becky to himself was because the one armed bandit, for the moment, had no need of her.

"PU . . *LEASE!* Just *what* was *that* about?" asked Gemma. "What does she *see* in him apart from rotten teeth that look like they're trying to commit suicide?"

Tom's face was ashen. The days of freedom from Becky and Nudge Canyon seemed to compress in to a few seconds. The poor boy couldn't take it. His ability to hold back high tide just crumbled.

"Tom, you ok?" continued Gemma, drawing attention to Tom and inadvertently applying more pressure. Tom said nothing. He stood, pushed passed Gemma and Kyle then hastened off.

"TOM!" shouted Gemma, with real care in her voice.

***

Half an hour later and the garage door at Tom's home was lifted open in one fell, heartbroken, swoop, allowing sunshine to gush in. The tarpaulin was torn off the one armed bandit by frantic hands and the machine was turned back away from the wall just enough to allow play to resume. The plug was hastily socketed.

A gasping, sweating, heartbroken young man named Tom stood with tears in his eyes, having just ran the three miles home without stopping. He leaned on the fatalistic gaming machine, wishing he was anybody else, any*place* else apart from who he was and where he was at that moment.

As for the one armed bandit, it jumped in to life eagerly, glad to see Tom back. The word "NUDGE" flashed brighter than ever as the one arm shook invitingly. Three love hearts sat, just one space too high, ready to fall in to line for the foolhardy. The machine seemed to speak to Tom:

*"Nothing has changed, **the deal is still on!**"*
*"You want Becky's love? **It's not too late!**"*
*"Pull the lever **and she's yours!**"*

The invisible countdown once again hit zero. Knowing fully that Nudge Canyon was no joking matter, having nearly died on two occasions and having lifelong wounds to show for it. Knowing fully that this time he would have to cross *three* miles of violent terrain to reach Clean Getaway and knowing fully that – if he made it at all – after 24 hours, Becky would tell him to get lost for a third time, Tom pulled the lever.

***

The echo of the gunshot – that had nearly blown Tom's head in half – at last had its day and smashed off the metallic confines of the steam engine cab, nearly drawing blood from Tom's ears as he landed with a thud and an awful grunt at the feet of the driver. The careering locomotive swept the darkness aside and immediately passed the CLEAN GETAWAY – 3 MILES sign. From the driver's point of view there had been a slight hiccup as Tom disappeared then reappeared one second later. This temporarily stunned the grease and soot covered who re-aimed down at Tom, convinced that the boy was Thomas Ketchum, the outlaw.

"Hold real still now till I plug me those reward dollars!" was spoken with a grin, revealing teeth that looked like they were the unashamed ancestors of Lenny's. Then came the tell tale click sound of his pistol being cocked again.

Tom, however, was now getting used to life on the run. The fact that he was back a *third* time clearly indicated Tom had not yet obtained his diploma in common sense but he *had* picked up some truths along the way.

With all his might, he swiped with his left leg and toppled the driver off his feet, causing the second shot to miss, lodging in the cab roof. The two grabbed each other in hateful reunion and rolled around for a few seconds. Near concussing head bumps and kicks went unnoticed as lives were on the line. Both grappled to their feet, inadvertently helped by the murderous embrace of the other. Gunshot after gunshot filled the enclosed space to bursting as Tom and the driver danced their macabre dance of life or death. The CLEAN GETAWAY – 2 MILES sign hurtled passed, unnoticed.

***

The first of the three love hearts now dropped in to position. Sheila was in the living room, about to make a phone call when she heard the same metallic clunk sound she had heard before. This piqued her concern more than her interest because plumbing is made from metal as are other important parts of any house. She laid down the receiver and went to investigate, instinctively rubbing her SOS pendant with her thumb, a stress deflecting habit she had cultivated not long after acquiring the medical medallion years earlier.

***

The engine driver punched Tom and landed a beauty. Tom fell back against the break lever, slamming it hard to the limit of its travel. Screeching, sparking, steel on steel fought against gigantic, stubborn momentum as the locomotive's wheels locked solid. The driver was thrown forward, hitting the front of the cab with a fat thud and an odd squelch of a grunt, buckling to his knees. Wood from the tender avalanched in to the cab, burying the driver who had been knocked unconscious. The wheel against rail screeching – that could shudder clenching teeth out of a corpse's mouth – went on and on like someone dragging their finger nails down a blackboard fifty feet long.

Finally, the train angrily halted, one foot past the CLEAN GETAWAY – 1 MILE sign. Somewhere, way off in another place, mercifully blessed with the bliss of ignorance, Tom's mum heard another clunk which led her on.

Tom, punch drunk and battered, now with new, splinter filled wounds swelling and old wounds opening up, struggled out from under the pile of wood and fell out of the cab on to the trackside. Was he dead? He didn't really know. Struggling to his feet, he staggered past carriage after carriage, along crunching trackside ballast and leaned on a carriage side. It went unnoticed by Tom but, a mile or so behind him, way way down the trail, a thin column of something, be it light or a more tangible substance, stood, reaching from ground level way way up through the evening's storm clouds, defying the naked eye by disappearing in to the upper infinity of distance.

Before him, he saw about nine or ten outlaws dealing very roughly with about eight or so passengers who had been forced off the last carriage at gunpoint. He was shocked to see a well dressed woman fall out of the carriage nearest him. She fell out face first with force. Immediately, an outlaw, the one who shoved her, jumped out with a "Yehaaaw!", landing with both feet astride the woman, who was sobbing and pleading for mercy, crying *"No, No, No, please No. Edgar, please do something"* over and over. Edgar, any present would assume, was the lady's husband and one of the male passengers – now also victims. Tom recognised the outlaw as one of the safari park monkeys he'd seen running along the coaches.

Now something odd happened.

The woman who had been shoved from the carriage saw Tom, and, amidst panic and pain, seemed to recognise him, but not in the way you simply recognise a friend you see in the street; more as if, out of all present, she saw Tom as a kindred spirit and the same species as herself. What exactly lay behind this recognition was a quick appearing mystery, a glint of something important that Tom had no time to delve in to. She pled her heart out to him.

"Help me! Take me with you, I beg of you! Take me and Edgar back to . ." A dirty, tattered boot stood on her head, blurring that "glint of something".

"You ain't cut out for the life we live, lady!" said the outlaw, thinking she was addressing him.

The entire scene was just rampant chaos. The locomotive chuffed sporadically, catching its breath. People were screaming and shouting. It was feeding time at the outlaw enclosure and nothing would stand between them and their evening meal of treasures. The continual clinking of someone's spurs, such a dainty sound amidst the uncouth, clinked out a morse code signal, saying – to whoever picked it up – what fun all this was. The outlaw stopped clinking his spurs for a second as he took aim at a cactus upon which sat a passenger's expensive bowler hat.

"*Reach for the sky!*" demanded Clinker. The cactus duly obliged, extending both green spikey arms skyward, then was duly shot.

At this point, Tom just completely lost track of his essence and totally forgot who he was and what he was. All passengers who had not already been shot – and a fair few had been – were lined up facing the carriage as two outlaws made their way along the line. These outlaws took uncouth to a new level both in manners and appearance. One word from a passenger earned a crack on the head from a rifle butt, be you male or female.

As he looked along the line, Tom saw several passengers crumpled on the ground, confirming the gangs modus operandi. There were no chivalry or heroics from male passengers under this unshaven and smelly dictatorship. Anything but total compliance summoned instant wrath. This was neither Hollywood nor a video game but was actually happening; really, actually, *happening*. Either Tom's head or heart thought that the best way to avoid violence was to comply so he turned and put both hands up and on the railway carriage as the other passengers did. Suddenly, the man who stood astride the poor woman spoke. His voice was coarse with a twang three inches thick.

"*Hey Tom, quit messin!*".

At the mention of his name, Tom thought he was home free and a smile at least *tried* to put in an appearance on his battered and bleeding face. It hurt to do this, which did not go unnoticed. The man took Tom's head by the chin and turned it this way and that without a by-your-leave, examining Tom's injuries. Tom winced a little.

"Wow, that driver got a few licks in by looks of you! You whipped him anyhow though!" continued the strange fiend of a friend. Tom started to sway and would have fallen but for the man catching him.

"Woah there buddy, you sure y'ok now?"

Tom was more compos mentis by this time and beheld his unexpected new ally. The man was about five foot seven and was as rough as it gets. He was sarcastically dressed in utterly filthy finery: trousers at half mast and a matching jacket maybe two sizes too small – with waistcoat – and the ragged remains of a bowler hat. He stank like a pile of decomposing rats. The man was simply revolting, yet, with Tom, friendly, but this was hardly the time for irony. Tom saw the train, he saw the crime in progress, he saw it all 20/20, but his eyes failed him when it came to seeing a way out.

There was a moan from the engine cab as some wood tumbled on to the trackside. The driver had come round, enough to crawl out. He got halfway out when Rat Pile shot him dead. Seeing this, Tom went so wide eyed there was almost nothing left to hold his eyeballs in his head. He staggered back against the carriage. Friend of foe, it was all or nothing with Rat Pile, who spat a sickly, syrupy splat of a spit on the back of the dead drivers head.

"Looks like *he* won't be comin' round the mountain no more, huh Tom!"

A gang member who had been going down the row of terrified passengers reached the woman Rat Pile had stood astride. The woman was beautifully dressed, which labelled the her a walking goldmine.

"*Give it up, lady!*" barked the stinking mass of crime and grime on two legs.

"All . . all I have are a few rings, a fountain pen and three dollars in my purse." she protested, still facing the carriage, leaning on it with both arms as instructed.

"Yeah, and I'm Abraham Lincoln!"

Tom looked on in shock as the woman was spun around by her hair and slapped to the ground. The outlaw knelt on the woman's stomach, pushing any air out that would have formed either begging or a scream. This was merciless dealings the gang were dishing.

The gang were about eight strong. Three sat on horseback while two stood with pointed rifles while three did the actual looting. Horses were skittish at this frantic event and tried to buck and rear, snorting madly in to the cold, moonlit night. With the woman nearly passed out and with her ribs surely breaking, the bandit tore off her gorgeous necklace and simply pulled, without hesitation, every ring off every finger.

The sound of dislocating knuckles and snapping fingers could clearly be heard as the rings were pulled. The woman moaned horrible, feminine moans of numb pain overload with each tug and snap. Her moans were of a woman in labour about to give birth to a new life of frugality as Finger Snapper robbed her of her treasures. When each hand had been looted, it was just dropped like so much rubbish. Both of the woman's hands now had fingers pointing in all directions and resembled white tarantulas splattered with blood. Apart from his utter mercilessness, the only things Tom could discern about Finger Snapper was that he stank like an open sewer and that nearly all his front teeth, top and bottom, were missing, along with his conscience.

"These'll do just fine when I marry Wyatt Earp's sister!" said Finger Snapper as he reached for the magnificent brooch she wore and tore it clean off her dress with two, lace ripping tugs. He stood up and glared at the jewellery; the woman didn't .. couldn't .. move and Tom hoped he was dreaming; hoped for it with a vengeance.

"C'mon, we're done here!" shouted one of the horseback raiders. The outlaw who had been repeatedly firing his pistols in to the air just kept up the pace, eerily never seeming to re-load. This agitated the already agitated horses that were kicking and snorting to explosion point, clearly wanting to distance themselves from the awful proceedings because animals just know things, don't they?

"Hey Tom, wat'ya doin? We gotta git!"

Tom looked round out of reflex upon hearing his name. Finger Snapper was indeed addressing him. This brought Tom fully in to the scene and confirmed that he was in the loop now and the only way out was to go right through to the other end, whatever that took. But can the end of a loop be found? For the first time, Tom felt the ground beneath his feet and truly realised this was no dream.

Suddenly he heard an odd sound. It reminded him of any given laser gun fired in any given video game at the arcade; other worldly and quirky. The sound came again and this time part of the carriage woodwork thudded and splintered with shock force. Finger Snapper fired three shots in to the night that lay over Tom's shoulder. Tom yelped and crouched like he was trying to hide inside himself.

Those mounted desperados echoed Finger Snapper's actions. Bang Bang finally stopped firing in to the air and sent some lead posseward because, right on schedule, the posse *were* coming round the mountain. Tom was so relieved his volatile colleagues never needed to re-load because at least they appeared to be on his side. The quirky laser sounds Tom had heard were, again, near missing bullets from a posse of vengeful hooves about four hundred yards away, three hundred yards away, two hundred yards away. The posse's reputation preceded it and arrived on the scene, causing a turning of tables and sheer pandemonium. Finger Snapper pulled Tom violently towards waiting mounts. The wind was fair rattling by this point. Tumbleweeds, out of their depth, hid where they could.

"Tom, mount up or die, buddy!"

Tom came up against a skittish and beautiful horse that he assumed was his. He found himself mounting with surprising ease either out of natural knack, adrenaline induced ability or pure luck. The horses, all of them, were glad the bandits were finally seeing things their way and took off away from the robbing, battered, moaning and groaning, gunshot mess; fleeing with all speed in the opposite direction. Tom glanced back and saw passengers either laying down dead or injured. Blood, missed trinkets and jewellery peppered the awful line of unfortunates. The steam locomotive, the good old 4204, chuffed weirdly like a steam starved death rattle.

The gang of desperados were just picking up speed when a bullet burst open one side of Finger Snapper's head. It burst with a sickly popping-squelch of a sound. Finger

Snapper slouched over the speeding horse then tumbled limply off the far side, to land and tumble in a pathetic heap of worthless stink. Now it was Finger Snapper's turn to moan as he fell. Poor Wyatt Earp's sister, a widow before her own wedding day.

Rings, brooches and all ill gotten gains, for there were never any *other* kind of gains, glittered in the moonlight as they fell, where they would remain until discovered by someone with a metal detector a century later. Tom, being behind, was splattered to an extent by blood as his horse galloped over the fallen criminal. It's odd, isn't it? . . the times we notice things, for through eyes stinging with Finger Snapper's blood, Tom finally noticed the column of something rise ominously in the distance.

The full moon shone down on to the railway track, lighting up the rails which gave off a blueish gleam that ran on and on to converge in the distance. The gang, however, did not follow this easy to follow metallic highway but veered off to the right, down through what was initially a dense wood that gave way to a narrow and very steep sided canyon. Tom heard the river again. Just where *was* that river that could never be reached?

Rat Pile galloped alongside Tom and he too had caught some of Finger Snapper's blood on his face. However, this indigenous citizen of the one armed bandit's world simply smeared it, war paint style, and let out a loud "Woooooo!" as if it was some adrenaline sport.

There was nothing half hearted in Nudge Canyon at this moment, as, no matter whose side you were on, a river of hurtling hooved, gunpowder flavoured menace stomped its muzzle-flash way along the bloodied track. From one end to the other, if there *was* one end and another, the whole place filled with flying clouds, flying bullets and moon dappled danger. Nudge Canyon was leading to something simply awful for one, few or the many. It was a careering one way street and that street was the only street in the world.

Clean Getaway, despite it all, had been coming closer all the while. It's amazing how nearly getting your head blown off by a greasy train driver, joining an utterly evil and utterly smelly gang and then being chased by people, who crave your death above all, can make the time just fly, for now Clean Getaway was in sight, just across a wooden bridge over a – finally found – river.

"Yeehaaaw! There's no place like home!" shouted Rat Pile.

Yes, Clean Getaway, safe haven for Rat Pile, Clinker and Bang Bang; portal back to the loving arms of everyday suburbia for Tom and where they would probably bury what was left of Finger Snapper's vulture gnawed and sun bleached bones, lay just yards ahead. The Main Street was void of people as folks in Clean Getaway went to bed at a sensible time, their collective clean consciousness helping then sleep just fine through the storm.

***

"Oh, its *you!*" declared Sheila as she stood in front of the Nudge Canyon machine, having finally located the source of the "clunks".

"You had me worried there for a second!" she laughed as she playfully slapped the one armed bandit. The machine stood, active but silent. Mum leaned over to see the reels.

"Aww, just lookee at those love hearts!"

There was, however, a very faint whirring sound coming from the machine, a very faint whirring sound accompanied by slow sliding and dainty mechanical manoeuvring as if the machine was up to no good and didn't want to draw attention to itself; tip toeing along, trying not to wake anybody's attention, like when you hear children playing. All is well until they fall silent. When *that* happens, it's time to investigate.

Tom's mum heard this faint whirring. She put an ear up close with a curious look. The machine sat as Tom had left it, semi pulled out, sitting roughly 70 degrees to the wall. Being petite in stature, Sheila easily slid in to the gap and saw the whirring was all three reels spinning painfully slowly . . snails pace slowly. She watched love hearts moved from view as the reels snailed their way to a perfect line of something indeed odd and out of place. Sheila peered then looked appalled as the reels showed three identical pictures of what was clearly a dead horse. The sight was shocking and she drew breath.

"Now just *what?* I mean who would *do* such a thing?"

*****

Clinker, that's who.

Tom heard the shots. He had heard little else for a while, but suddenly his horse crumpled underneath him. Yes, human nature, which can be a sinister lottery at the best of times, had a mighty hunger and was not satisfied with the carnage back at the carriages, for now Clinker yelled "*Reach for the sky!*" then deliberately shot Tom's horse out from under him in order to delay the posse. He would have shot Tom dead but taking Tom prisoner would take up more of the posse's time.

The horse and Tom just spilled and slid and tumbled and rolled in an avalanche of strewn, wasted equine strength and sandswept, dusty snort. Every ride at the fairground, twice, and every fall from his bicycle he had ever taken, was how Tom felt now. Concussion and contortion jumped on Tom from mesa height and stomped defeat down his throat and his all in to the trail. As Clinker rode past, he scuffed Tom's head with a spur, causing a gash to his forehead. A concuss of an injury, delivered with a dainty "ting" sound, closed the door to Tom's safe return by another inch.

In the total mess of it all, even a layperson could immediately see Tom's left forearm was hideously broken. It looked like a ghoulish prop bought from a joke shop for Halloween, which was fitting on this night of cowboy horrors. Sorry, no time for searing, blinding, thundering pain just now. That'll have to wait. Survive, survive, *survive*.

***

Mum stood, narrow eyed and curious. Like the machine itself, she was active but silent; drawn in to the machine's creeping tide of an embrace. She had given the one armed bandit scant thought almost since day one but now stopped her life and truly considered the machine full on. Woman's intuition? Hitherto undiscovered skills of detection? Plain old human curiosity? Sheila just *knew* something was afoot. The telephone receiver she had laid down started to buzz the reminder that it had been left off the hook.

And those "smooth and slick in their action" reels just kept on turning – ever so slowly – ever so quietly – all the while looking Sheila right in the eye with defiance. Gentle whirring and slow, sliding, turning, moved the dead horse from view, to replace it with a mighty river.

***

Lying there, broken, Tom had been crossing a bridge at the time of his betrayal. The extreme roar of the Rio Grande underneath frightened him almost back in to childhood. The Clean Getaway sign lay just fifty feet away.

Then it didn't.

Because it splintered in to nothing by a hurling lead volley from the posse. Tom screamed what he was sure would be his last and just threw himself off the bridge in to the raging – lesser of two evils – torrent beneath.

Churning white froth enveloped an injured and concussed Tom as the rapids dealt mercilessly with him; spinning him senseless, banging his breath out against rocks, hurling him on nearly as fast as the train. Totally defenceless in the river's wet fist, he bobbed violently. It was a mixture of submersion in to freezing darkness and being yanked up in to moonlit roar. Bent on his destruction, the mighty river of Nudge Canyon threw Tom over a 100 foot waterfall, discarding him like a chocolate wrapper.

A drop of 100 feet in to water comes with a lot of time to think about the impact and an age of submersion at the end of it. Tom entered the water with more of a crack than a splash, then down and dark, down and cold, oh so cold. Down in to the world of the muffled underneath sank Tom. Was this *really* the lesser of the two evils? Up above, just for a split second, he beheld the beautiful sight of chaotic ripples that broke the moon in to dancing nymphs of silver.

He surfaced and gasped all the air clean out of the world. Every second of life now had to be fought for. Now a single breath was the best friend Tom ever – *ever* – had. He gasped and clawed for his very life.

Then events seemed to take a step back as Tom found himself in a relatively calm lagoon before yet another massive waterfall. At the side of the lagoon was a sign and in front of the sign stood Becky. The scales of worth were teetering back and forth with the love of a pretty girl on one side and conditions most horrific on the other. The "thin column of something", going from ground to sky, was now noticeably closer. It had grown in breadth considerably and resembled a tornado, for it span like one. It had noise to it also, but, things being what they were at that moment, Tom had other things on his mind.

As he splashed a quirky survival stroke towards the shore where Becky stood, the river roar died down a touch and the water was really quite still. Oh stillness, how you command things sometimes with your mighty hush! How you bring order to chaotic hearts with your nothingness! Did you not quench the storm and polish the Galilean sea to a mirror finish? Stillness, you are, in ironic essence, nothing at all, but in effect, you are without peer or governor.

And this exact stillness permeated lagoon deep for Tom as he quirked and quirked towards Becky, who held out as substantial a dead branch as she could hold. Tom grabbed the branch as he felt boulders beneath his feet. A rough stumble beach but a welcome one indeed. Rise from the depths and drip, drop, drip, drop, fall to knees then flat on back. He fell at the foot of the sign and both feet of Becky. His arm really was smashed and shattered. Surrounding events had been a powerful distractant from pain. To give Tom peace now was to do him an injustice as that pain would be his death. It was misery at all points of the compass for the boy but at least the posse had been left behind.

He lay there for what seemed like an age, staring up at, yet not seeing, the crystal clear full moon. He lay there for what seemed like an age, hearing, yet not hearing, night creatures cavorting. He lay there for what seemed like an age, remembering, yet almost entirely forgetting how, one second before he pulled the bandit's arm, his life had really been pretty good after all.

In this soaked and battered and absent state, the eerie fact that Becky stood looking down at him without helping or saying a single word, got past him. She just stood staring down at him. No expression on her face. No movement. Nothing.

Finally, Tom was able to sit up. His clothes were already drying on him and felt stiff, slimy and just awful. Now he saw the moon but didn't care to ever see it ever again. He tried not to look at his arm which hung from his side like a weird creature from any given Hieronymus Bosch painting. He turned and rose to his knees, leaning on the one good arm.

Becky just stood and now Tom noticed this callous indifference on her part. Surely she will speak or help, surely. He didn't want to look her in the eye. Were the love of a pretty girl and conditions most horrific *actually* on opposite ends of the scales of worth? Like looking through binoculars and turning the wheel to focus, all Tom's senses were sharpening up now thanks to his rough recuperation on the rough beach.

Drawing in very deep breaths that would be fuel for the Herculean task of actually standing up, Tom glanced to the left. There, about a quarter of a mile away, infinitely massive in height, increasing in breadth by the second, swirling forcefully and perpetually, stood, and swirled, and swirled, and swirled . . . the tornado. Tom had seen tornados before on the television and two in real life, but this was in another, more terrifying, league. The main colour was sandy shades peppered with a multitude of slave driven debris imbedded therein. Plain old sand you trample underfoot, sweep from your patio and build sandcastles out of was now a frightening force to be respected and fled from. The sheer flexing muscle power of this desert entity was able to smash asunder a mountain range in a blink, drain any ocean bone dry in a moment and bore a hole clean through any given world. It stood majestic, it stood proud, it stood bizarrely hypnotic in swirling beauty and power, it stood just one quarter of a mile from Tom.

The pain of being on his knees on boulders broke the tornado induced hypnosis. One foot underneath, then push and hurt, creak, push, yelp, rise, rise then the other foot underneath. Finally, Tom stood tall. He towered over Becky, an eerie Becky not before known. What a novelty it was not to be running for dear life from things surreal and cruel. He stood, teetering, with his eyes closed and the arm shaped creature still attached to him. Finally, he looked upon Becky.

She was as pretty as ever but now as a stranger unto him. Her smile had long since fled the golden crop fields of amour, leaving those crops to rot in the rain, unharvested. Now she looked at Tom like she was turning in the street to confront a stalker. Her look said in the sharpest accusatory tone "What? What is it? What do you want from me?" Now

Tom's young and romance craving heart, which was the cause of all that had befallen him of late, beat smoothly no more. Instead, it jerked and squelched within his chest like a saddened and defeated creature from the same Hieronymus Bosch painting Tom's arm was from.

Becky the stranger ripped away and discarded Tom's wonderful memories of their time together as easily as pulling Velcro. Her eyes were still blue; but if before they were blue like the ocean, if before they were blue like a sapphire wave about to crest and if before they were blue like the lofty home of the albatross, now they were as enticing as blue flashing lights in your rear view mirror. Every crumb of comfort had been spoken for and pecked away by the ravens of distress and now Tom meant utterly nothing to Becky. Of all the places to go cold turkey from the love of a pretty girl, here and now wasn't it.

The scene was like walking in to a room and finding a chess board that had been abandoned mid game. You would wonder "Well, whose turn is it to move?" If the concept of "resolution" ever felt no one cared then this scene was the answer to all its prayers as it was sought after at this moment like air to the drowning. Movement from any quarter would have eased the pent up tension of the potentially explosive.

The stagnant stirred. Becky, holding Tom's gaze with her still pretty but blank and drab stare, stepped to the side. Tom was glad she had at last shown a little sign of life and even semi smiled at her. But then he saw the sign she had stood in front of. A single word was on the sign. Just one word on a rickety old sign.

Words, however, can be oh so powerful. Words are totally location independent and it is *context* that is the real home of all words. In the right place and time, a single word can rule your world whether that word sits on a throne or a vandalised and graffitied park bench. Words are like cats, independent and untrainable. The hunt is just built in to any given word. Words always seek a recipient, target or prey. Now Tom knew the power of a single word, and *this* word, the name of a town, had hunted him down and finally found him. The sign read . . JUSTICE.

***

Tom's mum jumped back slightly, bumping her head off the wall behind. As she "ouched" and rubbed her head, the pictorial bandit, without coin insertion, lit up and fled the posse as before. The reels of the machine stopped their creeping and went loud, spinning furiously in different directions, spinning with intent and glee. Faster and faster they span, generating heat, glowing bright. They stabbed to a halt simultaneously with a metal bending clank.

The pictorial posse caught the pictorial bandit. The three reels all displayed a tornado.

***

One lasso, then two, then three, all thrown by maestros in the art, snared Tom as the posse, appearing out of nowhere, finally caught him. The sheriff shouted at Tom with a voice that could make the Rio Grande flow backwards. It boomed out from somewhere behind a dust laden dam of a moustache and cast iron stubble you could nail a wanted poster with:

"You ready to meet yer maker buddy?.. cause he's been a waitin' for ya!"

The posse gathered around Tom, buffeting him with their horses and kicking him. Too gone in both the physical and emotional to react and with both arms pinned to his side anyway, Tom, from within, just blanked. He would have collapsed had the lassos not held him.

"Let's take him to meet the townsfolk!" cried a posse member.

Tom was dragged slowly, like a sodden rag, behind the posse. Becky was nowhere to be seen, unsurprisingly. Had she been there she wouldn't have helped anyway, unsurprisingly.

The posse began their psychological feast with a march of
triumph towards the town of Justice . . and the tornado.

8

Inside the Tornado

The road to justice is never an easy one. Anyone who has had to enter a courtroom in any capacity will tell you that. Tom had never seen the inside of a courtroom in his life. Mind you, it was a safe bet to say that everyone who *had* seen the inside of a courtroom had never seen the inside of a tornado like Tom would see, so let's call it quits on that score and move on.

Now joined at the hip to this maelstrom, Tom was heading for justice all the same and the road he trod was anything but metaphorical. Tugs from the three lassos were nearly dislocating everything in Tom that could be dislocated. If he fell there was no mercy shown, he was dragged over boulder, rattle snake and fallen cactus till he got to his feet again. His head wounds were swollen terribly. Only one eye could be seen through, the other hideously swollen. Gashes ran with blood, and those were just the *outer* injuries. If he made it back at all, these wounds could not be hidden by simply taking a shower and wearing a black t-shirt. Two months in hospital minimum. Tom was going crossed eyed with pain. Posse members taunted and kicked him. He yelped and moaned like the woman Finger Snapper stole rings from.

The track was well worn due to the constant flow of traffic. The reason for that is because the area surrounding Nudge Canyon was rife with crime. Rat Pile, Clinker and the whole gang, who eerily never needed to re-load and could only creep up on you if you were up wind, kept the posse occupied morning, noon and most nights. The worn path so dusty led straight to the tornado's base.

The tornado had grown heavily pregnant with expectation upon Tom's approach. It was now the width of about six city blocks and the tallest object Tom had ever seen. A skyscraper of power it was. Spitters of sand began to fall upon Tom's face as they drew near. Somewhere deep inside Tom, the obvious question was "Why head straight for something so overwhelmingly dangerous?"

Entering the tornado wall, debris now flew past at right angles to the posse's path but never seemed to touch or frighten them. Tumble weeds became hurtle weeds. The sheriff led the way, fading in and out of view amidst the grainy fog. The born with stubble law keeper, and his horse, never even flinched as violent debris rocketed by.

On and on.

Sand spitter on the face became marble sized, hitting Tom like small hammers. A scorpion slammed against his head, its tail curled right in to Tom's mouth. He reflex gagged and spat the ugly sting merchant back in to the whirl then heaved with disgust.

On and on.

All force swept Tom sideways, causing the lassos to jerk and jolt again. The ropes were taught to snapping point. Rope burns joined the list of his injuries. Marble sized sand bullets became fist sized as the tornado writhed and roared in the birth pangs of Tom's fate. The gale placed a sand blaster deep inside Tom's right ear and pulled the trigger, ripping his eardrum.

On and on.

Sand filled Tom's mouth. Oh!, this world where sand has outstayed it's welcome! Mouth filled with it. Teeth crunching it. Eyes stinging with it. Ears blocked with it. Nose stuffed with it. Hopes pummelled by it.

Yes, on and on and on. Just how much longer? Please, how much longer? Oh, the noise! Each step resisted by a hoard of opposition. Thoughts of Mum and Dad and pleasant suburban home life darted to mind but had the collective might of a butterfly to comfort in this and were blown asunder. If this persisted, the only thing holding the three lassos together would be Tom's shoelaces. Finally, Tom collapsed, dead. Darkness now, darkness and silence.

Or so he thought.

The silence, that was the eye of the tornado, by comparison, was proverbially deafening and caused fright, which summoned Tom back from the "Thought they were dead". Strange that, in the right context, you can frighten a person with silence.

The eye of the storm had indeed been penetrated now, and what is an eye for if not to see? Tom was now in the glare of the behemoth and well within the range of anything it saw fit to deal out to him. This entire phenomenon existed purely for *him*. One of the posse reached down and grabbed Tom by his hair, forcing him to his feet.

Looking through the eye not swollen, Tom looked up the inside of the funnel at a sight seen by extremely few people in any world; as rare a sight as seeing in to someone's mind.

Up and swirling up, it rose to near infinity; debris spiralling ever upwards. Dead centre of the opening was the blood red moon. Romantic silver was gone and the full red orb bulged with violence. The eye of this tornado was bloodshot and if the moon should burst, who would this blood fall upon?

And what of the town of Justice?

Well, here it was.

Like the town of Clean Getaway, Justice only had one street. Like the town of Clean Getaway, Justice sat in the middle of nowhere and also had its citizens, but here all similarity ended, for while the good folks of Clean Getaway slumbered, those of Justice were up – every single one of them. And it was not the Tornado that kept them up, it was the arrival of Tom.

In any town, anywhere, people to and fro. Paths may cross but objectives rarely meet in any other fashion than loosely. Your life is not mine and who is to say whose life is of greater significance.

But here, right here and right now, a town's worth of paths crossed and objectives wedded ever so tightly. As the posse dragged what was left of Tom along Main Street, the entire town had turned out to line the street as if fully expecting him. A good few held burning torches. They spat and jeered at what was left of Tom. Not one voice stood out from among the rest amidst the noise and clamour. This guard of dishonour – a carnival of carnivores, for all cried out for Tom's blood – had started while still a hundred yards from the first building. People cursed Tom as he passed then ran on ahead to re-join the hateful throng, cursing Tom again. A torch was shoved in to Tom's face. This was knocked aside by a posse member.

And what do you say exactly if you are on the receiving end of all this? To whom do you turn? From childhood, are we not trained to act a certain way? We needed no "training" as such for we all knew instinctively what to do. Tom acted accordingly now.

"MUM! MUM! HELP ME!"

"Your Mamma won't help you now!" mocked a dusty sheriff.

***

But maybe she *will*.

Jaw still open at witnessing the unruly behaviour of the one armed bandit, Sheila slapped the machine for making her bump her head.

"Don't you *DARE!*" she declared with that laugh/frown combination we use when a bizarre situation arises, like going for a walk in the park where you slip and fall and hurt quite a bit but then realise you slipped on a $100 note.

"This garage ain't big enough for the both of us!"

The machine ignored the pun and proceeded with its hidden agenda. With a foot in both camps and an eye on both worlds, this bandit was tugging marionette strings woven from intangible dark to make all spiders jealous, jolting lives this way and that, because this was all second nature to the Nudge Canyon machine.

***

"WAIT, WAIT . . I'M NOT ONE OF THEM . . YOU'VE GOT THE WRONG GUY!" screamed Tom, but he was in a world inhabited by a tribe called "Enemies" which, like all isolated tribes, couldn't understand Tom's mother tongue dialect of "pleading".

The halfway point of Justice Main Street was reached. The sheriff raised his hand and once again the justice machine halted.

Three blocks away, in every direction, the tornado did what tornadoes do best – look utterly utterly terrifying. Where the town of Justice sat, where the halfway point of the Main Street was and where Tom trembled in the middle of it all, was the very epicentre of the storm's eye. The one armed bandit was bestowing on Tom way in excess of his 15 minutes. So injured that nobody who knew him would ever recognise him, he looked like a scarecrow that hadn't slept for a month. Even Heironymus would balk at giving Tom canvas space now and a murder of crows would feel the alien sensation of pity – hesitate – then after furious, fickle feathered debate, fly off to ransack someone else's field.

The courthouse stood on one side of the street with Town Hall on the other and what better way to complete the "Town of Justice Collectors Set" than with a gallows ready and waiting in the middle? Two posse members held Tom up. He saw the gallows. They were indeed ready and waiting.

***

Sheila looked around gently but purposefully. Silence now. Silence in the garage. A gust of wind suddenly blew across her face, then another the opposite way. She gasped and teetered and, as she teetered, heard sand crunch beneath her step. No sand to see as yet though. She felt that all was gone, as if the house was gone, suburbia was gone, all purpose was gone.

Still so silent. Something was drawing near. Such an eerie herald, *such an eerie herald,* for a storm will always arrive at your door uninvited but never enters without knocking.

With a sweet and dainty clink, a coin dropped in to the payout slot of the machine.

Go on!

It was the very same coin Tom had used that day for the first ever spin.

Go on!

The chime made by the coin was saturated in flirtation, as, some may argue, *all* coinage is.

Go on!

Sheila looked down to see the coin dance then settle.

Go on!

It looked so lonely and out of place, just waiting to be used.

Go on! Go on! GO ON!

"I hope this doesn't become a bad habit!" she said, picking up the coin as she half bit her bottom lip. There was a hint of the mischievous in her words. Hang around long enough with anyone and some aspect of them will rub off on you. Tom's mum; ideal wife, mother and friend, for a mere 60 seconds, fell in with the wrong crowd.

But sometimes 60 seconds is all it takes.

She slotted the coin and pulled the lever, still jumping with a start at the gunshot sound effect. Lights lit, noises noised, reels reeled – the usual story. Sheila was flying solo and, to be honest, it was a thrill! Spin mesmerise, spin hypnotise, spin tantalise! Why are spinning objects so absorbing *now*? Spinning car tyres are boring as is a tumble dryer. It was all a matter of *context*, you see.

WALLOP . . the first reel zipped to a halt. No picture this time, only words. Sheila muttered the words. The words were:

***

Tom is pushed and dragged up the steps to the gallows platform. Unbelievably, he noticed the fresh and beautiful smell of the pine wood used. He kicked against each step, arching his back as the crowd cheered a disgusting sounding cheer.

"*MUM!*" cried the poor boy again. In this, the crowd saw an opportunity and all shouted "*MUUUM!*" in mocking unison.

***

The second reel thumped to a stop and Sheila spoke the words plainly this time, "SAVE TOM".

***

At the top of the steps, Tom was presented to the baying, torch lit crowd.

"*We got 'im!*" shouted the sheriff, unfurling a wanted poster and holding it up to the crowd.

"*C'mere wi' that.*" continued the sheriff to a posse member. The man gave the sheriff his torch. The wanted poster was held up to Tom's face and set alight. As it burned, Tom read the name "Thomas Ket . ." before it was consumed. The townsfolk of Justice united in a chorus of hatred for the the captured and condemned Tom.

***

The third reel hammered to a stop with "SAVE TOM" one space too high.

Sheila shouted "*SAVE TOM! WHAT DO YOU MEAN "SAVE TOM?" HE'S AT THE MALL ISN"T HE?*"

She sprinted a few panicked steps away from the machine with sobs coming instantly to the fore. Running to the kitchen, she picked up the phone on reflex, not knowing who to dial. Dropping a dangling receiver, she hurriedly returned to the one armed bandit and stared at the reels. Whoever's side the machine was *really* on, it was an integral part of what was happening now, maybe the very centre.

In less than a second, this was confirmed. A nudge was now offered by the machine. To Sheila, this was a known face in a world of strangers. The bandit's arm shook and lights flashed. And really, what choice was there? . . save Tom or *don't* save Tom? Never having so much as touched a gaming machine before, being someone who considered listening to two episodes, in a *row*, of the radio drama "Barwick Lives" to be riotous living and certainly not knowing what she was letting herself in for, raging motherly love pushed Sheila over the precipice of decision. She pulled the lever and the nudge was granted.

"OH NO! . . *OH NO!*" a strange woman's voice shouted in total desperation, covering her mouth with one hand.

"Is he *yours,* that young man I saw?" the stranger continued, "Tell me . . *is he yours?* He looked *so* handsome!"

The alien voice, with its immediate, blundering manner, shocked Sheila. She stood for a second then crumpled to her knees with eyes spinning at the sudden relocation.

For, as Tom had been transported by the pull of the lever, his mother, too, had now been transported. As the view span and re-span all ways, causing giddiness, Sheila saw half a dozen or so people in front of her. The woman asking the panicked question was dressed in historical elegance and held Sheila in her arms, stopping her from hitting the floor, but the questioning, and the worry it brought with it, continued.

"He *is* yours, isn't he? He *must* be or you would never have come here."

Not quite with it enough to answer, Sheila swayed on her feet, aided by Elegant Lady and one of the men present.

*This had better be a dream. It **is** a dream, right?*

No Sheila, this is *not* a dream.

One layer of reality was gradually lain on top of another, reinforcing the tangibility of the new situation. She looked in to the eyes of Elegant Lady then in to the others then at the surroundings.

Sheila now stood in a railway carriage from years long gone. The carriage interior was extremely beautiful, all so plush and inviting. No one, however, could take up that invitation for sheer worry.

Some of the people standing before her were dressed in extreme finery; clothes from years also long gone. Others wore clothes from just a few decades ago: the 50's and the 60's at first glance. From the sounds of some of them and the expressions of every one of them, hope, like their fashions, was also long gone. Had Tom been present he would have immediately recognised Elegant Lady as the poor passenger Finger Snapper had robbed of her rings and treasures so joint dislocatingly cruelly. She had been left for dead, or as good as, but now she stood complete and physically intact; fingers, rings, brooches and all.

"I *knew* he was not from here. He just had that look on his face." Elegant Lady continued, "Could I be blamed for seeing him as a way out of this?. . a way to get back."

"WHO?" blurted terrified Sheila?

Her question bounced off any non-plush surface it could find and came back with the answer: "YOUR SON TOM".

Elegant Lady began to change tac, mystifyingly now more interested in her own bejewelled hands. Sheila grabbed her and spun her back around.

"TELL ME, TELL ME, I HAVE TO HELP HIM. IS MY SON TOM HERE?"

The lady answered with a now up beat and seemingly irreverent cheeriness while still gazing at her rings. Just what was *wrong* with this elegant woman?

"Yes, I heard two of the outlaws call him by that name! And a fine name it is too!"

In contrast, the atmosphere in the carriage was so somber it would have been considered too dank even for the funeral of the last person on Earth. The aura was so somber that it coolly read between the lines and answered the myriad of screaming questions Sheila would have avalanched forth concerning her son's safety. Sheila crashed back on to a seat, imitating death perfectly as Elegant Lady gave near mocking comfort. A male passenger then gave the macabre welcome speech to Sheila.

"We are all here through trickery. You are here through trickery and deceit, are you not, Madam? Did the machine find out what you hold dear and then used the potential loss of that treasure to land you here with us? We are prisoners, unable to escape this plush and comfortable prison. Soon we will be robbed again by the gang of outlaws. Oh, how they enjoy hurting us! We are robbed so violently then a blurring and a painful mending and untwisting and undoing and we return here once more. We dread the firing up of the engine. Time after time we await the pain of it all with the blackest acceptance."

Sheila lay sprawled across the seat in a sort of wide awake coma, breathing frighteningly heavy, her heart having suffered the same fate as the Portland Vase.

***

Normally, people scaling a building or construction, even for serious purposes, cannot help but admire the view, but what Tom looked down on now was a world of hate looking back up at him.

Upon the creaky scaffold, he gazed down on total un-reciprocation. *One* friendly face, surely? A courtroom is not the best place to win friends and if that be the *courtroom* demeanour then what of the *scaffold?* Who wants to stand atop such a construction?, yet, if Tom should slip, he would be torn asunder. The phrase "Between a rock and a hard place" didn't even begin to cover it. The guard of dishonour Tom had been led along by the posse was now a mass of righteous indignation that circled the scaffold and cheered another disgusting sounding cheer with every jolt and injury Tom suffered.

There was a mighty crack, a breaking, a jolting. Something was happening. The tornado picked up speed slightly and began to shrink in diameter. The calmness of the eye was losing that calmness. The tornado diameter shrank slowly, moving towards Tom like the faltering steps of regimental pallbearers at a state funeral.

A boa constrictor with rough, hurting, scales of hemp, that tightened with excitement, the noose was placed around Tom's neck. Being only 18 years old, there was not really that much of Tom's life to flash before him, but this was hardly the time for reminiscing. The tornado wall reached the buildings of Justice at both ends of Main Street.

Total smashing and upward wrenching took hold as wall after wall was broken asunder and lifted, with massive noise, effortlessly, in to gargantuan and sand impregnated up-swirl. Roofs, shingles, any metal fittings, boardwalks, every room and everything *in* those rooms, shot obediently skyward at the merest wink from the tornado.

But what now? What was this? Confusion was the only emotion not residing in Tom's heart as he stood on the pine gallows, but now that confusion jostled inside. The reason? Now every person present turned outward to face the tornado. All but Tom himself turned to deliberately face that from which people normally flee with all their might. He would have sunk to his knees had he not been noosed. He looked directly up and saw the blood red moon. The red ripened orb was the only thing around not in danger as the tornado walls closed. A red deathly light, at the end of a violent tunnel, made a sight not seen in a billion lifetimes. Indeed, in another time and place, what Tom beheld would have been a Pulitzer Prize winning photo in perpetuity.

All citizens now raised their arms widely to embrace inevitable fate. They whipped up in to the tornado wall like the feathers they were by comparison. Blown away and up into the wind wall like confetti thrown from a speeding train. They had turned to face the tornado, showing no fear and throwing arms wide because they had obviously been through this before. Most of the posse were included in this, horses and all. All but Tom were adept at this ritual. The scaffold began to tremble and creak as it tried to flee.

But then the tornado seemed to go in to another gear. It idled, literally idled. No self respecting tornado is given to this as its very nature is wanton carnage, but now the threat retreated slightly, or rather, halted momentarily. The citizens and their splintered town had all disappeared moonward. Was the tornado full? Had it dined to contentment?

No, it was stepping aside for dignitaries.

For, you see, there was a ranking in all this. There was a hierarchy, for what is cruelty without irony to twist the blade? What is more distasteful for a soldier of life; an outright enemy or a traitor? Does an insult from a stranger hurt as much as that of a spouse, or your child? A fate you see coming has no shock value like the fate you never saw approaching from a formerly trusted source. Such garnished and seasoned awfulness, carefully and meticulously put together for your delectation and hurt.

With the tornado idling, the scaffold creaking its distress signal to anyone who could understand it and Tom standing on a trapdoor that opened to eternity, a new circle of people now surrounded the scene. Not many, but, even here, it was quality not quantity.

Standing around the base of the scaffold were the lorry driver from the lemon spill, the manageress from the "King for a day" experience, and both Becky's parents. All stood calmly as if they had the collective consciousness of those who had never sinned.

Tom saw what he saw and he saw that the eyes of every person were gone to be replaced with gaping holes of blackness the size of that persons fists. To make eye contact, if it could be called that, even fleetingly, with those black chasmic portals in to the head of any one of them was to totally rip the lid off Pandora's box. The look of these people now had a eerie dignity, unlike their chaotic, almost comical, previous demeanour back in suburbia. Regimented and purposeful they stood. Tom knew the sheriff was standing next to him and dared not look round lest he see the same blackness up close and his heart fail him. These things were indeed one thing, but what Tom saw next separated the men from the boys.

For Becky stood directly in front of the gallows about 10 feet from the steps. A ghost of a girl now was the maiden. The former dream girl was now a nightmare. Black gaping holes for eyes also she stood. She beheld Tom who couldn't look but had to look. Her look did indeed rip the lid off Pandora's box, and when all calamity had flown from within, the mocking dregs were scooped and bourn towards Tom upon her ferocious gaze. Black portal eyes were one thing, but place them within a frown and betrayal now had a face – betrayal now had an expression – betrayal was now personified. Every moment spent with Becky had been a house of cards built by trembling hands on shifting sands and Tom's love for the girl had been the all too eager architect. This was the time for *italicised thoughts.*

"Is this really happening?" Yes Tom, it is.

"All this just for me?" Yes Tom, all of it, just for you.

"But I have a life!" What about it, Tom?

"Becky never loved me at all!"

There was never *any* "Becky".

She began to walk towards the gallows and temporarily disappeared from sight. Then Tom heard the first step creak. Oh, must Tom go through the agony of anticipating her reappearance? The tornado swirled on. Slowly came the steps, creak after sadistic creak. She began to reappear but looked straight ahead, robotic like. Some people fear speed, they would fear slow also if they teetered where Tom teetered, for it was the drawing out of all this that was the killer.

Once on the platform, she turned to face Tom and step towards him. She utterly stank, for what can come from Pandora's box but foulness? Tom was both ends of the magnet now, unable to conform but straining to take flight. Those surrounding all snapped their heads back and began to cry out together. Mouths opened unnaturally wide. Awful voices made a siren harmony akin to an off tune air raid alarm. Becky stepped on till she was face to face with Tom.

They had once gazed lovingly at each other but that felt so long ago now that it seemed like it happened before they had invented history books. They had once embraced and been welded together by puppy love softness but said puppy was now a wandering and savage feral thing that would eagerly bite the hand that fed it and war with all. Becky, in reality, had never existed. She had been a cavalcade of lies sculpted to look like a dream come true, and what a sculptor the one armed bandit had been!

From the very start, Tom had been well journeyed within events, and he was surely at the centre of it all now, with no more North, South, East or West to travel. The bright lights we see in life are merely distraction, in truth they do not care. Alluring words clamour for our attention every day but in truth they do not care. The bright lights, alluring words and the sea of smiles we swim in, all too often come with small print written in invisible ink. Invisible, that is, to the young and short lived. Age should, in theory, force the world's deceptions out of the shadows and in to view, their cover well and truly blown.

Becky stood and stared at Tom and stared at Tom and stared at Tom. His memories of happier times flew through the air and lodged in his feelings as arrows made from the Mocking Tree. Becky was the archer. As each arrow hit its mark, Tom saw flashes of his old life and the friends who would help him in all this if they only could.

Oh, the pain of pleasant memories! In what awful world can even the lovely and sweet be used as implements of torture? Rather to have lived a more miserable life from the get go than to have tasted of friendship and kinship then have these things withdrawn. The niceness of the past was now a dirty and hateful bloodhound that tracked Tom, even here, and the present situation was a total smash in the face. With a past that now hates you and a present that also hates you, would you really want to see in to the future?

Becky stooped and reached for the trapdoor lever. Tom rolled the dice one last time and screamed his head clean off:

"BECKYYYYY!!!"

She kept hold of the lever but looked round very very slowly at Tom. Oh, was there a crumb of something there? Were there the remnants of a bond? Her face of horror, for horrific it truly was to see, for a few seconds, halted its intent. No arrows this time.

All sound ceased, every bit of it, and in the pin drop silence, eyes locked. Becky then said "Tom" in a frighteningly deep, slobbering, genderless voice. Her head snapped back round as she pulled the lever and the trapdoor swung open with might, relieved to be discharging its duty. In order, the last things Tom heard in that pin drop silence were:

creak

whoosh

grunt

break

And, as simple as that, because lies are lies, Tom was dead.

The lights in the plush carriage, where Sheila was, suddenly burned extremely brightly, way too brightly; enough to momentarily give off unpleasant heat. Then it went pure black, pure black and cold. Before the darkness, Sheila had seen the unnerving sight of every passenger turning to look at her. They knew something, something they had learned the hard way, and when you learn something the hard way, you are so full of that awful experience that, with one look, you can make the telling of it spill out through your eyes and make the novice learn, oh so well, without uttering a single word.

Sheila was learning the dialogue of hopelessness, quickly. The past half an hour had been a steep learning curve of near vertical wall aspect. All that could come out of her mouth in this place was the native tongue of despair. The light level rose a touch.

"It's Tom, isn't it?" asked Sheila, knowing the answer already.

Elegant Lady and a young couple looked away but a few others continued to stare. They knew that to offer even the tiniest crumb of comfort would be closing the stable door way way too late, knowing what they all knew. Ambiguity can be a cruel master, denying Sheila satisfaction.

"*It's Tom, isn't it?*" A bit louder this time.

Sheila now knew what she had never been taught. She had reached an emotional location without the required journey. She saw an irreversible situation without opening her eyes and she had become a forever changed person without that ambition.

Elegant Lady, "Welcome Speech" man and a few others gathered round Sheila, putting their arms around her. Others just sat in their own seats with their head in their hands, listening to scream after scream.

Sheila moaned when Tom was being born, now she screamed to the contrary upon his demise. The others held her as she writhed and thrashed and screamed and screamed and grappled with the serpent of culture shock and its detestable slithering colleagues: regret, anguish and despair. No words were spoken by the others as they knew this was a right of passage for the poor woman.

Suddenly, outside, the scene was one of total normality. The carriage was sitting at a platform from many years gone by, bathed in sunlight and happy activity. Prospective passengers and their loved ones and friends strolled happily to and fro, some carrying luggage. Children ran around. The station was adorned with hanging baskets laden with all gorgeousness. And the sound, oh, just to hear the sound of the normal was a drink from a lofty alpine stream.

Sheila, hearing and seeing this, clung to this visual driftwood. She turned and banged on the window.

"HELP ME, HELP US! HELP US!"

The woman never knew she had such strength as the window bent to near shatter again and again. A woman on the platform stopped dead in line with Sheila and approached the window with intent, muttering something.

"YES, YES, IN HERE! IN HERE! HELP US!" screamed – utterly screamed – Sheila.

The woman looked with concentration straight in to Sheila's eyes, then simply began adjusting her hat. She had just been using her reflection to preen herself.

"Shhh, my sweet! She cannot see you!" said Elegant Lady "She cannot see or hear you or *any* of us."

"BUT SHE DID, SHE DID . . SHE MUST!"

"Re-set has happened." continued Elegant Lady. "We have your reluctant arrival to thank, for it is only when a new passenger joins our ranks that we are given this view of the station. Normal re-set takes place out in the desert. In a few seconds an ever so sweet little boy will bounce a ball off the window next to her then be reprimanded by his father."

Sure enough, exactly as predicted, the little scenario was acted out. Sheila leaned against the glass, steaming up the window as Welcome Speech continued his fatalistic monologue:

"We may be privy to the world you see outside, but we are not part of it. We are prisoners on this carriage. The one armed bandit tricked us also, you see. We, as you, have all lost loved ones to this land of lies. You, as we, will now be robbed repeatedly, beaten repeatedly, only for re-set to happen. Broken bones will mend, riches will be restored, false and hollow hope will squat within this carriage and the cycle will begin once again. More will come here, as you have, and what will you say to them, my tragic dear? Will you say "Cheer up, friend!"? Would you *really* say that to the terminally devastated? Did we say that to *you?* We held our peace and trod gingerly on what was left of your feelings. We writhed and thrashed and moaned as you did, but now we have graduated, now we are the graduates of the most bitter academia."

A young woman a few seats away stared oh so blankly at Tom's mum.

"Welcome, freshman." she said.

Outside, the conductor's whistle blew and kisses and hugs and promises loaded the platform to breaking point. The engine fired up and chugged like the awakening sloth it sometimes was. Soon, only waving loved ones stood, blowing kisses as the train moved slothly away. Platform and small town gave way to desert and still more desert.

"We will be alright until darkness falls." said a man from the other end who had not spoken before. "All the same stations, all the same people. We see their ever repeating happiness. It mocks us and causes us to wonder about our own loved ones. You will even start to wonder about the lives of the people you repeatedly see, but eventually that will pass. You will be concerned above all with nightfall, and when it will come. It comes at different times, random times, playing Russian Roulette with our nerves. When we see the shadows shift and light start to fade, we know that violence is coming for us again."

So there it was. All within the carriage now took on a loosely uniform look: seated, heads bowed in resignedness, individualism crushed to nothing, ignoring spectacular scenery moving past, and a sun that would eventually set.

9

Afterwards

It was about 5 hours before the disappearance of Tom and his mother courted worry.

Another 1 hour and the police arrived.

Two days later the local news and then the inevitable national news.

One year later saw the filming of a documentary for any given channel on satellite. Because great was the mystery, a mystery perpetually kindled by absence of any motive or rhyme or reason. Simply baffling. Into thin air. Simply baffling. A great deal of involvement, most of it sincere, but no resolution. Hopefully one day. Hopefully closure one day.

Tom's dad, Andrew, had been through the grinder of primary suspect, emotional stress, public opinion and public judge, jury and executioner. He still lived at the same address, which still received anonymous hate mail, though thankfully that was petering out. The house was now basically a mess inside and out. He was well underweight.

Lisa, Gemma and Kyle took it badly. Lisa sobbed for a good while after the fact and only went to the mall if necessary. When the three of them got together, for a long time, Tom was the only thing they could speak about. They had wanted a candle lit vigil on the anniversary of Tom and his mum disappearing but none had the courage to get the ball rolling on that score.

Tom was still in their hearts but real life was under their feet and they were caught up in the flow of that life. Kyle went to college across country so was gone for long spells anyway. Gemma took a job at the mall. She was a waitress at a burger bar on the ground floor where, in between admiring herself in any given reflective surface, she actually served customers. She eventually got a boyfriend but, unbeknownst to anyone except the vain but loving girl herself, Tom's disappearance hit her hard and she was never truly the same again. She would one day have a son she would name after her missing friend.

Rotund Al had followed the story as he sat in the arcade change booth. The sad frown on his face as he read about it revealed that he was anything but the gangster "Heavy" who stood on lookout as someone got shot to bits. He remembered Tom kindly. One day, completely spontaneously, Al emerged from the booth, unplugged the game that was Tom's favourite and turned it to face the wall, then went out back – where it all started – for a "cig". The cabinet game sat like that for about a month.

So this had been a year of hardship on many levels of intensity for those who knew Tom. That's a lot of time and a lot of happenings. When "a lot" meets "a lot" it is very easy to overlook the odd thing or two.

And one thing had slipped through the net of attention entirely was that a lorry, just a normal goods lorry, had been abandoned by the side of the road a mere two miles from Tom's house. The driver's door was open and by the time any form of authority investigated, the radio had already been stolen and the seats slashed because some people just like doing that kind of thing. The driver was never traced as there was no company name on the side, license plate or any paperwork inside the cab. All that could be discerned was that its last load had been lemons, due to the citrus splattered rear goods bed, confirmed by the smell of said fruit.

Also, although not considered investigation worthy, the manageress at the store who welcomed Tom at his "King for a day" experience, never turned up the next day. No one had asked her her credentials as she had simply "turned up" that morning and everyone assumed the regular manager was off sick. This one day stand-in "supply manageress" was never heard of again. When the *actual* manger came to work the next morning, he thought people were pranking him about his day off and could not account for the missing day.

Just a few streets from Tom's house there was a play area. Just picture any play area and you have the general idea. Ask anyone in town and they would say it had been there for years. Ask anyone in their 20's and they could even remember playing on it themselves.

At the time of Tom's disappearance, Becky's house had stood there. The house and its occupants, the Hart Family, had been erased from all existence and knowledge. No one spoke of them as no one remembered them. "What Hart family? It's *always* been a play park".

And as for the "Nudge Canyon" machine . .

On that first night, the night of disappearing and worrying and police calling, the machine had been sitting exactly where it was the moment Tom's mum pulled the lever: half facing the wall with a tarpaulin semi-draped over it.

Then, choosing its moment to perfection, amidst police and sniffer dogs and a pacing, fretful husband, it just vanished. No lights, no fanfare, just gone. The tarpaulin that was draped over it crumpled to the floor.

The view now was one of rising and rising, at speed, further away, up and up and up, through clouds, until the view was one of looking down on the country from a very great height. Then a rapid moving across country – a real high speed journey – suddenly halting at another part of the country many miles away.

Descending now, at high speed, down and down, through clouds, until the view poised 100 or so feet above a suburban area similar to the one just left. Looking down, much activity could be seen on a glorious afternoon. It was apparent there was a communal event taking place. Down to ground level now.

Yes, the scene was one of weekend relaxation and small scale trading. One particular close in this town was holding its own yard sale. There was quite a big turnout, rivalling the 4th of July, such was the thronging merriment. It was easy, from a central standpoint, to view each driveway full of household items for sale. Armchair experts perused and haggled over that lamp they've always coveted that sat in their neighbour's front window. Children ran and laughed, adults just laughed. Some people turned up to buy, others just to eat and gossip. Three dogs sat near the barbecue, hoping to dine on the 4th July atmosphere.

At the far end of the close there was a small selection of goods for sale labelled as "Miscellaneous". Here were the rejected of the rejected, items even the most covetous would spurn: an amateur painting from evening art classes, a red jumper with a creosote spill on one arm, and other such forlorn items.

Suddenly, without any flashing lights or sound, the Nudge Canyon machine appeared among the outcast objects. It looked at home among the other oddities. Just then a little girl, holding a balloon, ran past. Two accompanying adults were just behind.

"Now Honey, don't get too far ahead OK!" said Susan, the girl's auntie. The little girl ran off anyway, maybe she had seen a school friend.

"*I said . .*" Susan hurriedly walked off in pursuit, leaving husband Paul in her dust.

"*I'll just take a look here! Go buy her an ice cream. Get me one too will you?*" cried Paul, stopping next to the miscellaneous items. He stood and scanned the rejected of the rejected, feeling like he had entered the town of Lonelyville.

"Boy, I almost feel sorry for you guys! He picked up the amateur painting and couldn't contain a laugh.

"You gotta be *kiddin!*" he exclaimed as he looked over his shoulder in case the artist was watching. Paul continued to wander through the shunned items, ignoring their silent pleas. He stopped in front of the one armed bandit. It was a one armed bandit in near mint condition, Tom had done such a good repair job on it. A labour of love it had been. Did first impressions count?

"Now hey, just *wait a minute!*"

Obviously they did.

***

A week later and a group of friends stood in front of the Nudge Canyon machine, which Paul had bought at the yard sale. It was a Saturday evening and he and Susan were having a party. Four or five friends stood, forming a semi-circle round the machine which Paul had placed in the hallway. Most held drinks and the sound of the party hubbub mixed with music, Susan's choice of music, was in abundance. *Good times!* The bandit was a real talking point.

"Couldn't you have just bought a piggy bank?" quipped a friend.

"He just wants us to pay for these drinks!" quipped another.

"Is it the real thing? I mean . . does it work? asked someone, reading everyone's mind. Susan took her cue:

"It better, cause we've got a pile of bills!"

Paul spoke like a salesman, "Well I've loaded it up with 99 one dollar coins so you're all welcome to go for it!"

"Why 99?" asked a guest.

"Because this was already in the machine when I opened it up." answered Paul as he flipped a coin a few times. "If you clean me out I won't complain! You're about to witness the first play!"

He slotted the coin, yes the same coin, and pulled the lever. The gunshot sounded and the bandit and posse set off as before, repeating history.

"*Go buddy go!*" cheered a friend.

"I'm on the side of law and order!" said another.

The reels sequentially and daintily clicked to a stop. No win. The posse apprehended the bandit. Raucous cheers from, nearly, all present!

"Well look who fought the law and look who lost!" quipped the quipper. All that could really be said by Paul was what Paul, in truth, had expected to say.

"Aw *c'mon!*"

"I knew it! It's rigged, like everything else in life!" said Susan.

"Anybody got a screwdriver, I mean a *real* screwdriver!" quipped the quipper again. They all turned and wandered away to join the party.

"Well I suppose it ain't called a bandit for nuthin'!" said Paul laughingly.

To look at the reels closely and what symbols they were covered with was an insight in to the mind of the deceiving machine. Gone were the lemons, crowns and love hearts used to lure Tom to his doom; now different symbols, innocent to the rest of us but what would hold great significance to the new owner, Paul, were visible. No good using love hearts on Paul because Paul was forever in love with Susan. New symbols to be seen were roses and doves, among others more cliché. Dollar symbols could also be seen here and there, because everyone likes cash, don't they?

So the party continued and the fun simply went on and on till the sun began to rise.

But somewhere else,
in a desert land filled with outlaws and sheriffs,
tornados and scorpions and wandering trains,
the sun would soon be setting.

10

Moving on

Clearing up after a party is a hangover all of its own, isn't it?

Throwing a party, even a fairly *small* party, is basically inviting some power to empty a dumpster right on your living room carpet. At first glance, the furniture is so rearranged that you could be in another house. You went and let a lot of cats out of the bag, didn't you? And what's the saying about putting the Genie back in his bottle? Just think, before the party started, didn't you put extra effort in to making your house look a lot more tidy than it usually does? – as if you were readying it for prospective buyers – only so other people can make it a lot messier than it usually is. So much has changed that the only thing the same is your actual address. No more parties ever ever *ever*.. until the next one.

Paul and Susan set about just this very task on Sunday mid-morning. Susan was like a whirlwind, literally. Anything she came near to vanished in to a black bin liner vortex. She held the bag, a detergent spray and a cloth all at once, juggling them as if she was auditioning for the Cirque de Soleil. Paul had a ringside seat and watched the whirlwind, watched the master at her work. He was *so* glad this wasn't a race!

"Check down the back of the sofa, honey!" said Paul.

"I will, when I find it!" she replied as she continued her audition.

"Well we got lucky last time hon, didn't we?"

"Yeah! Finding that thirteen dollar bill was a beaut!"

The sofa was eventually found and put back in place. No money found though. Maybe someone should start a "Down the back of the sofa" app so that party attendees can actually leave money for the hosts. Paul stopped tidying, as usual, and wandered up to the Nudge Canyon machine in the hallway. Susan watched out of the corner of her eye, her expression and energy depleting somewhat as she saw the look on Paul's face.

She had seen this expression before, a long time ago. She stopped abruptly and sidled up to her husband. In the silence, Paul turned and looked deep in to Susan. She reciprocated and both read the other, two stories synchronising perfectly, word for word. Paul sighed a few times as Susan placed a comforting hand on his back. He had an arm on the machine and was staring at the reels as if they were actually speaking to him. Turning, Paul hugged Susan very tightly, which she enjoyed on several levels. She placed a hand on his cheek.

"Was this really a good idea?"

Paul sighed and stared downwards, shaking his head. "No, not really." he replied, momentarily stuck in a swamp called "The Past".

You see, Paul was a reformed gambler.

He had become a gambling addict towards the end of his student days, only just managing to graduate in History before the addiction swept to victory by a landslide and ruled his life. Believe it or not, long before they were properly introduced and later married, Susan had actually taken bets made by Paul when she worked part time at the local bookmakers during *her* student days, a fact they both loved to laugh about. Yes, it was easy for them both to laugh *now,* but back *then* . .

Paul had really sunk to the lows. He himself had fallen "down the back of the sofa". His new "Friend" – gambling, was extremely high maintenance and didn't like being disappointed. Paul sought a divorce from gambling through the court of "sheer willpower" but gambling's counsel used the slithering counter argument of "Just one more big win then I'll stop" to keep Paul in wedlock. When you finish a box of cereal, what do you do? You throw the box away. When gambling had devoured all Paul had to give, it simply threw him away. Instant decree nisi. *This* was the look Susan had seen a long time ago, a look she still, unfairly, blamed herself for. Still in his 20's at the time, Paul had a truck load of youth on his side, a good education under his belt and loving people in his heart to help him recover. He was now a teacher of history at the local high school. He stood looking at the one armed bandit, wistfully.

"I only bought it 'cause . ."

"I could hang my handbag here!" interrupted Susan. She had started hanging her handbag on the bandit's arm – a very ironic place to hang it – immediately it had arrived. Paul laughed, "Boy, this guy's good! He got your handbag and never even threatened you!"

"Well all that's in there is my lippy, a video rental card and a 13 dollar bill!"

"I'll ask around here and see if anyone wants to buy it."

"*No way, Hosé!* I want this three reeled rascal *outta town!*" said Susan with a thumbs up "take a hike" gesture.

"Yeah, by sunset!" chuckled Paul. "Ok, I'll put an ad in the paper first thing tomorrow."

With that, the whirlwind went back to tidying and Paul, well, Paul *didn't*.

***

Monday afternoon, the best *part* of Monday afternoon, arrived when the school bell rang at 3:30pm. From whatever side you viewed it, teacher or pupil, you were saved by that bell at 3:30pm! Long after you had left school/retired, 3:30pm would never lose its significance to you and, in a subliminal way, you would react to it the same way as hearing your name called out by a friend while out shopping.

Paul had enjoyed the day, to be honest, despite having to deal with the usual cast of class "clown", class "beauty queen", class "look what I snuck in to school" and class "look, I'm just not interested in history, OK!" In front of him were stacked essays to mark from several of the day's classes, making his desk look like a cityscape. He had just been so caught up that he forgot to advertise the Nudge Canyon machine. There were always about 15 minutes before the cleaners arrived and Paul always took that time to just, well, *recover.* Usually, Paul would do the marking in the staff room so when he got home to Susan he was just *free,* but this time he decided to take it home as he wanted to catch Susan before she went out with some of her girlfriends. The desk cityscape was crammed in to his case with some under his arm and off he went.

***

Mmmmm, that "Welcome home" hug from Susan was just *so nice!*

"How'd things go at school today, Mr Teacher?" Susan's arms were round Paul's neck like a necklace of soothing balm. Will women *never* share the secret ingredient?

"Not too bad, actually." replied Paul "Somebody in class learned something!"

"*No way!*" exclaimed Susan "I *knew* it'd happen one day! And what did they learn?"

"Well I teach history, don't I?"

"Yep"

"Well I learned that, in all history, no man has ever loved his girl as much as I love you right now!"

Susan's "first crush" style excitement disappeared to be replaced with silent, appreciative sobbing. The soothing necklace became tighter, a lot tighter, as she burrowed her head in to Paul's chest. Paul *would* have loosened her grip and said more but it seemed that the necklace of soothing balm can only be detached by women also and it's doubtful they'll ever share *that* secret either. Locked in each other's arms, Paul and Susan both turned and stared at the beautiful sunset. Had this been a romantic comedy or some other such, the scene would have faded out at that point, the cinema audience would have cheered and end credits would have rolled.

Because sunsets are simply magical, aren't they?

One gigantic, frameless painting they always are; going, as they do, from red to orange through yellow and cyan, ending on darkening blue. You would think, just for a second, that the rainbow has toppled over or has simply lain down to rest at the end of another day. The world population stands at 8 billion and not a single one of them has anything bad to say about a sunset.

A sunset can wear anything and look good, for whether you see one playing peek a boo with you behind a ripe harvest of skyscrapers or stare across the top of a forest at one as you walk hand in hand with your sweetheart way out in the country, eye to eye contact with a sunset is always ever so easy. One can view a sunset in one of two ways for it either declares the day almost done or a night still so young; and if a single *sunset* can mean so much to so many, what about the *rest* of creation?

But, the appreciation of anything depends on context, doesn't it?

***

Sheila stared out the railway carriage window at the sunset. She leaned against the glass which fogged then cleared then fogged then cleared with each breath. Her eyes were

139

extremely blearily red and teared out completely. The *chug a ch chug . . chug a ch chug* of the train were as the drumbeats on a slave galley. She sought meagre comfort in the continual circular rubbing with the thumb of the SOS pendant around her neck. The pendant suddenly became some sort of executive toy to distract. Horizontal sunbeams touched her face, warming her teary visage and throwing the look of despair into sharp relief with ever so cruel and mocking, nearly artistic, emphasis.

Chug a ch chug . . Chug a ch chug . .

The sun played peek a boo behind mesa after mesa then sank its last behind distant low mountains.

Chug a ch chug . . chug a ch chug . .

Anyone seeing this woman's plight, be they friend or complete stranger, would immediately lay etiquette aside and put their arms around this saddest of women.

And other people *did* see her. The woman who had bid Tom's mother futile, and odd, welcome and indeed had met Tom himself - "Elegant Lady" - looked at her with solemnity. Any word spoken would have been too futile, too weak in themselves to carry even the lightest hope. To offer *any* hope in this place, be it through word or touch or gesture, would have been as useless as lying to the dead. The carriage was full to bursting point with culture shock that never lost its cruel novelty. No one spoke, no one mingled, all sat apart and isolated.

For, apart from one, all knew what was coming. All, save one, knew they were in a world where any sunset may accidentally take a wrong turn and find itself truly spat on by the coarse. The rainbow does not sleep *here* – the rainbow dies.

Chug a ch chug .. chug a ch chug ..

The rising moon stopped utter darkness from gaining sway. Always stealthy, always so full and all too rapid and bang on time, the silver disc would not shine down upon romantic walks or bended knee proposals but on repetitive mindless violence and ever recurring screams, gunshots and tornadic, nasty, mayhem.

The first gunshots were heard from way behind the carriage. This was the cuc for behaviour, long learned by the passengers, to begin. Sheila had no choice but to witness it all; witness as a nearby woman in 50's attire closed her eyes, gritted her teeth with a grimace worthy of any gargoyle, clenched both fists and started banging the table in front of her. Elegant Lady, sitting nearby, never flinched but simply sat, caressing her own ornately ringed and dainty fingers as if seeing them for the very first time. "Welcome Speech" man went to a window and started loading up his six shooter, then lost all inner impetus and held the gun vertically, letting all the bullets fall to the floor. He just stood there, full of resignation. Another man scooped up the bullets, grabbing the gun from Welcome Speech.

"*Well they ain't taking me. Not this time they ain't!*" he proclaimed loudly. His ineptitude at re-loading the revolver, however, proclaimed a different future for him.

"*C'mon, what've we gotta lose?*" the man continued. Hearing this question, in this place and at this time, couldn't even muster the reaction you get when you tell your favourite joke to someone who had heard it before you were born. But Sheila *hadn't* heard the "joke" before and actually reacted. She stood abruptly.

"Yes, YES! We have to do *something . .*" as she slapped the window.

Elegant Lady herself now stood, but slowly. More gunshots, louder and closer and . . wait . . a horse sped by like a crack through precarious ice, carrying a gun blasting creature that was maybe once human.

Chug a ch chug . .

"*WELL COME ONNNN!*" screamed Sheila, terrified by hyperactivity outside the carriage and complete, resigned lethargy within.

Chug a ch chug . .

Elegant Lady put her arms around Sheila in a vice like grip, semi wrestling with her while forcing her to sit.

"Sshhh my dear. There there now. Sit with me!"

"WWHHAATT . . BUT . ."

Chug a ch chug . .

"They only want to rob us."

"WWHHAATT! WHAT DO YOU MEAN "ONLY?"
DO SOMETHING! THIS CAN'T BE . ." Oh, but it *was!*

Chug a ch chug . .

Gunshots and galloping hooves sounded like heavy rain. Mr Bravado, the gun grabbing dreamer, smashed a window and fired and fired as did another man way at the end. Objectively; good on them! Subjectively; quick, put one in your own head.

Bullets now struck inside the carriage which caused splattering of anything they hit. Blood, glass, wood, all exploded, shattered or poured depending on their material composition. No one helped the fallen, no one. The inevitable wanted on board and the slowing train was being forced to oblige. The only one who screamed, properly, was Sheila. Well, who *wouldn't* scream their lungs out at a baptism of fire like this?

"They only want to rob us, my dear. You sit with me!"

Chug a ch chug . .

"We'll be alright again soon. You'll see!"

Elegant Lady tightened her embrace as the gang finally boarded. Sheila simply fainted. Quite what horror caused the faint was anybody's guess as this larder of terrors was jam packed with all horrors.

Chug . . . a . . . ch . . . chug . .

Chug . . . a . . .

Chug . . . and one almighty HISSSSS as the train finally stopped.

The rude awakening was only just beginning. Upon encountering any given member of the gang, it was difficult to determine which of your five senses were activated first. Did the utter stink of Rat Pile hit you before the sight of him blew your optic nerve to bits? Did gunshot deafened ears ring with blood dripping rupture before you felt violence or tasted, if you were a woman, a forced and slobbering kiss from Finger Snapper as he ripped you, your dignity and your treasures asunder?

The status of "Human" was not recognised by this gang. All passengers present were just "things" that existed for the profiting and furtherance of outlaw life and thus, all things were tossed around on an outlaw storm. Most were pistol whipped heavily before being tossed off the carriage. There was much motivation behind the rough treatment, for the gang knew they were on a timer. Each outlaw had an invisible noose around his neck at all times that tightened just a little every second the posse drew closer. The Hangman of

Nudge Canyon slept little at night, such was his excitement at hanging the whole awful gang one day.

Rat Pile swiped the floral hat off Elegant Lady, who was still hugging Sheila; grabbed her by her beautiful hair, struck her with his pistol butt and dragged her to the door; Sheila automatically going with her, the futile hug they shared woefully lacking the power to comfort. Out they sailed and *CRUNCH*, both crashed trackside, hurting both immensely. Sheila lapsed in an out of consciousness, in and out of black, in and out of black. She came to only to see a woman being struck full in the face with a rifle butt and two men shot in the head. Suburban Sheila just screamed.

This attracted the attention of Finger Snapper who, momentarily forgetting outlaw etiquette, left the corpse he was robbing before he'd finished robbing it and strode towards the futile ladies. He was in such a hurry to reach these new spoils that his moon shadow fell two or three paces behind. He didn't hesitate and shot Tom's mother in the knee. All five of her senses tried to flee the scene but were stuck fast.

The baptism of fire burned onwards.

Finger Snapper strode round the back of Sheila and began to strangle her with the SOS pendant she wore. He would have garrotted her for sure but the gold of the chain was something else that got his attention and, in Finger Snapper's world, gold trumps rock, paper *and* scissors.

"Wellll, I used to have *teeth* like this!" he croaked, jerking the chain heavily three times. The only reason Sheila didn't die right then was because the chain broke before her neck did. Finger Snapper, dropping the woman like the broken toy she was unto him, stuffed the chain in to his ghastly mouth as if the links were teeth. He gummy chomped the gold chain and chuckled loudly, smiling as if posing for a camera obscura selfie.

But then, a very short and sharp gust of wind hit the back of Finger Snapper's head. He span around very quickly, wide eyed and scared. All uncouth activity ceased instantly. The gust repeated again, only more sustained and up a notch in ferocity.

"Saddle up, its *them!*" shouted Clinker.

The posse were approaching, flushing evil doers from the valley. This posse held no jail cell keys or handcuffs, just loads of firepower and righteousness indignation with which they wiped out what they saw as undesirable.

Panic took hold now, horses reared.

In the gale, dropped paper money stumbled around the track as if drunk. Finger Snapper ran to his horse, spitting the SOS necklace in to the saddle bag as he mounted. Two already mounted members of the gang tumbled to the ground as long range shots from the posse beat the law of averages and made bullseye headshots. Such was the all around racket of the scene that it was hard to tell when the gang had actually fled but, five seconds before it reached critical mass, flee they did and were gone.

So history repeated itself. There was no democracy here where a person could vote for a world where history could *not* repeat. The line up of passengers was now a sight no one should behold. The dead lay next to the nearly dead who lay next to the wished for death. The silenced lay next to the comatose who lay next to the moaning. The posse never at any time stopped to help victims but rode past without even a glance downwards. Greed had dined once again and some supernatural force would now clear the leftovers.

✳✳✳

The skyscraper of homework was slowly bulldozed by Paul and the day's happenings at school finally bit the dust. He stretched a most enjoyable stretch and looked at the clock. Still easily 1 to 2 hours before Susan returned from bowling with her friends. In the homely silence, an unfulfilled commitment finally got his attention as he realised he'd not advertised the Nudge Canyon machine. Paul tutted himself and rose, going to the bandit. It had proved a big hit at the party and was indeed a ripe and most excellent acquisition, but this time, history would certainly *not* be repeating itself. Paul had loaded the machine up with $1 coins and they were still inside so it was time to "rob the bandit" and retrieve the money.

Opening the Nudge Canyon machine was, mechanically speaking, about the same action as opening a fridge door for a beer, but, in this case, no *cold* air poured out. Instead, something different flowed forth and got Paul's attention. An *atmosphere* flowed and spilled out like a secret that had been held for so long, making Paul feel like *he* was the cold beer. This atmosphere had a tangibility of its own, akin to shifting sands, cradled and borne on soft and wooing winds. The warmth Paul now bathed in was not any by product but was, it seemed, a friendly gesture, a welcoming handshake, a congenial smile. It seemed that, right there on his knees with a screwdriver in his hand and without so much as a third party to introduce them, Paul had just made a new friend.

Wait a minute Paul..

No one else in the room, yet Paul smiled. No one else in the room, yet Paul very nearly said "Hi", such was the tangibility, and friendliness, of this new flowing atmosphere. Momentarily taking on the aspect of a cannabis vending machine, the one armed bandit offered Paul a portion of illicit satisfaction. Closing his eyes like you do when tasting something extraordinarily delicious, Paul breathed deeply.

Now, Paul, c'mon buddy..

Paul was edging closer to a line, some sort of line. Oh yes, the friendliness he was feeling was very much "in your face" but this line, this threshold and precipice, was a velveteen chameleon and trod, oh so softly, towards Paul's heart, intent on releasing his former, captive cravings for the thrill of the gamble.

Paul, look out Paul..

He opened his eyes and gazed at the innards of the machine. No daggers here, just cogs and levers and those coins to be retrieved. This was not an iron maiden. Nothing to hurt a soul. As if closing a newly filled sarcophagus, Paul closed the front of the Nudge Canyon machine with near reverence. The machine took on the semblance of a child's toy full of chocolate coins and what harm is there whiling away the time playing with a child's toy?

Paul, oh no, don't!..

"CLUNK" and the machine closed. This was not Las Vegas. There was no "House" waiting to take your last dime. This was here, now, in the front hall and Susan will be home soon, so just go *on* already!

So Paul *did.* He slotted a coin which slid and bounced down the metal oesophagus. Paul pulled the bandit's arm and the three reels span, stopping at a perfectly aligned row of roses; beautiful - red as can be and simply dripping with romance - roses.

"Oh, I like it!" smiled Paul.

See, not so bad after all, eh! He waited for a payout, like the machine's former owners had all waited, but none came. Slight, respectful thump to the bandit but still nothing, nothing but a sigh from Paul. The bandit's arm refused to move even slightly now. Don't force it.

"Hey there, buddy," said Paul slyly to the Nudge Canyon machine, "you're booking your own spot on Craigslist, you know that?" He was just about to open the machine and finally get those coins when Susan arrived home. In a trice, she was inside and cuddling Paul like the whirlwind she was. Smooch smooch etc etc. As she hung her handbag on the bandit's arm she noticed the roses.

"Oh wow, are those for *me!*"

"Yep!" said Paul, and that was the last thing either remembered.

***

Susan struggled to breathe.

There was an overload of some nasal sort but, if so, why didn't the smoke alarm go off? Whatever it was filled her nostrils and on up through the front door, right in to her dreams. It may have been overpowering but it was pleasant beyond description. So strong was this olfactory joy that it had its own punch and one breath too many punched Susan wide awake.

She awoke to the sight of a most beautiful rose positioned on the pillow just below her nose. The rose was deep wine red, thornless and just at the very moment of bloom burst. Held snoozily in the flimsy petal vice, Susan smiled and stretched in anticipation of Paul appearing with breakfast in bed; although food, drink and shelter are no longer necessary for the one who dwells bosom close to *this* kind of thing.

Just as Paul snored a little, revealing his exact and disappointing "You won't be getting breakfast in bed, after all" geographic location, Susan looked and gasped to see the whole bed covered in roses, the whole *floor* covered in roses. She sat up and roses, by the dozen, toppled off the bed. Too stunned to wake Paul, she climbed out of bed, standing on the soft and wetly-cool, inches thick layer of deep red roses. The cold petals and leaves slid up between her toes, thrilling her. The thornless stems were soft and spongy underfoot. Yes, they were just *everywhere*! What a concentrated burst of niceness this was! Oh, the scent, oh, the *scent!* The tongueless beauty of the scene spoke shatteringly loud to Susan's heart, tearing away all cares, drawing a big thick line under the indifferent minefield of her past. *Paul, was this your doing? Was this your brainchild?* Well, Susan, just whose else could it *be?*

Paul struggled to breathe under an overload of some nasal sort. Who goes there? Who thinks they have the right to intrude so? No dream is ever *this* powerful! Oh, but wait, this is pleasant also! With an extra loud intake of a snore of a semi cough along with a clenched fist weak punch towards an invisible enemy, Paul awakened to Susan holding a breakfast tray laden with breakfasty delights!

***

Downstairs, Susan held as large a bouquet as her hands would allow, holding the bouquet as if it were a newborn. The roses, or rather, the unspoken sentiment *behind them,* had touched her heart and, as the heart and the face are linked in that oh-so-human way, a smile would be her de-fault setting for roughly a week. The bouquet was like an elaborate magic wand that turned all it touched in to something enchanted as she ballet danced around, humming some catchy tune, quite clearly auditioning for the Bolshoi. Sorry, Cirque, you had your chance! Paul simply looked on with a smile. Somewhere in his mind, a penny was stuck.

Now gifted suddenly with astonishing balletic ability, Susan pirouetted over and over right on to Paul's lap.

"That was some neat and clever idea, sweetheart!" she said, drinking up rich rose scent. Paul, of course was in the know of the situation or rather he was in the *don't know* of the situation as he had no idea how the roses appeared but didn't want to spoil the moment. All he knew for sure was that he did indeed have *somebody* to thank for this.

"Did you rig it?" asked Susan.

"Rig *what?*"

"Our one armed friend! I always had my suspicions those things were rigged."

Susan saw the puzzled look on Paul's face so dragged him to face the Nudge Canyon machine. She pointed to the reels like a she was choosing a ten million dollar engagement ring because it went well with her Lamborghini. Susan's penny *had* well and truly dropped.

"Those!" she gushed, pointing to the perfect row of roses on the one armed bandit. A clunk of some sort sounded somewhere as the penny now dropped for Paul also. Was he in the know *now?*; well, maybe. He smiled broadly and just managed to put 2 and 2 together in time to use the "Bro Code" on himself.

"Oh, what?, oh yeah *yeah*, I *thought* you'd like that touch!"

The spell of it all was so strong for Susan and Paul didn't want to spoil the moment for his wife, who, it appeared, was the first person in all history to actually find the end of the rainbow. Blinded by it all, Susan never noticed that she hadn't asked Paul how much all those roses cost and Paul hadn't noticed she'd not asked. The moment was the moment. He turned to look at those reels and tasted something, a taste from the past.

***

"So they're *fixed*, right?"

It was Monday evening and Paul was, again, opening the Nudge Canyon machine to empty it and prepare it for sale.

"Yeah, they're fixed. They *all* are!" he said in answer to Susan's persistent question. "There's no gamble with these things, it's strictly business." He pushed a lever and the metallic waterfall of 100 one dollar coins gushed in to a sack Susan held. This was open heart surgery on the machine, a wealth transfusion from it to Paul and Susan. Surgery over, Paul closed the machine. Susan took one of the coins from the bag.

"Leave one in for the next owner, huh!"

"Yeah, why not!" said Paul.

He took the coin and played the machine, not expecting a win because "they're all fixed, right?" The gunshot sounded, bandit and posse did their thing, as did the reels, which stopped on a perfect line of white doves.

"Aw now, *c'mon*, you're playing tricks on me again! *Enough already!*" tutted Susan.

"NO look, I promise! I don't know how . ."

"Well they're very pretty, Mr Merlin but those doves are gonna fly this contraption right outta here!"

"You bet! Buyer's coming tomorrow."

But "Tomorrow" had plans of its own . .

***

Paul arrived at school. He sometimes thought that, if *he* was in charge, he would re-name the school "Bittersweet Academy". This was from the standpoint of both teacher *and* pupil. There was much good to be found in the school by both groups: education, friendship, a sense of belonging and achievement; but for all too many, accessing these wonderful things meant running a daily gauntlet of distractions in the form of youthful, misdirected exuberance. Imagine having to cross a mine field to get to your favourite restaurant; well, *that* was day to day life at "Bittersweet Academy".

Echos abounded in the school. This was ok if the sound rebounding was Mozart but it was instead yelps, whistles and shouting teachers calling for order. A teacher's first port of call was to the staff room to draw up battle plans, shout "Semper Fi" with any other staff present then off to the front line.

As Paul walked towards his class, carrying that skyscraper of marked assignments, he thought something was amiss. Had he forgotten some announcement that class would not be in that day? Normally, Paul could tell what year he was teaching that particular period by the sound alone. He could tell if the class clown was in or off sick by the decibel level. The presence/absence of the class beauty queen was identifiable due to the presence, or lack of presence, of too much perfume wafting along the corridor. Just like a mechanic gets to know all the sounds of a sick car and can diagnose a fault in 3 seconds, so Paul knew these class quirks.

But all that was absent. The silence that oozed from the class, before he even got to the door, was like walking across country fields. He slowed his step in trepidation and peeked through the doorway. Yes, the class was there, the *whole class* was present!

All sat in silence at their desks. Most looked up at Paul and smiled. Paul was truly taken aback and said "So, you're all here!"

"Good morning Mr Smith!" the children replied in near perfect unison as if rehearsed. Paul dumped his things on the desk and waited for the punchline, for this just *had* to be a prank, surely. Usually the class was a microcosm of its own, with all aspects of human disrespect represented from 0 to 10. Certain areas of the room were like parts of a neighbourhood that you really shouldn't venture in to unless you wanted a parental confrontation later on in the day because, it would seem, pupils *gain* more rights every year and teachers *lose* more rights every year.

But wait .. wait .. no, this *wasn't* a prank. For 40 minutes, Paul strolled across those country fields as the teacher taught and the learners learned, absorbing everything he said. This was so unusual that Paul found himself more than a little distracted, looking at the class with his inner eyes narrowed in suspicion, but why argue with a genuine $100 bill inside your birthday card?

Class after class came and went; classes that were now, inexplicably, fully focused on their education. When each class ended, the moment they crossed the threshold, all reverted instantly back to the expected norm, bouncing and jostling around as usual. Paul was a teacher of history and it seemed that now, misbehaviour, right along with the Declaration of Independence, was a thing of the past, the occurrence of which was something to be celebrated annually.

***

"Did the buyer cancel?" asked Susan at the dinner table.

The Nudge Canyon machine was still standing where, by this time, it shouldn't have been. Paul was indeed eating but was also quite clearly somewhere else. He was still in school or the school was still in *him*.

"The oddest thing happened today." he said, still ambling across those sun warmed country fields.

"Oh yeah, do tell!"

"Well every class I taught . . just got to it and *worked*. There was no misbehaving at all. I've never had it so easy."

"Well is there a test coming up or something?" asked Susan.

"No . . no . . that's just the thing. There was no earthly reason for it. I mentioned it in the staff room but all the other teachers reported just the same mob behaviour in class. It made me feel a bit embarrassed to be honest."

"Shame, isn't it?" said Susan.

"What?"

"That good behaviour is such an oddity these days!"

Susan was rejoicing with Paul, but, in reality, it was a "You had to be there" kind of an experience and Paul *had* been there. He glanced over Susan's shoulder at the one armed bandit, remembering, and deeply feeling, the near human friendship the machine surprised him with when he had opened it. Those roses had come from *somewhere*, hadn't they?, and no earthly power has yet been invented that can entice every class Paul taught to behave itself for no reason at all, has it? But the icing on the cake had been . .

"So, *did* the buyer cancel?" asked Susan again.

Yes, right out of the blue, the buyer *had* cancelled and now there was no going back.

The trap was sprung.

11

Long time, no see!

Not really a full moon but good enough to stare up at and ponder serious ponders.

It was 2 am. Paul lay warmly in bed next to Susan. An odd encounter was on his mind. He had glimpsed an old friend, albeit a "Fair weather" friend recently and, as happens, thought about past exploits with that person. As they had passed, Paul's former friend had nodded and stopped, inviting conversation. So they stood a while and just chatted about the old days. Anecdotes were exchanged. Oh, how friendly was the friend! A way back in to the past was, due to this encounter, handed to Paul on a plate. Upon parting, an arrangement was arrived at whereby Paul and his old friend would meet up again. It was *this* meeting that Paul was preoccupied with, there in the mild moonlight.

It was Friday night in to Saturday morning. Paul slid out of bed and went downstairs. He switched on the kettle for coffee then went in to the living room where he opened a drawer and delved. A plain cardboard folder was found and retrieved. Hard for anyone to know what lay in the folder due to no label and the fact that it was buried drawer deep. Some facets of life will slumber and be of no embarrassment or painful reminder at all as long as you have a deep drawer somewhere.

The folder's contents were the culmination of Paul's 24 weeks at GAM ANON, short for Gamblers Anonymous, a group set up to help with gambling addiction. The group had met fortnightly in a church hall. Paul had been glad at the time as the hall was nearly 30 miles away and, theoretically, out of range of any "gossipy neighbors" radar.

The first meeting was a nervous one but the common bond all attendees shared meant no ice ever formed so there was none to break. Everyone in the group was exceptionally friendly. Paul had been acutely embarrassed to be the youngest by a long chalk, well he *looked* the youngest anyway as the addiction had obviously taken its toll, physically, on several members who were probably younger than they looked. What every attendee wore however, whether they knew it or not, was the sheen of honesty. None had the cool outfit or a comic named after them, all those amazing gadgets or any super powers at all, yet they were heroes unto themselves.

The kettle clicked. As Paul made the coffee, he heard movement. Peeking round in to the living room he was shocked to see his former friend sitting on the sofa, casually browsing the GAM ANON literature and progress chart.

"WOAH!" gasped Paul. Friend looked up and smiled.

"*Wait a minute!*" exclaimed Paul in hushed yet very assertive tone, nearly through clenched teeth. "Just *how* did you get in here? We hadn't arranged . . "

"I passed and saw the door open, so I thought . . " said Friend, very casually, still smiling.

"But all the doors are locked! It's 2:30 in the morning!"

"Now, *Paul*," said Friend with a single raised eyebrow, garnishing words with just a touch of mockery; a mockery which, Paul felt, had always tainted the friendship, "You *know* what door I mean! C'mon now!" Because there are doors and there are *doors,* aren't there? Paul saw the point well, nearly in 3D if truth be told. He slouched to the sofa and sat, head fallen, letting out a long sigh as he stared at his feet. He could feel Friend looking at him as if *he* was the owner of the house and Paul was the guest.

"Did you like the roses?" asked Friend in a very up beat tone, both eyebrows raised this time.

"Where have you been?" asked Paul.

"Oh, I've been making friends all over. I'm not the bad guy people make me out to be!" said Friend as he perused the literature that told of Paul's pathway to victory over his gambling addiction. He stopped reading, looked Paul right in the eye and asked in a tone that was neutral laced with just a hint of the sinister.

"Why did you get this folder out tonight, Paul? Was it nostalgia or something less romantic?" Paul simply sat with head bowed. The teacher felt like *he* was now the pupil. Just then, Susan spoke groggily from the head of the stairs.

"Paul, you ok honey? I heard you speaking."

"Nothing, Susan. Just thinking out loud. Be up in a jiff!" Susan retired.

"Why did you lie to your wife, Paul?"

"I didn't."

"Yes you did. You told her the buyer for the Nudge Canyon machine had pulled out, didn't you?" Paul didn't deny this accusation. He tried to parry the incisive attack from Friend. It was a blunt parry but needs must.

"Look, I don't *want* you here or to *see you again, ok!*"

"Well that's what you *say* Paul but you lied to your wife about the buyer and now you dig this old folder out! When you lied to Susan I heard the door unlock and when you got this folder out I heard the door creak open. C'mon buddy, why'd you *really* do these things?"

Paul felt surprise courage leap from somewhere.

"GET OUT . . JUST . . JUST . . GET *OUT!!!*"

"OK OK *OK!*" blurted Friend, standing abruptly, holding up two defensive hands, "I'm *going*! Some thanks I get for giving you peace at school, huh!" Friend was referring to the doves of peace on the reels which had given a day of peace in all classes which Paul had more than more than *more than* enjoyed. That day had been followed by 2 more of the same. A day per reel. Paul marched to the front door, stood, and held it open. Friend took the brutal hint.

"Ok Paul, you win, but just to show there's no hard feelings!" Friend stood in front of the Nudge Canyon machine and waved a beckoning hand. Paul stood in no man's land; at a fork no man's land.

Be careful Paul!

Friend continued to beckon. Paul stood, sighed and contemplated.

Paul, Paul, be careful now buddy!"

He closed the door and walked over to Friend.

"A "Parting gift" shall we say, old friend?, to show there's no hard feelings! What harm?" said Paul's unwanted guest.

Friend tapped the Nudge Canyon machine and that one coin Susan suggested be left for the next owner clinked in to the payout slot. Friend took the coin and held it up. Paul saw the gleaming coinage flipping along and back across Friend's rippling fingers. Paul took the coin, slotted it then pulled the bandit's arm. Doves disappeared, taking wing and flying off in a cylindrical rush of colour, which clunked, one by one, on three dollar signs perfectly aligned. The machine locked up as before. Paul looked at the win. He looked and looked and looked at the win, standing alone now, for Friend had left through the same "door" Paul had opened for him to enter. This was one tug too many. Somewhere, a knot that had been cleverly and patiently tied, loosened utterly. When that happened, GAM ANON oaths and pledges went in to free fall.

***

"Couldn't sleep last night, Darlin'?" asked Susan at the breakfast table.

"No . . I mean yeah . . no . . yeah"

"Well that's two "No's" and two "Yeah's" so let's split the difference and say you were sleepwalking!" joked Susan. Paul just sat like an uncompleted statue some sculptor had grown tired of carving; forlorn and wistful. His conversation with Friend had knocked planet Earth off its axis and it's asking a lot of anyone to put that particular needle back in the groove quickly and without help. It took every ounce of Paul's character not to glance repeatedly at the Nudge Canyon machine as, knowing Susan like he did, she would have noticed it immediately and dominoes would have started falling. More subterfuge Paul? More slight of hand to distract your beloved Susan?

"Who was your guest?" asked Susan with raised eyebrows. That question certainly put life in to the statue.

"WHAT?" whisper gasped a now wide eyed Paul, forcefully. Cutlery jumped and clinked with a jolt.

"Well there were two coffee cups on the living room table!"

"WHAT?" in ditto tone of voice.

Susan laughed heartily "Hey, *relax*! A full forensic of the scene failed to find any lipstick!" She alighted her chair and kissed Paul's forehead. The kiss was a shot to his arm and he smiled up at her. Susan lifted her handbag off the bandit's arm. She had not noticed the three dollar signs.

Don't run and stand in front of the reels. Let them hide in plain sight. Act casual.

"Hey c'mon gorgeous, let's go shopping for happiness!" laughed Susan.

Oh Susan, that's right. Do what you do best and joke me back to the land of the living!

Paul smiled freely now and took a mouthful of cereal. *Yes, get out for a while and mingle with the world.* He went to put the bowl in the sink but Susan grabbed his arm.

"Leave it! There'll be no happiness left. It'll be sold out! We gotta hustle!" She dragged Paul to the front door as if the house was on fire. Opening that door revealed an official looking person about to ring the door bell. Susan jumped with a "YIKES!"

"Gosh, so sorry to alarm you Madam. Is this a bad time? asked the suited.

***

So, just what *can* you do with five hundred dollars?

It's a good amount, isn't it? You could put it towards that holiday that never seems to get any closer, couldn't you? You could go for two, maybe three, romantic meals *and* throw in a surprise gift of jewellery for Susan, couldn't you?, because happy *wife*, happy *life*, remember! Apply those five hundred dollars to your relationship, like water to any thirst you care to mention, and just see those sparks fly again! The question is; does five hundred dollars become a family member or does it just come to stay for the weekend? Is it to be tucked away or just .. well .. *spent!* Being the tantalising amount that it is, neither chicken feed nor a massive amount, doesn't the wad of cash shout "*Aw, c'mon, just have fun!*"

The "suited" visitor had been a representative from an investment firm. Apparently, an unknown benefactor had started a fund for Paul that expired after 20 years. The $500 was the total amount plus interest. The rep said that instructions stipulated the money had to be given as cash, not a cheque. Paul signed for the money, the rep left, stunned silence, garnished with a wallop of joy, filled the room, and that was that.

"*WOW,* I mean just *WOW!*" gushed a "16 again for a while" Susan as she fanned the cash out. Paul basically did the same. It felt *good* being 16! And like most 16 year olds in a good mood, "*Celebrate!*" by Kool & the Gang was played on repeat for the next half an hour as the two danced and rained cash upon themselves. Was the mystery benefactor discussed? . . are you *kiddin'*? The timing of the money's arrival, just as Paul and Susan were going out the door to buy "Happiness" was extraordinary to say the least; a story straight from the best anecdote factory in the country!

***

Car headlights swept across the living room as Paul and Susan returned from their windfall tour of all their locality could provide. All talk had been of the temporary, but fun, side of life.

Oh, how the fleeting rushes along and catches you in its breeze as it passes; your hair blowing in those sweet and short lived adventures! Your heart drinks its fill of exactly what a thousand doctors ordered! There is no "waiting" in this land neither do people stand in queues but all access to all the joys of the fleeting are right there for you! Gravity is on your side, time is on your side, the realisation that you really *are* as young as you feel is on your side. This party is for *you* and in *your* honour so don't look, just leap, leap with a shout!

Susan took off her shoes and ran upstairs for a shower as was her habit. She carried two new outfits bought that afternoon. Paul followed at a more leisurely pace. It felt exactly as it does when you get home from a wedding; you have been so unusually engrossed and active for the previous 12 hours that it will take an emotional runway 50 miles long to land, fighting the crosswinds of reluctance, and come down safely from the high.

He reached the top of the stairs and couldn't remember if he'd locked the door so turned and started down. He stopped suddenly as he thought he could smell coffee. A few more steps and, to his horror, Paul saw Friend sitting where he had sat before. Friend sat with his back to Paul but, somehow, knew Paul had "joined the party".

"Well Paul, how was your day out?"

Paul rushed down and stood in Friend's personal space, hoping it would send a message, which it didn't. He noticed two hot cups of coffee had been served by Friend, who never even looked up or flinched, indicating in a subtle way that he felt he had a right to be there and was, once again, in command.

"Now LOOK!" seethed Paul, glancing towards the stairs, fearful that Susan would hear. Again, Friend, without looking, knew.

"She can't hear us Paul. We can speak freely!"

"Look, I don't WANT to speak freely, GET OUT!"

"You see, Paul, you're not actually *speaking* to me, you're *thinking* to me. Granted, you may think out loud and be heard occasionally. And you thought to me today, didn't you?" Paul's initial Rottweiler approach had not worked and he had nothing left in his arsenal but exhaustion, so, exhausted, and in no fit state for a quarrel, he slumped on to the opposite seat. Friend looked up and made eye contact with a smile.

"Susan will look great in either of those new outfits we bought her!" Paul looked up with mouth slightly agape and lurched forward.

"We?.. WE?" I mean two's company but three *is* a crowd.

"Yes WE!" said Friend, wide eyed and laughing quite heartily. "Is that such a surprise, Paul? It did cross your mind, didn't it?" Paul drew a long breath and sighed for his country.

"I was genuinely flattered I was in your thoughts. I love you too!" continued Friend. Paul reached for his coffee.

"All work and no play, Paul!" said Friend as Paul sipped his coffee, which was, unsurprisingly, delicious.

"Such a huge payback for so little investment." Friend continued "And look at how safe it is this time round! Look where you are, you're at home! *You're* in control this time Paul. You've come so far! You're not that guy you were back then. One coin at a time, buddy. I mean ONE .. COIN .. AT .. A .. TIME! Your biggest loss would only ever be ONE COIN! A pack of chewing gum costs more, doesn't it!"

Paul just sat there, absorbing the sales pitch like a 6 year old hearing a promise from Santa Clause. His expression was that of a person on a hitherto successful diet looking through the window of a cake shop; one of a man flirting with the past.

"Why?" asked Paul.

"Because it's what I do. Call it nostalgia if you will." replied Friend, looking himself momentarily wistful. "I don't let go of people that easily." Just then, Susan called from upstairs. "Paul honey, get yourself *up here* and check this outfit OUT!"

"Tell her you'll be .. "

"*Up in a sec.*" shouted Paul, completing the sentence. Friend smiled broadly and nodded knowingly then rose and walked over to the one armed bandit. One tap, and, in more than one sense, a penny dropped.

So the path right back to where he had come from 20 years earlier – a gambling addict – was just a few steps across the living room for Paul. It would have been funny had it not been so potentially disastrous, but, to be honest, which one is quicker to do, climb the Matterhorn or take a zip wire down the other side?

In a trice, Paul slotted the coin and, in a trice, the efforts of the past were forgotten. The three reels span their dance of spin, slamming to a halt at 2 perfectly aligned dollar signs with the third just one space too high. Immediately a Nudge was offered. Susan called from upstairs.

"Paul honey, the last time I looked *this* good was yesterday! Get yourself HERE!" But "Here" could wait.

"I'm so glad we're friends again Paul!" said Friend.

"Yeah, me too!" answered Paul as he pulled the bandit's arm and accepted the nudge. After all, all he could lose was one coin, right?

***

WALLOP!!!

Paul dropped from about an awkward height or so on to bare floorboards that were covered in sawdust and some sort of slime that were missed shots at a spittoon. It was fortunate for Paul that it was fairly rickety floorboards he landed on as they had a good amount of "give" which softened his arrival, at least on a physical level.

"UUGH . . WHAT . . *WHAT* . ?" he gasped.

This wasn't his living room! In the dizzying moment, lying there on the rickety, slimey floor, all Paul was aware of were other people's feet, and not a few. Wherever he was more or less heaved with people. The noise of the boisterous, for that is who these people were, mingled with the sound of a piano belting out some cheery ditty. As he partially raised himself up, the pain of Paul's rough delivery in to this world set in and he rubbed the side of his face as he winced. Attempting to get to his feet, he slipped and again, from a combination of shock and floor slime, re-adopted his arrival posture on the floor boards.

"Woah there, sonny, you look like a new born colt findin' his feet!" chuckled a friendly voice. A middle aged and slightly built man began helping Paul to his feet. A woman also took Paul's other arm and assisted. The look on Paul's face helped write the lines spoken.

"Ain't seen you here before honey. You sure, y'alright now?" asked Carla. Paul never answered, he just stared at the unbelievable, for it was all utterly unbelievable.

"Did you take a whoopin'?" Carla continued, waving her hand in front of Paul's face. Paul looked at her then at the man, who was the barman. Yes, Paul *had* taken a "Whoopin'" of some sort but none of the three of them could put their finger on it.

"Well I ain't served you a drop all night so y'aint drunk!" said the barman.

"And I don't see no twinkle twinkle little stars zippin' round yer head nor do I see a wound but you look like you just fell off a wagon!" added a forward but caring Carla as she gently sifted her fingers through Paul's hair like a nurse. Carla's voice was laden with twang and laden with a genuineness that penetrated Paul's emotions effortlessly.

It was immediately obvious when you saw her that Carla was an employee of this establishment and was dressed to please the eye, but her genuineness made her a textbook example of "Never judge a book by its cover". She didn't realise just how accurate her last "wagon" statement was. Finally, Paul became a naturalised citizen of the moment and spoke.

"Where am I?" he stammered, becoming a little concerned when Carla and the barman looked at each other wryly upon hearing his question. It was a small mercy for Paul that he never thought to ask what year it was, for if he had, and they had told him he was now back in 1901, 50 years before he was born, he'd have been comatose by now.

"Don't y'know, buddy?" asked the barman. Paul shook his head which seemed to awaken the first rumblings of what promised to be a monster headache that the sheer noise of the place didn't help. Carla had put a chair underneath Paul and gently lowered him on to it.

"You're in the saloon, honey." said Carla, "You know, the Rattler's Tail Saloon."

12

The Saloon

The "Rattler's Tail Saloon" sat on the main street of the small town of "Nickel" which, in turn, sat somewhere – just "somewhere" – in Nudge Canyon. A mostly forgotten dust bowl of a place, Nickel was colloquially referred to as "Coin Toss Nickel" by many, as, depending on who you were and how you saw life, you were either delighted or regretful to have encountered the town. It was also sarcastically known as "Dropped Nickel" because, on your dying day, if you realised you had dropped a nickel at some point of your life, would you really be all that upset about it? For the same reason, if you had traversed Nudge Canyon your entire life and never so much as *heard* of the town of Nickel, would you really be all that upset about it?

And why call it the Rattler's *Tail?* Should it not have been called the Rattler's *Fangs* or some other scary name? Well, you see, the first thing you know of a rattle snake's presence is that rattling tail. The snake doesn't want to be friends with *you* any more than you want to roll with *it*, so it gives you a chance to back off. The noise, and we're talking *noise,* and the smell, and we're talking *smell,* spilling out those waist high swing doors and on to the street, were as the rattle of the snake's tail. You *were* warned, pardner!

Not much, in fact, *no* action within during the day, as, like all "places that exist in life but really shouldn't", it slept the entire day and hissed at night. But for the saloon, Nickel *could* have been a thriving and prosperous place, but, it only takes one to ruin it all, doesn't it?, and there's *always* "one", isn't there? The Rattler's Tail Saloon *was* that "one".

Inside, beyond the snake's tail, lay the dark brown, wooden, dungeon like world of false pleasures. During the day, it was hard to tell what let in the most light: the windows or the 20 years worth of bullet holes in the ceiling. But the Rattler's didn't do "daytime".

Places like the Rattler's Tail were something of a topsy turvy world where everything was back to front, for in *this* world, robbery was perfectly legal. Well, just ask yourself, have you ever seen a posse storming a casino? In fact, bizarrely, people would travel for miles and queue up to sit at a poker table and simply lose it all. The continued piano playing attempted to put a veneer of fun and hence, respectability, on the whole scene, but, whether you were robbed by the gambling or robbed by the alcohol or robbed by the painted ladies or just robbed of time as you stood and watched, you exited Rattler's a lesser person. This was a "Wild West" saloon in the truest sense of the word and as "Yehaaaw!" as it got.

In corner of this bustle, Paul, thanks to his two new friends, began to acclimatise to this new altitude, be it higher or lower than the "Sea level" of his living room. He went to rise but then the fear of the new hit him somewhat and he walloped, with a real "creak", back in to the fairly rickety chair. The barman had made some sort of makeshift cocktail, which was all water in to which he'd squeezed the juice of an entire orange. He handed it to Carla.

"Here, honey, drink this. What's yer name anyways?" she asked, rubbing her hand back and forth along Paul's shoulders with that sweet forwardness of hers. Paul took the drink and gulped half of it down, along with two pips. The barman and Carla stood and waited for the placebo effect to work, which it did.

"Thanks to you both. My name's Paul."

"*Paauull!*" exclaimed Carla like it was some awesome revelation. Her tone of voice was also a placebo. Paul gazed around and saw the bustle of distraction as people sought for meaning and relief. He looked Carla in the eye for the first time. She smiled broadly for her patient.

"Please tell me how I got here." he asked.

"Well we were kinda hoping you'd tell *us* the answer to that!" chirped barman. Paul reached out and squeezed Carla's arm. She laughed.

"I'm quite *real*, Paul, well least ways I sure *hope* I'm real!"

Paul was just so relieved to be treated kindly. Carla was just pure *warmth* in all facets of her being. Just a few more gracious minutes and he'd get this astonishment sorted and head back home to Susan. He reached in to his back pocket and got his wallet to pay for the orange flavoured placebo. The wallet was crammed with much cash, the remainder of his windfall day out with Susan.

Cash was the very life force of the Rattler's Tail. It held the building together better than the nails. In fact, cash had designed and built the place. To walk through those waist high swing doors with any amount of the stuff was to invite the vampiric to waltz with you – fang deep. No invitation to dance, with either a lady or an establishment, was ever declined for the man who had cash.

"Mr Paul, you and your friend better skidaddle right quick." said barman, referring to Paul's wad of notes. "There's lots of critters in here and they only eat that kind of paper."

Honestly; out in the surrounding wilderness, *critters*; and inside, *critters!* Is there *any* safety in Nudge Canyon? The helpful nudge offered by the Nudge Canyon machine had indeed helped in the sense that it enabled Paul to bypass those waist high swing doors and – now – the Rattler's Tail Saloon worked its magic on Paul.

Slithering enticeties, in the form of a poker game he saw in one corner, and the hiss of that *atmosphere!* Carousing has a draw all its own, does it not? After all, what excites more interest, a soft breeze or a storm in the offing? Search the entire world and you will never find a "soft breeze" chaser. Merriment also has a draw all of its own, does it not? After all, which would you rather attend, a memorial service or a wedding? Search the entire world and you will never find *anyone* who has gatecrashed a memorial service. The saloon Paul was in was the amusement arcade of the day and offered joy at every turn; surface and temporal joy maybe but, well, joy *is* joy.

With his hand on Carla's shoulder, Paul stood and, even though he was standing, was still up to his neck in a world of temptation. He got his first good look at the layout.

As you came in those swing doors, the bar ran along almost the entire length of the left wall. The bar stopped just short of the far wall where the stairs were. These stairs led up to a balcony that ran right around the four sides of the saloon and had two doors apiece. What these rooms were used for were anybody's guess; let's just say there were "rooms" and leave it at that.

Back on the ground floor, men played and drank; elaborate ladies soared around, looking for pickings. There were five or six tables which were given over mostly to gambling and in fact three games were in progress. At the other tables were those just drinking. The piano player was on the right, next to the swing doors to enable the music to spill out and lure.

Two of the three poker games were full up as far as Paul could see at first glance, so he made for the one that seemed to be missing a player. This table was right up against the right hand wall. He made for the poker game, teetering slightly. Oh, how good it felt to take caution and just lob it in to the swirling thermals! *You've spent too much time in the classroom, Paul; relax, chill and be your old self again!* How friendly was the friend!

"Paul, honey, you oughtn't to be goin' over there." advised Carla as she placed her hand on Paul's forehead. "C'mon, me and a friend will walk you home. Wadya say? Let's get some air!"

But, you see, Paul, *this* Paul, the Paul of here and now and his student days *was* home and whether this sudden new world was real or not, Newtonian laws still applied, for Paul was simply drawn to the poker table. Carla tentatively half took Paul's arm as if she was half his girlfriend and towed along behind him. Bartender stopped wiping the bar for a second and watched then continued serving the thirsty as he whistled along to the piano playing.

The poker game wasn't much to look at at first glance. Three players sat; one with his back to the wall, the plumb seat, flanked by two more. The player on the left looked ridiculous. This slightly built individual wore what appeared to be an elongated top hat that was fairly bashed and resembled either a chimney or an upturned spittoon. He wore an officers jacket from the civil war but, in this place, the place which invented the phrase "No questions asked", you could wear a bright red jacket and nobody would argue that you were a tomato. The chirpy piano playing only added to the ridiculous sight.

The opposite player was well overweight with a wide, *wide,* open waistcoat that seemed to impede arm movement more than it enhanced appearance. He wore a pristine bowler hat that looked like it would one day belong to another overweight man named Oliver. But, judge these men on how they looked to you, both carried guns.

Paul sat at the vacant spot and the three were now four. None of the two flanking players even glanced at Paul, but the third, opposite player, looked up momentarily. Paul never knew it, but he was sitting opposite Finger Snapper, who was in the Rattler's Tail gambling away all the spoils from the train robbery. Although Paul may have felt intimidated by these sudden and fantastic surroundings he found himself in, a poker table held no fear from him, for Paul was now, fully, the "Here and Now" Paul of many years ago. A bit rusty but quick to re-adjust, Paul saw the previous hand was coming to an end.

The frankly pathetic pile of well soiled cash in the middle was swept homeward uncoothly by Finger Snapper as he threw down his winning hand. Paul saw the winning hand was just the low ranking "High Card" which immediately bolstered his confidence, but no bravado just yet, eh Paul? There was then an awkward pause in proceedings.

"Well, you in or out?" asked Bowler Hat, still without so much as a glance at a glance. Paul knew he was being addressed and threw a $5 bill in to the pot. Suddenly a finger jabbed in his direction, at full arms reach.

"You wan' in on this you gotta prove you can dig yer way out! *Show us!*" blurted out Finger Snapper, who rarely "spoke" but simply blurted his way through life and if you couldn't understand him, you answered to his guns.

Another emotion threatened to show on Paul's face now, but as he picked up the face mask of "shock" in order to put it on, found his "poker face" lying just underneath. He could now hide fear and bewilderment quite well, as the "poker face" mask, unused for 20 years and covered in the dust of time and rehabilitation, slipped on snugly.

"Paul, c'mon, honey, don't do this. Don't tangle with these people." advised a worried Carla as she leaned in to Paul and put a hand on his back. Paul looked up at her and smiled then turned and locked eyes with the hard core desperado, simultaneously drawing his wallet and showing the cash. Carla kept her hand on Paul's back.

So, just what was it like to look Finger Snapper in the eye?

Imagine you are standing, alone, on a flat, vast, featureless, plain. You look all around and see a lion some way off, at least half a mile away. Just one thing matters to you now; has the lion seen *you*? You are torn between two choices; the obvious need for flight or standing suicidally still in order to know if you have been spotted. Suddenly, both those options become utterly irrelevant because you *have* been seen, and it's as good as over for you. Examine your feelings at such a moment and you will know how it feels to look Finger Snapper in the eye.

However, a thick wad of notes, almost anywhere or time, will get you a first class ticket to the calm eye of any storm or cause Niagara Falls to flow upwards. A thick wad of notes will turn swords in to ploughshares right before your eyes. A thick wad of notes and suddenly, standing on that flat, vast, featureless plain with a lion closing in, you remember you are Samson and those long, flowing locks of yours are nicely intact.

Now the game was underway, Spittoon Hat doubled Paul's bet, taking the minimum bet level to $10. Bowler Hat had the deal and automatically dealt 2 cards all round with astonishing dexterity. Finger Snapper continued to eye Paul, the rudeness of which, as you'd expect, unnerved him a touch. It seemed as if Finger Snapper was perceiving something about Paul and, for a few seconds, forgot the game in hand. Skidding cards, however, snapped the snapper back to the present and he checked his hand as did Paul, who realised he had 2 nines. This would have been a terrific first hand at any time, but for a first deal at a first sitting at a poker table in over 20 years!

Finger Snapper reluctantly threw a soiled, greasy "You don't know where it's been" $10 note where his gummy, neglected, mouth was. Paul noticed Finger Snapper's moment of reluctance and that is *everything* in the world of poker. Finger Snapper, it seemed, like all cowards, was good at snapping innocent fingers, but little else. Bowler Hat completed the round and stayed in the game by matching Finger Snapper's $10 then dealt three cards, face up, onto the middle of the table.

All players now had to make as good a hand as they could with the two cards they held in combination with the three face up cards. Paul saw another 9, checked his poker face, which was still snug and threw in $10 then raised another

$50. This brought a gasp from the moderate crowd which had gathered.

Spittoon Hat gasped a different kind of gasp as he threw in his cards and folded, which caused Paul's poker face to go through one last stress test before it passed, successfully, through quality control. Oh Paul, if there was one statue in the whole of Nudge Canyon at that moment, *you* are that statue, my friend! Pull the cheery piano stitching from the scene and the tension would have gone through the roof.

Finger Snapper now had to either fold or match Paul's $50. Not used to being caught on the back foot and realising he had to win *without* the help of his guns; honest actions seemed to choke him, causing him to slug . . and slug . . whiskey. Living the life he had lived, and *loving* the life he had lived; all at the expense of trembling and defenceless others, Finger Snapper was experiencing a culture shock. Having all the poker face of a circus clown who had just won the lottery, it was *his* turn to feel claustrophobic, trembling and defenceless. He hurriedly threw what cash lay before him and raised by throwing items in to the pot. What he had thrown were several rings and a pearl necklace. No other player argued with this action. Paul didn't want to argue the point either as obviously house rules allowed that but it was obvious something was at explosion point.

Bowler Hat was now looking at Finger Snapper out of the corner of his eye, the first ounce of body language he had shown. A trail of sweat ran down his temple, the glint of which Paul missed but Carla and the others saw. No wonder the man sweated, it's hot sitting next to a spluttering, whiskey sodden volcano. Bowler Hat never had much of a poker temperament either, his statue like presence at the table being down to the fact that he was essentially an emotionless individual to begin with. But, whatever was going on in his head and despite the fact that he had a gun, Bowler Hat drew back from the edge of this awakening volcano and folded.

He was, however, nailed to the seat by the fact that he had the deal, and now dealt another card face up with the other three. This extra card offered Paul no assistance with upping his hand but he knew those three 9's were a three barrelled "Gun of Fortune" pressed right up against the outlaw's head so threw in another $50.

Bartender reached under the bar then surreptitiously made his way over to the game as the balcony above now creaked under the weight of people who had come out to watch and nobody had noticed the piano playing had stopped. When there is a total eclipse, everything, including happiness, stops to see it.

Finger Snapper went to stand, then sit, then stand, then sit. When he stood, Paul caught sight of his firearm, which was rarely given a chance to cool down. Some in the crowd ran outside before the Rattler could bite.

Still standing, Finger Snapper threw down all the cash he had. This never matched Paul's bet but before that could be pointed out, the fully agitated and set to blow outlaw reached into his saddle bag and pulled out more trinkets and a few dollar bills then threw them hurriedly in to the pot as if he was glad to be rid of "Hot" merchandise.

Bowler Hat dealt a final card face up. No joy again for Paul but Finger Snapper suddenly sat down and focused. This would have been a tell tale sign for Paul, and a worrying one at that, were it not for the fact that, in the previous rounds of betting, Finger Snapper had shown all the poker mystique of a 6 year old playing Ker-Plunk. Paul picked up caution by its lapels and hurled it out the window then slapped down $200, which out eclipsed any total eclipse, put even more strain on the balcony and automatically cocked the three barrelled Gun of Fortune.

A now wide eyed and slobbering Finger Snapper frantically thrust his arm deep down in to the saddle bag and found a gold coloured pendant. It was all he had left. This was the SOS pendant owned by Tom's mother. Throwing the pendant down in the most backhanded manner, he was now cleaned out . . and it was showtime.

Finger Snapper hurriedly and worriedly showed his hand which made a pair; a fair hand but a low ranking one. All eyes were on Paul now, including any termites who happened to be watching. Oh, how sweet the moment! Oh, how friendly was the friend!

Paul had never owned a firearm, but a marksman he now was as he pulled the trigger and shot from the hip, throwing his three of a kind in to public view as he reached out and scooped the pot into his personal space, tucking the SOS pendant in to his shirt pocket.

Only Finger Snapper himself heard the three barrelled Gun of Fortune's report and went for his impatient sidearm immediately. The Rattler's Tail, maybe not for the first time nor the last, was suddenly full of the screaming and the fleeing. Finger Snapper took aim at Paul, not so much because of the monetary loss and accompanying indignity, but because he knew there was something strange and out of place about Paul that was a real threat, so simply wanted to kill him.

Suddenly, Finger Snapper was thrown against the wall by a shotgun blast. He slumped and was gone, as was a portrait and a fair amount of the wall behind him. Bartender, an old hand at all this, had seen the end from the beginning and stepped in to do everyone a favour, not just Paul. The slightly built barman, who had made the effective orange flavoured drink for Paul, staggered backwards a few steps from the shotgun's recoil then righted the chair Finger Snapper had been sitting on, more concerned if there had been any damage done to the faux elegant furniture than to the nuisance outlaw, now splatteringly deceased.

***

With a thump and an awful grunt, Paul landed on his living room floor, right in front of the Nudge Canyon machine. Three seconds only had passed since he accepted the bandit's nudge. He lay, shocked in the truest meaning of the word, under the pile of cash and trinkets won at the poker game, some notes fluttering down onto him like autumn leaves. The three dollar signs on the reels were now neatly in line.

"OK buster, if you won't come to me then . ." called Susan from upstairs.

Paul's head just span like a reel on the machine as he frantically stuffed all jewellery, bracelets and any other such thing in to his pockets. He'd never felt so ill in his life. It was some kind of surreal jet lag with a nasty twist.

" . . I'll come to *you*!" Susan appeared at the top of the stairs, saw Paul lying under a heap of cash and burst out laughing as she ran down. Ignorance really *was* bliss for her as she assumed all the money was the leftovers of their day out on the town.

"Oh wow, let me join you there, honey!"

She lay down next to Paul and threw the money over themselves over and over, laughing hysterically.

"Ooh, your breath smells orangey nice! Let's just sleep here, right here tonight!" she said, reading Paul's mind. She obviously meant it because she rose, took two cushions from the sofa, produced a blanket from nowhere – another talent women seem to have – placed them behind their heads then snuggled up to Paul, who, still tasting orange drink in his mouth, wondered if he'd ever sleep again.

13

Don't bet on it!

Paul had had a fairly good sleep, considering where he was sleeping. His dreams had been of the kind that he didn't know if they were dreams or if his mind was actually "thinking" and turning events over as he slept.

Where he lay; the Nudge Canyon machine on one side and Susan on the other, was highly symbolic of the situation he was now in. He couldn't see the reels on the machine from where he lay, but he knew they showed three dollar signs in a perfect row. The one armed bandit had indeed kept its part of the bargain; Paul did indeed have more treasures than before but his visit to Nudge Canyon had been a nasty revelation that the gaming machine came with small print.

There had been guns where Paul had been. There had been nasty people where Paul had been and he could have died, he really could have died. Susan could have come to the top of the stairs to find his corpse laying in front of the Nudge Canyon machine with bullet wounds. Imagine the awful mess of unravelling all that, what with Susan's broken heart; not to mention Susan herself being suspected of Paul's murder. All that for some money.

***

"I'm quite real, Paul, well least ways I sure *hope* I'm real!" said Susan, repeating, verbatim, what Carla had said to Paul when he had squeezed her arm.

"WHAT, WHAT DID YOU SAY?" asked Paul, desperately. Not exactly the correct tone of voice for the breakfast table.

"Hey, relax! I just said that I'm perfectly real, that's all. Why d'ya squeeze my arm anyway?" exclaimed a now defensive wife; defensive and inquisitive.

Paul had been subconsciously checking his surroundings all morning; touching this, touching that, staring at things that ordinarily never received even a glance; behaviour which had not gone un-noticed by his wife.

"What's gotten *in to you?*"

Quite a lot, Susan, if truth be told. A whole lot had gotten in to Paul and Paul had gotten in to a whole load of *it.* Someone's mask had slipped and another person had seen that someone's true colours and now that other person was somewhat shell shocked. It was lucky indeed for Paul that it was Sunday because he certainly needed the day of rest. Unable to just blurt out to Susan what had happened in those 3 seconds he left this world and landed in Nudge Canyon and needing the time to complete the massive task of coming to terms with it all, Paul simply went upstairs and lay down.

The sound of Sunday activities; mowing the lawn, washing the car and impromptu, laughter filled barbecues mingled in to one sort of familiar suburban melody that put Paul to sleep rather effectively. Susan peeked her head round the bedroom door and smiled as she shook her head and rolled her eyes. Paul had still not really acknowledged her new outfit so she grabbed her bag and car keys then headed off to her best pal Edna for a few hours.

***

"You don't get outta here so easy, buddy!" said the outlaw as he jabbed his pistol very hard in to Paul's chest, right over his heart. Paul was standing in a desert place and felt the jab oh-so-much and the fear it caused. He was unable to speak for some reason but noticed Carla and Bartender about 100 feet away, chatting to each other. They didn't look his way or seem to care. The gun barrel hurt so much that it seemed it was going to kill Paul by stabbing, not shooting. The desert world span, sounds jumbled and clashed . . then Paul woke.

The "gun barrel" was the SOS pendant that was in his breast pocket. Paul had rolled over on to his front and the mini nightmare had graciously incorporated that pain in to the script. The dream confirmed that what had happened had indeed happened. Paul sat up on the edge of the bed and rubbed his hand on the indentation on his chest caused by the pendant while removing the object from his shirt.

"What am I going to do with *you* then?" muttered the bewildered history teacher.

Then, a viper of the past, a strange viper creature with both fangs and talons, sank all it could in to Paul, causing old cravings to surface, old cravings that were the "Fun of Gambling". Paul stared at the pendant. Yes indeed, the visit to the Rattler's Tail Saloon had been fraught with danger, but that danger had only highlighted the drabness of Paul's everyday life. Sitting on the bed, it was now the dreaded "comedown" period. Safe, rock solid safe, in pleasant suburbia, Paul still felt bored out of his mind with it all and wanted another hit. Where that hit came from, Paul didn't care that much.

"I know what I'm going to do with you!" said a more purposeful Paul as he went downstairs, opened his briefcase and put all the jewellery inside along with the pendant. Susan never looked in the briefcase but he scrambled the combination locks anyway, after changing the combinations, which was a feature on this briefcase. The beautiful case that Susan herself had given to Paul for his birthday was now full of school stuff, Nudge Canyon stuff and lie upon lie. The elegant black leather belied the Pandora's Box that Paul had just closed the lid on and was more than happy to open again; now that, as far as he was concerned, thrill outweighed consequences.

***

Elegant Lady held her hands one inch in front of Sheila's face and slowly wiggled her fingers, causing near hypnosis to the newcomer. Dainty fingers, that were a real treasure themselves, wore yellow gold rings, as they waved slowly like ripe corn in a gentle breeze.

"See! Look my dear, all's well again, isn't it!"

She was referring to the mending and resetting of broken bones of all victims of the outlaws. Tom's mother could not argue the point and even if she could, was too stunned by it all to respond. She leaned ever so slightly to look over the shoulder of her new friend.

"Yes dear, them also!" said Elegant Lady.

Indeed, some sort of reset button *had* indeed been pressed. Not a "Release" button, mind you, just a "Reset" button. Sheila gazed in near admiration at the scene. All health and finery, all poise and dignity, all that these people possessed at this point in their lives had been carefully restored to them. But, as the train, that was in no particular hurry to go anywhere, trundled on, it was apparent that the mood was no different.

Outside, the intensely beautiful, mesa strewn and cactus adorned scenery rolled by on the sunniest of days. Sheila looked out the window for a moment or two then re-focussed on Elegant Lady. It was clear to her that the cheeriness being shown by the ring wearing woman was the result of one too many raids the poor soul had endured and that she had become unhinged to some degree, but her cheery demeanour was sincere and totally appreciated.

"Look my dear, look!" said Elegant Lady, glancing down with a nod. Sheila looked down quickly, ready to swat away a fly, but saw the SOS pendant hanging like it always hung. She gasped and grasped the amulet, and, as she gasped and grasped, she remembered and hurriedly felt her knee that Finger Snapper had nonchalantly shot near off. For the first time in all this, she smiled. It was a "bottom drawer" smile that a person uses when there is no real joy behind it. Real, full on smiles require a horsepower that, unsurprisingly, none in the carriage could produce.

Now, in the calm *after* the storm, Sheila viewed her fellow captive travelling companions. She counted 9 in total; 6 men and 3 women. To look at them you would think you were flicking through the pages of a history book, for the attire of all were markedly different. Elegant Lady wore an expensive looking floor length dress in crinoline that was straight out of an episode of the Waltons. Her hands glittered with those gold rings. Add to the picture her earrings and brooch and she became something of a chandelier.

Two seats behind her sat a young man who had not spoken as yet. He wore jeans, t-shirt and trainers. Although he too had been hurled off the train by the gang, he had, apart from a rough body search, been basically left alone by the outlaws as he never had any spoils on his person. He sported either a beard or everyday stubble that looked like it was his first; Sheila clearly saw his eyes welling up. She thought of Tom as she gazed at the obviously broken young man and wondered if *his* mother was pulling *her* hair out over *him*. A young woman wearing a brightly coloured hooped top and blue jeans put an arm around this other, stubbled Tom. He unashamedly buried his head under her chin and started crying. It was only then that Sheila noticed both she and the boy were dressed in 50's fashion.

And so it went on; the further back you looked, the further back in time the passengers were dressed until all 9 – 10 including Sheila – were accounted for. This would simply never happen under normal circumstances. It was a sign that some higher power was playing games with people. What she observed really and truly spoke to Sheila and spelled out very clearly the mess they were all in. A juxtaposition of non concurrent lives had been wrenched from their time zones and forcibly thrust in to cruel confines to satisfy a detestable whim. Could it be that, whoever it was, had created an entire world just to hurt others? The train would stop at a station now and then which would only tantalise the prisoners as they beheld normal passengers alighting and embarking. To be so close to normality and everyday life, yet unable to join in and just run from all this, was exquisite torment.

"There now, that's better! You'll soon get used to life with us!" said Elegant Lady, meaning well from the bottom of her heart. This statement, however, at best, only confirmed the mental state of the elegant inmate; at worst, it truly meant there was no way out, ever.

***

Monday morning at school was like any other. Lots of people, mostly very young, blabbering on about the weekend. For the young, Monday had not yet taken on the somber "obstacle to happiness" meaning it will take on, later on down the line. Monday, for the present, is basically just another chance to hang out, catch up and chill with your buddies, only it's done in a school, not a nightclub or house party. The half a dozen staff undertook another week of attempting to lasso and corral this haywire crowd that had moseyed in to "town". All staff knew, by this time, that being a teacher meant you also on occasion had to double as ranch hand, law keeper and sheriff.

Of course, truancy was a problem as some pupils were hooked on that "Friday feeling" and couldn't face the "come down" of a new week. These absconders were thankfully few and far between and were dealt with swiftly by a single phone call to parents. Repeat offenders would get their 15 minutes a few years later on "Most Wanted".

But there is truancy and there is truancy.

Paul was in the betting shop, having called in sick. He knew the pupil/staff ratio well and surmised it could stand his absence for a while. There were two betting shops in town and Paul, as if on some covert spy mission, patronised the more "back alley" of the two.

This place really was a dive. There was so much cigarette smoke in the air that it practically jammed the door shut. Hunched and unkempt figures, numbering roughly four or five, stood in this fog, leaning over betting slips. Another handful stared with all their might up at television screens that blared racing odds and results from different races incessantly; making an unintelligible white noise mockery of the English language. Unlike Paul's fellow members of GAM ANON, there were no heroes unto themselves *here,* just those resigned to life in the thicket and caught in a thicket these people were. The betting shop was a bar that sold adrenaline and sold it neat. The disappointment of losing never dissuaded any drinker, it only heightened the sweetness of the next adrenaline shot. Nobody in the room wanted to know anybody else, a fact that Paul embraced as it made him feel more chameleon like and at ease. Because Paul, good and decent Paul, was now back in the saddle and how ironic for Paul that the word "Saddle" contained the word "Sad".

He had already lost a total of $100 on two races, but that, to the gambler, was only half the point. When you are dying of a particular kind of loud and demanding thirst, you will chew on raw nettles to get the juice. The thrill of the chase, the thrill of that which tantalises and the thrill of being lied to by the whole set up – and choosing to believe those lies – was the pitch black cocktail, garnished with a sprig of belladonna, that Paul loved the taste of. This drink was so hideous to behold that it relied on being unseen for its consumption and just as well for Paul it was, for, if it *could* be seen, there wouldn't be a gambler to be found on planet Earth. He glanced at his watch.

"Time sure flies when you're having fun!"

It was Friend, who appeared out of nowhere and was conspicuous by his immaculate appearance and dignified manner. Paul glanced up at him then semi face palmed himself while letting out a sigh from the old days. He never spoke as, by now, there was no point arguing with Friend.

"You know," continued the immaculate advisor and confidant, "I might just have a flutter *myself* one of these days! It looks fun!"

It was *designed* to "Look fun". *EVERYTHING* is designed to "Look fun", just ask any fish caught by a fly fisherman. The mocking, patronising tone in Friend's words gave voice to the four walls of the betting shop with cruel eloquence. He wandered around, perusing the other gamblers like a scientist walking among his guinea pigs. Not a single person noticed Friend's presence and that was just fine as they were all obedient to the call of the gamble and needed no nudging in the right direction. Patrol completed, Friend stopped in front of his crestfallen charge.

"Don't worry Paul, this is why they invented ATM's! C'mon, let's head over to the bank!" Paul glanced at his watch again with a swithering look on his face. He had called in sick and sick people don't usually recuperate in the high street, where the only ATM was. Also, it was near school out time. Honestly, a *real* spy on a *real* covert mission never had as many social avoidance issues to deal with.

From somewhere deep down inside, a lighthouse called "Common Sense" swung its wide beam over Paul, bathing him in delicious hope that all he had to do was walk out the door, go back to Susan and awake from all this. Oh oh oh, was that escape route *really there?* Yes, it *was!*

The door of the betting shop burst open as Paul exited with all his might, nearly stumbling. Combine that sight with a veritable entourage of cigarette smoke trailing after him and you'd think he was escaping a burning building.

Yes, I'll go home to Susan and just tell her everything . . EVERYTHING.

***

The desert is a beautiful place.

In essence, it could represent the average human mind. Many many acres of clear, gently undulating dune rises and falls are the idle thinkings of a person with towering mesas the worries over problems we all face. Breezes are the kindness of strangers while sandstorms are the hurtful memories we must ride out occasionally. How easy it is to be lost in these undulating, sandy thoughts! If you can get lost in a forest then fair enough, but if you can be lost in a crowd – a crowd slap bang in the middle of civilisation – and if you can get lost in your thoughts – your very own *thoughts*, then gosh, how easy is it to be lost and what fragile, wandering creatures we really are.

And *that* was basically the way it was on board the last carriage. The dust had settled now for Sheila. Not the dust of the outlaws violence, that was another entity completely, but the dust of seeing how it just "went" with all on board. All those she observed were so utterly lost in their own thoughts, their own worlds. They drew on memories as water from a well. All stared in to the past as they chugged towards an unavoidable future too repulsive to behold. Any spark to initiate an escape plan had been, quite literally, repeatedly beaten out of them all by the outlaws. She beheld all this as she thumb stroked her SOS pendant that had magically returned to her. She turned the pendant over and over right along with her thoughts as she gazed at her somewhat unhinged friend, Elegant Lady, who was writing something. Pieces of some puzzle fell in to those turning thoughts and, because coincidences *do* happen, they fell almost perfectly in to place.

"Would, you like to read some of . . ?" enquired Elegant Lady in ever so genteel manner, leaning over.

"SSHHH!" hissed Sheila, as she raised her hand to halt her friend's speech, not wanting to scare away the timid bird called "Hope".

"I love to write poetry!" gushed the genteel and elegant, "It does help so!"

Sheila gave her a smile and wondered if she herself would eventually be lost in the desert of idle, childlike thought mingled with memories. The prospect was truly frightening. Elegant Lady had obviously been a robust and independent figure in her former life and commanded an enviable level of respect, but the finely dressed poet was now reduced to near childhood in manner. This thought made Sheila very angry but she did not let her elegant friend know.

She opened up her pendant. Inside were properly printed instructions for anyone coming upon the taken ill and also a hand written note telling of next of kin. The pendant had been stolen clean away but had then been returned – with all inner documentation and handwriting intact – by some higher power. She looked at Elegant Lady with serious inquisitiveness.

"What's your name?"

Elegant Lady smiled and sat semi to attention. It had been so long since she had been asked that and the sheer normality of the question, here, in this place, was such a welcome reminder of a former life that it stole the thunder clean away from the shred of kindness it inadvertently contained.

"Melanie Carter, how do you do?!" she replied, extending a white gloved hand. "And you are?"

"Sheila, I'm Sheila Burness. Melanie is my *middle* name."

At any other time, shaking hands with someone from the past – *truly* from the past – would be a fairly mind blowing experience, but Sheila was more focused on a solution to all this than on potential future anecdotes.

"Ooohh well there you go!" replied Melanie. "We were destined to meet, it would seem! I am Melanie and you are Melanie of *sorts!*"

"Yes, it would seem that way." said Sheila with as much excitedness in her voice as a schoolchild reciting a multiplication table; obviously more aware of – and immediately concerned about – the reason they had met than poor Melanie was. She glanced down at the fountain pen Melanie held. It was as ornate as the lady herself and no doubt contained ink from no less a source than the fabled Ink Fountain in Never Never Land. Melanie noticed Sheila's interest.

"Beautiful, isn't it?! My husband, Walter, gave it to me for Christmas so I could write my poetry. I often .."

Frowning Sheila intruded, taking the pen. She saw it for what it was, just a pen. Yes it was indeed just a pen, but a spark that is just a spark can ignite all the gunpowder on earth and blow the most stubborn mountain range asunder. Laying the pen down, a pen so ornate that no matter what angle it lay at, it simply could not roll away, Sheila took off her SOS pendant and opened it.

"Did your sweetheart give you that?" asked Melanie. Sheila made no reply as she picked up the pen and did a small test squiggle.

"What's your name again?" she asked Melanie. "Oh, wait, just write your name on this."

She handed Melanie's pen back to her along with the blank paper from the SOS pendant. Melanie righted and adjusted herself as if she was about to be one of the signatories on the Declaration of Independence. There was *nothing* informal about Melanie. She signed her name, slowly reading it out as she wrote. She spoke like a child speaking to an imaginary friend. Sheila could see, looking at it upside down from her viewpoint, that Melanie's handwriting was utterly beautiful and curvaceous; a style of handwriting that had indeed been lost to history and replaced by the hurried scribblings of the 20th century.

"There!" smiled Melanie, holding up the paper, awaiting further instructions. Focused, Sheila rose, taking pen and paper and set off down the carriage. Swaying slightly from the carriages movement, she approached the tender young couple a few seats along.

The girl, who looked to be about 16 or 17, compassionately sat with her arm around her friend, the young man in jeans and t-shirt, also 16 or 17. The sight of the fragile and scared young man caused Sheila to show great tenderness in her expression. Yes, he reminded Sheila of her Thomas oh so very much and it hurt oh so terribly to behold this shattered youth. To look upon him was like looking at a precious framed photograph that sits on a mantle piece. His was such an easy story to read. His emerging status as a man had been continuously aborted by the outlaws who were anything *but* real men. She slid smoothly in to the seat opposite to them and forced a smile. The girl, who was oriental, strainedly reciprocated Sheila's smile. It was the first time the young woman had smiled since this all began for her. It was very warm in the hypnotically wobbling carriage. The oriental girl spoke:

"I heard you talking to the other lady. I'm Lorraine." She saw Sheila held pen and paper. "Do you want mc to sign?"

"If you would." replied Sheila with a nod. Lorraine signed. Sheila then looked at the young man who stared out the window with teary eyes.

"Patrick, this is Patrick." said Lorraine.

"Boy, that's a real man's name if ever I heard one!" said Sheila, writing Patrick's name for him. Her kind words picked up a few forlorn bricks with which to begin rebuilding Patrick's shattered world. Patrick put his head in his hands and started crying. The sight and sound of this instantly conferred on Sheila the power of attorney to act in stead of, but not replace, Patrick's mother. She started crying also and leaned over to cuddle him.

"Shh, shh, shh, it's ok honey. It's ok. We'll get out of this, I promise!" Lorraine confirmed that and also held Patrick. The young man's tears fell in to Sheila's sweet oasis of positivity and that oasis grew a little in size.

This display of love and the sound of it all did not go unnoticed, for it was a true novelty in the setting. For those on board, hope was a memory you thought of fondly; another picture on the mantlepiece of the mind. Words were rarely exchanged by the travellers, let alone actions. From further along the carriage approached the others. They looked upon the scene with shockingly neutral expressions, scaring Sheila somewhat as they approached. In Sheila's actions did they see the naivety of a "freshman" or did they see the oasis? In Sheila's eyes, they had come to either break up the party or drink sweet water.

A middle aged man, the one who couldn't load the gun during the last raid, stood and stared. There indeed was compassion in the gentleman, for Sheila looked up and saw it in his eyes, and all had seen his bravado the night before, but his voice and the message it delivered came from a heart trampled underfoot just one time too many.

"You oughtn't to do that. It just makes it worse." he said, parentally.

"Well *someone* has to!" retorted Sheila, defiantly, as she cuddled weeping Patrick.

"You speak like the newcomer you are. You are an immigrant to our world, my dear."

"Sheila!"

"You are an immigrant to our world, Sheila." he said as he looked around the carriage, waving his tour guide hands. "New laws, new ways, new customs; they overwhelm you. No one likes change but once change has been accepted you become numb to it."

"But I saw you fight back!"

"Sheer boredom, honey. The outcome is unavoidable. We cannot escape. Please do not tell the lad otherwise, to do so is to drop him from a great height. He is not a donkey, he is a human being with feelings. Do not dangle a carrot in front of him."

Sheila frowned deeply in contention and covered Patrick's ears. The words coming from Defeat Personified would drive a nail made of butter in to a coffin lid made of granite. Carefully releasing Patrick with a kiss to his forehead, she detoured around her well meaning but overly pessimistic opponent and cut to the chase, loudly.

"I WANT YOU ALL TO SIGN THIS! DON'T ASK, JUST *DON'T ASK* OK!"

Sheila waved the pen and paper with concealed desperation. Two or three stepped forward immediately; they had seen the oasis and eagerly signed this quirky and outlandish petition Sheila possessed. One by one by one the signatures flowed from Melanie's pen. With a sigh and a "Why not!" Defeat Personified also signed.

Slumping back in to her seat near Melanie and returning her pen, Sheila folded the paper back in to the SOS pendant, kissed it several times, pressed it hard up to her forehead with eyes tightly closed for what seemed like an age then slowly hung it around her neck. She had done all she could and now .. now it was up to some higher force. Now it was up to some higher law or set of laws she hoped were benevolent. She had read the list of names but had not derived any pleasure from the reading, even when she noticed that Defeat Personified's name was, ironically, Victor.

14

Susan's day in town

Funny, isn't it?

Funny how a slight prod to one particular sense can stop you dead, lift you right out of your shoes and place you somewhere in the past with pin point accuracy. For many people, the smell of a newly mown lawn can evoke powerful memories of childhood.

Years later, while cutting the grass, maybe for your own children to play on, the unmistakable, ageless and nearly edible aroma opens up a photo album in a particularly precious area of your thoughts, maybe to your joy or maybe to your pain, as that is what nostalgia is.

Sitting by a stream with your first love and counting all else secondary to their presence, you never even noticed the waterfalls that were so beautiful they must have surely been on loan from a fairy tale. You took your love many miles to the nicest place imaginable, only so you could ignore it all, so absorbed were you with your beloved.

Pass a vaguely similar setting many years later, however, and hear some insignificant, trickling stream, you now – too late – hear it for the flowing enchantment it was on that juicy day and that opens up a photo album in a particularly precious area of your thoughts, maybe to your joy or maybe to your pain, as that is what nostalgia is.

We'd love, most of the time, to stay there – slap bang in the past – and weepingly apologise for taking it all for granted; but a ticket to travel "Nostalgia Class" is always a return ticket . . and life goes on.

All too often, memories are *not* so nice: that first bad fall you had when playing – your first, trembling, day at school – an incredibly sore throat/tooth you had once – falling out with a long standing friend – a cruel, unfounded rumour about you that circulated and the moment it dawned on you that in a world population of 8 billion, the number of people who would genuinely miss you if you were gone would fit comfortably in to your car. When a sight or sound or smell or anything reminds us of *these* things, do they not stub the toe of your emotions?

Susan was in town, heading to make a pick up from the dry cleaners. The look on her face was that of someone who had just stubbed their toe on something. She had received a prod to her emotions and that had opened up a photo album in a particularly sensitive area of her thoughts. Two days previous, she had been going through Paul's jacket pocket, looking for the car keys. The jacket stank of cigarette smoke at a level far more intense than "going out for a quick puff". The odour left her no choice but to remember something she simply didn't want to remember; that how, when she had first met Paul, it was in a betting shop wallpapered with thick, clogging, nicotine mist. Throughout her life, Susan had had her fair share of "newly cut grass" memories, but the overpowering smell of cigarette smoke, which meant only one thing, threatened to force a glimpse in to some dark archive never visited intentionally.

Paul had borrowed Susan's car on the odd occasion, claiming her car was "nippier" around town, which it was. It was also true that Susan's car was never seen parked in the school car park and would therefore not get a second glance should anyone from school see it outside any betting shop. Paul was taking a few days off sick and was basically out of it, even when Susan leaned over and kissed him before leaving then berated him for getting his beautiful jacket "smokey smelly", as she had put it.

She entered the dry cleaners which was called "Coming up Roses!" and showed her ticket to the lady who peered at it over, then through, then over, then through, her half moon glasses.

"Thank you . . uh huh . . Oh yes, yes, that's ready for collecting. Hold yourself right here, honey." said the lady as she momentarily disappeared. Susan smiled but never said a word. Sometimes there is a reason we speak and sometimes there is a reason we don't and both reasons can be massive. She just looked around and savoured the smell of "clean" that was in the air. The lady reappeared, holding Paul's cellophane wrapped jacket, moving it all around so efficiently. Rustle rustle.

"Heeere you go then my dear! That's a nice jacket. People should look after things more but we brought it back to the land of the living! What's it like out there today?"

"Fine, yes it's quite nice." replied Susan. What she really wanted to say was "Can we swap lives please? I'll work here and you deal with the dark archive."

"Oh, you wouldn't want to work here, honey! I never get out too often."

"*What!* Oh . . yes, fine!" blurted out Susan, who had spoken her thoughts by accident, just grateful that the lady never asked what the "dark archive" was. She paid by credit card and went to leave when the lady suddenly grabbed the jacket.

"Hold on, what's that I see?"

She pulled the jacket, and Susan, closer. There was a little post it note on the cellophane Susan hadn't noticed.

"Oh yes, hang on a sec." The lady reached under the counter and produced an envelope folded in half.

"Don't forget these! I found them tucked way down in a fold in the inside pocket. I think I got them all." as she handed Susan the little makeshift packet.

Susan looked inside and saw at least a dozen little tickets. Curiously and in total innocence, she tapped out a few on to her hand. It tickled slightly. Laying down the envelope and finger sifting through what lay in her palm, Paul's signature jumped out at her again and again, causing her breathing to deepen. Oh Paul, is *this* what you meant when you said you would go home and tell Susan everything?

The lady owner said nothing but just stood and read the sad chapter straight off Susan's face. Susan could see that one ticket and .. wait .. sift sift .. *all* tickets bore Paul's name and were for the pawning of women's jewellery. Rings, brooches, necklaces; anything and everything that could adorn the female body and thrill the female heart; all belonged to other women, for Susan recognised not a single item's description.

Other women .. *other women!*

To play second fiddle to an addiction is not a threat to your heart as you yourself are not being replaced in entirety. An addiction has no bodily form nor substance and could never be stepmother to your children. Your spouse may have forked on to a new path but that path runs parallel to you; you are still in the loop and active, if ignored.

To play second fiddle to a hobby or interest is not a threat to your heart as hobbies only respond when called upon, usually during spare time. They are timid and mild and normally easy to scare away with a little attentive effort.

But to play second fiddle to another *woman* is indeed to be replaced in your entirety. An actual government has passed a bill that outlawed contentment, ousting you from your comfort zone you thought you knew so well. An actual parliament has legislated for your extinction from the former relationship and ordered your loving heart to be removed. You are now a former species residing in a forlorn museum as a stuffed exhibit. Your body is in the display cabinet and your heart sits in a glass jar of clear preservative labelled "Contraband" because owning emotions is now illegal. Some kangaroo court, somewhere, put your feelings in to black bin liners and left them beside a graffitied dumpster and the first you heard of it was when you tipped those tickly little pawn tickets on to your hand and overheard their dying, blushing, paper whispers.

Susan's world juddered, causing her to sway a little. This was noticed by the lady, who said nothing, hinting towards the fact that over and through and over and through her half moon glasses, she had seen it all before. She reached out and gave a resuscitative squeeze to Susan's arm.

"You have a nice day now!"

***

The "nice day" was not over for Susan as she teetered back to her car. She felt detached from reality, like the side effect of some medication. An elastic day this was promising to be; one that stretched and stretched. Smelling Paul's jacket and the discovery of those pawn tickets had been the first two hurdles in a steeplechase Susan was now forced to run. Every mile she drove exhausted her because, as she drove, she ran the steeplechase.

The pawn shop, called "Pawn but not forgotten", was in another town miles away but was easy to find once there and was in no wise down some backstreet as Susan expected. Falling on hard times is a fact of life and nothing to be ashamed of. Pawning some personal treasure for quick cash didn't have much stigma attached to it these days and in recent decades, pawn shops had tiptoed out of the shadows and now hung out with more respectable shops just off the high street.

The old style bell sounded as Susan entered. Never having been in a pawn shop, the sight stopped her in her tracks.

Momentarily fooled in to thinking she was on a game show, Susan was surrounded by four walls filled to the ceiling with an A to Z of things that looked like prizes she could win on that game show. Baseball gloves, coffee pots, lawnmowers, old books, new books, record players, cassette players and on and on, filled the sight and attention to capacity. The smell of all this was neutral with a hint of museum. A thousand things from a thousand lives. If those discarded things could speak, no doubt their tone would be dejected with a hint of the vengeful.

The host of this particular game show came in to view. Like the lady at the dry cleaners, he read Susan like the wide open book circumstances were forcing her to be.

"Hi!"

"Hi!" replied Susan; still basically agog.

"Is it cash or stash?" continued the owner, knowing full well Susan wouldn't know. He had judged Susan correctly by both sight and demeanour. She just didn't belong there. Susan looked at him and tried to splutter a response but was seriously floundering, so the host threw her a life jacket.

"It's ok buddy. Cash or stash is what I say to all my regulars cause it's either cash on their minds or retrieving their previously pawned stash!" He smirked broadly then continued as he leaned forward, raising one eyebrow "Usually before the wife misses her earrings!"

Susan grabbed the life jacket. "Oh, I see." she replied. She held up the envelope containing the pawn tickets.

"I have these."

She handed them to the owner who frowned a little and spoke as if he was a doctor about to examine some injury.

"Okaaay, let's have a looky here."

He took the envelope from Susan so tenderly you'd think she was trying to pawn a bottle of Nitro Glycerine. He unfolded the envelope and tapped out the contents in to his hands. He had been expecting rare stamps to be in the envelope and laughed when a cascade of about a dozen pawn tickets lightly fell in to his hand. He never looked up at Susan, but what he held, and the person who had given them to him, simply did not match . . and neither did the signature. The dates on the tickets were all the same and were from three months ago. Sift sift.

"Well these are from months ago." he said.

Susan's mind became an instant super computer that tallied up dates and times and eagerly delivered the bad news to Susan's suspicions with unwanted efficiency. Sprockets of actions located themselves in to the chain of Paul's timeline. Susan's expression was now anything *other* than what an artist would want to capture in oils. Times – places – Paul's barely perceptible behavioural changes – and now this perfectly fitting piece to the jigsaw. The word "Eureka", at any other time, would have been ideal; but not now. The owner spoke on:

"No payment has been made at all and no extension sought so these things went up for sale, or rather *should* have gone up for sale . ." a look at the calendar ". . one, two . . three days ago. Man, nobody tells me *anything* around here! These things should be out on display. Hang on a sec." He stepped out of sight and, having worked in a betting shop, Susan heard the unmistakable sound of a safe being opened. The man returned with a steel deposit box about the size of a pencil case and opened it.

The sight Susan beheld was simply gorgeous. Jewellery and *what* jewellery! Gold and silver and pearls and rubies and emeralds snoozed cosily together and seemed oddly at home, happy in themselves and not really missing human contact. The one and only oddity was an SOS pendant. A "friend of an invitee" was the pendant at this particular party as it lay with social awkwardness at one end of the box, "in the kitchen" if you will. Such was the beauty of the sight that the owner himself went narrow eyed with admiration and for a moment or two or more, both stood speechless. The owner wolf whistled.

"*Wow!*" he said.

What neither knew was that, with the exception of the SOS pendant, these items had come not just from a bygone age but from another actual world. Designed, fashioned, seen and coveted by people dimensions away were these slumbering and self satisfied treasures. The true, unheralded origin of these items trumped in to embarrassment the most sumptuous tombs of Egypt and that to say "Wow!" upon seeing them was criminally inadequate.

But the path that led to the plain tin box they lay in had been one of stench, greed and merciless violence. Kidnapped from their rightful owners who had taken severe beatings and death or near death. Slobbered over and gambled away by mindless entities with track records that would make you vomit, maybe it was a blessing that this jewellery could not speak . . or scream.

This stun gun of treasures caused Susan to forget herself. She reached out and picked up a beautiful gold ring that was crested with emeralds alternated with what looked like baby pearls fresh from an oyster found only in flawless and friendly blue depths of saltwater peace. This ring, that had been torn from Melanie's finger with a screaming crack of searing, blinding, thundering pain, now slid on to Susan's ring finger as smoothly as a cat walks. Knowing only the tiniest fraction of the ring's history, Susan was nevertheless absorbed and lifted clean out of herself by the wonderful moment. The shop owner, however, spoke; automatically stamping her return ticket. Just his normal speaking voice, in this context, caused Susan to jump.

"Oh now, these are those medical things, aren't they?" said the owner as he picked up the SOS pendant. "Kinda important I guess. Maybe someone needs this. Is it yours?"

Because Susan never grabbed it with an "Oh, thank goodness!" he surmised it wasn't Susan's.

"This should be handed to the cops." he continued.

Susan never even heard the question. Her mind was being blown here and there by what she saw. Other things would dawn on her later. It's hard to juggle very heavy thoughts. The ring reluctantly released Susan's attention. She resurfaced and blinked a few times.

"How much for the ring. How much for it all?"

"Well now, let's see. It says that ring is valued at . ." he wolf whistled again, "Yikes! $2000 dollars!" Susan slid the ring off and laid it back with its friends. She shifted through the treasure with cold gold metallic jangles and pulled out a gold bracelet. It looked modern and un-adorned. The owner kept up with her.

"And that is . . is . . $50." Susan laid it aside, indicating intent. She sifted on and on, eventually forming a small, beautiful and chaotic pile of jewellery "laid aside". It all totalled $173. She then turned her attention to the SOS pendant.

"I'll take it to the proper authorities if you like. How much for it?"

"That's ok sister." replied the owner. "Let's make today "Civic Duty Day"! Wadda ya say? Just give it a good home!"

"Ok, thanks, I'll do that." replied Susan as she paid and closed the transaction. The elastic day Susan was living was by no means finished stretching. The owner continued:

"Imagine pawning something as important as a medical necklace. I mean, if you don't wan' it yourself then let somebody *else* have it! Tsk . . people huh!"

***

Melanie gazed through and through her wedding ring as she slowly turned it back and forth on her finger. The beautiful gold ring was crested with emeralds alternated with what looked like baby pearls fresh from an oyster found only in the fantasies of Neptune. It had been given to Melanie along with an oath of faithfulness and indeed faithful was this wedding band that always returned to its owner. Melanie was a good and diligent curator of her own hands.

"It's beautiful!" said solemn Sheila. Melanie smiled but never looked up, still absorbed with her twinkling digits.

Suddenly, all went pitch black on the carriage, causing Sheila to cry out, thinking the Sun had set in a hurry. The train had entered a tunnel and eyes took just a second or two or ten to adjust. The carriage was lit but fairly dimly and not in the same manner it was during the night time raids but the noticing of this aspect could have been due to the fact that there was no murderous violence pending. Sheila saw no reaction from any other passenger and Victor's addressing Sheila as "Newcomer" and "Immigrant" took on a new authority. Would this place *never* run out of surprises? Shelia cupped her pendant and closed her eyes as she thought of Tom.

Melanie blinked a few times, looked up at the window so black then beheld Sheila in her pain and wanted ever so much to tell Sheila how handsome her son Tom was, to talk of his wonderful manner and stature and his de-fault glowing future. She wanted to overload Sheila with verbal assurances; to send beautifully packaged gift after beautifully packaged gift to Sheila's heart concerning her sweet son but knew that, upon Sheila hurriedly tearing the picturesque wrap asunder, it would be found that the thin air of reality lay lonesome inside. Do not adorn disappointment with a bow of silken lies, simply tie it with the plain white and respectful string of truth.

Whether it was physics or chemistry or some surreal alchemy, Melanie had changed in an instant. The dimly lit carriage trundled and swayed, making it difficult for Sheila to focus on Melanie's face, which now bore an altogether different expression. The sudden change in the lady was astonishing in its forward manner and loving intent. While in the tunnel, the desert could not reach in – transmission was interrupted – so Melanie's true personality reached out and spoke words that she knew would hurt herself a lot more than they would hurt Sheila. The bejewelled lady did this because she liked her new friend oh so much.

"I have a son too you know, my dear." Plain and flat was Melanie's tone; plain and flat with a scream wandering somewhere within.

Sheila opened her eyes which, even in the annoyingly dim and trundling light, allowed a lacrimal flood to glisten her cheeks and chin visibly. Her eyes were now the gateway to her heart. Melanie – the *real* Melanie – it would seem, was a natural counsellor and had pushed that gateway open with ease. Such a fragile and rustic gate, such a gentle and tender visitor named Melanie, who spoke on:

"We mothers, it would seem, are the easiest to lure for we bore the missing in our bellies. The utterly helpless came to us, in fact, *out* of us, and didn't we hold them to prevent them from falling? We walked the path of unreciprocation gladly as our child took and took and took."

As she spoke, Melanie held up both her hands and wiggled her fingers, the jewelled adornments now unsparkling and asleep in the gloom and for a moment Sheila thought Melanie was about to break the spell of her own words and regress well back in to her previous, almost childlike persona, but the bejewelled lady continued:

"See these rings? Oh, how I adore them! Oh, how I look after and cherish them and the sentiments behind some of them! Such pleasure they give! But they never speak to me. They never show the least concern when I am sad. Was that not the way it was for you and I, my dear Melanie of sorts? We were satisfied because our offspring gave back so much by simply *being!*

And as they grew and grew, the taking did not cease, did it? The inbuilt thoughtlessness of childhood and adolescence pounded daily at our hearts yet these things were as a single worried and frightened snowflake that had strayed too far from winter and was no danger to anyone's summer. Our happiness, it would seem, reached well, well beyond any far horizon. Oh my child, oh my daughter, oh my son, you bless me by simply *being!*"

Melanie paused and stared and stared at Sheila, who was now glad for the gloom, for it stopped Melanie's stare from frightening, if that was the intent. Melanie spoke again.

"I remember well the day the walls of my heart fell. My son, Edgar, had become owner of the awful contraption that has brought us both here, my Melanie of sorts.

Before the trouble came, I had watched as an adorning and pious travelling companion through life called "Responsibility" adorned Edgar's emerging manliness. Where this glorious attribute had travelled from I knew not but I gave God thanks and, albeit with a touch of motherly prejudice, I declared to my glad heart that like attracts like! A guide so true had been given unto my son. With this companion by his side, I knew he would never be alone and I was glad. "Reliability" "Staunchness" and "Constancy" heard of my son's love of good and came courting my Edgar who set the table and welcomed each in full reciprocation."

Still in the tunnel, still in gloom and still herself for a while, Melanie now looked out the window at the near and rough darkness. This was no supernatural darkness but, as Sheila saw strainedly, a real rough hewn passage through some mountain oh so intimidating. Melanie was adrift on painful memories and to witness this, to be taken in to Melanie's confidence, was honour scarred and blighted by the occasion.

Sheila looked further down the carriage but the insufficient carriage lighting did not travel enough to show the others in any satisfactory detail. They all sat, strangely subdued, with minimal movement; dimly disconnected like the jewels on the rings Melanie wore. Were *they* changed also as Melanie now was? A stale and claustrophobic confessional was now forming and took shape as the two friends sat close. Just Melanie and Sheila, just Sheila and Melanie. The tunnel wore on and Melanie spoke on:

"I remember the day that awful whirling contraption was brought in to our house. Edgar showed it to me with great excitement but I felt an aloofness emanating from the whirling wonder, as least with regards to my presence. He demonstrated the method of the contraption to me. All that whirling and spinning and flashing, it made me quite giddy. And to think you actually paid *money* for the experience! I asked Edgar exactly how he had come owner to this. He said he had bought it from a friend and it really was the latest thing. That reply did not ring true, however, with my heart.

It was not long after that things began to change. Good fortune, it appeared, smiled on my son. Was I glad, my Melanie of sorts? You can answer that yourself, can't you, my dear? Yes I was glad and bemused, for Edgar had caught some plague, it seemed; a plague of good fortune; *abundant* good fortune! First, someone died and left Edgar a modest amount of money. Notwithstanding the unfortunate passing, to inherit money is a blessing to anyone at anytime. But the deceased was not known to Edgar or my husband or I or any close friend or relative; a "blue inheritance", if you will."

Upon hearing this, Sheila – memory jogged by Melanie's words – was carried away in her thoughts to the days her sweet Tom had what could only be called like good fortune bestowed on him. She sat, staring at the floor with a look way way way beyond any thousand yard stare; for how many yards must your eyes peer to see a past you curse yourself for not seeing at the crucial time?

She thought of the then comical lemon spill; she thought of king for a day and she thought of Tom's on/off relationship with Becky and the joy then pain then joy then pain it caused her son. Sheila looked back in her thoughts and inevitably began to blame herself. She looked back on her thoughts and saw nothing but the flaming arches of many burned bridges. To Sheila's thousand yard stare was added a frown; to the frown was added a tear soaked ladder with no rungs and to that was added eternity.

Melanie noticed this but continued to speak the language of loss for there was no other way of conversing truthfully.

"This did not end the peculiar as gift after gift came Edgar's way, causing his father and I feeling bereft of the ability to please our son as much.

But, my handsome boy was not himself anymore. He looked a touch ill and out of sorts. His mind, mood and general persona had been tampered with. He bore the aspect of the broken hearted and this, of course, broke mine. Whisky breath, body odour and dishevelment smeared themselves across all Edgar did, thought or spoke.

Arguments became common where they had never existed before. Both my husband and I knew the contraption was to blame and resolved to destroy the mechanical parasite but hesitated, fearing awful repercussions from our son, should we interfere. Oh, how I have reflected upon that hesitancy and regretted it so.

The day that brought me here started badly. Another argument, more pleading, more begging . . more apologising for any lack or negligence on my part. Edgar went to the room where the machine sat, and slammed the door. I heard movement both soft and hard, then nothing.

The door, surprisingly, was open just a touch and I edged forward and forward like a frightened child, only to enter an empty room. Edgar was gone and there stood the machine. It stood as if it owned the whole house and I had not paid the rent. I saw the spinning discs had **SAVE EDGAR** on all three, more or less aligned. The lever on the side jolted and clicked.

I screamed before I even tried to and grabbed and tore at the monstrous lever. I reached a level of emotion only equalled when I first held my newborn Edgar in my arms that pained and exhausting day. Throttling the machine I thought I was and relieved to finally be doing so. *A battle won*, I thought to myself as I screamed and jolted the metal brute's arm.

But . . and oh *but*, what a rude awakening took place, most cruelly thrust upon my heart with force, making all my life before, as real and mostly harmonious as it had been; seem like a fairy tale I heartbreakingly could no longer believe in due to growing up just that bit too far."

Sheila saw the pain and pending dam burst of tears formulating in Melanie's heart. She reached out and near grabbed one of her friend's tender hands with a squeeze. Melanie looked at Sheila and ever so partially smiled. Her face was a gloom within a gloom. Warm, worried and wearisome hands joined and squeezed. Gloom sodden Melanie continued:

"The next I knew, my sweetest Melanie of sorts, the room was full of that accursed contraption, for the room twirled and danced within my dizzy head. For one such as I, who could not even brave a ride on a happy carousel, a teetering drunk I now appeared to be to any upon seeing me.

However, my shock and anger – for I knew the machine was to blame – were both swift to strengthen my resolve and confer sea legs upon me. The bravery of Geronimo became mine. I had anger enough to squander a hundred times over but the arrival in this world, where you and I now sit without aim or hope, silenced my smouldering breast for a season. I fell on to the floor of this carriage, crying for my Edgar again and again. All on me and within me was unbridled and galloped in a storm all mine. Those already here, namely Victor, grabbed me in my thrashing and held me till I was calm. Yes I was calm, my dear, but not because of happiness but because of brokenness.

When you arrived, my dear Melanie of sorts, you were a mirror held up before me. You were an echo of my colliding arrival. You were an artefact of my past that, through no fault of your own, was laden with detestable history. You, at once, were the dearest of friends that brought the baddest of news. We are, all of us on this carriage, from the same tribe. We have each other and the power of such to warm any heart, but each other is all we shall ever have."

Sheila went to speak but Melanie placed a finger up to Sheila's lips. The rings were still dormant in the gloom so Melanie continued:

"The first time we were attacked all hope was nearly slain. Why do I say "nearly"? Because when I was not among the dead then hope, or a good imitation of that emotion, tried to find moisture in my heart. Only upon malicious repetition did that hope wither to naught.

But what happened to me next killed all. What happened to me next put a seal upon a seal upon a hot red wax seal of a warrant for more than death itself; for as I lay trackside with broken fingers I saw my dear Edgar sitting on a horse, gazing down at me. He was one of the outlaws now, turned in to such by the machine with one arm. He never participated in any violence. He did nothing. When I cried out to him, he did nothing. When he saw me beaten and snapped, he did nothing, nothing but stare. Child of my body, oh child of my milk, you impassively watch as she who raised you with delicacy is violated so.

The first time this happened my heart became arid and how can hope take nourishing root in the arid? Everything fell, it all fell. The beauty of the past was pitted against a monstrous present and was slain. It was the nothing of it all that destroyed my everything, for my boy did nothing to help me. The walls of my world fell at a whisper, they fell at nothing; complete and perfect nothing. A nothing dagger from a nothing sheath. A nothing bullet from a nothing gun. A fist not raised at all. A person could rule the world if they mastered the art of violent nothing as my Edgar had mastered it."

The pitiful sight and sounds of Melanie describing rage filled pandemonium in such a calm and eloquent manner was, in an off centre way, beautiful in its irony. It shocked and surprised Sheila to realise that, as Melanie finally fell silent, both women were in an embrace; locked in each other's arms in true friendship. As they separated slightly, Melanie reached out and wiped Sheila's tears away with several surprisingly firm strokes of her dank and dimly bejewelled hands. This made Sheila sob some more and Melanie wipe away tears some more. Melanie had a true motherly look on her face as she looked after her sobbing travelling companion.

"Sshhh now my dear . . sshhh!" said Melanie.

"But . . but . . Melanie . . your son, your very own . ."

"Sshhh my sweet! See, we are together, alive and whole for a while."

Although coming close to doing so, Melanie's dam had not burst and, now that Sheila knew what she knew about her elegant and peculiar friend, she could only guess at the amount of hurt the sumptuous lady carried in her heart.

And in it all and having divulged what she had just divulged, it was Melanie who cupped Sheila's face in her hands when it should have been the other way around.

And in it all and having divulged what she had just divulged, it was Melanie who wiped Sheila's tears away when it should have been the other way around.

A cementing of friendship had just taken place, the like of which is usually only captured in novels and paintings by authors and artists long gone, leaving those born in following years tantalised. Melanie was the most unique person Sheila had ever met, not because of the sand storm of a world they were both in but because, whatever the occasion and surroundings may be, Melanie, the *real* Melanie, was quite simply an outstanding and remarkable person.

Suddenly, Sheila was blinded by a flash. She startled back a few inches. Another flash . . then another. Blinded for a moment by persistence of vision, Sheila could not see the broad smile now on Melanie's face. The train was leaving the tunnel and the light blocking rocks were becoming more intermittent. Daylight pirouetted outside the carriage before unceremoniously rushing in. Melanie's ringed fingers were awakened, bringing joy to their host. She wiggled her fingers, letting them out to play again.

"Oh look! Look my dear! Look!!"

Sheila heard the voice of her friend Melanie, but it now lacked the solemn, adult tone and conviction of seconds before. Regression in to near childhood had once again taken over as Nudge Canyon found her. This hurt Sheila who now felt bereft of her friend who was still right in front of her and conversing no less.

"MELANIE!" shouted Sheila as if searching for her friend on a foggy day, but Melanie made no response or gave an upward glance. She held both her hands out in front of her, wiggling her fingers to induce sparkle, giving the appearance of playing an imaginary piano. The light had also seemingly reanimated the others in the carriage. Reanimated them, that is, in their inactivity.

A bubbling, gurgling of emotions were inside Sheila. Everything in this place was geared to emotion provocation. It would light some fuse in you then stamp it out. Most of her travelling companions clearly displayed signs of repetitive conditioning. They had become submissive to the point of re-entering childhood. Others such as Lorraine and Patrick did not follow the expected behaviour patterns for, although seemingly helpless, they retained their own original humanity. Neutral, it would seem, was the gear to be avoided. Extreme emotion, good or bad, seemed to protect a passenger from succumbing to the brainwashing spell. Even defeatist Victor at least had been compos mentis enough to argue with Sheila.

Before she had returned the pen to Melanie, Sheila had taken a scrap of paper and, limited space permitting, wrote as dramatically and to the point as she could concerning the plight of all on board then put the note in the pendant along with the list of names. She looked down at her previously shot knee, now perfect again, and just didn't know what to think one way or the other. Suddenly, Melanie, still not looking at anything other than her ivory tinkling hands, spoke.

"Do you notice anything?"

"Yes, my knee is . ." Melanie finally looked up at Sheila, smiled and spoke in fluent unhinged:

"No no, my dear! Outside!" Sheila looked and looked.

"The shadows, my dear! The shadows are getting longer!"

Sheila momentarily displayed fright and true nervousness because whether in this world or the other, lengthening shadows mean approaching sunset. This sudden face slap of fear startled and disappointed Sheila, which she hoped Patrick wouldn't notice. Melanie beheld her suddenly distraught friend with a smile then started filing her nails.

***

Susan stood out in the rain, and it was raining heavily. She leaned against her car, staring down at the jewellery she had bought from the pawnbrokers: the gold, unadorned bracelet, a pair of teardrop earrings and matching brooch. Her honeymoon with the jewellery was over and it was no good blaming the rain, which, for the most part, ruins everything. If you had been standing next to her, you would have heard what she heard; splash mixed with passing traffic.

But Susan was hearing a different sound, for she was now a good way down in to those dark archives no one visits intentionally. There, way down there, a single drop of rain can drown an army. There, way down there, and not even yet at the terminus, a continent of experience, and we're talking the entire landscape of experience with her husband, was in real danger of shattering. All the items Paul had pawned were from females and Susan knew Paul was no Casanova. Yes, every item in the box of treasures were female adorning and even the SOS pendant, although not known yet, belonged to a woman.

Still blind to the downpour and now soaked thoroughly, Susan turned and twisted the SOS pendant. It opened fairly easily, making it even more remarkable that, up to that point, no one had actually thought to look inside. It contained paper, causing Susan to finally leap in to her car. She closed the pendant again and wiped it bone dry before re-opening. And when she opened it again, she reached the terminus of a thousand midnights. The little paper item inside folded out concertina style and was quite long.

The pendant belonged to a woman named Sheila Burness and had her signature. The pendant hurriedly told that Sheila suffered from diabetes and gave first aid instructions and next of kin contact numbers. The pawnbroker had muttered "People, huh!" but this was far more serious than a cliché admonition of fellow man. Drowsiness swept over Susan. Her emotions were running a marathon in bare feet. She closed her eyes and leaned her head against the car in the hope that the mini cocoon would change either her in to something else or change all outside into something else.

One thought arose now, presented itself, slapped Susan in the face and would not be denied; did Paul, yes *Paul,* steal the jewellery from these women and, in doing so, did he hurt them?

Oh Paul!, I love you Paul! You are my everything. Did I ever mean.. DO I mean anything to you? Are you behind this? Tell me it's only a matter of your gambling addiction and that you didn't hurt these women.

But, all things considered, it looked unlikely Paul, yes *Paul,* would spill the beans in any direction. Only one thing would eventually cause a coughing up of the truth; *time.*

***

As Sheila lapsed in and out of consciousness her world became a montage of a spinning full moon – the taste of trackside ballast – Melanie screaming – strangulation – foul language cranked up to ten – Melanie screaming – foul outlaw body odour cranked up to eleven – Melanie screaming.

Yes, the sun *had* set and yes, it had all happened as before. Clinker had pistol whipped Sheila and grabbed her SOS pendant from behind. Clinker was also experiencing some sort of macabre montage and Melanie's screams had no place there so he shot her in the region of her vocal cords. Melanie slumped and as she slumped, the moon caused her beautiful rings to twinkle just for a second. This twinkling spoke an odd fact that none present picked up on; Finger Snapper was not present at this raid so Melanie's rings remained Melanie's.

"Wanna see a trick I learned?" asked Rat Pile of Lorraine and Patrick as they lay, timid and broken. Neither answered so Rat Pile stomped on them both while screaming at the top of his villain voice:

"DO . . YOU . . WANNA . . SEE . . A . . TRICK . . I . . LEARNED?"

He then began spinning his gun on one finger like in a show. The gun that never needed to be reloaded went off repeatedly as it span like a Catherine wheel on the Fourth of July. Lorraine and Patrick slithered and jerked around amidst near misses as Rat Pile roared with laughter, oblivious to the fact that he could have blown his own head off.

The timer hit zero and one of the mounted outlaws was hit. His horse reared violently, dumping the corpse. This freed the horse from any contractual obligation so it fled in to the night and good luck to it.

As ever, the outlaws had outstayed their unwelcome and were now crashing through the thin ice they perpetually walked on. With the wind in its sails and those sails stretching to ripping point, the posse of Nudge Canyon sent lead calling card after lead calling card towards the gang.

ZZZINNNGGG went bullet after bullet.

Weird, high impact thuds were followed by rapid exhalation groans as life was rudely stomped out of outlaws. Ballast flew up like shrapnel at near misses. This mad and frightening sight became a new part of Sheila's montage she was forced to witness. She was sitting awkwardly, being held upright as Clinker pulled the SOS pendant tight around her neck as he beheld the approach of his wind borne enemies.

With one near garrotting tug, Clinker wrenched the pendant from Sheila's neck, mounted up and fled. Sheila slumped next to the slumped. Melanie was dead and others were dead. Two wounded members of the gang staggered and fired before being swamped by the now arrived posse who had the two wounded desperados hog-tied in a blink.

Moments before lapsing into unconsciousness again, Sheila couldn't help but notice Melanie's windswept corpse, the fact that trackside ballast tasted very salty and the sheriff's magnificent walrus moustache.

***

Susan had been sitting in the car for well over an hour. She was parked in the police station car park, a maelstrom of thoughts swirling in head and heart as she turned the SOS pendant over and over, over and over. After leaving the pawn shop with a niggling feeling, she had gone straight to the library where, with some assistance from staff, she had used the microfiche reader to sift through back copies of national newspapers from a year previous.

What she read resuscitated memories from twelve months earlier that had, up to that point, been an inch from extinction. The niggle was laid to rest as the newspapers confirmed that it was a Sheila Burness who had gone missing with her son Tom. They also confirmed that Sheila was a diabetic. The pendant was the property of a missing, presumed dead, woman. The casual turning of the pendant conferred a "heads or tails" aspect to the object which was utterly ironic and indicative of present feelings.

Such a history, such a marriage, had been lived with Paul, a history of emotional richness which had near effortlessly trampled underfoot life's endless supply of problems. That would all be gone in a blink if she entered the station with her discovery, for even if her suspicions were ultimately unfounded, the damage would be done. One single blink.

But, the coin had two sides, didn't it? The name in the pendant simply could not be ignored. Her thoughts had constantly been with Sheila as cries for aid never cease till aid is given. The pendant and the name were a conscience all of their own that would not hold its tongue. A hand was reaching out from somewhere. It grabbed Susan before she could go home and confront Paul, which would have been fairer to Paul, as we all like, even though we don't always *deserve*, to be given the benefit of the doubt.

Susan was the gambler now. She was about to gamble that Paul really *had* obtained the pendant and other treasures innocently; clandestine but harmlessly. If it was truly nothing more than a gambler's relapse, Paul was in the clear. Did Susan *really* know Paul well enough, I mean *c'mon* Paul was *Paul*, right? The attention this would get, even at the most discrete level, was daunting enough to measure on a Richter scale. The hand, that reached out from somewhere, pulled Susan out of the car and both led and pushed her to the station door. The elastic day she was living finally snapped.

The precinct was fairly quiet, well, quiet for a *precinct*, that is. There were three uniformed officers to-ing and fro-ing. A telephone rang and rang which nobody was in a hurry to answer. A typewriter clicked and dinged from the desk in the corner at which sat a bespectacled woman who glanced up at Susan then continued typing.

Dead ahead was the front desk and a man smartly dressed in black jeans and sports jacket had his back turned while talking to the officer on front desk duty. They were looking at paperwork. The officer looked up and saw Susan which caused the man in the jacket to look round. He approached Susan and smiled.

"Hi, can I help you?" asked Detective Jerome. Susan held up the SOS pendant. Jerome glanced down at it.

"Looks like one for lost property." He motioned to the officer he had been talking to. "Just leave it with my colleague and thank you for your good citizenship!"

Susan made no reply, simply staring at the pendant with all her might, looking as if she had just been hit by a car. Jerome noticed Susan's absorption with the pendant and also the look on Susan's face. The detective spoke two languages fluently: English and Crime. The language of crime was more than just the act itself, it had various dialects in the form of the knock on effect the "act" has on those directly affected and those indirectly affected. He knew, from all those years of conversing with crime, that Susan was the latter. Jerome put a hand on Susan's shoulder and cradled the pendant with her.

"You ok?, is this yours?" Still no reply.

"Here, step into my office. Here you go." Jerome tenderly led Susan in to the office and closed the door while gingerly taking the pendant form her. Both sat.

"I've seen these on TV, a good idea if you ask me!" said Detective Jerome, trying to start a party and mingle with

Susan's thoughts. Finally, Susan spoke, her answer lagging behind the present.

"No, it isn't mine. It belongs to another lady.

"Friend of yours?"

"No .. well yes .. sort of .. kinda .."

"Well now that's some good info you've given me there!" Mingling a bit more now.

"Look inside." said Susan, who still not had made eye contact with Jerome.

"Oh, so these helpful little guys have a message do they? Wait, what am I sayin', of *course* they do!" He opened the pendant and read the message. He read the name out loud in a strange, almost eerie way.

"Sheila Burness .. Sheila Burness .. She .. la .. Bur .. ness." There was a terrific silence which gave the impression Jerome was thinking thoughts that were inside thoughts that were inside other thoughts.

"I came here to help her if she's still alive." said a choked up Susan, making eye contact with Jerome for the first time. Jerome saw her tears.

"Do you know this woman?"

"I think it's that woman who went missing with her son about a year ago. I found a pawn ticket among my husband's belongings." Jerome pushed an intercom button and uniformed officer Elaine entered. He dangled the pendant up for her perusal.

"You seen one of these?"

"Yeah, I think so. What of it?"

"Find out who it belongs to, rapidly. And bring me any missing persons files from about a year ago that are still open." Elaine left with the SOS pendant. Susan felt relief that didn't show. Relief that the ball was finally rolling and *something* was happening.

A filing cabinet's tinny sound of drawers opening and closing is unmistakable. Open .. close .. open .. close .. finger tips rifling through cardboard files .. close. Elaine re-entered and handed a file to Jerome who opened it and began to read as if cramming for an exam the next day because *that* was Jerome; work hard, play hard. He squinted and sifted the documents of the missing, puffing out his cheeks.

"Mother *and* son, you say?"

"Yes. I remembered it because it featured on a true crime show. It happened way across country."

"That's probably why I'm not seeing it here. You a fan of those kind of shows?"

"Yes, maybe too much of a fan I think sometimes." Jerome sat back in his chair, defeated in this immediate battle but not in the war.

"Well it's a good thing you *are* else we wouldn't be having this conversation. We gotta get on this if there's a chance or no chance." The "Elaine" button was pushed again.

"Elaine, get the FBI on the phone then bring . ."

"*Susan*"

"Then bring Susan coffee."

Jerome picked up the phone casually, semi holding it to his ear, occasionally looking up at Susan, checking on her. Again, the open book that was Susan was easily read by Jerome, as it had been by the woman at the laundromat and the owner of the pawnshop. The detective sifted through the year old files as he waited for the call to come through.

Susan looked at the Jerome's blank expression that was simultaneously loaded with intent and worried at just how Paul would be treated by both the detective and the system. She now bitterly regretted not giving Paul the benefit of the doubt by talking to him first. Sheila was indeed Sheila but *Paul was Paul* and each case should be treated on its own merits. The thought that she had basically been Paul's judge, jury and potential executioner, when she should have first been his loving wife, now made Susan so ill she wouldn't be able to drive herself home.

But an avalanche had been set in motion. There was a wrong and a right to all this. The "best of intentions" and "civic duty" make uneasy bedfellows with "family loyalty" and "cherished love". That precarious relationship was about to rub off on married life for Paul and Susan.

That had been quite some day in town. The rain sodden pages of the book called "Susan" had been read ever so easily by everyone she had encountered until there was simply nothing left to read. That book was now closed.

Now it was time to open and read the book called "Paul".

15

The rubber meets the road

"Where *were* you? demanded Paul.

There was no answer. If you'd been standing outside the bedroom door you would automatically have thought Paul had lost his mind with his constant asking of the same question over and over, each query slightly angrier than the previous one and each silence more pitiful than the previous one. Finally, Paul ran out of steam. Friend now spoke.

"You didn't need me Paul. You were *home!*"

Friend was referring to Paul's visit to the Rattler's Tail Saloon, which nearly ended in tragedy.

"I WASN'T HOME AND I NEARLY DIED!" screamed Paul.

"But you *didn't!*" countered Friend. "*Nearly* isn't *actually* Paul, is it? You were too good to make a mistake. You were in your element. Now please don't tell me it didn't feel good! Please tell me you didn't feel at home, perfectly at home!

Go downstairs, Paul, in to your living room and tell me what you see. You see a cell in the prison of relentless, beige suburbia. You see the things you've acquired on the tread mill of routine. Your television is not a television, it is a flimsy black plastic trophy handed to you to make you feel of value and to stop you wanting to escape. It is little more than a hamster's wheel. You have warmth and food, but so does any given pet. You live in a "house" on a "street" in a "town" full of people who are also blissfully unaware that they are forever under house arrest and that the desire to feel satisfaction on any level other than the very basic is to invite frowns and suspicions of mental illness.

When you were in the saloon, you were on the other side of the "grass is always greener" fence, weren't you Paul? And wasn't it luscious! You made friends there, didn't you, Paul? They liked you and you belonged, you really *belonged!* You were that dropped and lost piece of the jigsaw unto them that was at last found and placed. The balcony creaked because of *you*, Paul. The unstoppable piano stopped because of *you*, Paul, and now, *right now*, the Rattler's Tail Saloon is a lesser place, frequented by people who miss you and all you brought to them. Why not go again? After all, it *is* your home!"

Paul's body language confirmed Friend's summation of the saloon visit and his life in general. An accomplished artist simply cannot hide raw talent even if they paint with their other hand. Likewise it just couldn't be hid that Paul – nearly killed Paul – had loved the taste of the pitch black cocktail garnished with a sprig of belladonna. It was a pricey, potentially fatal drink; but oh, that *taste!* The mere memory of beating Finger Snapper. The mere memory of the fun hustle of the saloon and Carla's kindness. The mere memory of the balcony creaking win – at the first attempt – in a strange land – and barely getting away with it – blasted another life force through Paul like a stitched together man creature brought to life by every ounce of voltage in a thunder storm. Paul smiled up at Friend.

"You know, you're a real tonic! Where would I be without you?!"

"Don't think about that," replied Friend, "concentrate on where you *will* be!"

Paul smiled again, feeling a lot better now. A photo album in a particularly precious area of his thoughts opened up. As he turned page after page of cellophane encased photographs he thought he'd never see again, Paul saw just how happy he was. No job to eat your time. No bills to eat your money. No "Nag Nag" of that back seat driver called "Responsibility". He saw a young, long haired Paul who just lived for the moment, and just how many moments can you cram in to forever?, because, being the age he was, Paul had forever!

When your "Nostalgia Class" holiday is over and you've used your return ticket . . just buy another ticket!

Just then, there was the sound of two cars pulling up at the house. Paul, staring at those photos, never noticed. Friend went to the window and looked. The first car was Susan and out of the second stepped Detective Jerome. Friend didn't like Detective Jerome or people like him. He had never actually met the detective but knew what he represented. Now *Friend* had the look of the "toe stubbed". The front door opened with a muffled thud and comical squeak that was a door bell all of its own and usually heralded the arrival of warm cuddles from a loved one. A fantastic sound it was! As Paul went to the top of the stairs, he heard two voices. The smile on his face fell and landed on the carpet where it dissolved without a stain. Seeing what he saw, Paul never anticipated any cuddles.

"PAUL, YOU UP THERE?" The tone of Susan's voice opened up another photo album. The photos inside were from Paul's childhood. Every photo was of Paul misbehaving and being called to account by one parent or the other. Those memories had tracked Paul down and found him because, even when some memories are so old they need a wheelchair to pursue you, it's still a case of "You can run, but you can't hide." Stand still long enough and they *will* find you.

Susan ran and met Paul halfway down the stairs and threw her arms around him.

"Oh Paul, I just didn't know what to do! I love you Paul . . I love you Paul."

Bemused would have been an understatement and "understatement" would also have been an understatement as to how Paul felt. What on earth called for such a forceful declaration of love in front of a complete stranger? Jerome just watched and waited for his cue. He showed his badge and set the scene.

"Hi Paul, Detective Jerome. Please don't be alarmed. I'd just like to ask a few questions if that's ok?" Paul looked at Susan in disbelief. Jerome was the prompter at this drama and reminded Susan of her lines by simply speaking them out loud on her behalf.

"Pawn tickets, Paul. This is about some pawn tickets your wife found in your jacket pocket."

Paul's head dropped immediately for a few seconds then he looked at Susan again with another look from the catalogue of looks that is issued to everyone upon birth. Still in Susan's arms, the pair stumble-plodded down the stairs.

"Take a seat, Paul." said Jerome, "Just a few questions and we can get this cleared up." Paul sat and Susan sat, squeezed up against him, holding his hand, smiling and crying. Jerome produced some jewellery and placed it on the coffee table.

He then produced some more and then some more, all the while remaining silent, looking at Paul, who sighed and fidgeted. The whole scene resembled a chemistry experiment where Detective Jerome was the scientist. Take unexplained evidence, mix them with a fragile man named Paul, and see what happens. Jerome sighed and smiled just a touch.

"We are all on the outskirts of some great mystery here, Paul." continued the detective, "It's tantalising, believe me! I'd like you to tell me how you acquired these items." There was the usual, expected, slightly too long pause. Sometimes, being blunt, well, it just gets the job *done* and this was a case in point.

"I know about your gambling addiction, Paul, but I don't know where you got *these*," Jerome then pulled Sheila's SOS pendant from his pocket and placed it on the other items.

" .. and in particular, *this*."

So now sat two people facing each other who knew things, important things. Detective Jerome knew almost immediately that Paul was no criminal. Caught with his fingers in the cookie jar .. yes. Caught with hands dripping with blood .. *no!* But what Paul knew was truly something else or rather some*where* else. What Paul knew was what the pawn shop owner didn't. Yes, Paul knew exactly where all that jewellery came from and all he had to do was tell Jerome. All he had to do was tell Jerome he'd won those things playing poker in another world; another world, that's all; and all Jerome would have to do is have no problem believing Paul had won these things playing poker in another world; another world, that's all.

The pause went on for a bit more. Paul chewed on his bottom lip while looking Jerome in the eye, Susan rubbed Paul's back so maybe the truth would burp its way out and everyone could go home. It was easy for Jerome to see the truth would be forthcoming and that it was "when" not "if". He thought he'd get Paul talking about something . . . *anything*.

"So, Paul, your wife tells me you're a teacher!"

"I won them playing poker."

"Ok" replied Jerome. "I believe you. Never played myself, well maybe the odd hand when I took an unauthorised day off school, if you catch my drift!"

"I've been doing a bit of that myself recently." said Paul who was, only to the detective's well honed eye, loosening up a bit. The "when" moment was near.

"I know, Paul." said Susan, "The school's been calling over and over. I just kept saying you were sick."

Listening to Susan and Jerome reminded Paul of the care he'd received from Carla and the bartender. He seemed to taste orange in his mouth. Add to all this the impressive speech Friend had given a few minutes earlier and Paul truly didn't know which world he belonged in or truly came from. Susan and Jerome were sowing seeds of cooperation so Paul decided to help them bring in the harvest.

"A saloon .. the game was in a saloon." Jerome went wide eyed with surprise.

"A *saloon!* When you say that I straightaway see those waist high swing doors!"

When Jerome said that, Paul looked up at him very quickly, his breathing becoming deep and deliberate and Jerome knew he'd touched a nerve. Experience told Jerome not to divulge the pressing magnitude of the SOS pendant just yet. Why pay over the asking price for good information? If there was ever a timetable of truth, it now proved itself as, now – bang on time – the truth arrived, just when Jerome *knew*, and Susan *hoped*, it would. Paul stood.

"I'll show you, Detective." he said, motioning for Jerome to follow. Jerome began to gather the jewellery items in readiness for following Paul's car to somewhere. Paul waved a halting hand.

"No, Detective, over here." He led Jerome and Susan over to the Nudge Canyon machine and rested his arm on it.

"*Here!*"

Now Detective Jerome was your classic "firm but fair" character, both in law enforcement and in his personal life, but there was a side of the man you just didn't mess with, both in law enforcement and in his personal life. Susan saw the look suddenly on Jerome's face and stepped in to be an impromptu intermediary between the two.

"Paul, honey, this is serious. *This is serious.*"

"I AM serious!" retorted Paul, looking back and forth at the two. "I AM serious."

Jerome, despite his experience, didn't know if Paul was being defiant or was truly mentally ill. He certainly couldn't smell alcohol on Paul's breath. He *did* know, however, that Paul was about to step over a precipice that would land him at the precinct for a night or two at least while the system sweated the truth out of him. He was one second from drawing a verbal slap from its holster but the one single ounce of intrigue that was suddenly in the air drew faster and pulled rank on the detective's professional wrath.

In the silence, Paul plugged in the one armed bandit. The machine jumped in to life, glad to see Paul back, like a particularly friendly and loyal breed of dog. He slotted a coin and set the reels spinning. Jerome had had enough. Susan screamed Paul's name as she saw Jerome reach for his handcuffs.

"Ok pal, I tried to be nice, didn't I?" The reels stopped with one dollar sign in line and the remaining two one space too high. Jerome saw this.

"See, your out of luck, Mr Teacher, now give me your hands." But before the law could touch Paul, a nudge was offered. Paul swatted away the detective's handcuffs and pulled the lever. Jerome had wanted answers.

And in 3 seconds, he would get them.

***

If a melody is fast and beautiful it is called "Catchy". If a melody is slow and catchy it is called "Beautiful". What Paul heard was slow and scary, not beautiful. What Paul heard was a piano tune that sounded like it was traveling through treacle and the treacle was successfully slowing it down, which, in the real world, it couldn't.

Each note was a thump-bang which sent a shock through you like the authorities hammering on your front door at 2 in the morning. Every thump-bang was the stomping of a giant who had found you. The world just span and span. An overly abundant leaf fall of memories of close brushes with the bizarre poured down on to Paul as he entered the world of the one armed bandit a second time. He heard his name being called over and over by someone.

Things began to solidify. Some force of some science of some world took the whole environment and clenched and squeezed, forcing shape on to the formless. Chaos was conscripted in to order. Paul heard his name louder and louder. *Nearly home, nearly home.* The end of the macabre birth canal was reached with a dam burst as sweet refreshing reality gushed forth with a . .

"PAAAUUULLLL!" shrieked Carla.

The jubilation in her voice was a monument to something people seek but rarely find. A few others nearby jumped with fright. Paul was once again in the Rattler's Tail Saloon and Carla was, once again, right in his personal space.

"Oh Paul," wept Carla with a smile, "I thought I'd never see you again!" She hugged Paul very tightly around his waist and pressed her head against his chest. Her forwardness was no big surprise as, in the Rattler's, *everything* is ramped up to 11. Paul was only too glad that this time he had arrived standing on his two feet to receive Carla's million dollar welcome.

"After that smelly varmint was killed, I turned around and you were just gone! We looked all over town for you!" continued Carla, nodding towards the bartender. "Then tonight I turned around and you were back!"

Carla's statement, that she'd been all over town looking for him, blew Paul away on a mini-nuclear level. While Paul had been skipping school, in the betting shop, lying to Susan, lying to himself, eating, drinking and everything else;

someone in another world had been caringly searching for him. Paul looked towards the bartender.

"Thank you for saving my life the other night!"

"Should've done it years ago!" he replied as he wiped wet whiskey glasses dry, "Was thinkin' of puttin' a new door there anyway!"

Paul looked over to where his fateful game of poker had been played. The table was still there at which sat chatty drinkers and chatty, ever so temporary, girlfriends. Behind where Finger Snapper had been sitting there was a clumsily repaired hole in the wall that was a pinch to Paul, confirming that what might have been a dream had really happened. Paul looked around and all he could feel was joy!

Have you ever been plucked from bottomless gloom by the soft embrace of a peculiar setting? That which is intangible and out of reach came rushing out to meet you, smothering you in ghostly kisses! The sheer joy that Paul felt was far beyond exhilarating. It pushed the envelope of joy and meaning and purpose and belonging to a place where only weeping solidly can begin to describe it. It seemed that Friend was right, the Rattler's Tail Saloon *was* home!

Well, the Rattler's Tail Saloon had not been built to simply keep people dry when it rained but to serve its purpose; its purpose being cheery robbery with a side order of genuine danger because nasty people like to win money too. Yes, Paul had felt joy but there was a hierarchy to the joy he felt and gambling owned the moment. He focused on one game of poker going on and chose it because of the huge pile of cash in the middle of the table. In a place like this other world saloon, and maybe even *all* saloons, a pile of money *that* big indicates that those playing are either seasoned experts or veteran losers and to sit amongst them was yet another gamble for "gamble loving Paul". Carla saw Paul's intent.

"Oh now Paul, lookee what happened last time. C'mon handsome, sit with me and chat a while! If you need money, I can give you some! Don't be goin near them critters."

But Carla, bless her, never knew Paul's back story and with her utter sweetheart of a voice tugging him from behind, Paul nevertheless made his way over to the table.

If his class could see him now!

Had Sheila or Melanie or Lorraine or Patrick been there, they would have fled the place, dragging Paul with them, as they recognised Clinker and Bang Bang sitting at the table. Spittoon Hat was nowhere to be seen but Bowler Hat was again present. He looked up at Paul and some measure of ambiguous emotion flitted across his face. Paul, bolstered on by his lecture from Friend, felt that dangerous lie of an emotion called "Invincibility". He took a seat.

Now Clinker and Bang Bang never owned the place, but the look both gave Paul turned the entire floor of the Rattler's Tail Saloon in to one great big "Unwelcome" doormat. Neither spoke because, you see, in the world of the mindless and the violent, spoken vocabulary cowers in the shadows as grimaces and actions alone are required to go through a lifetime playing grotesque charades. Words are forbidden as words may lead to conversation which may lead to reasoning and the resulting peace and loss of the spoils of crime. Bowler Hat looked again at Paul as he took his seat. He remembered what happened the last time Paul joined in and suddenly wished he had followed his parents advice to be a doctor.

Once seated, Paul saw that the centre of the table was a dog's dinner of soiled notes, coins, trinkets and poker chips. Jerome's words "And in particular . . *this!*" came to mind but Paul could not see the SOS pendant and, not knowing the "reset" aspect of this world, never expected to. Clinker noticed Paul's concentrated scanning of the table.

Like the late Finger Snapper, Clinker instantly knew there was something different about Paul that either commanded respect or disdain. The outlaw, whose only contact with water to any part of his body was when it rained – and how often does it rain in a desert? – stared at Paul as he slowly drew the dog's dinner towards himself as if he was indeed a dog and it was indeed his dinner. Suddenly, Paul saw Friend standing behind Bang Bang, who looked like an animal that had come to a fancy dress party dressed as a human.

"Go for it Paul. You can take both of them!" said the enticer with a smile that would fall in to any number of categories, all of them just plain wrong. Paul held Friend's gaze for a trice then stared Clinker right in the eye.

So, what was it like to look Clinker in the eye?

You're out in the countryside at a popular beauty spot, just wandering and strolling with your thoughts. You are happy with much to look forward to! You see couples arm in arm, obviously in love; but you have your own happy dreaming to keep you company. All the while the Sun has slid across the sky.

Still absorbed and hence absent from the real world, you have watched car after car depart. The last car, save yours, departs as does the tired Sun, now on the fall. Darkness tip-toed along while you were dreaming and takes its place at the head of the queue and now you know you really should be getting home. You are on the brink of seeing a side of that beauty spot that it likes to keep hidden.

Eerie takes the stage, acting as the warm up man for the pending night. Daytime shift has ended and you are there alone. Lengthening shadows unite to form a dark tribe and you are there alone. The sounds of nature's thrive and people in love have left the darkening scene and you are there alone. Examine your feelings at such a moment and you will know what it is like to look Clinker in the eye.

Carla placed her hand on Paul's shoulder as the piano churned through its ever repeating conveyor belt of the catchy.

"I like his taste in jewellery!" she whispered to Paul as she nodded at Bang Bang who was wearing Sheila's SOS pendant around his neck. Paul remembered it firstly because it had appeared seconds before Finger Snapper was killed and secondly for the semi-scolding look he had received when pawning the potentially life saving item for cold cash, an action he now felt bad about. He was surprised to see it again but . . there it was again.

"You sweet on me or summin?" croaked the animal in human garb when he noticed Paul's stare.

"Your pendant, I'll play you for that." replied Paul, pointing straight at it across the table. The outlaw then glanced up at Carla and assumed she was Paul's girlfriend. He laughed through a cavernous, tooth forsaken mouth.

"Oh, you wants it for yer gal?"

Maybe he had heard Carla's mention of Bang Bang wearing the pendant and – surprise surprise – never realised she was being sarcastic.

"Well, strikes me it'd look better on a lady. I just want it. You up for that?" said Paul.

"What y'got for the pot, high roller?" asked Clinker as both he and Bang Bang laughed one mighty mock of a laugh. Their tone was comical but all the while laced with pure nastiness. Paul put his hand in his pocket then realised everything he had won the last time was ever so slightly out of reach on his living room table in another world. He had no money, not even enough to buy a "Canyon Sunset" – the orange flavoured placebo invented by the bartender.

Just for a second, Paul felt his poker face take a blow and hit the canvas. Carla saw Paul's predicament and immediately took the elaborate butterfly clip from her sumptuous hair, allowing a true midnight of dark locks to tumble around her gorgeous face.

"Here, Paul darlin', use this!"

"You sure, Carla?" asked Paul.

Carla answered in kind by placing the magnificent hair clip on the middle of the table. The clip, whether real or not, was a wolf whistle of an adornment; a real magpie lure if ever there was. Being the horrific magpies they were, the outlaws had no problem accepting the odds. Clinker roughly relieved Bang Bang of the pendant, threw it along side Carla's hair clip and the game was on. Bowler Hat simply started dealing, thinking the twirling cards would distract and intercept any vocal escalation. Thankfully, they did.

All cards were viewed but not a face muscle stirred. In the middle of the "Yehaaw!" of the Rattler's Tail Saloon, a micro world of hush and concentration covered the table like a glass dome. Both Paul and Carla simultaneously noticed that Bang Bang kept one arm out of sight, below table level, when he had been moving both arms easily moments earlier.

"Paul . ." whispered Carla, who had both arms wrapped around Paul's shoulders, her head snuggled against his. Her perfumed embrace was a necklace of something utterly fantastic.

"Yeah, I noticed." whispered Paul.

Now in poker, there may be skill in the bluff and the calling of that bluff, but there is no skill in being dealt the ideal hand. Just the feel of the cards in his hand made Paul feel he was handling something he'd normally scrape off his shoe. This shoe scrape of a hand was a 2 and an 8, both different suits. A bit disappointing but potential is all in poker.

Bowler Hat then discarded the top card form the pack and dealt three more cards in to the middle of the table. No luck for Paul in improving his hand but Clinker seemed to know something the others didn't because, well, no one could be the person called "Clinker" and simultaneously be *that* optimistic about life. Along with Clinker's knowing demeanour, Paul heard a definite "*click*" sound from under the table. That click caused Bowler Hat to squirm. Paul knew Bang Bang, under the table, had his gun pointed at Bowler Hat, forcing him to deal from the bottom to favour Clinker's hand.

Clinker saw Paul's moment of realisation and it all hit the fan. He stood and drew, getting off a shot before anyone got off a scream. A second before, Paul had grabbed Sheila's pendant, some trinkets and soiled beyond belief notes; just as much as a "quick grab with one hand" would allow and instinctively dove to one side, taking Carla with him. Clinker's shot missed but clipped Bartender before smashing the long mirror that always hangs behind every bar in every saloon ever built.

Bang Bang got with the program and started blasting with guns that never needed to be reloaded. They *did*, however, need to be *aimed*. He stood there like a rabid firecracker as shots spat in to every corner of the Rattler's. Fleeing people were hit in the back and fell dead. Two on the balcony were hit. Suddenly . .

"PAUL . . HERE!" Carla had run behind the bar and retrieved the shotgun. She threw it to Paul. Now, holding a shotgun was alien to Paul, but to be thrown one in the middle of gunfight carnage in another world was exquisite newness upon exquisite newness.

He caught the weapon with the same level of expertise a person would catch an octopus, were one to be thrown at him for the very first time. Grapple with the shotgun over, Paul turned to face the outlaws with the appropriate level of dexterity for a suburban dwelling history teacher in his first shootout, pulled the trigger and hoped the recoil wouldn't jolt his hands off.

Well a shotgun – very definitely – comes under the category of "You supply the trigger finger and we'll do the rest!" Using a shotgun at close range is a "Win Win" situation, like riding a bicycle with stabilisers. A cavalry charge of lead shot rode forth in triumph from the shotgun barrel to rescue Paul, speed smiting Bang Bang, who span around violently and fell, spinning blood all over the wall, shooting his last shots. With the very last bullet Bang Bang would ever fire he ironically shot himself in the foot.

Clinker, taking the brunt of the shotgun blast, hopped back a step then bent double immediately and unceremoniously as if he was snapping shut. He fell on to the table which reared up then flipped and fell over him. Everything went everywhere, including people. Paul found himself lying on his back, still holding the shotgun which had no trouble knocking a firearms novice like Paul clean off his feet. The last thing he heard was Carla shouting "PAUL, PAUL, PAUL" over and over. Each time she shouted, she shouted her own echoes as her voice grew fainter and fainter.

With a thump and an awful grunt, Paul landed in front of the Nudge Canyon machine. More to the point, however, was that he had landed right in front of Susan and Detective Jerome. Susan just screamed and Jerome took a staggering step back, almost pulling his gun. He gasped the inevitable line . .

"WHAT . . I mean just WHAT!"

He had wanted answers and boy, *did he get them!* Three seconds only had elapsed. Jerome saw the shotgun and drew his piece; shouting . .

"DROP IT . . DRO . ."

Paul lay gasping very heavily. Jerome knew Paul and the firearm were strangers to each other so re-holstered his unique looking gun. He stepped over and took the shotgun from Paul, looking at the firearm which was, suddenly, an antique. Notwithstanding what and where he had just experienced, Paul was obviously very much the worse for wear. Susan dived forward to help her hurting husband.

"NO . . . WAIT . . . WAIT" shouted Jerome, halting Susan's approach.

The detective's natural drive for justice took precedent over Paul's physical condition and he knelt beside Paul, or rather he knelt beside the person who was holding the SOS pendant. The detective's world halted utterly for a split second at seeing the pendant. Was it the same one Susan had come to the station with? Was it another one entirely? Either way, Detective Jerome knew the pendant and its repeating role in all this was considerable, so gently unwound it from Paul's grasp and pocketed it.

As incredible a learning curve as it was for the two of them, Susan and Jerome had seen what they had seen and now knew what they both knew. They were both now fully paid up members of the "Need to Know" society. Paul gasped and thrashed, nearly fighting off his own wife as he spluttered his inevitable line . .

"I NEARLY DIED . . I COULD HAVE DIED . . I NEARLY DIED"

Susan and Jerome helped Paul on to the sofa. They both stared at him as if they had never met him before. The bad after glow of Nudge Canyon permeated the air thickly through Paul, who was some sort of umbilical cord between two worlds. Jerome could smell gunfire about Paul. He could see that Paul's reappearance in to the world was not merely a case of his being dragged through a hedge backwards but one of facing and enduring a given level of violence. Susan smelled Carla's perfume. She had smelled it before and naturally feared the worst, but the events of the last ten minutes put things in to a whole new perspective and, at least on an immediately selfish level, she felt more relieved, despite the fact that, as she and the detective helped Paul to the sofa, one of Carla's earrings tumbled on to the carpet, having come detached from the western beauty when Paul grabbed her to dive under the table.

Somber silence descended. When you have just been missed by a truck while crossing the road, you don't really feel like a chat. The next hour, however, saw Paul spill every bean in a family sized tin to Jerome and Susan. His tale was fantastical; his tale was brutal, tactless and confessional; yet every word was believed by Susan and Jerome because they had seen what they had seen and were now members of a very exclusive club.

And on the Nudge Canyon machine, conveniently ignored by all present, three dollar signs now sat perfectly in line, lined up by the deaths of Clinker and Bang Bang.

16

Revelations

Well, what more was there to say?

Paul lay on the sofa. Susan knelt next to him and held his hand. Every bean Paul had spilled had been absorbed by both herself and Detective Jerome. Paul had finally kept his promise to himself to tell Susan everything. This was no time for accusations, finger pointing and "Why didn't yous?" as a raw open wound requires a bandage, not sandpaper. The first bandage applied to Paul was the fact that he knew his story was believed. The second bandage was Susan by his side and the faithfulness her presence declared. The third bandage was the fact that, in another world, Carla was again searching for Paul, the mercurial love of her life, and the faithfulness *it* declared.

Hour after hour passed and the Sun eventually rose, bringing with it a new day on many levels. Paul awoke to find Susan lying on the floor next to the sofa. He looked at the Nudge Canyon machine and resolved to utterly destroy it this very day. Susan awoke and bypassed the groggy stage, throwing her arms around her husband like that necklace of soothing balm. Paul fell on to her and they both lay crying over it all.

Well, women being women with their seemingly bottomless bag of tricks, Susan rose and pulled Paul with her. She went to Paul's briefcase and took a black marker. Leading Paul to the calendar that hung in the kitchen, she took Paul's hand and wrapped it around the maker then wrapped her hand around Paul's and drew a big line under the calendar, going over it over and over before taking the calendar and throwing it across the room. She grabbed Paul's lapels and shook him lovingly.

"Our lives start from this moment on, ok? OK? OKAAAYYY?"

Paul's reply, the most meek utterance of "ok" ever uttered in history, was the most momentous thing he had ever said.

***

Back at the precinct, Detective Jerome stared at the two SOS pendants lying before him on his desk. One pendant was the one Susan had brought to the precinct that odd day and the other was from Paul's visit to the Rattler's. Both were 100% identical and both had a few scratches . .

. . 100% identical scratches.

He'd been up all night; cramming, if you will. What he was studying left him speechless at every turn and caused him to seriously question his day to day world. Upon opening the SOS pendant, the one Paul had reappeared with, Sheila's note and list of personally signed names had jumped out with a gasp, as it had been inserted in a cramped manner by the distraught.

On one little piece of paper, designed to give helpful instructions and ask politely for assistance, a roaring message of such pleading and troublesome magnitude, screamed the solutions to several unsolved missing persons cases. The little piece of paper was way out of its depth for such information and wilted with frightened meekness in Jerome's hands, glad to be passing the torch to somebody . . *anybody* else. Uniformed Officer Elaine leaned over Jerome's shoulder and wrote each name down, speaking each name slowly and respectfully out loud as both read. Melanie Carter . . Patrick McIntyre . . Lorraine Huang . . Victor Johanssen . . the list went on, with all names immediately significant.

Your name is your unique social fingerprint in this world. From birth, you hear yourself being called that name over and over. It is written on your birth certificate and on your first and subsequent birthday cards but it goes much deeper than that, doesn't it?

Your name was chosen for you by a small but intense council with much care and thought and love, it was not picked out of a tombola. Over time, you absorb your name to such a degree that hearing your name called, even in a noisy environment, will cause you to look round instantly as surely as if you'd been tapped on the shoulder. Hearing your name, spoken in your ear in the form of a harmless kitten of a whisper, will send a jolt of just "something" right through you. That particular sound, the sound of your name, will correctly pick you out of a line up of a million people every time.

Any middle names you may posses have in all likeliness been bequeathed to you by your grandparents and theirs and theirs, making you an ambassador for family history. You see, whatever you are called, in certain circles, your name carries more weight than any power could lift and remove from history.

Jerome was well trained at absorbing everything the awful side of life could throw at him. He had been around the block so often that they really should have named the block after him, but what the awful side of life conjured up *now* was so unexpected and surreal that you'd be tempted to take it as a joke. Every signature was different but with the same pen. Again, it was fairly easy, even at first glance, to see that the signatures appeared to come from different, some *way* different, periods in history, but that to voice that observation would surely be to invite ridicule. With the names read, attention was given to the desperate and annoyingly smudged message:

Help, please please help. We are all trapped on this railway carriage. We cannot escape and are robbed repeatedly with great violence. It repeats and repeats. I was tricked to come here. The bandit machine is responsible. We cannot come to you, please come to us. The violence hurts so much. Sheila Burness.

Elaine took a seat at the reading of this. Jerome whistled a slow whistle that was morse code for "Boy oh boy!" The writing was adult but so off kilter that it looked like it had been written by the non dominant hand, such was the plea amidst horror that flowed and mingled in with the black ink.

"You ok?" asked Jerome.

Elaine was visibly shaken. She was dealing with what she had just read but she had not witnessed what Jerome and Susan had. Jerome knew that this cry for help had not come from one end of a call to 911 but had come from another world where joy and pain flow from person to person like the loose change in your pocket changes owners ten times a day.

"Step outside for a while Elaine but this doesn't leave this room ok? Least not till I say it does."

Elaine stepped out and Jerome began the process, the potentially enormous process, of helping the distraught Sheila and the others, *if* they were still alive to be helped. As always, due to the march of technology and police protocol in general, this began not with the loading of a gun or the sound of a siren but with the switching on of a computer. As he had witnessed what Elaine hadn't, Jerome knew every single name would check out. Of that much he *was* certain. Elaine re-entered:

"Sir, they're here."

***

Detective Jerome ushered Paul and Susan in to an interrogation room that appeared to be stripped of everything but air. All parties involved in this meeting were innocent but Detective Jerome sensed the need to avoid too much informality – considering the backstory – so did not use his more welcoming office. Sometimes you just have to get down to business.

Three minimalist chairs scraped the bare floor as all took seats around a minimalist table. Not even an ashtray. At no time did Susan let go of Paul's hand. Paul and Susan, within the precinct, were two fish out of water, let alone their recent experience. Jerome saw this so corralled their nervousness with a smile and coffee.

"Ok folks, thanks for coming. Please excuse the décor but the room's more about talking than looking!" The couple opposite didn't respond either way so Jerome produced an envelope from his jacket pocket and slid the SOS pendant on to the table almost surreptitiously, along with Sheila's plaintive notes. *Tread firmly but gently, Jerome.* He smiled as he spoke.

"So, Paul, can you tell me how you came by this?" Paul nodded assertively.

"Yes, I won it."

"Playing poker?" Paul looked at Jerome for what seemed like an age. The detective continued to smile.

"*I killed a man!*" came Paul's untainted testimony without so much as a knock. Susan let out a scream but moved even closer in to Paul's personal space, which spoke volumes.

This was news to Jerome and Susan. Jerome, however, did this for a living and Susan, well, Susan *didn't*. He had wanted to ascertain the presence of the shotgun Paul had reappeared with but Paul had totally cut to the chase. The thousand yard stare fluttered around the room, spoiled for choice as to whose face to settle on. It settled on the detective.

Jerome stared at Paul then the pendant then Paul. The see-saw went on for a full minute.

Innocent until proven guilty, Jerome; remember that.

The detective let out a sigh which was the equivalent of an elongated haunted house door creak in that it built suspense.

"Did you kill him with the shotgun?"

"Yes."

"And how did you *get* the shotgun?"

"A woman threw it to me."

Jerome's eyes darted to Susan who increased her grip on Paul with a jerk. Jerome would have usually asked Susan to let go of Paul but hoped her boa constrictor hold on her husband would squeeze more truths out. It did.

"I was in a card game and it got nasty."

"Ok."

"It was them or me."

"*Them?*"

"Yes, there were two. I knew they were cheating and when they knew that I knew, they tried to kill me."

Susan never reacted to Paul's statement that Clinker and Bang Bang had tried to kill Paul as she was already at the summit of Mount Distraught.

Jerome had no problem believing all this. He had been present and saw that, although Paul had reappeared with the shot gun, he had not *entered* with it. On *this* side, things were, physically speaking, as normal but the detective knew that, back where Paul had been, there were innocent people in grave danger. *Move on, Detective Jerome.*

"Well I've no jurisdiction in any other world apart from this one so you get a free pass on that." Paul nodded his appreciation of Jerome's understanding and professionalism.

The detective drew attention back to the SOS pendant. He turned the notes round to face the couple and motioned them to read. As they read he continued:

"You see, Paul, this pendant belongs to a missing woman. Her name, Sheila Burness, is on that list as you can see. Both she and her son Tom went missing a while back. All those names on that list are real people. Every single name checks out. They are all people reported missing, some as long ago as a hundred years."

"*What?*" exclaimed Paul.

"And it doesn't end *there.*" Jerome continued, "We've checked out what signatures we could from official records and personal effects. To our satisfaction, those very people, and get this, all signed their names *in person!* Science lab confirmed that all, and I mean *all* names were written using the very same pen filled with ink not produced for best part of fifty years. Several of those people, if they'd gone missing or not, should have been dead anyway . . a long time ago."

"*Wow!*" said Paul.

"To put it mildly!" replied Jerome. "You mentioned a woman throwing you the shotgun. Was that Sheila, Sheila Burness?"

"No, that was Carla . . a . . a . . woman who . ."

Susan had released her grip on Paul but still held his hand, never flinching at the mention of Carla. Paul smiled at her, appreciating *her* understanding and professionalism. Jerome rescued Paul.

"She saved your life, right?"

"Yeah, she did *that* alright."

"Well look, Paul, as off the wall as this seems to be, you, I mean *this* pendant with its plea for help is the only link to solving this. Someone needs to go back in and confront this."

"NO!" shouted Susan.

"Not *Paul,* Susan. *I'll* go. It has to be me as no one is going to believe this story anyhow. I know I wouldn't have."

The next hour saw Paul briefing Detective Jerome in as much detail as possible on the set up in the Rattler's Tail Saloon. To listen to Paul speak, a bystander would automatically think Paul was telling Jerome about a western movie he'd seen at the cinema, and that it had made a big impression, such was the conviction in Paul's voice as he effortlessly described various characters and setting in great and convincing detail, the telling of which would have been genuinely exciting had it not been so momentously serious.

***

Well there's getting dressed and there's getting *all dressed up* and then there's . .

Back at their home and directly in front of the Nudge Canyon machine, Paul and Susan sat watching as Detective Jerome, aided by officer Elaine, kitted himself out in readiness for entering the Rattler's Tail Saloon. A macabre gent's outfitters this was, bespoke in the most down to earth way it could ever be. A somber, wordless, mime act.

The "BOO!" of a ripping sound, as hook and loop was attached then re-attached, repeatedly, was highlighted in the officious silence as officer Elaine unapologetically span the detective around to make his bullet proof vest snug.

At the same time, Jerome checked his weapon, the Gavel Gun. As he clearance checked the outlandish firearm, he looked at Paul and Susan and knew what they were thinking. What they were thinking was that Jerome was dressing to confront tangible and nasty evil with as much worry on his face as if he was putting on pyjamas.

"You two ok?" asked the detective.

"Yeah, just about." answered Paul.

"Good!" replied Jerome with a slight smile and a wink. To the uninitiated, like Susan, this was cold comfort but to fully in the know Paul, a quite unbelievable gesture.

To speak such words at such a time was testimony to the degree of tempering the detective had undergone as part and parcel of stopping, or at least hindering, crime, for many years. This profession had aged the man, who looked roughly 10 years older than his actual age but this, again, went with the territory. Every day since leaving uniformed life behind and becoming a detective had been a non stop head on collision with crime. He really had seen it all and although *this* particular case was actually set in another world, the characters and events Paul had described to Jerome were, apparently, no different. To Paul and Susan, the situation was a monster but to Detective Jerome that monster was no more than an imaginary monster under a child's bed.

A bystander to all this was the Nudge Canyon machine; sitting, unplugged and harmless, almost a wall flower. So unobtrusively sat the cause of all this that you'd be tempted to think it was a case of "You've got the wrong man, Detective." So innocent and fun looked the one armed bandit that, if it was involved *at all*, it *surely* didn't know what it was doing and, in some bizarre court somewhere, could easily claim "Diminished Responsibility".

Preparation over, Jerome put a slight smile on his face, more for himself than anybody. A nod to Elaine then . .

"Ok Paul, plug it in."

Paul plugged in the machine, which immediately went in to its default setting of "Attract" mode, a beautiful and hypnotic chase of lights, flowing silently round and around the exquisitely rendered face. Silent, oh so *silent* beckoning, like the curl of an index finger saying "Come here!". The former wallflower of a machine now bloomed and like any bloom, looked so desirable that you just *had* to interact with it.

The Nudge Canyon machine simply stood looking at the four people it had turned in to marionettes. There is no emotion in any machine save what some human has built in to it and this one armed bandit had none, simply none. Its blinkered existence had seen many people come and go. Its only master was itself. Its only need was to do what it did. It was like gravity, it was like electricity, it could and would entertain; but its nature, its *true* nature, like that of gravity and electricity, approached without safeguards, would not hesitate in destroying you without blinking. Jerome went to slot a coin but the slot was closed fast.

"Here, let me." said Paul. Again the slot remained closed. The machine's slight electrical hum belied the pressing need of the moment. Jerome reached out and took hold of the bandit's arm. A loud crack of some electrical whip bit the detective's hand with a white spark, throwing the detective's arm back with force. Jerome yelped as he was thrown backwards several feet on to the floor.

Suddenly, the electrical hum stopped, as did Attract mode. The one armed bandit fell silent and unexcitedly dark and drab. Because the machine didn't care anymore. It knew that they knew. The honeymoon period had long since passed. Elaine helped Jerome to a seated position as he shook his electrically whacked hand.

Now the word "NUDGE" began to pulsate dark to bright to dark to bright, very slowly and in utter silence. Paul knew this offer was for him alone, as did, instinctively, the detective. Elaine rose and put her arm around Susan as Paul reached for the lever.

"WAIT!" shouted Jerome. Paul hesitated then moved his hand very slowly. The bandit reciprocated and moved *it's* arm towards Paul's hand.

"I SAID WAIT!"shouted the detective.

***

"Well you're not going in there again without *this*." Jerome said as he took off his bullet proof vest and started to put it on Paul, turning him around as a tailor proud of his work and, as it always goes with bespoke protection, the bullet proof fitted perfectly. Susan, held by Elaine, just stood and sobbed, reaching out and touching her husband as he was equipped by Jerome.

"Don't take this off for any reason." ordered Jerome and the dressing was complete. To the untrained, it looked as if Paul was sporting nothing more than a body warmer while camping. All sounds of preparing Paul for "doing what a man's gotta do" seemed to be magnified.

Ever notice that the best part of a choc ice is the very last bite? Why didn't you enjoy it all to the same degree? It was because when you knew you had more to come you got all blasé about it. Only when you saw the end approach did you set phasers to "Appreciate". Susan threw herself between Paul and Jerome. She hugged what she thought was her last bite of the choc ice and wanted it to never melt. She wanted it to last forever. Her love for Paul basically welded her to her husband.

"Oh Paul, Paul, sweetheart, darling . . you come back to me ok? YOU COME BACK TO ME . . OK?

Jerome looked up at this moment between Paul and his wife and for a second was reminded that there was a world outside of crime. He span Paul around, checking all was in place then bent down and attached an ankle holster to Paul. Susan screamed at this action and hugged Paul in an embrace only love could exert and that love alone could break.

"Don't forget, this little lady will be there for you in a tight spot." said Jerome, referring to the sleek little bomb of a pistol he now handed to Paul. A feisty little weapon this was. Minimal in design but maximal in purpose.

"She's best concealed so you don't appear to be a threat."

If it has to come, you want a private, candle lit date with trouble, a confrontation on *your* terms and easy to handle; not a heaving barbecue with half the town.

"You've got six shots plus these two clips." continued Jerome as he slipped the ammo clips into a secretive pocket on the vest. "Remember how to re-load?"

"Yeah."

"Well show me again!"

Paul ejected the little clip from the little gun. Susan turned her head away sharply. Detective Jerome caught the clip before it hit the carpet. He noticed that Paul's expression was "pommeled" garnished with "determination" and was pleased with his pupil who, until that very afternoon during a practice session, had never held or fired a gun; at least not in the real world. A new magazine was inserted and the little gun was clearance checked, impressively. The sequence of masterful actions then hit a dead end as there was no imminent threat. *That* lay waiting in another world.

"Check the safety, Paul". Paul tutted himself then set the safety to "ON" then "OFF" then repeated this several times. Safety was now ON.

Jerome stood and stared Paul right in the eye, trying to impart courage in to the history teacher. The detective looked at Paul then at Susan. To Detective Jerome, to the Nudge Canyon machine and to the whole potentially check mate of a situation that it was, Paul and Susan stood like the rank rookies that they were, conscripted and press ganged in to the goings on of another world. A moment for being not quite so officious presented itself but had the door closed in its face by Sheila's scribbled pleadings; this, all present, knew.

Jerome slowly turned Paul to face the machine.

"We've got to at least try to get them back, Paul. You know that."

"I know that." nodded Paul.

Susan tried to stop Paul but Jerome barred her way with his arm. She turned and ran outside, sobbing, followed by officer Elaine. Paul never even glanced back at Susan's actions. He lowered his head with eyes tightly shut and silently blamed himself for the whole show. He put his hand on the one armed bandit's arm. No need for a coin and nothing special on the reels, just pull the now invitingly jolting lever. Jerome shook his head a little in disgust at the machines cunning.

Paul moved the lever an inch . . then another inch . . then all the way.

***

"AAAAAGGGHHH" shouted Paul

He did this because he had re-entered the bandit's world in the middle of the day; near noon, in fact. The brightness of the scene hurt his eyes a lot. He stumbled, again, on his arrival, falling on to inches thick, dry, dry dirt and dust that had been turned in to a semblance of a high street by horse and foot and occasional carriage traffic. Deep ruts, made when it rained and, for the present, caked bone dry, made the surface a joke to behold.

The sounds of the old and near deserted west, much the same as the modern west but without any technology and vastly less people – more nature than humanity – were about him. Paul knew only too well he was back in the other world.

He wondered for a moment just how far this world went. Were there seas to cross to other countries? Were there libraries with books which told the history of this peculiar world? Were there stars with constellations unique to this world and universe upon unreachable universe out there also? But deep thoughts would have to wait. Paul stood and looked around, still squinting in the boiling, sandy town. He heard commotion.

Turning, he saw Carla running out of the Rattler's Tail Saloon and over those caked ruts towards him, nearly stumbling herself. She grabbed Paul round his neck and squeezed as if she was making a Canyon Sunset. The silence was profound. Page after page of sincere silence turned over and over as Carla's feelings for Paul were conveyed without a single word.

Paul, who had spent his life up to his neck in books, stood and read – and read – the silent and unwritten pages of the scented book that held him close. She loosed her grip slightly and stared in to Paul's eyes for an age then out-beamed the Sun with her smile, making Paul's heart squint. She was gasping as she placed both hands on Paul's cheeks.

"Oh Paul!"

Paul knew that Carla loved him and knew that Susan had her suspicions about her rival from another world. He also knew Carla had no idea of his real life or situation and was acting in all innocence. Faint and cheery piano playing wafted over the touching scene, easing any awkwardness and hinting at the next chapter in the strange saga. Carla was herself again now, a self who even *she* never knew existed before Paul came along. She firmly took Paul's arm in the most romantic way and led him to the Rattler's Tail Saloon. Honestly, were there no other places to go apart from that death trap of a building?

But, it *was* shady inside and an escape from the desert sun. The saloon, like Nickel Main Street, was nearly empty and the piano player stopped, finally, for a break. This allowed the sound of the persistent desert wind to be heard as it made the waist high saloon doors creak back and forth.

Carla, who now wore a smile you couldn't blow off with dynamite, led Paul to a table in the corner then plonked herself on to his knee, her body language shouting to the world "You've gotten away from me twice, you wont get away a third time!" As far as Carla was concerned, it was open season on Paul so she planted a smacker of a kiss on his lips in much the same way a cattle rancher will hot iron brand his cattle. This was a land rush for Paul's heart in which the only participant was Carla herself and she wanted *every inch* of romantic acreage. Another friendly face approached:

"Here, son, thought you'd like one of these again!"

Bartender had again made Paul a makeshift but effective drink which was all water in to which he'd squeezed an entire lemon. This was a "Canyon Sunrise", the water with orange drink Paul had previously being a Canyon "Sunset". This was all so friendly and appreciated by Paul from another world but neither Carla nor Bartender knew about Sheila and the others and their living circle of torment out there somewhere. He would have smiled sociably but simply couldn't. Carla saw this and, now her feelings for Paul were as good as written in to the Constitution, she stroked his cheek with a smooth and dainty hand moulded from pure, refined, oestrogen.

"Darlin', you ok?"

***

Powerless, and not liking the feeling, Jerome stood and stared at the Nudge Canyon machine. When he had joined the force, the detective knew what he was signing up for but *this* had not even been mentioned in any small print.

Like Paul arriving on Nickel Main Street and wondering; Jerome also wondered just how far this story would go. The reels span then slowed and stuttered then span too fast then and then and on and on. This was a clear indicator that there were happenings in another world. Jerome leaned against the machine, the alluring reels and lighting reflecting off his concerned features. He muttered "C'mon' *C'mon.*" through gritted teeth over and over. Three seconds had elapsed five minutes ago and Paul should be back by now. Susan returned from sobbing in the garden and now sobbed as she knelt before the machine. It hurt both to know that Paul was in there on his own, facing danger on his own. Both stood holding the crumb of comfort that was the fact Paul had returned twice – alive – and that was *without* a bulletproof proof vest or weaponry.

***

And both would have been further comforted by the fact that Paul was with his two friends, even if one of them was a woman as gorgeous as a woman can ever get and sitting on Paul's knee.

"Boy, what is this shirt *made* of?" asked Carla as she tapped Paul's protective vest. Carla was in Nirvana now and her head was full of thoughts of her future with Paul, who looked around at his surroundings. Sure enough, there were the gunshot damaged reminders that he had indeed been in the Rattler's – twice before – and escaped by the skin of his teeth – twice before. His chat with Jerome down at the station came to mind. He took Carla's hand, which she definitely appreciated.

"Do any trains come through here, Carla?"

The countenance of the dark haired and sumptuous beauty on Paul's knee fell a few feet. Her eyebrows furrowed as she squeezed Paul's hand way out of its comfort zone.

"Why d'you ask? Oh Paul, y'ain't fixin' to run out on me again are you?"

"No. It's just there are some people who need help."

"Friends of yours?"

"Well no, I've never met them . ."

"Well how d'you know they need *help?*"

Carla's interrogation, which had only one purpose, to determine if Paul was already spoken for, reached the really tricky stage when galloping hooves, that clattered with sheer panic on the horse's part, careered up to the the swing doors of the Rattler's Tail Saloon. The approach was so fast that the horse appeared to skid to a halt, if horses can do that sort of thing. The horse and rider didn't come alone, for the wind jumped up the Beaufort scale like a gazelle, blowing the doors clear open, making way for the rider who obviously thought nothing of riding his horse past the point of death for the poor animal.

Carla loosed hold of her sweetheart for a moment; obviously, she knew who it was. Paul saw the look on Carla's face, which was a Beaufort scale all of its own, and knew trouble was here. The wind continued to hold the swing doors open, causing a tornado of dust to blow not only dust, but tables and chairs around with that horrible scrape. Sheet music on the piano flew everywhere as if alive and on the wing. Rat Pile entered – all goodness fled.

You see, the thing with Rat Pile – and there were lots of "things" with Rat Pile – was that he was basically a walking talking Pandora's Box. Now the world has heard of Pandora's Box and no doubt imagined it to be some beautifully ornate masterpiece of carpentry or stonework, at least on the outside, when the reality would be more like the physical appearance of the stinky train robber. Only unpleasant surprises came forth from the ridiculously dressed desperado; only unpleasant surprises. To have even the remotest contact with Rat Pile was to risk lifting the lid, the ever so easy to lift lid, and unleash your doom. Carla frowned in disgust, wafted her hand and said an emphatic "Phew" then cuddled Paul's neck tightly, seeking safety.

Rat Pile scanned the near empty saloon for a second then marched over to the only table still un-blown out of place by his windswept arrival ceremony. He sat down with his back to Paul and Carla. Suddenly the piano started to play a tune only Paul could hear. It was Friend, who was tinkling the ivories. He played "Chopsticks" in an infantile, clumsy manner and spoke to Paul while looking at the keys.

"I never did like that tune, but then again, piano playing isn't really my thing. I see we've found *love!*" Paul knew Friend was referring to Carla.

"Don't worry, I won't tell Susan if you won't!" said Friend, with a light laugh. His tone was like he was telling a beautiful joke that had an ugly punchline you didn't want to hear but were going to hear it anyway.

"Paul, sweetheart, what's wrong?"asked Carla, who saw Paul staring at the piano where sat nobody.

"I know why you're here, Paul." continued Friend, who now turned to face Paul. "You're here for those on the last carriage, aren't you? Yes, I know all about them!" Friend said with boast in his tone. "I know about them and you and Susan and Detective Jerome and Sheila with her stupid little SOS pendant." Paul's jaw dropped, causing Friend to again laugh more heartily as he spoke.

"You should be teaching mid morning history right now Mr History Teacher, shouldn't you . . SHOULDN'T YOU!!!!"

Paul stood up sharply for no other reason than it was his only defence against Friend, who, upon seeing Paul stand, laughed all the more.

"What, are you going to throw me out, Paul? We're not in bland, living room, colour television, hot showers suburbia *now!*"

Paul sank back on to his seat with a creak-whump as, defence blown away, it was all he could do. Carla cradled him from behind, offering up the Canyon Sunrise to his lips, deeply concerned at Paul's actions and expressions caused by, from her perspective, nothing at all. Carla knew that when

Paul began to act a little frantically then he would act more frantically and then would disappear completely and *that*, she did *not* want.

Friend rose and walked over to the bar. He started to prepare a drink. Paul watched as the "Gambler's Doom" cocktail was put together very skilfully and with surprising delicacy. Friend turned waiter, the waiter no one could see but Paul, and brought the drink, the drink no one could see but Paul, and placed it on the table next to the Canyon Sunrise.

To behold this malicious drink was to gaze upon the hideous. To behold this drink was to force your eyes to see all negative in liquid form. Black, near solid tar was this beverage that had spikes and barbs throughout, moving and crawling with hopelessness, despair and extinction. It sat on the table like any impediment to happiness you could name in life. Paul tried to appear un-shocked but found himself leaning back in the chair out of reflex.

"You think I'm going to *drink* that?" he said.

"It's lemon this time, honey!" said Carla in all innocence. Friend stayed focused.

"I'm not showing you what you have to drink, Paul, I'm showing you what you've been drinking *all along!*"

"Well not another drop, OK!"

"Orange more to your taste then sweetheart?" said Carla, rising to go and get Paul a Canyon Sunset. Friend watched her then looked again at Paul.

"Click your fingers, Paul."

"What?"

"Yes, you know . . "*CLICK*" . . click your fingers!"

In no mood to argue or even joke, Paul clicked his fingers. Nothing happened. He felt slightly embarrassed.

"Don't be embarrassed, Paul, what did you expect? Now, let's see what happens when I click *mine!*"

Friend clicked his fingers and a bubble rose from the bottom of the black drink on the table. When it burst on the surface, the level of the drink went down by a whole third, that third going down Paul's throat and nearly inducing vomiting. Paul went ashen faced and looked 10 years older for a few seconds. The barbs and spikes threatened to lodge halfway down and call for surgery to remove.

Friend seemed strangely compassionate at this point and waited till Paul's colour returned before clicking his fingers twice more. No child will play with a broken toy and Friend's compassion was simply because Paul was no good to him dead. Carla returned with the Canyon Sunset. She went to sit on Paul's knee again but Paul had just drank a nightmare which was liquid at room temperature. He stood abruptly and headed for Rat Pilc's table.

"Paul honey, don't be goin there. *Please* Paul sweetheart!" cried Carla as she ran after Paul, pleading with him all the way round to his seat.

The gamble loving Paul, who had yet to be slain, had been electrified in to life by the Gambler's Doom cocktail. This, undesirable Paul, now stood nose to nose with the "Good" Paul who had come on behalf of those in the last carriage. The immediate moment was ruled by "Gamble loving Paul", who was back in the saddle now.

Back in the saddle and, in some loathsome way, *loving* it.

17

The Final Game

So it was with a large measure of ease that Paul took his seat opposite Rat Pile. The black drink of barbed worthlessness did what it said on the tin and blinded Paul to the potentially lethal situation everyone he cared about were now in.

The odour coming from the outlaw was just awful and it seemed that you would require a tetanus shot for simply saying "Hello" to the criminal. You could play as cheery a ditty all day long on the piano and every note would clash with what you saw in the man. A friend of the scorpion and a friend of the shadow dwellers of Nudge Canyon was Rat Pile. The clothes he wore no doubt once belonged to some unfortunate victim. The money he had on his person was no doubt stolen as were his guns but one thing was for sure, Rat Pile's disdain for any being other that himself was all his and always had been. Rat Pile treasured his personality and rejoiced in the fact that it was a treasure no one wanted to take from him.

Paul sat and thoughts flashed across his mind for a second of the prisoners on the carriage, causing him to look down and lose track of where he was. He felt Rat Pile staring at him and that feeling snapped him back to the present.

So, what was it like to look Rat Pile in the eye?

Was it easy to look at that beautiful bed of roses the last time you meandered through the park? Captivated by all that beauty, weren't you? Locked in silent conversation with the effortlessly beautiful, you drew nearer and nearer. You knew about thorns and other such things but counted a close brush with real beauty to be more than worth it.

Was it easy to go swimming in the sea on that hot summer's day? Did the muffled crash of those waves on to that wide and peculiar street of deep pile sand tempt you beyond measure? You knew about the sign, warning of undercurrents, but counted that a trifle against the sensation of azure embraces.

And what exactly was it like to drive along the Las Vegas strip the first time? The entire rainbow, in neon attire, towered above you. The restless juxtapositioning of deliberate dazzle made you gasp, did it not? An easy gate to open and step through.

"Come this way, friend!"

"Over here for fulfilment!"

"And you thought nobody loves you!"

You well knew these places are simply robbery laced with the hypnotic but decided that giving your money clean away is fun if it comes with a side order of adrenaline. Examine your feelings and motives at these times and you will know what it is like to look Rat Pile in the eye.

Rat Pile smiled a lot, it was just in his nature and make of his smiles and smells and fluctuating moods what you will. Friend took the cards and shuffled.

"Ok Paul, here's how it will go *this* time. We'll simply cut the cards!"

Carla watched but seemed to be just "out of it" and dislocated from the reality of it all. Paul noticed this and was glad for her as he felt this would protect her from any unpleasantness.

"We'll cut five times, gentlemen, Aces high. We can't have any draws so suits rank from Spades through Hearts then Diamonds down to Clubs. If Paul is the first to three then those on the carriage will be freed and Paul gets to go home. If the opponent wins then those on the carriage will stay forever and no one will pass back through the portal to their own world."

It was quite something to hear someone talking about the eternal fate of a group of people with utter nonchalance, but there it was.

***

"He should have been back by now, shouldn't he?" asked Jerome of Susan as he glanced at his watch.

Way more than three seconds had passed since Paul re-entered Nudge Canyon. The reels continued to spin sporadically as if the machine was ill. Detective Jerome tried to see some form of hidden message in the one armed bandit's behaviour. He tried to "read between the lines" of it all; something years as a detective had trained him more than sufficiently for, but nothing was jumping out at him and you can't exactly take an antique one armed bandit down to the station for questioning, can you?

Susan, beset with worry, idled up to the machine. She thought back to the day when she and Paul had agreed to sell the Nudge Canyon machine and wondered what exactly had scuppered that plan. Susan had been through so much recently that the answers she craved, if she ever got them, would fill an encyclopaedia. Oh, how she wanted those answers but her first desire was for Paul.

Suddenly, all the reels stopped dead. Susan shrieked and lunged at the machine purely out of reflex and not knowing what she was doing. Jerome barred her path.

"WAIT, JUST WAIT!"

He had wanted meaning to all this and the machine now accommodated him, for the three stationary reels all said HELP PAUL, with one reel sitting just one space too high. Immediately, a nudge was offered. The out of line HELP PAUL clicked and jittered repeatedly, crying out to be added to the line. Susan stopped reacting involuntarily for the briefest moment and read the reels too.

"WHAT, WHAT, HELP PAUL, AAAGGGHHH!" she screamed.

Jerome had to zone Susan out of this and focus. The HELP PAUL message had *definitely* not been on any of the reels up till now. The world of reality and logic were, again, being forced off the stage by the supernatural and the surreal. Jerome knew this and drew back from it but also knew he had to push forward. There was just so much at stake. He turned to officer Elaine.

"Officer, if I'm not back in five minutes, call back up."

"Ok, Sir . . are you *sure* about going in?"

Jerome squeezed Elaine's shoulder.

"No, officer, I'm *not* sure. But when I joined the force, I signed my name on the dotted line and I meant every stroke of that pen."

He took his detective's shield and gave it to the officer and suddenly Detective Jerome wasn't Detective Jerome, he was a husband and father. All the experience of the last few days had brought Detective Jerome's humanity to the fore and he had felt humbled by the whole surreal saga. He stood like this for a few seconds, then pulled the lever.

WWHHUUMMPP! Jerome landed face down in the carriage isle. Sheila screamed and Melanie yawned. The further you went back down the carriage, the more indifferent the reactions were. The carriage rumbled on, loudly and carelessly.

Sheila immediately went to help Jerome to his feet. The detective was not really hurt but was culturally shocked, in *spades*, as he raised himself to all fours, utterly wide eyed and gasping, head darting in all directions in seek of bearings. He looked frantically for Paul but could not see him. Shadows in the carriage were long and the light possessed a beautiful orange hue which indicated either the start or the end of the day. He saw Sheila approach and immediately saw the SOS pendant, which spoke with a glint.

"*Are you ok?*" asked Sheila, firmly, arms outstretched. The look on Jerome's face at that moment would have over qualified him for a place on Mount Rushmore. He grabbed Sheila's arm and raised himself, grabbing her pendant with a tug. He looked Sheila in the eye.

"ARE YOU SHEILA?" he asked with more than a little demand in the tone. One second of 24 carat dawning realisation followed, then . .

"YES! YES! I'M SHEILA! HOW DID YOU KNOW?"

Jerome tried to explain the inexplicably vast and unexplainable in a nutshell:

"I'M FROM OUTSIDE OF HERE . . ANOTHER PLACE . . SOMEWHERE ELSE . . WHERE YOU COME FROM . . I GOT YOUR MESSAGE."

"YOU GOT IT! YOU GOT IT! *YOU GOT IT!*" screamed Sheila, looking Heavenward, clasping her hands and closing her eyes in exhilaration. She sank to her knees. Jerome looked round at the others, knowing they were the ones in Sheila's note. He recognised Patrick and Lorraine immediately as he shouted over the repetitive rumble.

"ARE YOU ALL HERE FOR THE SAME REASON?"

Only Lorraine answered in confirmation. Jerome did not know what to make of the apparent apathy of the others in the swaying carriage as he was not yet acclimatised to the oh so very real surreal. He turned and lifted Sheila up roughly.

"WHERE IS PAUL, WHERE IS HE? HOW DO WE GET BACK?"

Sheila began to pull at her own hair with white knuckled fists as the pent up came forth . .

"PAUL . . *WHAT* PAUL? THERE IS NO PAUL HERE. WE CAN'T, WE CAN'T GET BACK."

"See, now you've upset my friend!" chirped Melanie.

"WHAT?" shouted Jerome. He looked out a window and saw they were way out in the desert. The carriage of the entombed hopeless was surrounded hook line and sinker by an entire atlas worth of the inhospitable. He ran up to the front end but there was no door. The rear yielded nothing better. Jerome took aim at a window.

"Save your bullets, son." said Victor, "You'll need them in a little while."

"WHY?"

"For the welcoming committee. They like things loud!" said Victor as he started laughing like a hyena that had just gotten the joke. Jerome put a hand on Sheila's head as she sat weeping. He turned and everyone saw the resolve on his face.

Standing up to his neck in passenger apathy and possessing an utter hatred of injustice, Jerome shouted his own declaration of independence for an atlas worth of desert to hear:

"WELL I'M NOT BUYING THAT. WE'RE ALL GETTING OUT OF HERE AND WE'RE ALL GOING HOME."

When Jerome said that, Sheila looked up at him and nodded vigorously. There was the sound of guns being loaded, and this time, no bullets were dropped. Somewhere in the land, a tornado was ignited. Nudge Canyon had detected a foreign body within itself.

Melanie yawned.

***

Well there's always some sort of breeze blowing through the town of Nickel, whether it's literal or metaphorical, as when rougher elements ride through, so the first yawn of a tornado as it awoke would not be noticed initially. Today was no different and *CREAK CREAK CREAK* swung those waist high Rattler's Tail doors. Honestly, 30 seconds and a can of oil would end the annoyance but, hey, that's somebody *else's* job, isn't it?

Suddenly, those little dolls house of doors blew open and right back on themselves, holding that position for about a minute. A very stiff breeze intruded with rudeness. What could be moved – moved – as it had when Rat Pile had arrived. Paul was sitting at the far end of the round poker table and in order to get to him, the wind had to pass Rat Pile. Normally, a filter will remove any impurities before allowing progress but this was the opposite. The waft of every ounce of scum of everything you'd ever find wrong with a desert land, blew across Paul, who closed his eyes as he teetered on his seat. Friend looked toward the still agape doors. Paul saw his expression and, although unable to translate it word for word, knew that something serious had just happened.

"Well, it seems the detective has joined us!" said Friend.

Paul took heart at this statement and tried not to let the moment slip, even when Detective Jerome didn't come through the doors with the his gun in top gear to end all this as he hoped. Friend brushed the obtrusive moment aside, deftly concealing the fact that he knew he would now be fighting a war on two fronts.

And that was just *it*; because Friend's gaze remained on the door or rather what he knew was way way beyond it. Paul saw on Friend's expression that Friend had not been expecting this turn of events and this had seriously distracted him as he now pondered a new attack or defence. Yes, Paul saw this and now knew that Friend was not infallible. A few more seconds of distracted-ness then Friend regained his cocky composure.

"So, to the game, gentlemen!" chirped Friend with a light clap of his hands. "I'm sure none of us wants to be here all night so let's keep it simple. Both of you will cut the cards a maximum of five times. Best out of five wins the loot. Remember, first to win three rounds wins all!"

This was fairly familiar to mild mannered Paul. Sinister house rules were dictating how it would all go down and Paul knew that even if he was in his own living room in suburbia he probably wouldn't start to kick up a fuss, much less in an actual other world, and a violent one at that.

***

"WHATS HAPPENING?" shouted Jerome, who had his gun drawn.

Now Jerome's gun was something else. It was a piece of bespoke weaponry with its own aura. A buffalo of a hand held weapon, the pistol was an apex gun in that absolutely nothing was beyond its thumping reach. It looked at least two sizes too big for any human to wield easily, but in a land where crime put its feet up, thinking that it owned the whole world, this piece of chrome and faux pearl reassurance, that swelled, glinted and throbbed to bursting point with law keeping power, was the minimum requirement.

The train was slowing down as per usual. Those aboard knew Jerome was about to climb the north face of a very steep learning curve and tried to help *he* who had come to help *them*.

"WE'RE ABOUT TO BE ROBBED VIOLENTLY. REMEMBER MY MESSAGE?" screamed Sheila.

Yes, Jerome *did* remember. He noticed that there was no station awaiting the train's arrival and that this impromptu, substitute station was going to be miles and miles of cactus covered, scorpion infested, bone dry wasteland.

"WHEN DO THEY COME?" shouted Jerome.

"NOW" shouted several in staggered unison.

At that moment, a volley of gunshots shattered every window on one side of the carriage.

"GET DOWN, GET DOWN" bellowed Jerome.

All were diving to the floor anyway. The noise was frightening in its suddenness quite apart from its actual volume and answered every question Jerome had, or ever would have, about the situation.

Loud smashing everything flew everywhere and every bit of it was out to get you. Jerome took a bold graze to his left shoulder which spun him round even though he was on the floor. A monsoon of glass shard and wood splinter rain poured to its hearts content upon the passengers. Guns that never needed to be reloaded spat and spat upon the scene.

Then, suddenly, total silence, a real *"Bang"* of silence.

Jerome, however, knew one single, lonely second of silence, in a situation like this, was a doorway of action to enter, so he stood and threw himself through the opposite windows with a smash, falling 8 feet on to the track side, landing on his back with a thump and an awful grunt.

The detective's head struck a rail, concussing him. The first 60 seconds of this experience had so much crammed in to it you'd think Nudge Canyon had shot its bolt and was out of "bad", but the macabre canyon always did its guests proud and more was coming.

***

Paul reached out to cut the cards when Rat Pile shot his arm out, blocking him. The outlaw gave Paul a "Go on, I dare you." look, then cut the cards. It was a Jack of Clubs. The Jack itself seemed to have a smirk on his face. In Nudge Canyon, even inanimate objects made you feel unwelcome.

***

Jerome lay trackside, wishing it was a hospital bed. Hysterical, male, unwashed laughter mingled with mostly female screaming as the gang boarded the train. The oral cacophony of it all, like the shard and wood monsoon, was a monsoon all its own.

The sound coming from the carriage would scare the bravest in to flight. You would think that possessing guns that never ever needed to be reloaded, the outlaws would simply kill everyone on board then proceed to rob them but all work and no play . .

Detective Jerome was now sitting up and groggily looking up at where he had fallen from. His taking advantage of that one single second of "nothing" and throwing himself through the door it opened, now bestowed upon the detective – and those he came for – a treasure so small you can't see it with the naked eye, a treasure as important as it is small, that treasure being a glimmer.

The whole scene was truly a 50/50 situation. He was out of sight and knowledge of the outlaws and now rose, rounding the end of the carriage very tentatively. The potential energy within the detective was dangerously immense.

A quick, viper fast, glance round the end filled Jerome in on the scene. All were now off the carriage and the nightly festival of looting had begun. Three of the gang were on horseback as they always were. The wind was getting up. A tornado, unsurprisingly unnoticed, was on the way.

Detective Jerome was no stranger to coming eye to eye with the "wrong" of the world. In the interrogation room, he'd sat many a time across the table from assorted culprits and had stared every one of them under that table. Jerome was indeed a father and husband but, as much as he loved the loveable, he hated the hateable. He stepped round in to full view of the crime in progress.

The report of Jerome's gun fell like repeated strikes from a judges gavel. Every single sleeping creature within a mile awoke and panicked. One horseback rider was shot dead forever in 2 seconds, the other two riders fled immediately. All looting abruptly stopped and all victims were dropped as the remaining outlaws focused on this new threat. They seemed to stagger as if drunk. This new silence was traditionally "deafening".

Jerome retreated round in to the shadows. He heard clumsy footsteps above him and saw the moon shadow of one of the carriage riding outlaws stumbling along the roof like a novice. Jerome stepped out and the Gavel Gun blew the carriage monkey to oblivion. The body fell over and down the far side to lie with dead passengers, whoever they were *this* time round.

If they had kept their ignorant mouths shut, the outlaws might have fared better, but knowing only two modes of operation – sleeping and wild behaviour – they may as well have put their guns down and shouted "Over here, over here!"

Shouting orders to each other as to how to get Jerome, and nobody knowing who was in charge and just whose order to follow, the outlaws themselves were Jerome's very own Sat Nav.

Jerome looked under and through the wheels just as an outlaw did the same; only Jerome, however, got back up again as the Gavel Gun spoke out another guilty verdict and blew away the culprit, smashing a cast iron carriage wheel in half at the same time. Only at this stage did Jerome turn for a second and notice the tornado wall about a mile away. He span round in incredulity as it dawned on him the whole tornado wall surrounded the train but was still some way off.

Ducking again quickly to peer under the carriage, Jerome saw no enemies. A bullet struck the detective in the thigh, toppling him immediately. The distraction caused by the tornado had tipped the scales of opportunity towards the outlaws who had rounded the rear of the carriage.

Jerome cursed himself for negligence as he fell. He lay full out on his back facing away from the enemy. More shots rang out and Jerome was hit again in the same shoulder as before, throwing up a huge mist of blood and desert dirt. The arm was now void of all feeling or use. Tilting his head way up to look, the approaching killers were upside down from his viewpoint.

***

Paul, still under the menace gaze of a face that never needed to be reloaded, reached out to cut the cards. Senses are heightened at such times and, all at once, Paul was acutely aware of, and processing, both love and hatred standing close by, for he was genuinely surrounded by both those forces. Carla helped her darling and rubbed Paul's back as he cut. It was a Queen of Clubs.

***

With the roughest of awkward and hindered aiming, Jerome teeteringly raised the Gavel Gun and just blasted and blasted. Out poured the death verdict on the criminals as a lead tsunami swept them out of this life. They crumpled in the most hurried fashion amidst splatters and groans.

All outlaws were now dead.

The detective just lay there gasping and fathoming the scene. He heard a large group of horses arriving at the scene as the posse duly sped past, chasing the two mounted members of the gang who had fled.

Turning his head and re-loading with any dexterity broken bones will allow, the detective looked through the carriage wheels to see others in a similar state.

***

"Well, Paul," said Friend with raised eyebrows and a sly smile as he picked up the pack "you win the first round! Did it feel good?" He shuffled the pack again and placed it on the table.

Black . .

Black . .

. . then reset and rush back in to the world.

"WHATS HAPPENING?" shouted Jerome as the train slowed down.

"WE'RE ABOUT TO BE ROBBED VIOLENTLY. REMEMBER MY MESSAGE?" screamed Sheila.

Jerome looked through Sheila and through Sheila again. His hand shot up to his wounded shoulder which was now not wounded. A look of incredulity told the others Jerome was struggling with the birthing of realisation.

"WHAT . . *WHAT*? spluttered the detective, scanning around to see everything fixed up and renewed. Sheila tried to help him up the slippery learning curve he was on.

"REMEMBER MY NOTE? THIS REPEATS AND REPEATS"

Jerome was stumped, just *stumped*. He started to un-holster his gun, always a good idea in such situations.

Rat Pile reached out and cut a 7 of Clubs. Paul reached out and cut a 5 of Diamonds.

The volley of outlaw gunfire again near smashed the entire side off the carriage. Jerome was hit immediately and fell dead, as did Sheila and Patrick. Murder and looting ensued. The timer hit zero. The posse gave chase, leaving a hideous scene of robbery and death.

"Well, that's one *apiece* gentlemen!" spoke Friend, smoothly.

Again, the cards were shuffled and placed centrally between Paul and Rat Pile. The piano player came through a door and sat, ready to begin. Friend merely looked towards him and, without seeing Friend at all, the piano player got up and left. Paul looked in astonishment. Friend mockingly imitated Paul's expression perfectly for a second then continued;

"We can't have any distractions Paul, can we? Now cut!"

Black . .

Black . .

. . then reset and rush back in to the world.

"WHATS HAPPEN . ." Detective Jerome had to adjust supernaturally quickly to this nightmare. The pinnacle of Mount Learning Curve was reached but the view was horrendous. Reset had happened. He still staggered a bit as he checked himself for wounds, a habit the others had long since conquered. All aboard were whole and well as the train slowed down. No more learning, just act.

Save them Detective Jerome.

The usual sound of slowing steel momentum, a cruel wake up call to the others, was drowned out by some terrific roar; a freeway of a roar; a Niagara of a roar. Jerome, still in many ways a novice, despite his baptism of lead and cackling cactus catastrophe, noticed this also. But what had come before may come again so . .

"EVERYBODY DOWN"

All dove, but no gunshots. Some screamed, probably out of tradition rather that fear. Still no gunshots. The carriage began to wobble as if a wheel had been bent and de-railed. Jerome rose and looked to see the tornado touching the end of the carriage.

Now this was truly a frightening sight and the detective really had to fight to stop from showing shock.

When does an assertive wind become a wall so tough you couldn't drive a tank through it? When does a blustery day go from making you want to fly a kite to making the most experienced pilot too afraid to fly a passenger jet?

Jerome stared at the wild wall of hurtling sand that no law enforcement agency had as yet tamed and knew when to cut losses. Sheila, Melanie, Lorraine and Patrick all huddled as the vibrating carriage turned rodeo horse, trying to throw them all off.

Jerome knew that, despite already having tried, the only way to safety, even for a moment, was to get to the next carriage along. He stepped over the timid and got to the blank and black wall which he pistol whipped with ferocity.

Paul could feel the gaze of Friend and Rat Pile, he took that as a cue and cut. An Ace of Clubs. This turned a dial somewhere deep within Paul, releasing a valve which brought such a feeling of relief with it that it could induce sleep.

Third blow from the butt of the Gavel Gun, and two shots, made a slight gap. Jerome kicked and smashed the gap until a makeshift doorway was formed.

"QUICKLY, EVERYONE GET TO THE NEXT CARRIAGE, MOVE MOVE"

Amidst the roar, the four huddlers staggered and fell through to the next carriage. Jerome stood by the doorway and shepherded everyone through. Such a rough transition it was, for "panic" and "politeness" may sit fairly close in the dictionary but they are poles apart in truth.

Jerome had to push the pile of people, causing it to topple fully in to the next carriage. The carriage they had come from was smashed to smithereens with ease like blowing out a birthday cake candle. The juddering stopped but the fleeing didn't as all made for the far end of the next carriage.

Rat Pile, who hadn't said a word for the last 10 minutes, had a strange look on his face. Paul watched as the outlaw turned and looked to where Friend was standing. He looked up and down and it was obvious he was aware that someone he couldn't see was standing next to him. This sober behaviour was out of character for Rat Pile and told an ancient legend that there was maybe a spark of humanity in the bandit. Friend watched and laughed at the bewildered lump of stink.

"He doesn't need me like you need me, Paul. He was born during a hold up. He was robbed of a normal life and has spent the rest of his life trying to rob it all back." He snapped his fingers and Rat Pile snapped out of it, reached forth a hand that perpetually looked like it was holding an invisible pistol, and cut.

Suddenly, in the carriage, in the midst of pandemonium and in the middle of blood, sweat and tears, there was silence. This silence hurt. It hurt because it was such a change to the setting. What you saw and heard clashed. It hurt because it appeared to withhold the end of it all from coming and it hurt because you just didn't deserve all this. Not a sound from the outside and hateful world. This was a silence that had stepped on to the stage to introduce something else waiting just out of view.

The door to the next carriage along disappeared, and not just the door but the entire door wall also. The carriage the desperate passengers stood in now blended in perfectly with the next carriage, forming one. This happened again and again until at least ten carriages became one long corridor. All, including Jerome, noticed this. All, excluding Jerome, failed to view this as escape being made too easy.

Patrick took Lorraine's hand and started to run along this sudden pathway to freedom. Jerome, being the wrong side of the mountain of people, couldn't stop the fleeing from possibly running themselves in to trouble but his voice could outrun the swiftest.

"STOP .. STOP .. PATRICK STOP"

But, unsurprisingly, no one was listening. Jerome pulled his gun and fired a shot. The fleeing couple stopped abruptly as the detective pushed past the others and the young couple.

"Just let me go first, Patrick." said Jerome, giving Patrick's arm a slight squeeze.

A strange and rhythmic sound could now be heard way way off at the other end of the tempting corridor of freedom. Jerome's head turned to see some sort of a bobbing mass coming towards them. The uneven beating was like the heartbeat of this whole situation, possessing a rhythm indeed but one that contained a prophetic message to it, like war drums of an enemy, designed to defeat you before it even reaches you.

On and on came the form and louder grew the bizarre and off kilter heartbeat. Every beat was a rude awakening. Melanie screamed and her scream lit the fuse which Jerome knew would detonate mass panic if he didn't snuff it out.

"SHUT UP" he shouted. Shelia grabbed Melanie and put her hand over her friend's mouth.

The form came on and it was now clear this was a rider on horseback, the heartbeat being awful; just an awful, awful sound. It all came closer but the rider failed to take on any more definition, remaining an unidentifiable black form. Never having been encountered before by anyone, the creature's reputation still preceded it, running ahead with nothing but bad bad news.

The rider raised an arm high, the arm swaying like a tree in wind. Glinting came from this raised arm and Jerome saw it was a lasso. Gold and silver glints hypnotised all who gazed. Slowly swaying and slowly turning, slowly galloping and slowly but unstoppably coming on .. and on .. and on. The carriage thumped and juddered violently to the hoof beats. The detective raised his gun and aimed at the approaching.

"Forgive me, friend." whispered Jerome as he shot the horses head, a course of action he'd never have taken but for the circumstance and cramped conditions.

Loud, so loud and commanding was the triggered declaration of the Gavel Gun, jerking the detective's arm sharply up with the recoil. Accurate, oh so very accurate was the aim as the bullet hit the horse between the eyes.

The horse tumbled head over heels, taking the rider with it. Both tumbled at the pace of the eerie. All watched as the horse and rider rolled once in a jittery way as if every few frames of a film had been removed. Then both righted again and the oncoming came on. A second blast from the Gavel Gun caused an exact repeat.

Still a good three carriages away, with a scream as long as a piece of string, the rider threw the lasso. The silver and gold threaded rope spat forth from the rider's hand like a vipers "faster than the eye" kiss.

Immediately, every passenger froze solid as the loop reached them with a surreal spark. Jerome fought and strained and struggled with all his might to fire but could not. He was underwater; a strange water made of hostile air that slowed everything, making him feel like he was trying to run in a dream in another dream.

Rat Pile, like Paul, cut an Ace but an Ace of Hearts, out ranking Paul's Ace of Clubs.

Extreme disorientation and a numbness of perception exploded cruelly on the group of lassoed and paralysed passengers as the tornado, the sound of which literally exploded back on to the scene, tore the back off the carriage. The last thing any of them were aware off was one second of noise as the tornado swept all aboard to their deaths.

Paul's countenance sank. Carla applied the necklace of soothing balm to her boyfriend but it had no effect. Friend quipped:

"Does Susan know about your girlfriend Paul? She smelled your girlfriend's perfume, you know! 19th century lipstick on your 20th century collar!"

Paul closed his eyes slowly, a sign of defeated realisation. He had never thought about Susan suspecting Carla. Friend, who was up to date with the happenings on the carriage, looked over at Paul with a knowing expression. Paul stared back and didn't mind the awkwardness.

Friend left Rat Pile's side and walked to the bar where he started to make another Gambler's Doom cocktail.

"You look like you could use a drink, buddy!"

Paul, finding a flash of backbone up in the attic of his personality, kept up the stare at Friend. Everything had been stripped away from the situation. All pretence and flattery and enticements had been filleted out and now, in the cold light of Friday night promises and Monday morning lies, Paul sat cutting the cards for . .

and was one inch from losing . .

everyone on the carriage.

Black . .

Black . .

. . then reset and rush back in to the world.

Jerome stared at Sheila and Sheila stared at Jerome as the train swayed and rolled on. All that was outer about this place and experience was not to be tasted of, or savoured. All passengers knew this and, in time, had fled to their inner personalities for sanctuary.

Some people, however, upon looking within, did not find the inner strength they required and had been crushed by it all. Not dead within but barely alive within, the weak turned off all rationality and went in to the exile of true hopelessness. Jerome's declaration that they were all going home had stopped the pilot light from being snuffed but could not fan the flame in to a robust blaze; however, that pilot light flickered on. All aboard, collectively, were a machine, fighting for freedom, that had been pummelled and pummelled, but was so well made and oiled with defiance that the fight was not by any means over.

There was nothing to do for any of them. No rallying of the troops, no drawing up battle plans and tactics or even the tending of any wounds as all had been healed upon reset. The constant repetition of the wildly different thwarted any attempt at organisation.

Jerome looked around. Lorraine still held Patrick, at least to some degree, Victor almost seemed to have a smile on his face as he paced up and down his little part of the carriage. It was impossible to know if the smile was hope or resignation. Melanie turned and twisted her rings on her bejewelled hands. She was so far out of it that it was a blessing in disguise for the poor woman. Jerome was now one of them, a naturalised citizen, fully aware of the laws governing the set up. He looked at Sheila and asked a well intentioned but ultimately futile question.

"You ok?"

"Yes" replied Sheila, stepping towards the detective. It was Sheila's ingenuity that had brought it all to this stage, something that Detective Jerome admired. He knew that Sheila was his most capable ally. Sheila fought very hard indeed to keep her "inner" from being affected but it was a battle all its own and here and now another battle was not needed. Tom raged in her heart and the absence of Tom broke her heart. She really didn't know if she wanted to be here or to just not exist at all. As the rhythmic swayed and swayed and rolled on, Jerome allowed the merest flicker of a smile onto his face.

"Hey, we're all going home, remember!"

Sheila smiled a half empty, dredged up from somewhere, smile and hugged Jerome. With a killer tornado a mere hundred yards away, he held her as she sobbed and sobbed.

"Well Paul, feel the thrill yet!" said Friend.

"What thrill?" answered Paul through semi clenched teeth.

"The thrill of the chase! C'mon now Paul, remember who you're talking to! I introduced you to all this decades ago, didn't I? I saw the look on your face when you won – oh that *look*! – and I saw the look on your face when you lost and, to be honest, there was all the difference that there is between 99 and 100. "I'll get it back! . . I'll get it back! . . Just one more . . Just one more . ." became your mantra, didn't it? Susan ruined it all and we fell out but she isn't here. Yes, you've got your new girlfriend and I've got your stinking outlaw opponent but basically it's just you and me in this one horse town and the name of this particular horse is "Addiction"!"

As he was saying all this, Friend had finished making the cocktail of bad weather and had strolled over and placed it on the table to Paul's right. Paul looked away from the drink which actually moved with black tentacles and had some sort of disjointed humming sound emanating from it. Friend resumed his position next to Rat Pile who was somewhat subdued, perceiving maybe, that Friend was running all this.

"Going to play then, Paul, or do you need help" said Friend, gesturing towards the tentacled drink. Paul stared at the table as he attempted to think of every ramification that would come his way of he didn't oblige Friend, the primary thought being of Jerome and the others. He wanted to return Carla's perpetual smile whenever his eyes met hers, which they were now doing as he glanced up at her, but just couldn't. Her perfume and touch stood sentry on Paul's nerves and were fairly effective.

"Ok, I'm in."

"*Attaboy!*"

Friend had no sooner said that than Rat Pile reached and cut, eager to win. Paul looked to see what the card was but Rat Pile looked at the card then pressed the card to his chest. This could be interpreted as very good or bad news. Rat Pile's face was indecipherable at rest; a dam that held back just *something* and as long as "just *something*" remains so, it is almost impossible to prepare oneself for what may come, for coming it was.

As Jerome held Sheila, a shot came through the roof and hit Melanie in the knee. She cried in pain and tumbled off her seat. Sheila screamed and ran to help her friend. Another shot came through the roof but missed any target.

Jerome unloaded the Gavel Gun upwards but the downward shots just kept coming. The detective ran and opened a carriage window, climbing out as the train rolled on. The outlaw firing down just kept at it and as Jerome clambered up and out he heard shouts and screams as before but knew that pushing on would yield better results than retreating to help his fellows.

Almost up and atop the carriage, Jerome was spotted by the outlaw who strode forward, grabbing the detective and pulling him up and out the window, slamming Jerome down on to the carriage roof. The brute strength in the villain was astonishing. A shot from the outlaw smashed Jerome's wrist, causing the Gavel Gun to tumble from his grasp and fall trackside.

Rolling on to his back, in total pain, Jerome clutched his smashed wrist. This very wrist was stomped on by the outlaw as Jerome wailed. The outlaw stood astride the detective like the Colossus of Rhodes as a pistol was raised and pointed between Jerome's eyes.

Paul cut the well soiled deck, cut a 2 of Clubs and now everything in the Rattler's Tail Saloon changed.

For Paul had lost.

If ever a pack of cards had any "dregs" then they were what Paul held now. The lowest card of the lowest suit.

Whatever card Rat Pile held, it would automatically out rank Paul's. Carla and Barman froze, not out of shock but they actually froze, statue still. Sound froze also. Not any ringing in your ears or your own heartbeat. Hope froze. Friendly "Hope" was now encased in clear preservative, an emotion to be seen and longed for but never again experienced.

And upon Friend's face now sat his true personality. For the first time ever in their turbulent "on/off" relationship, Friend now stopped lying to Paul and finally, with a single, well honed expression, told the horrific truth.

To destroy Paul was all Friend had ever wanted. The personification of all gambling addiction, that Friend was, had successfully coaxed Paul in to defeating himself. No more alluring banter and no more tantalising wins for Paul now, only death.

Jerome had signed on the dotted line when he joined the force. Yes it had been a rough ride up the ranks but what "Rank Ride" isn't? When it came to dealing with crime, this detective took no prisoners and never gave any lawbreaker a single inch. Jerome now side swiped with his leg and toppled the outlaw over and off the carriage. Guns are not the *only* weapons.

Suddenly, right in front of everyone, Paul's 2 of Clubs changed to an Ace of Spades, a Royal Flush of a card in this situation. Whatever card Rat Pile held *now* would lose to Paul's. Friend's look of triumph changed to anger mixed with great disappointment. He drew a long, nasal breath to quell an outer explosion as he looked way past the waist high doors.

"Nice one .. Detective!" said Friend with an equally long exhalation. Paul closed his eyes, some illicit emotion within savouring the taste of such a near miss.

"IDIOT!" shouted Friend as he slapped Rat Pile on the back of his head. The outlaw took the slap like a righteous rebuke and didn't even wonder who or what had slapped him.

Friend picked up the cards and began to shuffle. He shuffled and as he shuffled he stared out past the swing doors. He would shuffle then pause then repat and repeat and all the while staring out there across the desert. He turned to face the table but with a look so far away and suddenly Paul felt so insignificant, such was Friend's concentration on events far afield. The cards were placed on the table but no eye contact was made.

"Two each now then." said Friend, almost mumbling the words; still semi gagged by disappointment. "This is the end of the line, gentlemen."

He looked out across the desert again with a look of rabid determination and a resuscitated smile flickered on his face.

"Yes, the end of the line!"

Rat Pile cut. A 7 of Hearts.

Another reset.

As Detective Jerome and Sheila held each other, there was one almighty CLANG and an immense jolt, knocking everyone off their feet. The last carriage had been uncoupled and was slowing. Jerome clambered to his feet and looked out the window. The scenery had changed somewhat and it was more mountainous now with crags very close by.

There was a sound that was at first difficult to pick out from the tornado. Knowing that every piece of everything was a potential foothold on the situation, Jerome put his head right up to a window. This yielded nothing so he smashed the glass with the butt of the Gavel Gun.

The sound of a roaring river flooded the carriage with all the power a metaphor could muster. It was a roar indeed. It was the roar of a venomous – now awakened from its slumber – liquid serpent. It was the roar of an entity that, eons ago, had taken an oath to be merciless unto all who try to pet it. It was the roar that could never created by mere water but by an actual personality dwelling within wet DNA. It was the roar of the mighty river of Nudge Canyon.

Jerome saw the mammoth careering river a mere 20 yards ahead and that the tornado had torn the bridge away. What good a gun now?

"EVERYONE JUMP . . EVERYONE JUMP . . JUST JUMP" shouted Jerome as he began to smash windows on both sides of the carriage. This new shouted order, as needful as it was, mixed with pending death, inadvertently created sheer panic which tied people into knots as they dove and slipped and scrambled for the windows.

Self defeat was the name of the game now and, before a single soul had got out, the sheer tonnage of carriage toppled over the brink and in to the depths of ice cold, ever so, ever so ice cold, glassy rage.

The carriage entered the water with a mammoth, wet, wallop, displacing so much water that any creature dwelling remotely near the river bank was soaked, including birds in trees. The 60 foot long carriage pile-drived itself solidly in to the river bed, standing near perfectly on one end. It resembled a tower block.

Sand, gravel and shale, a poor foundation at best, shifted, causing the carriage to topple ever so slightly and lean against what meagre scaffolding of the bridge that still stood. All on board plummeted like boulders to the bottom end. The sound of people falling, their fall being funnelled in to an area no bigger than roughly five telephone booths, has no description yet written for it.

No room now to swing a cat. No room now to roll those dice. No room now to let the most slightly built "church mouse" come and lodge. No room now for plans. No room now for time itself. No room now for your bucket list. No room now to even scratch your nose.

Because Nudge Canyon didn't need the help of outlaws to rob you. No, robbery was the bedrock of the place, the crust of the place, the mantle, outer and inner core of the place. Soar the sky and clouds will rob you. Dig right through and you simply dig a grave for "Hope".

Oh, the unfairness of all this, as Nudge Canyon breezed through an audit of all it could dish out and proved, by actual demonstration, that its existence was no urban myth. The canyon would laughingly pass all stringent scrutiny from all departments, be they scientific, archaeological, poetical or other and ate "litmus tests" for breakfast.

Screams, shouts, moans, smashes, cracking and contorting limbs; the sadistically rude juxtaposition of precious life with metal, wood and freezing water, and all of it without invitation, was the new normal.

The carriage speared the river bed by 10 feet. Jerome had been standing at the locomotive end of the carriage and had managed to smash three windows before the drop. One of these was now under the river bed and the other two now let the river gush in, eager to reclaim its territory and destroy the little group of odd but dangerous squatters.

The detective was midway down the plummet pile of it all and fought in a portrait of madness to get to the top. The unapologetic climb was completed but white water simply hurtled in through the two windows, knocking desperate breath out of most and seeing just how much noise the average ear drum can take. Jerome shouted but couldn't really be heard over the roar.

"C'MON .. WE'VE GOT TO GET OUT .. C'MON.. OUT .. OUT.

The sodden and the broken shifted and began to resemble a group of people. They helped each other as best they could, aided, either ironically or sarcastically, by what buoyancy the rising water gave. A few lights and other fittings, jolted free by the impact, dropped with cruel randomness, adding macabre suspense to the scene.

It takes time for confusion to evolve in to organisation and by the time bearings were gained, the water had already bypassed the two windows. The gush was silenced but not stopped and the quick water rose on. "Direct and violent water rush" was now "subdued but oh so insidious danger" coming for you. Escape through the openings was impossible due to the incoming water pressure.

Gasping Jerome rubbed his stinging eyes and looked directly up to see that the top end of the carriage – the new ceiling – was about 30 feet up. He tried to ascertain where the river level was so he could smash those windows. It lay three windows up. He addressed the others:

"LOOK, WE'RE GONNA MAKE IT . . JUST WAIT TILL WE RISE UP A BIT THEN SMASH AND ESCAPE . . JUST TRUST ME . . WE'RE GONNA MAKE IT . . IS EVERYONE OK?"

Sheila seemed to just know she was second in command and spoke as she looked around while holding Melanie above water. Some were injured. Oh it was a cram, a real cram of bodies but at least all were present if not correct.

"YES . . WE'RE ALL OK . . LEAST I THINK SO" she shouted.

Paul stared at the pack but the pack wasn't going to cut itself. One wrong cut was all it was going to take to lose an indescribable amount. People who had been missing – some for decades – would remain missing for all time. Mysteries that may be either crimes or genuine bizarre and outlandish happenings would never be solved. No reuniting, no closure and just no end to the pain of it all. One wrong cut and all that would fall on Paul and spray like a shrapnel of misfortune upon all involved.

His eyes darted back and forth to Rat Pile and Friend. Both were as a book with no pages; nothing within to read and void of any information. The weight of it all pressed down upon the history teacher like a wine press and forced a reaction to come forth.

"I'm out." said Paul.

Friend never budged an inch but Paul could see in his eyes a storm brewing. A macabre courtesy was granted by Friend unto Paul, a courtesy of no consequences as the seconds ticked by. Paul thought about the day he'd seen the Nudge Canyon machine at the yard sale and the invisible fork in the road it represented. He thought about his flirtation with his addictive past. He had been an adulterer of sorts but just because your actions fall in to the category of "sorts" does not erase deadly consequences.

Yes, Friend was his enemy, Rat Pile was his enemy but neither would have been encountered at all had Paul not been such a complete and utter fool. Susan, wherever she was, would have been tripsying around the house, wherever *that* was, at this very moment, looking forward to her girls bowling night instead sobbing for her husband a world away. Come back "drudge life of a history teacher", come back "noisy school", come back "just getting ahead then falling behind again". Please, all of you, come back because it appears I love you after all.

BANG . . Friend hammered his fist on the table. Paul really jumped out of his skin, making Carla jump out of hers.

And when Friend hammered his fist, the carriage was pile driven another 10 feet in to the river bed with what truly sounded like a gurgle moan.

Jerome and Sheila looked at each other, appearing to be the only ones to notice. The two windows that had been allowing water in were now under the river bed but the jolt smashed the next two windows and the deluge continued.

The rising of the water, which would have provided an escape, as Jerome knew, had been cleverly counteracted by Friend and now the near drowning were still below the river level which was, again, three windows away. The far end of the carriage, that was the ceiling, was now a whole 10 feet lower. Things had changed for the worse.

Paul tried to ignore Friend's hearty laughter at making him and Carla jump, especially as Carla couldn't see who had struck the table. Paul looked at Carla who seemed to be breaking under all this and righteous indignation now joined the game.

"I said I'm *out!*"

Friend once again seemed to show restraint despite obviously possessing powers Paul did not that could very well annihilate all present.

"Are you *sure* about that, Paul?" asked Friend ever so calmly.

"Yes, totally!" came Paul's reply.

BANG . . Friend hammered the table.

The carriage sank into the river bed another 10 feet. The ceiling was now only 10 feet above and dead level with the river surface. Sheila, a rock and an anchor of a woman her whole adult life, started screaming as she knew what was happening. Jerome looked at her and drew the Gavel Gun out of reflex, intending to just blast the ceiling to smithereens.

"COVER YOUR EARS!!!" shouted Detective Jerome as he took aim at the ceiling. His shouting order went unnoticed in this situation. He looked around and saw near everyone crying, including Victor. None could tread water and it was the sheer crushed together aspect of the people that stopped them from sinking. Patrick and Lorraine were as one, as they had been since the start. Melanie and Sheila hugged and closed their eyes.

"Cut, Paul! Just cut the cards and we can all go home! When I say "Home" I mean that loosely of course!" said Friend.

At the same time Friend said that, in another world, Susan stood in front of the Nudge Canyon machine, which she utterly hated. The reels slowly span, ignoring Susan and just doing their own thing. Full of grief and rage, a formidable cocktail of its own that Susan, like Paul, had been forced to drink, she spat on the one armed bandit.

"The dominoes have nearly all toppled for the detective and those others, Paul." said Friend, forcefully. "How ironic for them to die a watery death in the middle of a desert! You've never faced such stakes as these, Paul! Now we are pushing the envelope way beyond the manufacturer's recommendations and twisting it in to new, teetering contortions! You are a pioneer! You gamble as none other! You sit here because you wanted to. All I did was show you the doorway in. That's all I *ever* do, show the foolish the doorway in! I did it with poor young Tom. I've lead so, *so many* to ruination but with no other save yourself have I ever managed to manoeuvre in to *this* position.. **NOW CUT!!!**"

Yes, Friend said all that, and it hurt, but there is no honour among thieves and Paul, again, mentally stepping aside for the briefest moment, realised he *had*, without anyone holding a gun up to his head, been a thief of happiness, not just to himself but to others. He sat in a one man circle in an empty village hall at an impromptu meeting of GAM ANON and finally owned up to it all. One advantage this immediately gave him was that, if he *was* a thief, he was under no obligation to act honourably. Now in an attitude of lawlessness, Paul just went for it.

"NO" he shouted at Friend. One smouldering second then.. **BANG**, Friend hammered on the table a third time.

BANG The Gavel Gun spoke and its voice blew a hole in the ceiling at the same moment the ceiling dropped another 10 feet. The drop hit most of the crushed and compacted passengers, hurting them and forcing everyone under water. Absolutely no way out now. A world of thrashing and holding and twisting and turning and all of it experienced through blurred and blood filled, underwater vision. A liquid car crusher was this. Life for all was down to seconds.

The hole made by the Gavel Gun was only big enough to put an arm and shoulder through, which Detective Jerome did. Muffled, bubbling screaming could be heard amidst the violent twist of it all. Adrenaline was in it all somewhere but you cannot breath adrenaline. Flashes of life memories jumped through minds but you cannot breathe memories. So much of life left undone and so many words that needed to be spoken now unspoken. The mass moved and twisted and strained and thrashed.

Suddenly, the detective felt a blow to his face which reeked of unfairness. The school bully of a blow came from something outside of the surrounding mayhem. It snapped the detective's head back and forced upon Jerome a huge gulp of river down his throat accompanied by a blue flash and the reflex need to vomit profusely. Blood from a broken nose flooded Jerome's bubbling, underwater and chaotic view.

At the same time he felt a vice grab his protruding arm. WALLOP . . another blow . . WALLOP . . another. Friend had bi-located and now stood on the end of the carriage as well as in the Rattler's. He stomped on Jerome's face then upon the carriage end, smashing the hole bigger; just bigger enough to lift Jerome up and through it with incredible strength.

Jerome was lifted right out and slammed on to buckling legs in front of Friend. He flailed like a fish just landed but still hooked. There was roughly 10% of the detective left for the fight now and he screamed with pain as Friend snapped the detective's left forearm with a crack.

"PARDON ME DETECTIVE, BUT I DON'T RECALL DIALLING 911!!!" shouted a gritted voice above all the sheer noise. Jerome's left eye was already beginning to swell horribly as he wailed in pain, a pain exacerbated by seeing his lower left forearm at near right angle to the rest.

"I said **NO!**" shouted Paul.

He felt Carla's finger nails digging in to his shoulder at this emphatic show of dissent. Friend still had his fist on the table. He had an expectant look on his face like that of an emperor used to getting it all his own way.

Still holding that expression, Friend straightened himself. He snapped his fingers and, as if in some trance that was not a trance but her own free will, Carla left Paul's side, rounded the table and stood next to Friend, the person she could not see. She stood, smiling at Paul with love. She stood in blissful unawareness.

Then Friend snapped his fingers again. The shotgun that hung on the wall behind the bar and just below that long mirror, flew through the air and in to Friend's hands. In a blink, Friend held it up to Carla's head, all the while giving Paul the "Emperor" look. As the echo of this action faded, the room was filled with the sound of Paul's powerful yet restrained breathing.

"You wouldn't. You just *wouldn't!*" said Paul. The shotgun was cocked with force and again pointed at Carla's head.

"WOULDN'T I? **JUST . . *WOULDN'T . . I?*"** shouted Friend through teeth so gritted they seemed to crunch. Paul swallowed one of those awful swallows. Friend saw this slip on Paul's poker face and verbally pounced.

"AND AFTER I'VE DISPATCHED YOUR GIRLFRIEND, I THINK I'LL PAY A VISIT TO SUSAN!"

Time slowed down now; slowed down in to smaller and smaller divisions; each division buckling under the strain of being loaded with more than the previous one. The history teacher reached out to cut, glanced over at the whistling bartender who was wiping the bar, then smiled at Friend.

"Yes, I believe you really *would!*"

Paul's hand moved to the side and lifted the Gambler's Doom cocktail. Friend's expression never changed one bit and in that un-changing Paul now saw the last page of the story. In that un-changing Paul read and now knew "what happened right at the end" and exactly "whodunnit". Everybody dying and Friend living was what happened right at the end. Paul knew he was now a gambler par excellence as what he was about to do would, one way or the other, sever all connection with himself and all things momentous, be they the loved or the loathed of Paul's life.

Gambling is a road built deliberately with no end as any victim of the gamble will testify but, just for once and here and now, it really *was* the end of the experience. With no higher exhilaration to feel after this one and nowhere left but down, Paul stood at the summit of Everest.

Time in the saloon had now stopped dead.

"Where are my manners?" said Paul with a sarcastically quizzical look as he lifted the drink. With the war on two fronts going well, Friend was just so close to his own personal finishing line that it blinkered him to Paul's actions.

The look on Friend's face was an iron sleeper pin hammered right through the world and out the other side yet Paul, now standing on the captain of summits, felt the exhilaration of a thousand old days, felt the fearlessness that the moment bestowed upon him and realised that, after this extreme fizzing twist of everything that Nudge Canyon was, came only the secondary and all gambling adrenaline would be drunk dry because no one climbs Everest twice.

For the first and last time, Paul's gambling addiction became his ally and lifted the fear just long enough for decisive actions. Sensible Paul lay wounded by the wayside but reckless Paul, the Paul of yesteryear, sprang forth, took the helm . . and spoke:

"Where are my manners? Please, join me!" said Paul as he threw the drink in to Friend's face before he could react.

Black tentacles from the thrown, blackest of drinks, slithered and gripped the enticer, throttling him. The shotgun was dropped as Friend screamed and pulled at the tentacles, staggering backwards. This noose of tar tentacles then shrank several sizes, cutting in to Friend's neck like cheese wire. The enticer fell to his knees as he gagged and gagged. He grabbed at the death noose he now wore and tried to roar a stifled roar.

For the last time, Paul looked in to Friend's eyes. The look of shock was pitiful to see, even on an enemy. Friend, who had been so used to lording it over Paul, was now forced, in his final moments, to go cold turkey on that exquisite feeling of power.

Carla snapped out of her trance and could now see Friend. She picked up the shotgun and fired, the force of which blew Friend's belly clean out his back and sent him sliding across the floor and out of existence. The recoil of the shotgun hurt Carla as it pushed her backwards across the table in to Paul, who instinctively wrapped his arms around the western beauty as he caught her. Like before, Paul began re-entry in to his world and this time he had no choice but to take Carla with him.

Suddenly, as he gripped Jerome, Friend froze; he just froze in the middle of it all, staring straight ahead, becoming the only stationary thing in a 50 mile radius. He looked like he'd sampled a new taste for the very first time and the jury was out as to whether he liked it or not.

Then the jury was in.

Friend let go of Jerome's arm and raised his fist to strike the death blow to the detective in a last attempt to cut his losses.

"PAUL WAS ABOUT TO FALL OFF ONE WAGON .. *BIG TIME!!!"* shouted Friend as he grabbed Detective Jerome by his hair, **"NOW YOU'RE GOING TO FALL OFF ANOTHER!!!"**

Detective Jerome was dying soon and he knew it. An arm reached out from the hole in the carriage end and grabbed the detective's leg as others fought their last for life.

The last two chess pieces stood on a tornado engulfed board with one square left out of 64 and one of those pieces had to be evicted.

But, as on the carriage, Jerome had used that one second of Friend's inaction to raise the Gavel Gun, which, in his arrogance, Friend had ignored. Jerome now rammed that very gun up under Friend's chin as he shouted himself completely out of charge:

"I DON'T DO ONE LINERS . . I DO JUSTICE!!!" and all monstrous and deafening calamity ended with one firm pull of a trigger. The Gavel Gun barked before Detective Jerome had even finished shouting. Friend fell limply and impotent in to the torrent and was gone. Being borne aloft in to the tornado was far too poetic a death for the trouble maker called "Friend". No Valhalla for *him*, he was simply swept away like driftwood.

18

Hellos and Goodbyes

The bottom of the carriage, that held the drowning, gave way. All within plummeted down and out in to Paul's living room. The vertical carriage was now a birth canal. Susan had no time to react as a thousand gallons of river water, mingled with passengers, gatecrashed through a supernatural hole in the ceiling and in to her suburban world. It all dropped like a big wet rag, causing breakers of chaos.

For a moment, the room was filled as the carriage had been. Furniture was tossed around and smashed on the stormy and unexpected shoulder high sea. Susan, uniformed officer Elaine and another uniformed officer were toppled like skittles as a rude and unexpected tributary of the mighty river of Nudge Canyon stomped a wet stomp into sleepy suburbia and careered everywhere. Scream after scream came from Susan as she beheld the pile of the gasping. There was no time to think or be rational or lay down the law, only time to ride it out. The water flowed in to every room of the house then out the front and back doors. There were two squad cars outside and an officer immediately called for back up.

The sound of survivors drinking air they were thirsty for seemed synchronised and almost choir like as the gasping filled their lungs with extreme zeal as they twisted and turned to throw off death. Susan and Elaine staggered to their feet and immediately Susan recognised Paul, who had arrived, along with Carla, via a different route, dropping 6 feet in to the living room with a splash and an awful grunt. Susan just dove on to her husband.

"PAUL . . . PAUL . . ."

Paul said nothing, he just looked. A smile tried to get to the surface again and again as he closed his eyes and accepted Susan's power embrace.

Uniformed officer Elaine saw Detective Jerome and went to his assistance. He lay there, savouring that invisible drug everyone is hooked on called "Air". Water level lowering, Elaine helped him sit drippingly upright. She was shocked at the detectives battered appearance and broken arm. He looked at Elaine and all around then back to Elaine, reaching out and taking her hand, which felt so warm. She helped him stand and seated him on the flotsam of a sofa. She saw that her superior had been through a monster of an experience and put officer etiquette to one side. She hugged the detective very tentatively, seeing his terrible injuries.

"We made it . . we made it . . didn't we?" said Detective Jerome, punch drunk and holding Elaine as if she was his sweetheart. Elaine knew that it was the adrenaline of the moment that was keeping her superior from fainting but that it would come to that very soon.

"Yes Sir, you all made it. Welcome home! Look, help is already here! I'll alert your family."

"Help *them*, Officer, go . . *GO"* Their pseudo romantic embrace was separated by two medics.

Soon, the room was filled with survivors, police officers and ambulance technicians. The water was now down to six inches deep, making for a world of splashing and squelching as people to and fro'd. One by one, the survivors who were able, were placed on righted furniture on flooded floor. Sheila sat on a chair, a soft and comfortable chair and realised she was back in her world. Her head darted around just to make sure it *was* familiar suburbia. Her gazes were halted abruptly as her eyes fell on Patrick and Lorraine.

Both Patrick and Lorraine had aged 30 years and were now fully middle aged. The shock of this perfectly natural yet greatly accelerated process would have flummoxed the scientific world had they but seen it. Events caused by the unplanned collision of two worlds were creating a room full of never to be seen again happenings and those fortunate enough to be in the room at the time knew they'd never be believed. Everyone who needed it was now being attended to. Outside was a feast of flashing lights from squad cars and ambulances. Neighbours were now gathering and it would only be a matter of time before the media arrived.

Susan hugged and kissed Paul intensely, in between a paramedic taking Paul's blood pressure.

Paul suddenly spoke .. "CARLA .." He loosened Susan's grip and went to his friend.

Carla lay semi-comatose by her forced entry in to another world. What little she saw of Paul's world: people dressed nicely but strangely different, lights without flames, soft furnishings – albeit topsy turvy soft furnishings, a person who shone a little, too bright, light in to her eyes and just a different atmosphere to it all, put a bemused smile upon her face. Paul instantly saw that Carla was ageing rapidly but Susan, who had never seen young Carla as Paul had, never knew the difference, seeing an obviously late middle aged woman lying before her.

Carla's eyes met Susan's and both women smiled. Both knew instinctively who the other was. In an instant both knew that the other loved Paul but, here and now, it didn't matter in the least. Susan again smelled Carla's wonderful perfume and could now finally put a face to the fragrance. Despite being at a disadvantage, friendly and loving Carla spoke first with a struggle.

"Mighty right fine to meet you Ma'am!" she said to Susan.

"And lovely to meet you too!" replied Susan, taking Carla's hand. Carla raised her head a little and scanned her surroundings, strainedly.

"Is this your house? My, it looks lovely!"

"If I knew you were coming I'd have tidied up a bit!"

"Oh hush now, it looks just fine!"

Gone, finally gone, was the hurtful world of the Nudge Canyon. Here, finally here, was the care and love of another world; new for some, a taken for granted luxury for others. Tenderness replaced the scorpion's tail. Giving replaced robbery. The ability to smile replaced anxiety of heart. In this new world, with new rules, even a meandering tumbleweed could finally find purpose. Yes, a new and better world this indeed was; but it was not a perfect one.

Sheila was basically ok and went to Melanie's side as she was placed on to a stretcher, paramedics checking her vitals, an act they were unaware was of little use.

Again Sheila saw that, like Patrick and Lorraine, the years Melanie had skipped were not going to be denied and had caught up with her, taking her hurriedly down the path of extreme old age to death's door. She looked well over 100 years old. Melanie was on a well meaning but futile drip and clutched her very pretty handbag.

She cried "Wait!" loudly and the paramedics halted. This one word utterance by Melanie carried with it an air of confidence and sound health that, up to that point, it had not; giving again, like those few minutes in the tunnel, a glimpse in to Melanie's true personality, which had been insidiously pick pocketed from her psyche by her time on the carriage.

Sheila's out of time and bewildered friend, who had been such a comfort to her, opened her bag and took out the beautiful fountain pen, handing it to Sheila. This action silently spoke the fact that they were not going to meet again. Sheila's eyes welled up and overflowed unashamedly. She took the pen with reverence and kissed Melanie's hand, smiling broadly for her dying friend. Melanie once again reached forth, this time with difficulty, and, not so firmly this time, wiped tears from Sheila's cheeks when it should have been the other way around.

"Will you think of me from time to time, my dear Melanie of sorts?" asked Melanie.

"No, Melanie," replied Sheila, taking Melanie's hand and forcibly kissing her palm over and over, "I'll think of you from all the time to all the time."

By this time there were five squad cars keeping the crowd back, forming a semi circle, reminiscent of a melodramatic TV serial wagon train's defensive set up against "attacking" Native Americans. Three ambulances sat within this automotive cordon. The crowd was fairly large and, inevitably, the media had arrived. It wasn't the "Big Guns" media, more the local newspaper. Nosey, sensation seeking crews from the bigger news outlets would take longer to crank in to life but nosey, sensation seeking *neighbors* stood sentry during the interim. On the law enforcement grapevine, word had got out that Detective Jerome had returned, bringing much relief mingled with some incredulity and restrained excitement as the detective was well respected and liked. Back inside, activity had plateaued. Shock and fear had subsided to a great degree like the supernatural river deluge.

They had seen each other almost immediately but now for the first time in all this, Paul made eye contact with Detective Jerome. What do you say to a person after something like *this*? You say nothing, you just nod, which is what both men did. A world of ferocious activity and experience was summed up, almost insultingly, by the nod of a head.

Jerome continued to look, now a touch narrow eyed, at Paul as the history teacher interacted with others. The detective just wondered about the "all" of it and the "why" of it and in doing so, for a brief spell, Detective Jerome turned philosopher, theologian and poet as he sat, broken and smashed, pondering the layers upon layers of recent experience that clamoured for his attention and order. He felt a touch naïve and green, those feelings humbling the detective somewhat. Having been simply guzzled by an experience, all he did now, all he wanted to do now and all he *could* do now was think of his wife and two daughters.

The number of people in the room seemed to remain constant as departing patients and paramedics were replaced by more of the same. Officers came and went. Most entered the building just to see Jerome with their own eyes. They would speak in to their shoulder mics "Yeah, it's him!" then depart. Elaine was put out by this and, although understanding, vocalised her disdain to several officers as it was obvious by now that there was no "crime" to deal with.

Those survivors who could, regardless of their original "world", hugged, even if they weren't given to that kind of thing. Patrick and Lorraine were gurney'd out to ambulances. Jerome looked on as two of the carriage passengers had sheets drawn over their heads. Force of habit caused the detective to think of pending autopsy reports to discern if cause of death was drowning or accelerated ageing as with Melanie. His thoughts were interrupted by a concerned voice.

"Sir, we should get you to the hospital." said Elaine.

"Is that a direct order, officer?!" he smirked.

"Well you can take it that way and I'd appreciate it! So would the guys!" said Elaine.

"No that's ok officer. I'll go along later if it'll make you happy though!"

Elaine smiled and again forgot herself, kissing Detective Jerome on the head. She stepped outside. Jerome was just happy to let others do the work. He let his head rest back on the couch and felt sleep gaining on him.

There was a constant hum coming from somewhere that was hypnotic and eye lid closing, that only someone present, who was not caught up in the freneticism of it all, would notice. Detective Jerome noticed it now, as did Susan, who was in a silent, deep embrace with Paul. Susan, instantly recognising a sound that was not part of the usual living room menagerie of the audible, semi broke from Paul and looked around as the hum, mingled with slow, dainty clicking, continued. It was almost as if the sound was trying to tip toe past and avoid detection. She stood up, distracted. Jerome noticed this.

"What?" he asked briskly.

Susan headed for the Nudge Canyon machine. Detective Jerome zeroed in on Susan's look, posture, expression and thoughts all at once and immediately.

"WHAT? SUSAN . . WHAT?" he demanded.

"SUSAN SWEETHEART, WHATS THE MATTER?" shouted Paul. There was no getting through to Susan. Detective Jerome struggle-stood and followed Paul's wife. Susan stood in front of the one armed bandit. She gazed at it with utter disdain. Jerome and Paul stood beside her.

The reels on the machine were turning. The lights on the machine were turning on and off but with no joy or flow to their actions. The cockiness of the Nudge Canyon machine had turned to mourning. Sheila's SOS pendant note with its message came to mind for Jerome.

"I was tricked to come here. The bandit machine is responsible"

"Step back." ordered Jerome, ushering Susan and Paul away and backwards as he drew the Gavel Gun.

But the Nudge Canyon machine was a step ahead.

Immediately, the three reels span to a blur for a tenth of a second then utterly, and with a wallop, smashed to a halt. All three reels displayed total black around their entire circumference. Gone now the pictures and colours, black and only black was now the prize. All this transpired before Jerome could even raise his gun.

The portal in the ceiling opened up, and again, two worlds grudgingly rubbed shoulders. A roar came from the cavernous mouth like portal. The sound vibrated the entire room. All present, stood, frozen in shock, covering their ears.

Some fled and it would never be held against them. Paul grabbed Susan tightly.

Again, the portal roared an elongated song of deep grief then stopped, leaving a silence, nearly as loud, that heralded something awful was about to happen.

With a third roar, Rat Pile fell through and in to the living room. He crumpled in a huge heap. Detective Jerome turned and aimed his gun then lowered the weapon. He did not recognise the outlaw and assumed he had been on the carriage with the others. Sheila however, screamed and pointed at Rat Pile.

"HE'S EVIL . . HE'LL KILL US . . HE'S EVIL"

Before Sheila had finished screaming, the Gavel Gun was re-aimed at crumpled Rat Pile. The outlaw raised himself to standing, looking around, gagging psychologically as he was being force fed a new world, like his contemporaries who had come through before him. Jerome saw Rat Pile's side arm.

"DROP IT . . DROP YOUR WEAPON . . I SAID DROP IT"

Now Rat Pile had found his bearings and saw Jerome. His hand instantly moved to his side because that was the rule and that was the law and that was "just the way it went" with Rat Pile. Sheila screamed. Uniformed officer Elaine and three other uniforms rushed through the doorway, alerted by the commotion. They too saw Rat Pile and drew their weapons.

"SHEILA . . GET OVER HERE" Sheila ran the ten feet to Susan and Paul. They huddled down in a corner.

"DO NOT DRAW THAT WEAPON. I WILL KILL YOU" shouted Jerome, because that was the rule and that was the law and that was "just the way it went" with the detective.

But there was more chance of Detective Jerome winning the lottery on his 200th birthday than there was of Rat Pile not going for his gun that never needed to be reloaded. Outnumbered 5 to 1 and with pure death scraping its hoof and snorting at him from North and East, Rat Pile made to draw.

An ear splitting volley, wedded to smoke and a choke of gunpowder, erupted without apology from all law enforcement present. Rat Pile was hit by the flying lead plague. The volley span him somewhat but no more.

The reason for this was that Rat Pile had entered the world eight foot tall and proportionately wide. He staggered and drew at the same time. Rat Pile's Gun was now like a cannon, the circumference of its barrel was the same as a man's wrist.

Now the outlaw fired.

Jerome dove aside as the shot blew a four foot hole in the wall behind him. The only help this elicited from the outside was a flash as a photo was taken.

Immediately, Rat Pile turned and fired at the four officers. Two dove to safety but two were hit and killed. They did not slump but blew apart and through another four foot hole in the front wall. Mass screaming and panic began among the crowd outside, who had been all too eager to witness calamity as long as they were not involved. But now they *were* involved and conscripted in to proceedings. People scrambled up the grassy embankment that was opposite Paul and Susan's, slipping ridiculously, fingers digging in to the turf, standing and clambering over friends without a thought. No honour among thieves, or, it would seem, the formerly nosey, now deadly desperate.

Rat Pile emerged from the hole in the wall like a stinky animal whose hibernation in Nudge Canyon was over and stood to his full height. Officers, despite their training, gasped for a second before releasing another, more sporadic volley at the outlaw. More units were arriving.

The outlaw roared at the hits he was taking then fired at one of the flashing objects he saw in front of him which was a police car. One shot from Rat Pile's tank like gun and the car exploded. Bystanders and one officer were hit and fell as the gigantic flame flash lit up the entire street. A helicopter soared well above which momentarily attracted Rat Pile's attention. He didn't know what to make of it so ignored it, refocusing on ground threats.

One of the newly arrived units fired tear gas. The gas canister punched through the air with faint smoke trail, bouncing off Rat Pile, landing at his feet, hissing its smokey venom upon the outlaw. Again, Rat Pile did not know this object, kicking it slightly to one side as tear gas rose. He choked up and staggered a little then aimed and fired at the huge target of people and vehicles he saw before him, all of whom he now knew had declared war on him. Vehicles blew apart again and again and again, parts of which landed on neighbouring buildings. The human cost was keeping pace with destroyed property as people were falling like flies.

Paul, Susan and Sheila escaped through the hole created when Rat Pile had fired at Detective Jerome. They circled the house, emerging round the front, about thirty feet from the eight foot monster.

One snap of a head turn and Rat Pile saw them, in particular, Paul.

Temporarily relieved of any opposition due to the carnage he had caused, Rat Pile turned and strode teeteringly towards the trio, kicking the fallen and wounded aside. He aimed and fired. The tear gas had grogged him somewhat, causing the shot to go wide. The fist sized bullet blew asunder the corner of the house, making the roof slump to nearly ground level. The body of law enforcement started to regain composure and shots tore in to Rat Pile as he pursued Paul. Crimson splashes appeared all over Rat Pile's body that twitched and jerked with each hit.

It only took a few strides and the outlaw had caught up with Paul, who shoved Susan and Sheila aside. A limping and bloodied officer in a charred uniform grabbed both women and dragged them away, ignoring Susan's frantic pleas to Paul.

The history teacher knew his own stupidity and weakness had caused all this. He thought it could all be reversed if he atoned in kind. Paul sank his head and stood in a dock of his own making. He stopped fleeing and, as Rat Pile took aim, stood to hear the verdict of some intangible jury.

What was well camouflaged in all this was the fact that the bodies of three dead officers had begun to twitch and jolt. They twitched and jolted and slid towards each other, the bodies turning over disrespectfully upon hitting some minor obstacle such as a rock or divet.

Unceremoniously, the bodies rolled and contorted with desecration towards each other as marionettes in your nightmare. The flashing of various emergency lights made a mockery of the sight.

The three dead officers reached each other with flailing limbs. They stopped moving and rested in a heap of the disjointed and the blue. Then movement returned, but this time it was a slow slow deliberately pressing movement like an embrace. The three were dead but now, together, they at least did a good imitation of life. They entwined and rose, changing shape; not from human to something else but to something more human than human.

Up and up rose the limbed form, shedding its former and taking on the new. Many limbs became reduced in number but greatly increased in size. A new person, moulded out of human clay, began to take shape.

Two heartbeats later and a single eight foot tall person, *another* eight foot tall person, now stood. This person, this latecomer to the party, was the equal of Rat Pile in every aspect. He drew his first breath, opened his eyes and saw his first sight. The Sheriff of Nudge Canyon now stood complete, walrus moustache and all.

Rat Pile immediately recognised his enemy and turned to fire but the tenacious lawmaker had drawn already while in the womb of his creation time and fired his gun that never needed to be reloaded. Instinct within the law keeping DNA of the sheriff gave him a split second time advantage and he fired. The cannon of a gun banged for its life. Rat Pile took a hit to his left shoulder but returned fire.

For a history making 30 seconds that power chiselled memories in to all who witnessed, the polar opposites fired and fired. Bits of each would splatter and spray blood. Missed shots careered out and in to a new world, smashing anything behind. It was "all or nothing hour" at the "Last chance you will ever get . . *ever*" saloon. Blast after blast turned the immediate surroundings in to some sort of insane asylum. Nobody stepped in to call halt. Nobody *could* step in to call halt.

Suddenly, the shots ceased, but why? Not of *this* world came the ability to decide the end. The sheriff and Rat Pile stood, both wounded to the hilt. They swayed and teetered in the wind of death their actions had summoned. The sheriff, for the first time in his life, looked ill and defeated but never broke eye contact with the outlaw. Rat Pile's expression was one of defiance to the end.

The sheriff crumpled to his knees then fell forward with a wallop. Immediately, he started to change and reduce in size until the three dead officers again lay side by side. The corpses suddenly drew in massive breaths in near perfect unison and were alive again. Alive but in no fit state to enforce the law. Rat Pile, dying with wounds, turned to face Paul.

Suddenly, Rat Pile's stomach exploded outwards as Detective Jerome, emerging directly behind Rat Pile, unloaded the Gavel Gun to the fullest. The gun spoke, exhausting its leaden vocabulary. Paul was splattered with innards and for a brief moment, thought they were his own. Rat Pile sank to his knees. His muscles contracted, pulling the trigger. The shot twanged past Paul's head and hit the telegraph pole behind him. The pole severed. Jumping, imp like sparks, flew liberally with loud slicing electric buzz crackles as the pole fell. Ping after ping of differing octaves sounded as electric wires strained and snapped. Paul was grabbed by the bloodied officer and jerked to safety as all electrical landed squarely on Rat Pile.

The outlaw started to char instantly. He screamed and as he screamed he twisted and as he twisted he wrapped the electric cables around himself.

More tear gas poured in.

All around fled, leaving Rat Pile to his fate. He writhed and writhed the dance of the tortured and dying, becoming blacker and blacker, losing bodily definition. His electrical shroud embraced him tightly. All around where he lay was being singed to the point of combustion. Electricity arced from the fallen bandit to any un-damaged vehicles. It leap frogged along ten or so cars, setting off alarms.

But any dance lasts only so long.

Rat Pile's writhing dance of justice slowly subsided. He turned and moaned meekly, a burned out and unrecognisable black twist of burned flesh. The timer hit zero, as it had always done for the outlaws and now the last one of them – Rat Pile – was dead. He had rode the silver, moon soaked desert, dishing it all out generously and with zeal, now he had been dealt it in the same measure; electrocuted, gassed and lethally injected with lead.

Detective Jerome buckled to one knee as Elaine ran to his side. The detective had just had enough of this case and considering he'd been killed twice, that wasn't surprising. In a short time, ambulance technicians were able to assist and the detective finally allowed himself to be taken off to hospital. Uniformed officer Elaine rode with him in the ambulance. Paperwork could wait.

The scene now was one of fire hoses and life saving professionalism. Stubborn tear gas refused to discriminate and hung around to hinder where it had helped moments before. Sounds of car alarms and moaning people and burning buildings and collapsing buildings still seemed like near silence, coming after the mayhem as they did. On TV from one end of the nation to the other, sports games, celebrity interviews, lifestyle programs and soap opera cliff hangers were interrupted to bring news of events.

Paul held Susan and they both held Sheila as all three were ushered to a waiting ambulance. Suddenly, Paul thought of Carla, still inside the house.

"CARLA!" he shouted, running towards the hole in the side wall.

"PAUL . . PAUL . . *WAIT* . ." screamed Susan, fighting free from a restraining police officer and stumbling after her husband. They both re-entered and swooped on Carla, who was having difficulties of her own. Paul and Susan knelt on either side of her, trying to stifle the shock at what they saw.

Because Carla was now well in to her 90's and fading fast. Her sumptuous dark hair was now grey-white and flimsy, the butterfly clip she wore nearly falling out as it had no foundation to cling to. She was barely recognisable. Speeding age hurtled over her being. Her breathing was becoming obvious and obtrusive. She was a fish out of water that couldn't be thrown back. Her magnificent "Rattler's Tail Issue" dress remained unchanged and now looked several sizes too big and ridiculous on the body of a very old woman. She looked at Susan and smiled then, with great difficulty, reached up and took the wolf whistle of a clip from her straggly hair and placed it in Susan's hand. Susan just broke down at this gesture.

As she had held Paul lovingly in her world, so now Paul carefully cradled Carla up and held her lovingly in his.

Carla looked as deep in to Paul's eyes as she could. She looked at Paul and he knew she wanted to say so much to him but was unable to. She would twist in pain and arch her back as death pulled her from the world. Susan wept solidly, kissing Carla's hand over and over.

Again, Paul tried to do what a man's gotta do and spoke, violently forcing words past a barrier of emotional awfulness and a real flood of tears. The force required to speak at this moment robbed his words of the tender tone he wanted to impart.

"*Carla .. Carla ..*"

"I did it Paul,", replied Carla, in between dying, "I got you home!" Paul drew Carla close to him, totally close.

"Yeah, you did .. you said you would and you *did*, buddy! But I can't get you back!"

Carla placed her hand round the back of Paul's head to draw him closer, wanting one thing only. Paul looked at Susan, who was sobbing solidly. Paul's wife smiled as best she could, considering, and nodded as emphatically as she could, considering, giving her blessing on what Paul would do next.

Since the beginning, songs have been written about "two worlds colliding" and now, for the first time since the beginning, here it was, in the most literal and romantic way. Paul allowed Carla to pull him right in and they kissed their first – and last – kiss. They separated slightly but eyes remained locked. Carla reached up with an aged hand and stroked Paul's lips with her thumb then caressed his cheek.

"Darlin', I wouldn't *want* to go back!"

And when Carla uttered those – her last words – and died, Nudge Canyon claimed its very last victim. Carla slowly fell limp and died in the arms of her "darlin' Paul", the elusive love of her life. For Paul, Carla had searched twice and found twice. For Paul, she would have searched again and again, forever, in any and all worlds.

So, tell me, just how do you delve inside a person's heart? How do you make headway in to the secret place we all have? This cleverly concealed, yet massive garden, full of topiaried longings and neatly pruned and arranged beds of scented sentiment, is never open to the public. Do you need an invitation? Maybe but not always. To truly visit a person's heart it appears you can sometimes do it almost by accident.

You are walking along the street when you see someone approach. You have spoken to this person once or twice and initially got on well with them. You smile and they smile back. You both stop and you say how nice it is to bump in to them again. You show a measure of interest in their life.

Suddenly, with a gasp, you find yourself standing alone at one end of a long corridor; a long and virgin white corridor. You indeed gasp at these sudden and pristine surroundings but what is a corridor if it does not lead somewhere?

At the far end you see an ornate door, also white. The ceiling above you, the walls surrounding you and the floor beneath you are flooded with the ornate. Yes, the very floor of that corridor is so artistic you will surely be arrested for simply walking upon it, but it is yours for the taking so you walk towards that ornate door.

As you draw near you hear a sound. A flickering and flickering. Delicate is this sound so it intrigues but does not frighten. The door is so ornate that anything that lives behind it must have a magnitude clean off the scale. You press your ear up against the door and swither, not wishing to upset the fine balance of this unbelievable set up. But how did you get into that corridor? Just *how?* You must press on so you push the 20 foot tall door open.

And then you see a thousand and yet more thousands of sparrows flying round and round. The swoosh of their wing beats cools your brow and blows a charm upon you. The delicate whirlwind playfully tussles your hair with its bold whisper. Looking up, it seems you cannot see the end of this feathered funnel that appears to ascend upwards to infinity. Round and round and round flutter the tireless. One or two or three land on your shoulders and you begin to cry at their acknowledgement of you. Your eyes wander and suddenly you see the puzzle of it all.

These who live behind the ornate door are not trapped there, for they fly within a beautiful bandstand like room, open on all sides and leading out to the countryside on a glorious day. They fly with power but they do not flee. They are obviously born for freedom but do not take it. You stand perplexed. Then you realise that those sparrows are feelings, human feelings.

You see, you are standing in your friend's heart.

Those birds are indeed trapped after all, trapped by the fear of getting hurt. They have heard sad tales from the outside of just how awful it can be, so trade freedom for safety. Yes, we all know only too well why those sparrows reject their freedom, don't we?

Instantly, you are back on the street with your new friend. She smiles and says she hopes to see you again soon! You know from her smile and body language that she means it. Her words are the affidavit that you really *did* see those sparrows deep within the chambers of her heart and that you may be allowed another visit soon.

No one ever sees this amazing spectacle from one end of the year to the other .. but *you* did!

No one ever gains entry through slick television commercials full of small print or the half-hearted promises from "friends" who also come with "small print" ..

.. but *you* waltzed right in!

You wonder how you did it. It was the last thing on your mind. You hardly tried. It all just came naturally to you. You ponder and ponder but don't recall getting a gilt edged invitation in a sumptuous red envelope. You don't remember a limousine pulling up at your door to deliver a telegram. All you remember are your usual, mundane ways, peppered with a kind word here and there along with the odd joke thrown in.

On and on you ponder, unable to see the wood for the trees, never realising that as little as a single, or a few, kind words, will *always* gain you access to that magnificent room where flutter those friendly sparrows who perpetually shun their freedom.

In the chaos of the Rattler's, Paul had accidentally stumbled over the threshold of Carla's heart without even trying. Carla too had perceived that Paul was not of her world and her intrigue had hastened in to love for the mild mannered history teacher. Now, in a bomb site that the house now was, the seam of honest and true love that had lain untouched deep within Carla's heart and had been stumbled upon and effortlessly mined by Paul, yielded its last ounce of gold and at least a fair few feathered friends flew the feathered funnel, finally finding freedom and fulfilment.

As Paul held Carla and Susan sobbed for Carla, Paul looked over to the Nudge Canyon machine, his attention being gained by movement in the corner of his eye. This random movement, that spoke of panic and disorder, was accompanied by pieces of one armed bandit junk, colliding and scattering, ousted by an angry, dying, entity within.

Paul, as no other owner of the Nudge Canyon machine, now saw – because it was forced out in to the open – the true spirit behind the colourful and tempting giver of lemons and crowns and dollars and peace and pretty girl cuddles.

In amongst the smashed bandit remains lay a scorpion, the size of a man, a scorpion in the anguish of death, upturned and ugly beyond its norm, because if there is one thing uglier than ugly, it is upturned, exoskeleton ugly.

The scorpion's segmented legs jabbed and flailed upwards, pathetically seeking a foothold. Each leg seemed to die in its own right, jabbing and stabbing the air independently of the others, clicking and snatching for reality.

Slaves to their taxonomic classification, emotionless arachnid claws snapped shut again and again as the crowning glory of any and all scorpions – its tail – now redundant and unable to right the scorpion and discharge its awful duty, appeared to drink its own venom as it swung and stung with impotence and abandonment, scattering whatever got in its orbit. The upturned aspect of the winding down hideous indicated that the battle, as far as *its* involvement was concerned, was truly over.

Paul turned and, more gently than gently, lay Carla down. He stroked her lips with his thumb then lightly caressed her cheek, as she had done to Paul mere minutes before.

"All my love, forever and ever!" he whispered.

Susan and Paul both helped each other stand as paramedics knelt and dealt with Paul's sweetheart from another world. Carla was placed on to a gurney and taken away, taking a mammoth piece of Paul's heart with her.

Paul cupped Susan's face and saw that she had vicariously been through so much. This had happened because, when they were married, they had both made vows before God and, as such, had become one flesh. Paul's experiences in Nudge Canyon had had some sort of acupuncture effect on Susan and had dragged her in to it all on a level way more than just the emotional. Paul felt that many apologies, from himself to his devoted wife, whether called for or not, would be given to Susan in days and years to come.

"C'mon" said Paul, "Let's just go anywhere!" Susan smiled then buried her head in to Paul's chest.

As they turned to walk out and in to whatever now faced them, Paul once again glanced over to the Nudge Canyon machine. It surprised him, yet did not surprise him, that the scorpion was gone.

The one armed bandit was now a collapsed pile of wooden and metal junk that blended in with the suburban war zone. It lay there, a pathetic heap of outards and innards, not even good enough to build a dog kennel out of. A "bully that had been stood up to" was the machine. An "elected official, caught in hypocrisy and exposed", was the machine. It had died when no one, but Paul, was watching, so as to avoid the shame. Its home was now, fittingly, any given dumpster.

A lingering and hurtful legacy that would remain, at least for Paul, was the fact that the machine he had intended to sell . . but *didn't*; the machine he had intended to smash . . but *didn't*; had proved, by actual demonstration, that "saying" and "doing" are two different things.

GAM ANON would never have come in to existence if the temptation to gamble came with a glimpse of what Paul had just seen. Motive is behind any action taken in life and if your motives are fine then fine, but if they are essentially unkind and selfish, even slightly, then that requires a "Trojan Horse" approach.

Because, granted, a one armed bandit doesn't *look* like a scorpion . .

. . but it is.

19

Then what happened?

Considering his injuries, Detective Jerome, after a two night stay, checked out just fine from the hospital. He had a few good bruises and one cracking scar to show that would stay with him, but otherwise good to go. Six weeks later, his face was recognisable again and the cast came off his left arm.

Initially, he was advised to take additional time off. These few days turned in to a week that threatened to become forever as the detective seriously considered retiring, so he could devote more time to that wife and those two daughters and as much time, as his wife would allow, anyway, to renovating his '68 Dodge Charger. He chatted to this very wife about it and even took counsel from uniformed officer Elaine but, as happens, decided to continue on the force. At 51, Detective Jerome wasn't a young man anymore but neither was he a museum exhibit. He reasoned that he still had another ten years or so in him.

"When crime retires, so will I" had always been his mantra anyway.

The problem was, just how *do you* write the report?

As he typed, Detective Jerome occasionally thought he'd turned author, such was the outlandish and fantastical tale he lay down on paper. An outlandish and fantastical tale that had begun when a forlorn looking woman, named Susan, walked in to the police station, holding a scratched and defaced SOS pendant.

Lots of people saw eight foot tall Rat Pile, so there was no arguing about that; but only Jerome, Paul and Sheila, along with Patrick and Lorraine, had been to the other world and lived to tell of it. The police chief, although staggered by what Jerome's report contained, unhesitatingly gave Detective Jerome every benefit of every doubt, such was the respect the detective had reaped through years of battling crime.

Knowing the un-hesitating media would inconveniently act as a siren and awaken the slumbering entity of conspiracy theorists et al, who followed the story like bloodhounds, the two men decided to make another, more believable report and make *that* the official version. This fake and more believable report would be as a bone to those hounds. In the report, Rat Pile was now a drug crazed homicidal maniac who trifled with the law and got his comeuppance. An eight foot tall sheriff with a walrus moustache . . *what* eight foot tall sheriff with a walrus moustache? It all started with Rat

Pile and ended with Rat Pile. Case closed. No conspiracy here.

The Chief and Jerome visited all survivors and informed them of this "new" version of events. They advised all involved to resist financial inducements and to stick to the story. If asked by the media – and asked they *would* be – they were instructed to simply reply: "It's a police matter now. My involvement was minimal and I have nothing further to say".

With a wry smile on his face, Detective Jerome handed two SOS pendants over to Sheila.

"I believe these are yours!" he quipped. "Some good citizen handed them in to lost property! I've seen these on TV. Good idea if you ask me. I mean, just look what they did for you!"

***

And with the return of certain people came glorious reunions! For, to have returned unto you, that which you thought was gone *forever*, was nothing less than resurrection itself! To embrace what had become, for you, a misty image in your mind's eye. To feel, for real, that which had become intangible. To replace memories of being squeezed and squeezing with the actions themselves! A chance, at last, to say those things you regretted not saying and to hear your words echo in full reciprocation! A chance, at last, to prove your vows. A chance, at last, to plough new furrows of romance together. A chance, at last, to share. A chance, at last, to move on and on and on.

You lived without them .. now you are forever with them!

A solar flare of flashbulbs erupted the moment Sheila and Andrew Burness embraced for the first time in a long time. They just held on to each other as the media lapped up pure gold. Welded to each other it seemed, were the couple. The media in all its forms would orbit Sheila and Andrew for the coming months. Why explore outer space when life on Earth can be *this* interesting?

There was nothing to avert this attention quickly. The "slow escape" approach was adopted by the couple, which entailed simply giving in and neither running or attempting to hide. Let the world feast for a while and it will soon tire of you. Just let the novelty run its course and peter out naturally.

Because of Sheila's safe return, Andrew Burness was finally above reproach concerning the disappearance of his wife. Concerning this, there was now nowhere to go for the rumour mongers, both the garden fence variety and those who published magazines indulging in such. These now stumbled over each other as they slunk away.

It was safe to assume now that Tom's disappearance was probably not Andrew's doing either. A great burden was lifted from the poor man's shoulders. Andrew had lost friends, employment, health – both physical and mental – and the pleasure of anonymity. He had become accustomed to walking in to a store and everyone falling silent but now people could not look him in the eye out of shame and Andrew was the victor. His bona fide innocence came home at last and maybe – just maybe – he would know again what it was to sleep well.

The immensity of what Sheila had been through and the equal of it – what Andrew had been through – made words of any language redundant. For three solid days and nights the couple lay in bed, fully dressed, just holding each other, stroking the cheek of the other. Tom was, of course, at the centre of their thoughts; thoughts that were in perfect union. Both felt they were emotionally treading water with no coastline or lighthouse or beach to comfort. To be a complete family was the prize but to win you have to cross the finishing line and Andrew and Sheila, bereft of Tom, would forever be stumbled and fallen just yards from the white tape.

***

At the moment Rat Pile was defeated, as you'd expect, any person present couldn't really think straight, such was the blast to the senses the macabre occasion gave rise to. Things went unnoticed, the forces operating those "things" gladly taking opportunity to act while others were distracted.

Amidst the blue, strobed lit and tear gassed carnage, right out in the open, the area was cordoned off to even the police as people in bio hazard suits lifted Rat Pile in to a body bag and transported him away. Ambulances that had taken away Melanie, Victor and the others were intercepted and diverted en route down dingy back alleys by the suited and sinister. Paramedics were threateningly told they "Did not see a *thing*" as bodies were moved from ambulances in to bleak vehicles which moved off briskly in to the night, heading for inhuman compass points.

In the days that followed, Sheila went round every hospital in the area but could find no trace or record of her friend Melanie. She went to see Detective Jerome.

In his office, the same office where it all began for him, the detective, knowing exactly what lay behind the wall of secrecy Sheila was running in to, over a coffee and with as much kindness as he could muster, advised Sheila to drop it. They hugged for a moment and Sheila acquiesced.

Paul, as Detective Jerome, took a good bit of time off. Paul, as Sheila with Andrew, spent that time off solely with Susan. They had initially been assisted by the police department who booked them in to a hotel but press intrusion stalled any recuperation the couple sought so they ended up at Susan's parents. Paul would just sit staring at the TV screen that was not switched on. Changing invisible channels with the remote in an effort to change his past. He stared at the black television screen and Susan stared at her husband. Draped with the soothing balm of Susan's arms, he would engage in stilted conversation about anything mundane. Mundane, it would seem, might just be the one antidote to how his experience had affected him.

Because Paul really had a lot to deal with.

In a sense, time and dimension travel is the emotional equivalent to licking your fingers and sticking them in an electrical socket, in that some part of you, call it innocence, will die and what is left will never quite be the same again. It had been no "Hollywood Blockbuster" sight seeing tour which was the result of excitedly and naively tinkering with time travel. In the world of Nudge Canyon, Paul had been forced to look through a kaleidoscope of jumping, jolting, intoxicatingly shifting scenarios that had been both horrifying and beautiful. Paul had truly tapped in to every facet the desert dimension displayed. He had won the heart of a passionate and devoted woman and now that woman was dead. He had been rinsed clean of frivolity and his new and present longing for only the serious and touching would alter his demeanour from now on. The north face of Mt Recuperation, the summit of which could not be seen, fearfully and unapologetically rose and towered over Paul, as it did with all the other survivors.

Two months passed and Paul returned to work, feeling that being swamped with a world of educators, warring with those who resented being educated, would happily distract and heal. He received the expected speech from the headmaster about whether he was "ready to return" and the, also expected, blundering and over the top kindness, laden with pity, from colleagues.

As he entered his classroom, all fell silent. Stabbed with all those stares, Paul walked to his desk, placed his briefcase on the desk, turned and smiled at the class. They all smiled back.

"Good morning everyone!"

"Good morning, Sir!" That sounded lovely to Paul, not in a Mozart kind of way but in a "We like you!" kind of way. It was an anchor of a moment which Paul would utilise often in his memories. He turned to face the blackboard.

"Well, let's get down to busi . ." He went wide eyed and gasped. Hanging from end to end of the blackboard was a huge hand made sign that read:

WELCOME BACK, SIR!!!!

Paul's eyes instantly tear'd up and he blushed forcefully. He turned and sat down on the seat, head in hands, and started crying. With no Susan or Sheila or even Detective Jerome around to offer comfort, Paul felt isolated like he'd never ever felt before.

As he sobbed, he heard chairs scraping on tiled floor. Every pupil drew near to their history teacher and fell on his neck in a mass hug. Shrouded in the sincere teenage duvet of this collective embrace, a door slammed somewhere in Paul's being, shutting out Nudge Canyon forever. He couldn't help but think that it was Carla who had reached out from somewhere and slammed it for him. A last act of love from her to him.

Paul stood and hugged and thanked every pupil individually. He then took down the handmade sign, placed it in his briefcase, blew everyone a kiss, which they all caught, walked out the door and school, never to return.

He resigned . . and retired . . that day.

A few months later, Paul opened a satellite group of GAM ANON. The first time the group met, he thought the exact same people who had sat with him in the group he himself had attended had come to see him but then realised that these new attendees simply resembled the others in the sense that they all had the same monkey on their backs so resembled the others in numerous mannerisms, call them symptoms, if you will, such as shyness, embarrassment and the despair of thinking you were the only one in the world caught in this web.

Paul was now ideally equipped, in the most literal way, to take these people under his wing.

But, in history class, Paul had learned facts and dates first then went to work and passed those things on to others in as interesting a way as possible. He could speak of this event long gone or that bygone occasion that shaped the present world and he'd be believed. But here and now and to these people, he could only tell of how he felt in the aftermath of Nudge Canyon and never of the experience itself.

In the months and years that followed, Paul separated victim after victim from their gambling addiction, denying them entry through those waist high swing doors of their *own* "Rattler's Tail Saloon". He used his poker face just one more time when a middle aged woman began to attend whose name was Carla.

***

Patrick and Lorraine were married! Oh what a day it was!

If you are invited to someone's wedding you are a member of a very exclusive club and should indeed be thankful but, for some present, to be there *at all* was to belong to a species that came as near to extinction as possible. Sheila and Andrew, Paul and Susan, along with Detective Jerome, were guests of honour, the reason for this being known only to a very few present. There was some media attention and the wedding was mentioned on the six o'clock news. The happy couple were inundated with cards and gifts from well wishers and followers of the story from around the globe.

Now Detective Jerome was not exactly an unsocial person. He had a family of his own but never really enjoyed such occasions, preferring to socialise on his down time with television hockey and a six pack. This time, however, he made the effort to attend and was only too glad to do so and in fact had a dance with the beautiful bride Lorraine and two dances with Sheila. Sheila broke down repeatedly but discreetly and found the day very difficult to get through as her thoughts were of Tom.

What no one not "in on it all" seemed to notice was that, in the middle of the tables at the reception, there was another table at which nobody sat, the table being, understandably, lost in the midst of the unique day. This table was decked out as all the others with all the usual wedding feast adornments. It would have seated eight, had those eight been present. During the meal, in amongst the happiness and noisy joy of it all, a few waiting staff and one or two other guests who ambled past the table noticed that the place names read "Melanie" "Carla" "Victor" and several others.

Needless to say, Patrick never forgot what Lorraine did for him during their ordeal. He rewarded Lorraine by turning her in to the most loved wife that has ever lived! They decided not to have children and to just focus on each other.

Lorraine was now Patrick's main impetus and driving force in life and he made a definite point of taking her in his arms and sweeping her clean off her feet, every single day! For his darling Lorraine, Patrick made very very sure that:

.. every Valentine's Day lasted a week!

.. every wedding anniversary lasted a month!

.. and every "I love you!" echoed on and lasted forever

.. and ever

.. and ever!

20

Canyon Secrets

The mighty river of Nudge Canyon flowed on.

The slithering mass of water, unremarkable in places, unforgettable in others, patrolled the canyon repeatedly. Always on duty was the river of Nudge Canyon. Its origin was unknown as was its final destination. Not a seeker of friends was the river; it only sought to exist and assert its right do so. The river and surrounding desert never spoke to each other. No water gave even an ounce of life to a million acres of sand and no midday sun hindered by drought the flow of the river by even a drop.

Looking down on all this were the mesas. A scattering of dinosaurs, now solidified and locked in place, their wanderings forever curtailed with their last expressions captured for the record, *this* is what the mesas resembled. Unexplainable, mightier than mighty, rises of sedimentary rock that need never move to impress and awestrike anyone. Geographically indigenous the mesas knew they were and, come and go as people do, these harmless behemoths would never be ousted.

The full moon once again rose and shone down on it all and the Sun's needless rage was diverted for a while, making the whole scene appear just that bit more hospitable. The canyon and all within drew breath. If ever there was a nice side to Nudge Canyon, this was as close as you could come to seeing it.

On the flat top of one particular mesa there was something not one single citizen of Nudge Canyon knew of; not from lack of exploration but because the canyon guarded its secrets jealousy.

That secret was a cemetery.

Here, in rows of headstoned graves, surprisingly neat, lay the victims of the Nudge Canyon one armed bandit. Roughly 20 graves lay in somber regimentation. The names on the headstones were of a line of people stretching back 80 years. In another world, every one of these names had massive significance. Voids boiling with heartache, that these names alone could fill, walked this other world; the world of Sheila and Andrew, Paul, Susan and others from long ago.

The last grave to appear was very recent, it lay at the extreme end of the row. On the headstone there was no birthdate or date of passing, just the name "TOM".

21

Epilogue

The auction room was packed.

Much like the immediate vicinity had been packed the day they opened Tutankhamen's tomb. This gathering was more or less for the same reason. An elderly widow had died. This was no ordinary person. Not a celebrity as such, rather just someone who was known to all in the area, even if never seen or actually met by yourself or anyone you knew. She lived alone in an extremely grand mansion called "Provincetown" which was situated outside of town and up a hill.

This was the great great great granddaughter of two of those surviving 101 (out of 102) brave pilgrims who had disembarked the Mayflower in the early 1600's. Her great great great grandparents had fought against hardships and deadly uncertainties to establish a foothold in the country now known as America. The third Thursday of every November was a date especially revered by the sole and aged occupant of the grand mansion on the hill. She had had a good life and had found love but her husband had been killed in the Second World War. A rumour had persisted that the husband had in fact disappeared under mysterious circumstances. With no children or direct relatives to tempt her with staying on this side, she had passed, aged 97. The wealth she possessed had come from honest endeavour and shrewd investing by both herself and those before her. Not one to display wealth like a peacock, it was not until the executors of her estate entered her house to take inventory that the full extent was known.

Paintings by old masters, about half a dozen of them, adorned wallpapered, thick walls. More paintings were found in careful storage, the investment value of these being fully appreciated by the deceased. Tables and chairs of swirling woodwork and sumptuous beyond sumptuous upholstery, crafted to last an eternity, mourned in almost every room. A display case containing her grandfather's civil war uniform was in the hallway. Nothing frivolous lay within these walls, only the historically momentous. A museum unto itself was the house on the hill, now missing one careful, aged and widowed curator.

So the auction began and, one by one, the grand house on the hill, a mystery to all, gave up its secrets just like Tutankhamen's tomb did on that blisteringly hot Egyptian day. There and then you could look – but not buy – anything that the boy king had tried to take with him but, here and today, it was different. This was a yard sale of a different kind. Bidding went through the roof for painting after painting, chair after chair and anything after anything. People who stood no chance of even starting a bid had come just out of curiosity because people just *have* to know, don't they?

So much was up for grabs that, after an hour, all broke for lunch, then resumed. Another hour of emptying deep pockets until, finally, the dregs of Alladin's cave were reached.

"And now, miscellaneous items." loudly declared the auctioneer. An overalled worker walked out holding one antiquy thing after another, most of which were falling apart. Some of these items sold and some didn't. The worker disappeared and returned pushing a luggage trolly on which sat an odd looking item. Another worker helped slip the to be bid for item from the trolly and turned it to face the crowd.

All immediately recognised it as a one armed bandit. It was indeed at odds with everything that had come before and was most definitely in the "frivolous" category. It attracted the intense gaze of everyone by its sheer audacity. A mistake had been made, surely.

The name of the machine was "BITE THE DUST!" On the beautifully rendered front, above the reels, was a painting of two Wild West gunslingers facing each other in the middle of a gunfight. Lines of white dots, symbolising bullet paths, emanated from each gun, with some reaching and some missing the enemy. These white lines would light up during play and give either a hit or a miss depending upon a win on the reels or not. How the one armed bandit came in to the old lady's possession was a quickly asked question. The answer, however, would probably never be known.

The bidding started. The asking price was lowered and lowered and lowered but nobody seemed to want, at least publicly, to buy the third last item to be put up for auction that day. The two men carefully slid the machine back on to the trolly and wheeled it out of sight.

So it was a bit of a disappointment for the beautifully maintained one armed bandit; defeated, maybe, by its own quirkiness and for being, through no fault of its own, from the "wrong side of the tracks".

But all was not lost. Next month there was to be an auction of the more relaxed kind in a town about 25 miles away where quirkiness was more than welcome. Because this most entertaining of all antiques had most definitely not come to win any popularity contest with the crowd, neither had it come to make loads and loads of new friends . .

. . just one would do.

P.S.

Q: Whatever happened to 5 year old Cedric?

A: Well, in time, Cedric went on to become the first ever Mayor of Clean Getaway.

And boy, he did a good job!

Before long, dirt roads were tarmac'd, boardwalks became paved walks, street after street was added and a school and church were built. Clean Getaway became a prosperous and thriving town under Cedric's leadership.

As the 20th Century progressed, so did the march of technology. The "Wild West" slowly gave way to the more efficient, but, many would argue, the more noisy way of life, that machinery brought with it. The "Rough and Smooth" of the old west was consigned to history books, re-enactment enthusiasts and grandparents' tales, only to be replaced by the "Rough and Smooth" of the new, technological west.

For Cedric and his contemporaries, the romance of it all simply died.

In 1930 Cedric married the lovely Anabelle. They had no less than 7 children, resulting in 11 grandchildren and 5 great grandchildren, who, when Cedric would allow, played with the very soccer ball Cedric's parents bought for him all those years before.

Of course, as happens, Cedric saw the passing of his parents. This, however, Cedric took in his stride, due to the christian input of his mother. Happily, there was a slight hill, just outside of town, with one almighty oak tree at the modest summit. Cedric had this hill designated to be the town's cemetery, where he tenderly laid both his parents to rest. He named the cemetery "Calvary". It is still named such to this day.

In 1977 the Atari 2600 video games machine went in to production. It was a worldwide hit.

Knowing Cedric's love for new technology, and with more than a hint of mischievousness, his loving family bought him one.

And so, at the ripe old age of 81, two years before his own passing, for his birthday . .

. . Cedric finally got that games console!

For more information on Edward, St. David's
and future releases, please go to:
www.edwardstdavids.com